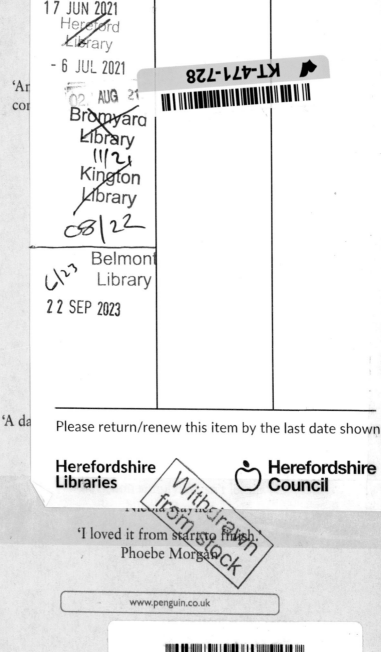

'Ar
con

'A da

'I loved it from start to finish.'
Phoebe Morgan

www.penguin.co.uk

Also by Emma Curtis

ONE LITTLE MISTAKE
WHEN I FIND YOU
THE NIGHT YOU LEFT

and published by Black Swan

Keep Her Quiet

Emma Curtis

BLACK SWAN

TRANSWORLD PUBLISHERS
Penguin Random House, One Embassy Gardens, 8 Viaduct Gardens,
London SW11 7BW
www.penguin.co.uk

Transworld is part of the Penguin Random House group of companies
whose addresses can be found at global.penguinrandomhouse.com

Penguin
Random House
UK

First published in Great Britain in 2020 by Black Swan
an imprint of Transworld Publishers

A CIP catalogue record for this book
is available from the British Library.

ISBN
9781784165253

Typeset in 11/14 pt Sabon by Jouve (UK), Milton Keynes
Printed and bound in Great Britain by Clays Ltd, Elcograf S.p.A.

Penguin Random House is committed to a sustainable future for
our business, our readers and our planet. This book is made from
Forest Stewardship Council® certified paper.

For Steve

PART 1

1989

1

Jenny

I LOOK DOWN AT MY ENORMOUS BELLY AND TOUCH where the baby's heel is pressing. It's getting on for midnight and my contractions are five minutes apart. The rain is illuminated by streetlights, glistening on the eerily quiet road. Leo darts a glance at me and I smile back. His concern is gratifying.

Ahead of us the traffic lights switch to red and Leo brakes too hard, startling a woman about to cross the road. She sends him a look of indignation and strides forward. Her short, belted coat looks inadequate. She's wearing extremely high heels. On her way home from a first date, I decide, as a gust of wind turns her umbrella inside out.

Has she been good? Or has she done something she might regret, like I have? I stifle the thought. Nothing is going to spoil this.

'Sorry about that,' Leo says. 'All right?'

This time my smile is through gritted teeth. 'I'm fine. Just don't kill anyone.'

3

The woman is still fighting with her umbrella as the lights change from red and amber to green. Leo grunts in annoyance.

'C'mon, for Pete's sake.'

I laugh at him, then groan as a contraction rolls through me.

'Breathe,' Leo encourages.

The wipers sluice the rain from the windscreen and I focus my mind on their steady beat. When the contraction has passed, I uncurl my shoulders and lean back with a sigh.

I'll forget what I did. It's in the past, it's gone. Constantly beating myself up over it will achieve nothing. Leo and I love each other, so why rock the boat? The truth can be so destructive.

I check his profile. Grim determination. My contractions are still five minutes apart, so there's no need for him to be stressed – certainly no more than I am. I place my hand on his thigh.

'We've got plenty of time,' I say, smiling. 'Don't worry.'

We pass Vauxhall and have a clear run along the Albert Embankment. Across the river the Houses of Parliament and Big Ben are lit up, their reflection a shimmering gold in the black water. I hardly have time to appreciate the beauty of it before we arrive at the hospital.

This is it. There will be three of us by morning, all being well: me, the baby and my husband. My heart constricts. I will make up for it. I will be the perfect wife. Leo needs to feel loved. And I do love him, so that part is easy. I'll support him too, and make sure the baby doesn't get in the way of his writing. I made him a promise and I won't renege on it.

Leo reverses into a parking space, switches off the engine and turns to me.

'Ready?'

I nod.

'Don't get out yet. I'll come round.'

He reaches for my overnight bag through the gap between our seats, narrowly avoiding butting me with it as he lifts it through.

He gets out of the car and runs round to open my door, tucking his hand under my arm to help me out. Another contraction. I lean against him, close my eyes and breathe, sheltered from the rain by his coat. The pain goes, and I straighten up and draw cold air into my lungs.

Kate's wrong about Leo. But Kate doesn't know what I did.

2

Leo

'SHE'S BEAUTIFUL,' THE MIDWIFE SAID. 'WHAT A LITTLE darling.'

The look Leo gave her was probably not what she had been expecting, but after Jenny's fourteen-hour labour he was blurry with exhaustion and his back was killing him. Added to that, his sense of betrayal was laced with a disconcerting euphoria, creating a wholly unexpected turbulence in his mind.

'She looks like her mum,' he said, pulling himself together and smiling down at the raspberry-faced baby swaddled in a blanket on Jenny's swollen breast. 'Hello, Sophie.'

It was the name they had decided on only yesterday. Jenny looked up and smiled at him.

'What's the time?' she asked.

He glanced at his watch. 'It's just gone half past three.'

He stroked the baby's cheek and pushed back the dark cloud. Funny that he had always thought he knew Jenny better than she knew him. Maybe that was just something he'd told himself because, after four years together, he was once again curious about his wife. He had to admire the sheer audacity of the woman.

What the hell had been going through her mind? Had it been passion, or cold calculation? Did she think, *My husband won't give me a baby, so I'll shop for one elsewhere*? He wondered about her conscience. She was probably consoling herself with the possibility that there was a one-in-a-hundred chance Leo was the father. She had no idea.

Whoever the man was – and Leo didn't want to know – he was probably married. Jenny's male colleagues tended to be. A European conference; a gathering of accountants. What was the collective noun for that? A calculation of accountants? A liability? He would have laughed if it hadn't been so sad.

He twisted the signet ring on his little finger. Hers had not been the only cold calculation. *I'm not losing you or what we have, Jenny.*

He had been arrogant and he had been humbled. Yet, despite the situation and his reignited anger, he hadn't been able to distance himself from what she was going through, or feel a torrent of emotion when she finally gave birth. She had fought through pain, she had reached for him as the agonizing spasms rolled through her. The undiluted love he felt had surprised him.

Leo reached into the pocket of the coat he'd folded over the back of the chair. He had taken the sensible precaution of bringing a bottle of whisky with him. He turned away from Jenny to pour a slug of it into the white plastic beaker in which his tea had arrived. He had earned it.

He felt something for the baby too, although he couldn't put his finger on what it was – protectiveness, maybe. Poor little mite. It wasn't her fault she was here, after all. But he wasn't besotted, like his mother had insisted he would be.

'You'll fall head over heels in love,' Lola had said. 'Especially if it's a girl. She'll have you twisted round her little finger in no time.'

When Leo had rolled his eyes at the cliché, she'd added wistfully, 'I wish I'd had a girl.'

The room was hot and smelled of blood and other bodily fluids. Leo wanted to open the window and stick his head outside, but he'd only be told off. It was pelting down out there.

Watching Jenny gaze at her daughter, something in Leo twisted. He'd found it hard to square living off his wife's money while he wrote his novels. Not any longer. He considered their bargain fair. She had the baby she wanted, he had a financial cushion that meant he could write full time.

Human nature was fascinating. It was so contradictory that the wrong someone had done you had the power to hold you to them as well as push you away. He put his hand on Jenny's shoulder and she looked up at him with eyes that shone. He couldn't say a word.

The door opened.

'Oh, Mr Creasey,' the midwife said. 'There's a phone call for you. You can take it at the reception desk.'

She didn't have any idea who he was. None of them did. Not even the consultant. Leo Creasey, author of *A Time for Bleeding*, meant nothing to them. That was going to change. One day they would tell their friends they had met him at the birth of his child. They would be asked what the great man was like.

'Leo!' his father-in-law bellowed down the phone. 'How are my girls?'

Leo held the receiver away from his ear. 'They're doing well. Have you booked your flight?'

'We're on the earliest one. We should be at the hospital by ten tomorrow. But that's not why I called. I've just got off the phone to James Turner.'

James Turner was Leo's closest neighbour to Sparrow Cottage, the Kent bolthole where Leo wrote his books. An over-anxious retired head teacher and local magistrate, James could be pompous, but he was also the helpful type. Leo didn't mind him.

'Oh yes? What did he want?'

'The storm's hitting the area hard. He very kindly checked on the cottage and there's a fallen tree. The sycamore.'

Leo groaned. 'Hell. How bad is it?'

'Some broken tiles and guttering hanging loose. He can't say without getting up there, but he's fairly certain a branch has gone through the roof. Sorry, Leo. I know this is the last thing you need, but what with the rain, someone needs to take a look before it does any more damage.'

'I'll go.'

'Gracious, no. I didn't mean that. I meant phone round, see if you can find a builder.'

'No. They're going to be busy enough. It'll have to be me.' He didn't want to sound too eager, so added a tired groan. 'I may have to stay the night.'

9

He glanced back at the door to the ward. He didn't need the aggro, that was true, but in spite of that he was elated. He could do with a few hours' break from all this.

'It'll be dark by the time I get there, so I won't be able to do much until morning, but at least I can put buckets under the leaks.'

'Good man. It wouldn't do to let the place deteriorate. It's been in the family such a long time.'

Leo set his teeth. His father-in-law was fond of reminding him that Sparrow Cottage belonged to Jenny.

'No problem.'

'But, darling, you're exhausted,' Jenny said. 'Why don't you go home and get some sleep? You can set off in the morning.'

'I'd better not. It sounds bad. I'll drive carefully, I promise.' He looked around, checking his pockets. 'Do you know what I did with my keys?'

'No. I was a little distracted last night.'

'Shit. Maybe I dropped them.'

'I doubt it. Try the overnight bag. Your dad is always losing things,' she cooed at the baby. 'Let's hope he doesn't lose you.'

'Found them.' He turned to leave.

'Aren't you going to kiss your daughter goodbye?'

Leo bent to kiss the baby's forehead, trying not to inhale her scent. He had made his choice, and he'd had months to ponder it. The baby was here now. It was real. This was his life. It was his job to make sure he used what had happened to his advantage.

3

Hannah

HANNAH SAT IN THE MINICAB, HER TWO-DAY-OLD
daughter swaddled in a hand-me-down blanket and
held firmly against her, her hand cupping her head. She
should have bought a car seat, but she hadn't been able
to afford one. The cab driver had protested, but they
were standing outside the hospital getting soaked, and
in the end he reluctantly gave in. It was pouring with
rain. The midwife had said the weather was going to get
worse before it got better. Hannah placed her hand on
the baby's chest, comforted by her animal warmth and
the rise and fall of her ribcage. Her mum, in a moment
of spite, had predicted there would be something wrong
with the child, but she was perfect – the most beautiful
baby ever.

Her heart swelled. So this was what love was. How
odd that her mother had put conditions on it. This baby
would be loved; she would never have to prove herself
worthy. She would be allowed to be whoever she wanted
to be.

This was not her fault. Hannah's parents had sent her to Michael Brady for counselling after she had been heard to question their beliefs, and even when she'd asked to stop going they had insisted the sessions continue. She had been too embarrassed to explain why she didn't want to carry on, and they hadn't bothered to work it out for themselves. Michael had seduced her, and she had complied because she wanted to rebel and because he told her she was torturing him.

She had been terrified when she realized she was pregnant, and had gone to him for help, only for him to wash his hands of her. He even said the baby wasn't his, that she was a little slut and if she told anyone they had been together, he would say she had tempted him to sin. He would tell them all the disgusting things she had done.

When her condition became obvious, she told one person the truth: her mother, who immediately accused her of lying to cover up the fact that she was sleeping around with boys from outside the community. It was better than facing up to the reality, which was that it was their fault for leaving Michael Brady alone with a naive and trusting sixteen-year-old girl. Michael was an elder and, as such, beyond reproach.

Even Hannah's best friend had ignored her attempts to talk to her. But then she was Michael's daughter. Like everyone else, Rachel assumed it was all Hannah's fault, and her father had just walked away, free from any blame.

The baby's eyes opened and Hannah saw herself reflected in them. She rested her palm over the fontanelle and felt its delicate pulse.

'Bit of a dramatic start to life, isn't it?' the driver said as thunder rolled. He kept flicking his gaze up to the rear-view mirror, curious about her. 'Fire and brimstone.'

Hannah didn't have anything to say, so she nodded.

She was awash with hormones and pain, from the ache in her breasts to an almost delirious exhaustion. The midwife had wanted to keep her in for an extra day, concerned that, despite being only seventeen, Hannah had received no visitors and no one had sent cards or flowers. It was impossible to sleep there, though, and if she did drop off, it was only to be jolted awake again by the cat-like cries of newborn babies, so she left.

'Got a name?'

'Zoe,' Hannah said.

'That's lovely, that is. My niece is called Zoe.'

'Oh.'

'You got someone at home, have you? Your mum or a friend?'

'My sister is there,' she lied, ashamed of being so alone.

She had told the midwife the same thing: her sister was at home but she didn't have a car, so she couldn't collect Hannah and her baby. She almost wished she had stayed when the midwife told her she should, because she was scared to death. What if she got everything wrong? She'd babysat Deborah's two plenty of times, but they were always asleep. She had never looked after them properly on her own; just helped her sister from time to time.

Twenty minutes later, the cab drew up outside the house, a plain redbrick affair built in the 1950s. Hannah didn't have enough for a tip, but the driver jumped out anyway and protected them from the rain with his brolly.

'You sure about this, love?' he asked.

It was obvious no one was waiting for her.

She nodded and shut the front door. The car's lights glowed through the window before they were swallowed up by the night.

The house was ice-cold. She balanced the car seat against the back of the sofa, fed the meter and turned on the electric fire before unstrapping Zoe and walking her from room to room. It was lovely holding her, getting used to her sagging weight and her warmth.

She showed her new daughter the bedroom she'd spent the last few weeks preparing; scrubbing the musty old carpet and washing the curtains. She hadn't been able to do anything about the nasty green-and-brown wallpaper, but she'd stuck pictures on it – cartoon animals from children's comics – to cheer it up.

The second-hand cot had turned up outside the front door one morning. Hannah had recognized it immediately. It belonged to Deborah. With it had been a pram, a high chair and a carrier bag full of her niece's baby clothes and bottles. Hannah hadn't seen her sister in months, but the gifts gave her hope that one day they might be reconciled. She missed Deborah more than she missed her parents.

Back downstairs, Hannah held Zoe in the crook of her arm and dialled the family home. The phone rang six times. She imagined her parents glancing at one another, as they always did, as if it were a surprise that anyone would want to call them.

'Hello?' her mother said warily.

Hannah closed her eyes, overwhelmed with home-sickness. She saw herself standing at the kitchen counter, chopping vegetables for the evening meal while her mother kneaded the dough for the next day's bread. She could almost smell the yeast.

'I had a baby girl.'

A sharp intake of breath at the other end made her skin prickle, then the receiver was replaced with a soft click. She sat on the bottom stair until she grew so cold she had to get up. It was like a bereavement, she decided. Perhaps it was easier to think of it that way. That was why people referred to their estranged relatives as 'dead to them'.

Her reflection in the window showed a girl with eyes still bruised and hollow with exhaustion. The raindrops raced down the panes like tears.

She turned away, shrugging it off. She would find a way. So far, the people she'd met over the last four months – the doctors and midwives, the staff at social services – had been kind. They had got her this house, sorted out her benefits, found her a job at the Birches – a residential care home for the elderly – and made sure she understood her rights. She had enough to live on, and when Zoe went to school, she'd get her job back. She liked it there. The elderly residents treated her with a respect that she'd never had at home. She didn't feel so lonely when she was with them.

At the hospital the midwife had asked her leading questions, wanting to know what the situation was, who would be looking after her, if she had friends, family or colleagues. Hannah had done her best, describing a life that included other people, people who cared what became of her.

'The community nurse will visit you tomorrow,' the midwife told her when it was time to leave.

'She doesn't need to. I'll be fine.'

She didn't want them to see how little she had, in case they decided to interfere and contacted her parents. What if they decided she was too young to manage and took Zoe into care?

'It's routine, my love. Don't worry, they visit all our new mums. She'll check you and baby and make sure she's feeding well. Now, have you got everything? Your child health record? The nurse will need to fill that in when she comes. And remember, sleep when your little one sleeps.'

Hannah fed the baby as she had been taught, snuggled on the sofa, warmed by the heater. Zoe suckled hungrily, sending shoots of pain and pleasure through Hannah's body. At least she was doing something right.

After Zoe's eyes fell back and her fingers lost their grip on Hannah's jumper, a trickle of milk soaking into her babygro, Hannah laid her on the sofa with a blanket around her and heated up half a can of baked beans. Beyond the sitting room, where the three-bar heater kept them warm, the rest of the house was freezing. She ate, with Zoe beside her snuffling quietly, then she washed up her plate and the saucepan and placed them on the drainer.

Her body felt heavy and drained of energy. She turned the heater off to save money, took Zoe upstairs to bed and closed the curtains against the slate-grey sky. The nursery was bitterly cold but Hannah's bedroom was over the sitting room, so it was warmer. She wedged folded-up pieces of paper between the windows and the frame to stop them rattling, then put Zoe down in her bed, took off her shoes and got in with her daughter, curling around her tiny body so that Zoe could draw warmth from her stomach, breasts and thighs. Zoe whimpered, her tiny fists flying up. Hannah laughed and kissed them.

'I'm your mum,' she whispered sleepily. 'It's just the two of us, but it's going to be OK. I'll make sure nothing bad ever happens to you.'

4

Jenny

'HUBBY GONE HOME FOR A KIP?'

'What? Oh, no. Well, yes.'

It isn't worth explaining. I can barely drag my eyes away from the baby suckling at my breast. She's here at last, she's beautiful and she's mine. I drift my fingers over her downy hair. I thought happiness was Leo, but I was wrong. This is happiness – this pure, unconditional state of love.

'Do you want these opened or closed?' The midwife indicates the curtains that surround my bed.

'Closed, if you don't mind.'

When we're left in peace, Sophie unlatches from my nipple and I cup her head in my hand. She has long lashes and a cupid's-bow mouth, more hair than I expected, and fingers that splay out and curl in, as though they're testing the space. I feel such joy it's almost painful. I am a mother. I have a year's maternity leave ahead of me and a house full of baby paraphernalia. I'm looking for-ward to bringing my daughter home and having my life turned upside down. I have a healthy financial cushion and a job to go back to. Leo has his work and a promise from me that things won't change. Of course they will, but by that time he'll have fallen in love with her, because that's how it works.

Sophie has fallen asleep. I'm reluctant to put her down in her bassinet, so I rest her in the angle created between my thighs and stomach. I can feel her chest rising and falling, and her heat seeping through the blankets.

It's still raining hard enough to hear above the other hospital sounds. I imagine the storm clouds gathering above London. When I was a child I loved thunderstorms, because I loved counting. I would press my face to the window and stare at the sky, not wanting to miss a single flash of lightning.

A worry nibbles at the edge of my mind. Leo's poorly concealed relief at having to rush down to Kent. Surely he could have phoned someone, and got them to go out and check? What was behind his willingness to leave?

Unless he knows.

But how can he? I haven't told anyone. And in any case, why would he have stuck around if he did?

He should be here.

I try to be reasonable: I've given birth, I'm bound to be feeling vulnerable. It's just Leo being Leo. I shrug off my unease and snuggle down with Sophie. Perhaps the experience has overwhelmed him. He needs space; he's a man and men are apt to be squeamish. He needs time to wind down without the midwives fluttering round him.

My mind refuses to shut up. It points out that I recognize Sophie's smell, even though there are three other newborns on the ward. I wonder if fathers have that ability as well. Does Leo sense, in some animal way, that something's missing? He would have said something, surely? Leo would never put up with another man's child. He would have left me if he had somehow figured out the truth.

I'm not by nature an impulsive person. I like maths. I enjoy working out problems, taking my time, ticking things off, teasing out solutions, but I had sex with a stranger I met at a conference. Gazing down at the result of that night, I don't regret it, but that doesn't mean I don't feel guilty.

My tiny newborn yawns and opens her eyes. I can tell she recognizes me because her eyes widen. Things feel so much simpler when I look into them. She makes me smile and she'll do the same to Leo. He has no reason to believe she isn't his, and after all, she might be. It'll be all right. In the meantime, it's raining cats and dogs, and she and I are snug and safe in here together. There's only one possible outcome and it isn't complicated.

I kiss her forehead and she flutters her eyelashes at me.

'Your daddy will never know,' I whisper, 'because I'm never going to tell him.'

5

Leo

LEAVING THE VICINITY OF THE HOSPITAL, A BOTTLE OF whisky set snugly between his thighs and Brahms playing on the cassette player, Leo drummed his fingers on the steering wheel, angry now that he was away from all that positive energy. Why did women assume men could be changed? It had happened with his first wife – she had assured him she didn't want children either, but within months of their marriage she'd had second thoughts. Her wheedling had driven him crazy.

After the divorce, he'd had a vasectomy. It hadn't been an impulsive decision – he had thought it over for several weeks, because he felt he had a duty to do so – but he knew he wouldn't change his mind.

He slapped the steering wheel hard, stinging his palm. How could Jenny have done this to him? Hadn't he shown her he loved her, over and over again? Why wasn't he enough?

When she had broken the news about her pregnancy he had reacted badly, demanding to know how it could have happened. Genuinely interested. Jenny grew flustered, burst into tears and said she didn't know, but that condoms weren't 100 per cent effective. Not only that, but she had also helped it along. That had been clever of her. He supposed he shouldn't be surprised that she had turned out to be so calculating. She was an accountant after all.

After the argument he had left the house in a fury, scared that he might actually hurt her, and roared down to Sparrow Cottage only to have his mother turn up on the doorstep while he was wielding his axe, taking his anger out on a pile of logs. He was angrier than he had ever been in his life. His wife had slept with another man. How could she? His loyal, funny and, frankly, besotted wife. It was so out of character, he couldn't believe it.

When he'd told her he didn't understand, he'd meant it literally. He'd had his pick of beautiful women but he'd married the uncool girl; the geeky one with the low self-esteem. In all relationships there's a delicate dance played out between the one who loves more and the one who is loved the most. He'd always assumed he had the upper hand in that respect. Well, the worm had turned, hadn't it? She must have wanted a baby very badly. Like a fool, he had underestimated that desire, just as he'd underestimated her.

'It's just a baby. It's not the end of the world,' his mother had said, keeping a safe distance from flying splinters in her belted camel coat and high-heeled boots.

He had put down the axe slowly and taken a deep breath. 'I'm aware of that. You didn't have to come all the way here to tell me.'

22

'I was worried about you.'

'Were you? Well, I'm OK.'

He had wanted to tell her to bugger off home, but he couldn't bring himself to be that unkind.

'It would make Jenny so happy.'

Why would he want to do that?

Lola had interpreted his silence as receptiveness; a mistake she often made. It always amazed him that she had so little self-awareness.

'She'll be a fantastic mother. She's so patient and loving. Honestly, darling, I can't think why she puts up with you.'

'Presumably because she's so patient and loving.'

'Grow up, Leo. Find some sense of responsibility before it's too late.'

That had been enough to make him erupt. He had slammed the axe into the block, startling her.

'Do not lecture me about my decision, just because it doesn't suit your world view. I can see no benefit to me in having a child – quite the opposite, in fact. All I can see is a shitty future, like my father had. That's not happening to me. Nothing is more important to me than my writing.'

Lola had looked as if she'd been slapped. 'Even family?'

'What do you care about family? Have you never asked yourself why Marcus and Jake moved so far away?'

His younger brother, Marcus, had emigrated with his Australian wife to Sydney, where he ran his own IT company, and the youngest one, Jake, lived off-grid in Wales with his girlfriend and their new baby.

'They have their own lives to lead,' Lola had responded, indignant. 'I've never put pressure on any of you.'

23

'You weren't interested in us, Mum. Not really. And Dad gave up his dreams because you wanted him to. Do you know how hard it is for children when they know a parent is unhappy? They spend their lives trying to compensate.'

Ben Creasey had been a writer with potential, a published novel under his belt, pegged as one to watch, but at the age of thirty-one, Leo's age now, he'd fallen head over heels in love with Lola and married her. All had been well until Leo arrived, followed swiftly by Marcus and then Jake, then Lola started to pile on the pressure and Ben became an English teacher. To his credit, he made a good fist of it, rolling up his sleeves and getting stuck in, swiftly rising to the position of headmaster, but it wasn't the life he had imagined.

'I did my best, thank you very much, Leo. And your father wasn't that great a writer. If he had been, he would have been successful and wouldn't have had to go into teaching. If he was frustrated, it was his fault, not mine. And it's not as if you've succeeded either, is it? The only thing you've done differently is marry a woman who's prepared to keep you. I wouldn't take her for granted, if I were you.'

Leo had held his mother's gaze, refusing to allow her to see that her barbs had hit home.

'Do not interfere in my life. Do not try to manipulate Jenny. Do not expect me to endorse the lies you tell yourself.'

'I'm sorry you feel that way.'

He was trapped. If he admitted he knew the child wasn't his and refused to have anything to do with it,

Jenny would leave him. He knew enough about women to understand a baby would win every time. If he left her, he would risk losing more than he gained. He would have to go back to teaching, and his bright future would shrink until it became a pinprick and then finally disappeared.

And now here he was, a new father. He was going to have the bright future if it killed him. He unscrewed the top of the whisky bottle and took a glug, tasting the bitter warmth in his mouth, feeling the heat bloom in his chest. His father had killed himself after the three boys left home. Leo had been twenty-four years old. At the funeral, he had pretended to be praying, when really he had been making a solemn pledge never to have children of his own.

Leo's windscreen wipers swept from side to side. He leaned forward, rubbing gaps in the misted glass with a square of chamois leather, staring narrow-eyed into the gloom, unable to see beyond the beam of his headlights. The idea of being poor, of scratching away at his stories in a garret, held no appeal and certainly no romance. The deadening mediocrity of it appalled him.

6

Hannah

MICHAEL BRADY WAS TALLER THAN HANNAH REMEM-
bered him. Her head used to come up to his shoulder, but
he seemed to have grown a couple of inches. She looked
down at his feet to see if he was wearing some kind of
heel, but his shiny black lace-ups were the same ones
he would always take off and place neatly at the end of
the bed.

He indicated that she take a seat, so she did as she
was told. She always obeyed him. The room they were
in was square and white with pictures of idyllic land-
scapes hanging from the walls: mountain streams and
majestic deer, a waterfall gushing down into a magical
glade. Two chairs were arranged either side of a table.
She was cold but she didn't like to ask if they could have
the radiator on. She could hear the rain, but as there
were no windows, she couldn't see it.

She twisted round in her seat when the door opened
behind her and several people walked in. First her parents,
then her sister Deborah, then Hannah's brother-in-law

Sean, and lastly Rachel. They lined up along the wall. The three men wore suits, the women plain dresses. Sean stood in front of the door, his arms crossed. Hannah sent Rachel a question with her eyes. *Are you with me or with them?* Her old friend sent her back a look of hatred. Deborah refused to meet Hannah's eye.

'Mum?' she asked.

Her mother seemed to sink into the wall, to grow faint with shame. She held out her hand to Hannah, but Hannah couldn't reach it.

'Hannah Faulkner.' Michael was leaning towards her, his fists on the table. 'You have indulged in immoral behaviour.'

He picked up a Bible and opened it at a page he had marked.

'Genesis 38:24. "However, about three months later, Judah was told: 'Ta'mar your daughter-in-law has acted as a prostitute, and she is also pregnant by her prostitution.' At that, Judah said: 'Bring her out and let her be burnt.'"'

'Mum,' she said. 'It was him. Michael is the father.'

Her mother sprang from the wall and slapped her in the face.

Hannah held her hand to her blazing cheek, tears starting. 'Why don't any of you believe me?'

'Michael is a good man,' her father said. 'How dare you tell such filthy lies?'

As she wept, she noticed her shirt had come undone, but when she tried frantically to do it up again, her fingers were made clumsy by anxiety. The buttons dropped off, one by one. The stitching must have rotted, she thought. Or Deborah had played some horrible trick on her.

Hannah woke with a gasp. Had she heard something? She held her breath, listening, but all she could hear was the wind and rain. How long had she slept? She could feel the baby's head under her breast, and lifted herself up, fumbling for the switch to her bedside light.

Zoe hadn't cried for her feed. With a flutter of anxiety, Hannah put her hand on the baby's chest and fear slammed into her. She threw back the covers and found Zoe flat on her back, her face an odd blue colour.

Hannah snatched her up with a wail, but Zoe's head flopped into the palm of her hand. She shook her then realized what she was doing, what it would look like if the baby was examined.

She had been taught CPR when she started working at the Birches. It had been on adults, but it couldn't be that different with a baby, surely? You just had to be gentle. She tipped Zoe's head back and breathed into her mouth, then compressed her ribcage.

Nothing. Zoe had gone. For a moment Hannah was uncomprehending, her brain unable to fix on what had happened, but then it sharpened into a searing, nauseating agony and she twisted away from the body and retched, coughing up scorching bile while tears streamed down her cheeks. She wailed at the incomprehensible enormity of what she had lost.

Hannah sat staring out of the window for a long time. Outside, the weather had worsened. The draught that had crept through the cracks and the gaps of the shoddily built house earlier had strengthened to a stiff breeze. She stayed there until she grew cold, then dropped her gaze to Zoe's face. Her eyes were closed. She looked unreal, not even peaceful, but like some kind of mannequin. She looked . . . She looked inert, and soulless.

How could this have happened?

When a flash of lightning illuminated Zoe's face, Hannah dived under the covers like a frightened child. She was only seventeen. What was she supposed to do? She didn't have anyone. Her life was over when it had hardly even begun. She'd had a baby to love and she had killed it.

She remembered that a nurse was coming tomorrow to check on them. She would blame Hannah. An ambulance would come, then the police – she imagined them tearing down the lane, sirens blaring – then social services. Her parents would be contacted and they'd say it was her fault because she was bad.

She could run, but where could she hide? She would be caught and they would think she had run away out of guilt. The only person who might help was the lady from social services. She had been kind. She had told Zoe that she could call her any time. Hannah had her number by the phone.

With Zoe's body clutched close to her breast, Hannah went down to the hall and picked up the receiver but there was no tone; the line was dead. She shuddered with relief at the reprieve. She didn't want anyone knowing. Not that they would care about her. As far as they were concerned, Hannah was an apostate – the worst kind of person, an infectious disease spreading lies amongst the faithful.

She thought she heard a noise and listened hard for something that wasn't her own heavy breathing, or the wind or rain.

Hannah.

She whirled round, petrified. She had been told that she had lost her chance of paradise, and that she would be destroyed in the Armageddon with the rest of the sinners. It all made sense: the death of her baby, the forces of evil gathering. It was starting. The house seemed to shake on its foundations. A loud crack sounded, and she screamed and ran outside. The wind tore at her clothes and whipped her hair across her face. She was soaked within seconds.

As she sprinted into the road, a car came round the bend too fast, its bonnet glancing off her thigh and sending her flying. Hannah lay in the wet, dazed, blinded by the headlights. Her arms were empty.

'Zoe!'

Hannah raised herself on to her hands and knees and felt around, until at last she touched a tiny foot. She picked the baby up and kissed her cold wet face, wiping away the mud with her cuff.

Through the windscreen the stranger looked like the devil, with his deep-set eyes and open mouth. There was no kindness in his gaze, just a horror that matched hers.

7

Leo

LEO SAT IN A DAZE OF STUPEFACTION AS THE ENGINE
ticked over. Brahms' 'Symphony No. 3 in F Major' filled
the car, the rain drummed its own beat, and his breath
heaved in and out of his lungs. Time came rushing back.
The digital clock on the dashboard moved at last, from
five minutes to six, to four minutes to. Leo groped around
the footwell for his glasses, found them and put them
back on, then peered out of the window. There was a heap
on the ground, half on, half off the verge. Jesus, he'd
killed someone.

All he could think was that he had to get out of there
or his life was over. He stretched his arm across the back
of the passenger seat, twisted round as he reversed, then
wrenched the Citroen into first gear. The prone figure
moved and Leo hit the brake with an oath. It got up on
its hands and knees then felt around for something,
drew it into its arms and stood.

At first he thought she was an older woman, but now
he could see that she was young, a teenager. Her face

31

was lit by his headlights, her eyes huge and dark in an ashen face, and the thing she was carrying looked very much like a baby.

Go. Leo gripped the steering wheel, his mouth tight. *Go, you wanker. You need to leave right now.* What was he doing waiting? His car was warm and dry and safe; out there was unknown. A different life, a different track for him. He understood that, even as he slumped against the steering wheel, his legs like jelly, his feet unable to work the pedals. He reached down, retrieved the whisky bottle, shoved it into his jacket pocket and got out.

'You gave me a hell of a fright,' he shouted, a note of hysteria in his voice.

The girl said nothing, just gripped the bundle tighter against her chest.

He took a tentative step towards her, his hands outstretched. They were both soaked, rain running down their faces, dripping from their hair and clothes, puddling at their feet. Lightning flashed, bringing into sudden relief the electricity pylons marching across the landscape.

'Are you hurt? Is that a baby? Is it OK?'

He stopped in his tracks when she screamed at him. 'She's dead!'

Leo staggered. He stared at her in horror.

'Are you sure?' he managed to rasp. 'She may just be unconscious.'

The girl's face was smeared with mud, rain and tears. 'You killed her. You killed my baby.'

'No.' He shook his head. 'No, that isn't true.'

He felt as though she had punched him in the stomach. He pictured the baby being tossed from her arms and hitting the tarmac with a stomach-churning thud, its skull splitting. He broke out in a cold sweat. What the hell should he do now? She was out of her mind, she had probably got it wrong.

'Let me see,' he said, resisting the urge to swear at her when she didn't loosen her grip.

She shuffled backwards. 'Don't touch her!'

'Let me feel her pulse at least,' he said. 'Come on. Please.'

Was his voice trembling? Yes, it was. He was terrified. She pulled back a section of blanket exposing the child's face. Its eyes were closed. It could be unconscious, surely. Didn't eyes open in death? This nightmare had to end. He placed his fingertips against the baby's neck, trying not to recoil. It had a clammy coldness that felt alien. He snatched away his fingers in horror and threw up on to the sodden verge.

Leo felt cold and shivery. He had got them both inside, though he barely remembered doing it. The girl was sitting on the sofa, the baby on her knee, staring into the middle distance while he paced.

He had killed it. He had drunk half a bottle of whisky and driven his car through a fucking storm. He had smashed into a young girl carrying a baby. Why hadn't he got the hell out of there when he had the chance?

A sudden burst of hailstones rattled against the window. He stopped and stared at the patch of dark-green and maroon carpet between his feet. She was watching him, her eyes bloodshot and swollen. He had no idea what to say to her, though instinct told him to keep quiet. *No comment. No comment. No comment.* He wondered how much she understood of what had happened.

His mouth felt like the inside of a vacuum-cleaner bag and a band of pain was developing around his head. He remained standing to prevent himself from succumbing to the powerful lure of sleep. He needed to keep his wits about him.

'You came out of nowhere,' he said. 'You ran in front of my car. I couldn't avoid hitting you.'

'You killed her.'

'What are you going to do?' he asked. 'I need to know what you're going to tell the police. My wife's just had a baby. This will destroy her.' He paused, gauging her mood. 'It was an accident. You understand that, don't you?'

'You've been drinking. I can smell it on you.'

'I . . .'

He could hardly deny it, could he? He tipped his head back with a groan. 'Are you going to call the police?'

'The lines are down.'

That would only delay the reckoning for a few hours. He felt another surge of panic. He searched for words, something, anything to crack some light into the fog.

'What were you doing running into the road on a night like this?'

She wiped her arm across her face. 'I thought . . . I thought someone had broken in. I'm hiding from her father. He'll hurt me if he finds me.'

She choked on her tears again and curled her body over in a paroxysm of grief. She lifted her head and howled at him. 'Look what you've done to me.'

'I'm sorry. I'm so sorry. If I could give you my baby, I would. I don't want it.'

The words burst out of him before he could consider the consequences.

There was a long silence. She pushed her hair out of her face. She looked like a child with her blotchy cheeks and tear-filled eyes.

'What do you mean?'

'It's not mine. I can't have children. I had a vasectomy before I met my wife. She doesn't know that.'

'What's a vasectomy?'

He raised his eyebrows. How young was this girl?

'It just means I can't have kids.'

'Oh.' She paused, sniffed. 'Is it a girl or a boy?'

'Girl.'

'Like mine.' Her bottom lip started wobbling again. 'You don't deserve her.'

'You don't have to tell me that, I feel bad enough as it is. But I'm still here, aren't I? I'm not a monster. I could have driven on.'

'Why didn't you?'

'Fuck knows,' he blurted out, exasperated. How could she possibly understand the complexities – she was barely out of school.

They lapsed back into silence. Leo slumped on the sofa, his mind settling into a dream where he was explaining to his mother how he came to be here. Then, suddenly, he was spinning round the bend again, the girl materializing out of the rain. He sat upright with a shout of horror, and found her staring at him.

'I feel like I've seen you before.'

'I don't think so.'

Leo closed his eyes again. The room smelled of warm, wet clothes. He imagined a passer-by looking through the window at the odd couple on the sofa. He got up and drew the curtains, then sat down again. He urgently needed to disentangle himself from this hideous situation, but there was a heaviness in his limbs that stopped him walking out. He didn't even know the girl's name. He opened his eyes and started to ask her, but she'd fallen asleep in the corner of the sofa, her dead baby tucked beneath her arm. He felt a thick torpor descend on him and didn't fight it. He too wanted to sleep for a very long time.

8

Hannah

HANNAH HAD DOZED ONLY FOR A FEW MINUTES, BUT it felt more like her body and mind had shut down through shock than actual rest. She lay like a stone, her eyes closed, wishing she had died when he hit them; that she was with Zoe in heaven. But Zoe's small bulk was still, and Hannah's heart was beating too fast. She had made him think he'd killed Zoe. It had been a spontaneous outburst, an instinct to survive at the expense of someone else. An entirely new experience for her. She sat up abruptly and stared at him. She had seen him before, or at least his face.

So what now? He didn't want his baby. She needed a baby. He thought he was to blame. A life for a life.

While he slept on, she cleaned herself up, brushed her hair, put in fresh breast pads and a maternity pad, then went downstairs and shook the man's shoulder to wake him.

He opened one bleary eye.

'I've remembered where I've seen you before,' she

said. 'I saw your photograph in a bookshop window. With piles of your book. Something about a cuckoo . . .'

She had been trawling the charity shops in Maidstone, looking for baby clothes, when she stopped by the window, attracted by the gold-embossed hardbacks, the little bird on the branch.

'*The Emerald Cuckoo*,' he muttered.

'Yes, that was it. I don't remember your name.'

He didn't give it to her. His eyes closed again. She nudged his arm and he jerked it away, grumbling, reluctant to wake up.

'We're going to get your baby,' she said.

His eyes snapped open and looked straight into hers. He wiped away the spittle that had leaked from the corner of his mouth while he slept. 'I beg your pardon?'

'You said you would give her to me if you could. Well, you can. We'll go to the hospital, and take her.'

He sat up straight. He didn't look so sleepy now. 'You can't be serious. You're not going to steal my baby, or any baby for that matter.'

Hannah's face heated. 'You don't understand—'

'Yes, I do.' He held out a hand and she looked down at it then up at his face. He dropped it. 'You're grieving and scared, but making another woman unhappy is not going to solve that. You can't go around stealing other people's babies, it's unthinkable. And you're certainly not dragging me into your lunatic plans.'

She pulled on her beige anorak, and zipped it up to her chin with fingers trembling with nerves. Her leg was agony but she didn't flinch. She needed to convince him she meant business, or he would realize she was weak

38

and in pain and would talk her out of it. She'd had more than enough of being talked out of things she wanted to do, or talked into things she didn't want.

'Come on,' he coaxed, making her feel like a hysterical child. 'You know this is impossible.'

'I'm doing it and you're helping me,' she said. 'If you don't, I'm going to report you to the police. You're famous, aren't you?'

'Not that famous.'

'But you'd like to be.' His guarded expression told her this was his Achilles' heel. 'Do you want to be famous for your books, or for running over a woman and killing her baby when you were drunk?'

His face turned grey.

'Think about it. If I do what you ask, it'll only make things worse for you in the long run. You must be able to see that.'

She didn't respond, because what was the point of arguing? He knew how to; she didn't. She had been brought up to agree with men. This one was typical of the males she had known: overbearing, smug and entitled. He reminded her of Michael Brady, with his shadowed eyes and heavy masculinity. She wasn't going to be taken in by that again. She had to stand up for herself.

'I'll tell you what we're going to do,' he said. 'We'll have something to eat and talk it over. Neither of us has had much sleep. We're not capable of making life-changing decisions, not until we have clear heads and full stomachs.'

'I could destroy you,' Hannah said. 'I don't want to, but I could. I need that baby more than you do.'

39

'More than my wife?' He spoke with a sneer, but he couldn't hide his terror from her.

She clung to her resolution, making her eyes meet his. He didn't care about the baby, and she needed it. No one would ever know. She'd be a mother; a good and loving mother. If she let this opportunity go by, she would have nothing and she might as well not exist. She couldn't go home, she had no qualifications, no friends, no purpose. The baby would give her back her self-respect and her life.

'More than her,' she said finally, stepping towards the door. 'I don't want to talk about it. We're going now.'

'If I don't eat, I'm going to throw up again.'

Hannah limped into the kitchen, untwisted the end of a bag of white bread, pulled out a slice and wrapped it around an overripe banana. It was the best she could do. When she handed him the sandwich, he raised his eyebrows, but he ate it all the same.

'I'm over the limit,' he said when he'd finished. 'What if there's another accident?'

'There won't be.'

'You do realize my wife had her baby in London, not Maidstone?'

It hadn't occurred to her and she wavered, but only for a second.

'It'll be OK,' she said. 'Let's go.'

She moved towards the door, but he grabbed her arm and swung her round. 'You can say you dropped her. You're only a kid yourself. They'll take that into account.'

'No, they won't. They'll say I murdered her.' Her voice broke. Zoe. Her baby, her future. She fought back a wave of despair. 'I know they will.'

'Then blame it on a hit-and-run,' he begged. 'You can say it was too dark, that you wouldn't recognize the car again.'

'I need that baby. There is no other way.'

They stared at each other for a long moment, then he held out his hands and spoke quietly.

'Please don't wreck my life.'

'You've wrecked mine.'

His shoulders slumped. 'Where's the baby?'

She swallowed hard, fighting back the huge lump in her throat. 'In your car. Once you've dropped me back here, you're going to take her away and bury her.'

He shook his head. 'No way. I'm not doing that.'

'I'm helping you.'

'Helping me?'

Tears sprang to her eyes, but she took a deep breath, wiped them away with her sleeve and picked up her house keys. 'This way we both get our lives back. I can't have her here, not with the new one.'

41

9

Leo

WHAT THE HELL IS GOING ON? LEO THOUGHT AS HE SWUNG open the door and marched outside. It was as though he'd hurtled into somebody else's life. He cupped his hands in front of his mouth and sniffed his breath. The trauma had sobered him, but there was whisky in his bloodstream. He needed Jenny, that was the horrible irony. He needed her wisdom, her calm, her tolerance. He needed to put his aching head on her shoulder and have her kiss him and tell him they'd find a way out of this mess. But he couldn't do that. He was going to have to lie to her for the rest of his life and, in his weakened state, the idea made him want to weep.

Once they reached the outskirts of London, the journey became easier – the roads were better lit and better drained. The suburbs looked as though they were under siege, hatches battened down, shop windows boarded up. There were more buses than cars, their windows fogged; beacons of warmth and solid security.

The girl's head was tilted away from Leo, cradled by

the seatbelt. Apart from the disturbing fact that she was holding a dead baby, she was ordinary. Her face was plump and lacked definition. Her mouth, slack in slumber, didn't have that mesmerizing quality some women's did. Her eyes, well, they were closed, and he had already forgotten what colour they were. She was nondescript, the perfect person to walk in and out of a hospital unnoticed, unquestioned and, later, unrecalled.

She opened her eyes suddenly. 'Are we nearly there?'

What was she? A child? Yes, he realized with a jolt, she was. A child he had hurt.

'Not far now.' He was shafted. Damned if he did, damned if he didn't.

'I've never been to London before.'

He didn't answer because he was too nervous, his stomach roiling. He had spent the last hour mentally rehearsing his arguments and now he had to do it for real. He owed it to Jenny to try one more time to make the girl see reason.

He kept to the back streets on the approach to the hospital, his knowledge of the area, first garnered when he was in his early twenties and doing his work placement at a local secondary school, precise. At Hercules Road he turned abruptly into Centaur Street, ignoring the no-entry signs. At this time of night and in this weather, no one was going to see him. The place was dead. He drove under the railway arch, pulled in behind an abandoned and wheel-clamped builder's van with a wad of parking tickets pinned under its windscreen wiper, and switched off the engine.

She glanced at him as she grappled to undo the buckle

of her seatbelt with one hand. He wasn't going to help her. He definitely wasn't taking the baby out of her arms.

'You don't have to do this,' he said. 'We can turn round and I can take you home.'

She didn't answer.

'What are you going to do with her?' He indicated the bundle. 'You can't leave her where she's visible.'

He sighed, took the keys out of the ignition and got out of the car. The wind almost grabbed the boot door out of his hand. The girl came round and stood beside him, then she put down the baby, making sure she was tightly swaddled, and stepped back. He slammed the door shut. The driving rain was already soaking his collar.

'Please listen to me,' he said. She was as white as a sheet. 'You need professional help. You've had a terrible shock and you're not thinking straight. You'll wake up tomorrow morning and realize you've committed an appalling crime. There's no coming back from that.'

She still didn't answer, but her face had hardened, her mouth set in a thin line.

He put his hand on her arm. She flinched so he removed it.

'Once it's done, it's done,' he said. 'But there's still time. It's not too late to change your mind.' He waited, then exploded. 'I cannot do this!'

'Fine,' she said. 'You can take me to the nearest police station, then.'

'Are you serious?'

'It's up to you.' She stuck out her chin.

Leo sighed heavily. 'All right.'

'All right go to the hospital, or all right go to the police?'

His fists tightened.

'The hospital.' He gave her directions to the Grosvenor ward. 'My wife's bed is the first on the right. The name on the baby's wristband is Creasey.' He spelled it out for her. 'C-R-E-A-S-E-Y.'

There, she knew his name now. He didn't want to know hers.

'If my wife is awake, you will abort this, won't you?'

She threw him a look. 'I'm not stupid.'

He breathed out slowly. 'Just hurry up. And for God's sake, don't limp when you're in the hospital. People remember that sort of thing.'

The car became cold quickly, but he didn't dare run the engine. Someone living in the Georgian houses that backed on to the railway line might hear. He contemplated borrowing the blanket in which the dead baby was wrapped, but his mind revolted at the thought. He hugged his arms around his chest and dropped his chin.

Twenty minutes. Chances were she would return empty-handed. He hadn't prayed since primary school, but he did now.

10

Hannah

IN HER BLUE TABARD, THE ONE SHE HAD FORGOTTEN to return to the Birches when she left, Hannah convincingly passed for one of the army of auxiliaries at work in St Thomas's. She was able to pass through the doors to the main entrance without having her right to be there questioned. She focused hard on walking normally.

It had gone eleven and the hospital was winding down but people were still milling around: nurses and doctors coming off shift, night staff coming on; weary relatives, new fathers and elderly wives seeking out cups of coffee and bars of chocolate from the vending machines now the shop was closed. Hannah kept her head down and followed Creasey's instructions until she reached the lifts. She was good at hiding in plain sight, good at effacing herself. Her mother had encouraged that in her.

Was it wrong to have lied to him? When she'd bolted outside the house, blind with panic, she'd thought that it had been the end of everything, but then the car had torn round the bend at that very moment, and she had been offered a way out, a second chance.

She could not and would not admit to her family and the community that her baby had died in her care. They had tossed her out like a piece of rubbish, so she wasn't even going to ask for their help. And she wasn't going to be accused of harming her own child either. People always thought the worst. She had no one on her side, not even her sister and certainly not her best friend. Rachel hated her. She choked back a sob. Zoe would have made up for all that she had lost.

She was doing the man a favour. He should be grateful. As long as she didn't think about the mother, she could pretend she didn't care about the pain she was about to inflict on her. The idea of holding a warm, solid little body and feeling that insistent, greedy sucking again made her breasts ache.

Hannah got out of the lift and followed the signs to the Grosvenor ward where the night nurse was engrossed in a book and barely looked up. Hannah walked straight on and through the next set of glass doors, where she waited out of sight.

Five minutes later the nurse put down her book, came out from behind her desk and crossed the floor to another room. This was her chance. Hannah nipped past the reception and quietly let herself into the darkened ward.

The curtains were closed around each bed, affording the mothers some privacy. Hannah ducked through the first set on the right, checked the woman was asleep and moved to the baby, who also slept soundly. If either of them had been awake, Hannah would have left, but she took this as a sign that what she was doing was right. She bent over the perspex crib.

There was a noise from the bed; a small sigh as the woman rolled over, with an audible ripple from the water-proof cover protecting the mattress. At the other end of the room, a baby started crying.

'Is it morning?'

'No,' Hannah whispered, petrified her legs would buckle. It was too late to leave now. She kept her back turned. 'It's only just gone eleven. You go back to sleep now.'

She waited until the woman's breath had deepened then she peeked out through a narrow gap between the curtains. Through the window in the door she could see that the nurse had returned to her station. It struck her at that point that she hadn't thought to bring anything in which to carry the baby. Stupidly, she'd expected to pick it up and walk out.

A leather overnight bag tucked under the bed caught her eye. She opened it and pulled out everything except for a pair of soft cotton pyjamas. Holding her breath, terrified of making the slightest sound, Hannah lifted the baby from the cot, put her in the bag, tucked a towel around her and zipped it up, leaving a couple of inches for air. She used the discarded items from the holdall to create a baby-shaped hump in the crib. There was even a brown teddy bear to serve as the baby's hair peeking out from under the white blanket. The rest of the belong-ings she pushed under the bed.

She waited, silently, for as long as it took, praying

the baby wouldn't wake. If Creasey had driven away by the time she got back to the car, then so be it. She would walk out of London. Two minutes ticked by before an elderly woman approached the reception desk. After a short conversation, the nurse led her back the way she had come. Hannah moved swiftly, leaving the ward and heading out through the nearest door.

She hurried down the stairs, her face tensed against the jarring pain in her leg, the bag clutched to her chest, the tap of her footsteps echoing off the walls. She was sure she would be pursued, but she wouldn't allow herself to run. She walked; her head dipped so low that her chin was on her chest. The baby was beginning to make noises, little protests that would soon escalate. No one looked at her, spoke to her or demanded to know what the noise was. She had already decided that if anyone asked, she would tell them it was her cat. But no one did. She was euphoric by the time she reached the main entrance and exited the building.

In Centaur Street the wind blew out the plastic sheeting covering some scaffolding and propelled Hannah forward, rain driving into the back of her head. It was as though she had sprouted wings.

By the time she reached the car, the baby was choking on its tears, its wail cutting through the noise of the storm. She got in, set the bag on her knees and unzipped it, lifted the baby out, pulled up her tabard and jumper and fumbled with the hooks on her nursing bra.

'What the hell?' Creasey spluttered, starting the engine and screeching into reverse to execute a three-point turn.

Hannah ignored him and, raising the baby to her nipple, sobbed with agony and sweet relief.

11

Leo

LEO TURNED ON THE RADIO. THE NEWS WARNED OF flooding in the South East. Two people had been killed in their cars by falling trees. Seventy-five-mile-per-hour winds had been recorded across the south coast. People were being warned not to make unnecessary journeys.

He laughed and Hannah's head whipped up.

'What's funny?'

'Nothing. No, everything. Life.'

Her gaze settled back on the suckling baby.

He was running on little sleep and too much adrenalin, and he wanted to wind down his window and roar, but he kept a tight hold on himself.

'Did anyone see you?' he asked, flicking a look at her profile.

'Your wife woke up, but I didn't turn round. She thought I was a nurse.' Hannah fixed her clothes and angled herself towards him. 'There were people around on the way out, but no one noticed me.'

'You have great faith.'

'No one would ever connect us, you know. We're complete strangers.'

'*Strangers on a Train*,' he said.

'What?'

'It's a Hitchcock film.'

'I've never seen a film.'

'No shit. You should get in the back and lie down. If the alarm's been raised, the police will be on the look-out. Stay out of sight.'

He pulled over as she twisted round, knelt on the seat then squeezed through with the baby and made herself small.

Leo drew a sigh of relief. He refused to consider the implications of what he had done until he got home. It was only a matter of time before the hospital discovered the abduction and then they would try to contact him. Fortunately, Sparrow Cottage didn't have a phone. He'd had it disconnected, not wanting any interruptions to his work, particularly from his wife and mother. He used the payphone in the local pub to call Jenny at seven o'clock every evening. That worried him slightly, then he reasoned that, in the circumstances, she wouldn't have been expecting a call tonight.

With any luck, if she already knew the baby had gone, the police and emergency services down in Kent would be too busy rescuing the elderly from their flooded homes to investigate before morning. He remembered the phone line had been down at the girl's house. Would that affect the entire area? It would be a piece of luck if it did.

On the other hand, a kidnapped baby had to be a high priority. The Metropolitan Police would contact their colleagues in Kent and ask them to break the news. If he wasn't where he was expected to be at this time of night, he would be in trouble. Panic invaded him and he put his foot down on the accelerator, reaching seventy miles an hour before the girl hissed at him to slow down.

The countryside sped by. Twice he had to take detours because more roads were blocked, adding half an hour to a journey that already seemed interminable. Where there were no trees to provide a windbreak, the car was buffeted by the gales. He had already lost the radio signal, so there was nothing to listen to.

Two years ago he had watched the Great Storm of 1987 with Jenny from an upstairs window. Dark banks of cloud had raced across the sky, illuminated every few seconds by sheets of lightning, accompanied by a cacophony of car alarms. They had enjoyed the drama. This was different, this was terrifying. This storm reflected the surreal turn his life had taken. Nothing would ever be the same again.

He was close now, ten minutes away from the diversion to her house if their luck held. He sped up as he drove under a narrow railway bridge.

'Shit.'

The road disappeared into a lake that spread out across the fields. He was in it before he could take evasive action, water pouring through the doors, rising around his feet. Halfway across, the car slowed to a halt and went silent. Leo thumped his fist on the steering wheel and swore. He twisted round to find the girl half standing, pressed up against the soft ceiling, clinging to the baby.

'We have to get out and push,' he said.

'I can't. What am I meant to do with her?'

'Stay there, then.'

He wound down his window and climbed out, dropping down into water that came up to his thighs. He waded round to the back of the car, set his palms against it, trying not to look through the window at the small corpse in the boot, and shoved with all his strength, but the car refused to move.

'You're going to have to help,' he shouted through the window. 'Or we're not going anywhere. Give her to me.' He stretched his arms in. 'She'll be OK. I promise.'

Hannah shook her head.

'Do it or you're going to lose that fucking baby too and we're both going to prison.'

She jerked but she obeyed, clambering back into the front seat and handing him the baby before emptying water out of the leather bag. Sophie was awake now, her body tensing before she started to cry, that weird seagull sound new babies make. He hadn't wanted to touch her, and this was almost unbearable. He held her away from him, grimacing, but her eyes had snagged with his and wouldn't let go. He couldn't help himself, he cuddled her against his shoulder, where she settled miraculously. He could smell her, and he was both repulsed by the odour and overwhelmed with emotion.

He thought about Jenny waking to find her gone and was speared by guilt. He looked back the way they had come. He could run. He visualized doing it, as he did with scenes in his novels before he wrote them. He watched himself taking off along the rain-slicked road.

But where to, for God's sake? He wouldn't get back to Jenny tonight, and if by some miracle he did make it and walked into the hospital drenched, muddied and holding a newborn baby, all hell would break loose. Not only that, Sophie was bound to get hungry soon and start screaming. Left alone, he wouldn't know what to do with her. His options had narrowed so quickly it was disorientating. He gritted his teeth. If they didn't get moving, all hell would break loose anyway. It was only a matter of time before someone else passed this way.

Leo placed Sophie in the leather bag and hung it on his shoulder, telling himself that babies in third-world countries survived worse. She started to cry again, building up to a wail. He could feel her fists pummelling the sides of the bag, her feet kicking as they had the inside of Jenny's abdomen not so long ago. She was a feisty little thing.

Something twisted inside him. It was the first time he'd attributed any personality to her. She was a human being. How the hell had he got himself into this? But it was too late for self-reproach; what was done was done. He had to deal with it.

The girl climbed out of the car with his help, falling against him and grasping his shoulders before righting herself. It was a strangely intimate moment, one that he instantly wanted to forget. She followed him round to the back and on the count of three they pushed. The vehicle edged forward then rolled back.

'Again,' Leo shouted.

They pushed and it moved. Leo strained, throwing every ounce of his strength into it, and then suddenly they were out.

'Grab the steering wheel,' he shouted at the girl, pressing his weight against the car to stop it rolling back again.

She ran to the driver's door, opened it and steered the Citroën into the side of the road as he pushed. The bag swung from the crook of his elbow, the baby screaming inside it. Dirty water drained in a rush, like a woman's waters breaking. He caught his breath, then hauled the girl out of the way, leaned in and pulled up the handbrake.

She stood panting, her face drawn with pain. He felt bad. She'd given birth only a few days ago, after all.

'Are you OK?' His glance lowered to her abdomen where her hand rested.

She took a long breath. 'I think so.'

'You'd better get back in,' he said.

He opened the door for her. She didn't look at him as she lowered herself gingerly on to the wet seat.

Leo eased the clutch down and turned the key in the ignition. The engine sputtered and died. He rested his head against the steering wheel.

'I want to go home.' Her voice was small and exhausted, on the verge of tears.

Extreme circumstances called for extreme behaviour. If they stayed and waited for help, they were fucked; if they walked together, they were fucked.

He turned to her. 'Listen, it's not that far to your house, is it? It would be safer for you to walk the rest of the way than risk getting caught here by the police. Do you think you could do that?'

She looked horrified. 'Walk? Won't the car start if we wait?'

'I don't know. It might after half an hour or so, but it might not.'

Just go, he thought. *Please just go.*

'I'll do it,' she said, seeming to shake herself out of her fear. 'I need something dry to wrap her in. She mustn't get cold.'

'OK. Good.' He breathed a sigh of relief.

He took off his coat. Underneath, his sweater was warmed by his body. He pulled it over his head and handed it to her, holding on to it, his eyes locked with hers.

'You will look after her, won't you?'

'I'll guard her with my life.'

She swaddled Sophie on her knee, tying the sleeves of the sweater to secure her, while he struggled back into his wet coat. He got out and opened the boot and the girl stared down at the corpse. She reached in and touched its head. Sheltering under the door, Leo took his wallet out of his pocket, extracted all the notes – about forty pounds' worth – and gave them to her. She sniffed back her tears and pocketed them without thanking him.

'Do you want to put her back in the bag?'

'No.'

She turned and marched up the lane, the baby tucked under that ugly beige anorak he didn't think he would ever forget.

He shouted after her. 'Hey!'

She stopped and looked back, her expression full of a childlike hope.

'If you do hear a car coming, for God's sake don't let yourself be seen.'

She paused, then walked on and, as she was swallowed by the darkness, he hoped fervently that he would never see her again.

She had gone, but he was still in trouble. If he didn't get to Sparrow Cottage soon, the police would arrive before him. What would they think when no one answered the door? He had to make it, even if it meant pushing the car the entire way.

He glanced at the dark mass of a building he had noticed further up the road, fortunately too far away for Sophie's screams to have been heard above the howling wind. It was tempting, but it would mean a witness to testify that he hadn't been at the cottage when his baby was abducted.

He tried the ignition again. Nothing. He didn't know much about these things, but he assumed something vital had been flooded. He pulled the lever that opened the bonnet and went to take a look. Steam was pouring from the engine. He leaned over, trying to figure out where water might have collected, but he couldn't see anything. The truth was, he didn't have a clue. He could jump-start an engine, but that was about it as far as he and cars were concerned. He wanted to weep with frustration and fear, but he would not let this beat him. If he couldn't use brute force, then he would use his brain.

The corpse had come unwrapped, left to roll and knock about in the darkness of the boot. He picked it up, trying not to touch flesh or look at that lifeless face. With his free hand, he opened the holdall, then lowered the body into its gaping mouth, covered it with the blanket and zipped it up with a murmured apology, tucking the bag into the dark space behind the passenger seat.

He closed the door and went round to the driver's side, leaned in and released the handbrake. Guiding the steering wheel, he turned it hard clockwise and propelled the car across the lane, then pushed it backwards into the hedge and yanked the wheel round again. Once he had it facing the flood he pushed it back into the water, then stood back and surveyed his handiwork. His story would be that he'd been caught out by the flood waters driving towards London, not away.

He walked up the lane to the farmhouse and crossed the muddy forecourt. A dog started barking when he rang the bell. A light came on in an upstairs window and feet pounded down the stairs. The door was opened by a tall man with tufty hair, wearing faded blue-and-white-striped pyjama trousers and a thick jumper.

'I'm so sorry to disturb you but the lane's flooded,' Leo explained. 'Like an idiot, I drove straight in and got stuck. My engine's waterlogged. I was wondering whether you could tow me out?'

The farmer didn't appear to be either surprised or angry at being woken in the middle of the night.

'Wind woke me anyway,' he said, pulling a heavy oilskin coat off the hook beside him. He shoved his socked feet into Wellington boots and crammed a broad-brimmed hat on to his head with a large hand.

They trudged back to the car, heads bent against the rain, accompanied by the dog, an elderly red setter called Champ. The farmer, who introduced himself as Martin, stroked his stubbly chin as he surveyed the scene, before coming to the obvious conclusion.

'That won't start. You shouldn't have switched off the engine.'

'I didn't have a choice. I was too far in before I realized what was happening. I was trying to get to London, but I'd like to turn around and go back home now. It was stupid of me – my wife's just had a baby and I wanted to be with her. I was a fool to even consider it.'

'Better late than dead,' the farmer said in a dour tone. 'How far do you live?'

'I'm out near West Farleigh. If you could tow me back, I'll gladly pay you.'

'No, you're all right. Might as well help a neighbour in trouble. Come on, Champ.'

He asked no questions, apparently uninterested in why Leo was there, and his wife and new baby were in London.

Leo sat in the front of Martin's ancient Land Rover, shivering with cold, while the farmer told him about the last time the area flooded, and the drama of facing ruin and losing his marriage. The dog lay between them, panting happily. To an author it was mildly interesting, but the writer in Leo had absented himself hours ago. Leo, the terrified, guilty-as-hell criminal, was shaking like a leaf.

He kept an eye out for the girl, but they didn't see her. Martin's headlights were on main beam, so she would have been able to see them coming from a long way off. They had to be long past her by now.

They pulled up outside Sparrow Cottage, unhooked

60

the Citroen and, out of politeness, Leo offered Martin a coffee or a tot of whisky, but to his profound relief, his rescuer refused and drove off with a cheery wave. Leo stood looking at his car, then made up his mind, retrieved the holdall from under the seat, brought it into the house and tucked it behind the armchair in the sitting room. That would do for now. He'd find a permanent solution later. For the moment, he had more pressing problems. The first being justifying his presence here.

Leo walked around the cottage and shone the torch up the length of the fallen tree. The damage was considerable. Broken tiles lay scattered where he was standing, the lean-to had lost part of its mossy, corrugated plastic roof, and a section of guttering was hanging drunkenly against the wall. There was nothing he could do until the storm had blown itself out.

Upstairs, he found water dripping through the ceiling above the smallest bedroom, where it had saturated the carpet. Left any longer and it would have leaked through to the sitting room, taking the ancient plasterwork with it. He placed a bucket underneath the drip then changed into dry clothes, poured himself a generous measure of whisky, lit the fire and flopped down on the armchair, exhausted. He couldn't remember where the day had started; he knew only that it had been the longest of his life.

12

Jenny

THE SOUND OF A BABY CRYING FOR ITS FEED BRINGS ME staggering out of my dream. It wakes the other babies too. My body is still sticky with dried sweat and flecks of blood, and I fantasize about having a bath as I wait for Sophie to join in. I listen to the rain, feeling lucky to be safe inside. Big weather always brings disaster for someone. I wonder how Leo is doing. I wish he hadn't rushed off, but I can understand why he grabbed at the opportunity to get away for a few hours. This has been a difficult adjustment for him.

Leo has never wanted children. He was clear from the beginning that he wouldn't sacrifice his writing for a child in the way his father had been forced to do. He is too selfish, too one-track-minded, too ambitious. I've always known that and yet I woke up one morning with an overwhelming urge to be pregnant, and in my naivety, I thought he loved me enough to change his mind. At first he was understanding, even good-humoured, but that ended when he realized I thought my recent bio-logical urge overrode his deep-rooted stance.

'We've talked about this,' he said.

'It wouldn't be so terrible, would it? I would do all the work. It wouldn't make any difference to your writing and you'd still be able to go down to Kent as often as you like.'

'Darling, I am not having a baby. I've explained the reasons. I thought you'd agreed.'

'I did.'

'Then what's changed?'

'I don't really know. I just know that I want a baby.'

'It's your hormones, that's all. It'll pass.'

'You understand about that sort of thing, do you?'

He didn't answer.

'Please try to see it from my point of view. I'm as des-perate to be a mother now as you were to give up teaching and write your books when I first met you. My income allowed you to do that – still allows you to – so why can't I have what I want?'

To me it sounded perfectly reasonable, but Leo let rip, accusing me of lying, of trying to trap him. He told me I would make a terrible mother, that I was emotionally crippled and more in love with numbers than I was with people. I had never seen that side of him before, and it frightened me. I didn't sleep a wink that night.

The following morning, leaving for a conference in the South of France, I had to be content with a hand on my arm and a brief, muttered, 'I didn't mean all those things I said.'

I nodded quickly, not wanting to cry again, and scuttled out of the door to the waiting taxi.

And then I met someone: a fellow delegate with time to kill in the evening. A nice, perfectly ordinary man. Not full of himself, like Leo, but interested in others – interested in me. My one and only one-night stand. I wince when I remember the lie I told him. It was so unlike me.

'Do I need a condom?' he had asked, as we kissed.

I can't even say I hesitated. 'No, I'm on the pill.'

It was a spur-of-the-moment decision. I wasn't on it at all. I took it when I first started going out with Leo, but the weight piled on to my hips, thighs and bum, and I stopped taking it after a year of increasingly mad diets. I justified the lie because I was angry and hurt.

On the plane back to England, I was sick with apprehension. Leo wasn't an idiot. He could add up. I needed a plan. In the chemist at the airport I bought a packet of non-spermicidal condoms and, once home, swapped them with the safer brand we normally used. Leo would never notice a detail like that, especially not in the dark. We had make-up sex that night and when he fell asleep, I took the condom into the bathroom, gingerly turned it inside out and smeared its contents inside me. Accidents happen.

I picked a Sunday morning in late July. I'd brought tea and newspapers up to the bedroom. Leo sleepily put his arms around me and kissed my shoulder.

'Morning.'

I allowed him a few minutes to wake up properly, to go for a pee and get back into bed, and then I told him. I will never forget the way the colour left his face.

'What are you talking about?'

I smiled uncertainly. 'We're having a baby.'

I hadn't expected joy, but I'd hoped for something instinctive to happen in my husband, for a chink to appear in his armour, the result of some chemical reaction.

The confusion on his face was not contrived. 'But I'm always careful.'

'Condoms aren't a hundred per cent effective.'

He frowned.

'I might have helped things along a bit,' I admitted. He had to be convinced.

I told him about the switch.

He got out of bed hurriedly and glared down at me. 'Why would you do something like that?'

'Because I wanted a baby.'

I looked up at him, at his handsome, mobile face, and saw an expression I didn't recognize. White-hot fury. For a moment I thought he was going to hit me, and put up my arm to protect myself.

'Christ,' he spat. 'What do you think I'm going to do?'

I lowered my arm. He was pulling on his clothes in fast, angry movements. 'Where are you going?'

'Down to Kent.'

'Leo, please. Let's talk about this.' I hugged the duvet around me for comfort. 'I shouldn't have done it, I know, but . . .'

He came over to the bed and put his hands on my shoulders. 'Who are you?' His fingers were rigid and dug into my muscles. Then he tore himself away and walked to the door.

'Don't go.'

He turned towards me, his eyes scanning my face, looking for something.

'I need to figure out who I married, and I can't think in this house. Not with you.'

'I'm the same person.'

'Then you've been hiding that person from me up until now. I never really knew you, Jenny.'

And then he went. I don't like remembering that morning and, after all, he did come round in the end. I think we're stronger now than we've ever been. And Sophie might be his. In fact, she probably is his.

Sophie is taking her time to wake up. I stretch out a hand, not wanting to disturb her slumber but needing to feel her warmth, to prove to myself that she's alive and well. I lift the edge of the blanket and scream.

Lying where my baby should be is the teddy bear my sister gave her. I experience a kind of wrenching, as if I've been yanked loose from my moorings. My world collapses around me.

I retch as the curtain is ripped aside and a nurse appears. When she sees the empty bassinet, her hand flies to her mouth. The next few seconds pass in a whirl of sound and movement: babies wailing, mothers gasping and sobbing, staff rushing in. I fight for each agonizing breath, convinced I'm going to die. One of the nurses holds me, pressing me forward, rubbing my back, urging me not to panic. Another barks questions in a voice clipped with fear and disbelief.

'Did anyone see anything? Did you hear anything?'

I can't speak. The only sounds I can make are painful gulps. I am an animal, not a human being. People are talking to me, but the words are muddled, just sound and intonation, like a foreign language I've never learned. I swing my legs over the bed, but the nurse restrains me.

'Mrs Creasey, please stay calm.'

'I need to look for her.'

'No, you need to stay here. Security are searching the hospital and the police are on their way. They're going to want to talk to you.' She swivels round and addresses the growing crowd. 'Would you please give us some space? Who was on duty last night?'

'Sally Mather.'

'Well, can somebody phone her and get her back here immediately.'

It's only then that I notice the pile of clothes and toiletries spilling out from under the bed. I slide to the floor and gather my discarded belongings, looking up at the nurse whose horrified expression matches my own. I'm uncoordinated and clumsy, and I drop things around my feet: a pair of pants, a roll of ultra-soft toilet roll. A bottle of shampoo bounces and rolls out of reach. The things I packed with so much thought three weeks ago, ticking them off on the list given out at the NCT class, seem to mock me. Any hope that a doctor might have taken Sophie off for tests drains away. She's been stolen.

'My name is Detective Inspector Liane Parker,' the officer says, taking a card out of her pocket and placing it on the cabinet beside me. She rests the tips of her fingers on it for a second or two, as if to establish its importance in my mind. 'And this is Police Constable Warren. We're going to do everything within our power to make sure Sophie is found. Are you feeling strong enough to answer a few questions?'

'My husband. He doesn't know what's happened.'

'Ah, yes. Where is Mr Creasey?' She looks around, as if expecting him to materialize in the tiny curtained-off space. 'Did he go home to sleep? PC Warren can call him for you.'

'There's no phone where he is.'

Her eyes narrow and I feel judged. 'Where is he?'

'There was an emergency and he had to go down to our cottage. We need to call the police station in Maidstone, or a neighbour.'

The logistics of getting hold of Leo calm me for a few minutes, and then the grief and horror sweep me up all over again. Parker tweaks a fresh wad of tissues from the box beside the bed and presses them into my hand.

'My parents . . . They're on their way from Portugal. How am I going to tell them?'

'We'll cross that bridge when we come to it.' Parker waits for the fresh bout of tears to dry up. 'I know this must be incredibly difficult, Mrs Creasey, but I need you to concentrate. What time did your husband leave yesterday?'

'I'm not sure. About four o'clock, I think.' I wrap my arms round my breasts to dull the growing pressure.

'And no one else visited you?'

I shake my head. 'The other women on the ward had visitors, though. Will you talk to them?'

'I have an officer putting together a list of names. Everyone will be interviewed. Staff and patients included. Perhaps you could tell me what you can remember from when you left the labour room until you woke this morning. Every detail. It doesn't matter how irrelevant you think it is.'

I describe being brought to the ward in the wheelchair by a porter, with Leo at my side and Sophie asleep in my arms. Leo took her from me and placed her in her bassinet, and then he and the porter helped me into the bed. The midwife outlined what would be happening over the next couple of days. Sophie woke up for her feed and dozed off again. There was the phone call from my father. I needed the loo but didn't want to leave her because Leo had gone by that point. The woman in the next bed offered to keep an eye on her.

'Apart from that, she wasn't out of my sight until I fell asleep.'

'Did you meet anyone between the toilets and the ward?'

'No, no one. But I don't think I would have noticed anyway.'

'I understand. Don't worry, Mrs Creasey. None of this is your fault.' She lifts Sophie's blanket off the teddy with her biro. 'Have you seen this before?'

'Yes. It was a gift from my sister.'

'Did she deliver it here, or did you bring it with you?'

'She sent it to me last weekend. I put it in the bag.'

'Her name?' She holds the pencil poised.

'Kate Hurst.' I reel off her telephone number while I try to imagine my serious-minded sister being part of a plot to take my baby. 'Kate has a baby and she lives on a farm in Northumberland. This is a waste of time.'

'Any information is valuable at this stage. Can you describe the bag your clothes were in?'

'It's a soft leather holdall with a tartan lining. It's my husband's.' I frown as an image forms and fractures in my mind. I feel a rush of adrenalin. 'I spoke to her.'

'To who?'

'The woman who took Sophie. I woke up and she was beside the crib. She was wearing some sort of uniform, so I didn't question it. I asked her what time it was. She said it was eleven and I should go back to sleep.'

The detective's eyes light up. 'Do you remember what she looked like?'

'No. She had her back to me.'

'Would you recognize her voice? Did she have an accent of any kind? Foreign or regional?'

I focus hard, my mind tuning in to that moment: the woman's back to me, her swift response to my murmured question. In retrospect, had she sounded scared? Maybe a little. Or is that just my interpretation now, because it makes sense? I can't be sure.

'She was English, softly spoken, that's all I remember. How could this have happened? How could someone just walk in and steal a baby?'

'I don't know. But we're throwing everything at this. Don't you worry, Mrs Creasey. We'll get her back.'

After they leave, the midwife appears with a breast pump and stays with me until I've got the hang of it. The sight of my milk slowly dripping into the bottle is the most depressing thing I've ever seen. I need my husband. I need Leo.

13

Leo

LEO JERKED BRUTALLY OUT OF SLEEP. HE WAS SLUMPED in a chair not a bed, which was bad enough, but also he'd been dreaming about something reassuringly normal – talking to Reuben about his edits. His life was never going to be normal again, though.

He wasn't sure what had woken him. Wind prying off more roof tiles? Branches tapping against windows? He heard it again, unmistakable this time. Someone was knocking at the door.

Oh God, the police. He checked his watch. A quarter to seven. What must he look like? He combed his hair back with his fingers, then held out his hands in front of him. Shaky. He had known this was coming and was ready to look shocked. For fuck's sake, he *was* shocked. The last twenty-four hours had been the most harrowing and catastrophic of his life. To be impassive was impossible.

Shit. He hadn't moved the baby.

He found a police officer in a black raincoat sheltering under the shallow porch.

'Leo Creasey?'

'That's me.'

'PC Shaw from Kent Police. Can I have a word?'

Leo smiled, although inside he was churning with alarm. 'I'm OK, the house isn't badly damaged.'

'I'm not here about the house, Mr Creasey. I'm afraid there's been an incident in London, at St Thomas's Hospital. Perhaps we could go inside.'

Leo ushered him into the house. 'I'm fine. Just tell me what's happened. Is it the baby? Is she all right?'

Shaw glanced through the open door of the living room.

'Come into the kitchen,' Leo said. 'It's warmer in there. I'll make some tea.'

He turned on his heel and led the way into the tiny galley kitchen at the back of the cottage, his heart thumping.

'I'm sorry to have to inform you that your baby has been taken from the hospital.'

'Do you mean by an ambulance? Is she unwell?'

'She's been abducted, Mr Creasey.'

'What?' Leo's hand gripped the edge of the sink and he let his shoulders slump forward.

'Mr Creasey?'

'Sorry. I'm just trying to take it in. How the hell did it happen?'

'I can't answer that question, sir. The Met will speak to you as soon as you get to the hospital.'

'I need to be with Jenny.' Leo took off his glasses, polished them on the edge of his shirt and replaced them. 'Shit. My car. The engine died when I drove into a flood last night. Can one of your officers take me?'

'I can't spare anyone, sir – the emergency services

72

here are stretched to the limit – but the Met are sending a car to pick you up. Their chap's having to come a long way round, I'm afraid – it's havoc out there. An hour or so, two tops. In the meantime, I need you to answer some questions. Perhaps you could make us both a cup of tea. You look like you could do with one.'

'I reached my house at about half past six,' Leo told Shaw. 'I had a look at the damage, and realized there was nothing I could do until morning. It was too dangerous to climb on to the roof, so I stuck a bucket under the leak. I sat down to do the crossword and fell asleep on the sofa. When I woke I had a feeling something was wrong.'

'A feeling?' the officer probed, noting down Leo's words. 'What kind of feeling?'

'Like something gnawing at me. I was hungry so I had something to eat, then tried to go back to sleep. I kept thinking about Jenny and the baby and wishing I hadn't made the journey. I couldn't shake the feeling that they needed me.'

'Why *did* you make the journey? Surely the roof could have waited?'

'In retrospect, yes. I wasn't thinking as clearly as I might have been. I'd found the birth traumatic, and I have a phobia of hospitals. All the blood and bodily fluids, well, they made me feel ill, and I needed some space. If I'm being honest, it felt like a gift.'

The officer made a sympathetic noise and Leo smiled sheepishly at him.

'Do you have children?'

'Two.'

'I expect you know what I mean, then. With the best will in the world, childbirth is very hard to watch. Anyway, at one o'clock I was still wide awake. I decided to drive to the local phone box, meaning to call the hospital and reassure myself, but the lines were down, so I just kept going.'

'Even though you were intending to fix the roof in the morning?'

'Yes.' Leo sighed. 'I admit there's no logic to it. But I had to make sure my wife and daughter were safe. Unfortunately, I didn't see that the road was flooded until it was too late and the water was pouring in. I'd passed a farmhouse just before I got into trouble, so I climbed out of the car window, walked back there and woke up the farmer. His name's Martin. The farm's called Westgrove. He towed me out and brought me back here.'

'Why didn't you keep going?'

'The engine had flooded. But even if it hadn't, I'd had a wake-up call and realized how stupid I was being, putting my own life in danger. It was a ridiculous idea that I could get back to London in that weather. Completely mad. I persuaded myself that my imagination was working overtime, my family was in good hands, and I needed to do what I'd come here for – cover the hole in the roof and phone a builder, then drive up to London in daylight.'

'Had you been drinking, Mr Creasey?'

Leo looked down at his hands, then up at the officer.

'I had a glass or two of whisky once I got in. I needed

it, frankly. I was soaked through and frozen, but I was stone-cold sober when I left the house earlier.'

Later, sitting in the back of the car that had been sent to collect him, Leo's thoughts were dark. What the hell had he done? He had handed his innocent child over to a madwoman. No, not his child. Never his. He must not start thinking about Sophie like that. She was someone else's. But never mind whose she was, he had done a terrible thing to his wife. What must she have felt when she woke to find Sophie gone? He needed to think about Jenny's welfare now. In swapping fatherhood for a lifetime of guilt, he had made a bad bargain.

14

Jenny

'OUR DARLING SOPHIE WAS STOLEN FROM ST THOMAS'S Hospital sometime around eleven o'clock last night.' Leo is speaking but it's going to be my turn soon. It's better, apparently, if the mother speaks. More poignant. More likely to find a way through the perpetrator's defences. I wonder how many times it has. I guess not many.

We've gathered in a cordoned-off area outside the main entrance to the hospital; Leo and I flanked by my mother and father on one side, DI Parker on the other. Mum is holding my hand. I feel a lung-crushing misery that I truly believe might kill me. The inside of my head is a fog of disbelief and horror.

Beyond the cordon of officers, a crowd of excited journalists jostles for position. It feels like being lost in a nightmarish fairground, with noise and flashing and gurning faces. I don't know where to look, so I fix my gaze on the dirty concrete paving. It's studded with flattened blobs of chewing gum.

My parents arrived with no knowledge of what had happened, happy and excited about seeing their new granddaughter, and were stopped by the police at the same time as Leo came running in from the car park. I can imagine how their words of congratulation shrivelled when Leo told them what and who the police presence was for.

Leo was beside himself, shouting at the staff, demanding answers, then breaking down as he held me, saying he was sorry, over and over again. He said it was his fault for leaving me. Dad had to take him downstairs for a coffee and a man-to-man chat. Leo's guilt only made mine worse. I was the one who woke up. I saw the woman and spoke to her. I allowed my precious baby to be taken.

Leo is holding the microphone in front of me, his hands shaking. I take it from him.

'I just want to say, please, if you know anything, please contact the police urgently.' I rush my words, forcing them out of my mouth before another wave of despair can overtake me. 'This is a mother's worst nightmare and the pain is indescribable. If you think you know someone who might have done this, please, please come forward. Or if you have Sophie, it isn't too late, you can leave her at any police station anonymously. We just want to find her. I just want my baby back in my arms. If you're watching this, I believe that you know how loss feels. You know what we're going through. Please give her back to us.'

I reach blindly for Leo as my eyes swim with tears. He puts his arm around my waist. I don't know which of us is supporting the other. The flashes start to make my tired eyes spasm and I hold up my hand to shield them. Detective Parker immediately steps in.

'Could you please desist from taking photographs now? This is extremely difficult for Mr and Mrs Creasey, and you're not making it easier. I think you probably have enough pictures already, to be frank.'

She speaks politely, but there's a hard edge to her tone. It's effective. There's a general, disgruntled mumble but the photographers lower their cameras. It's almost worse because it means I can now see their eyes.

'We need the public's help to find Sophie Creasey,' DI Parker continues. 'As you can imagine, time is of the essence. This crime happened late at night, but hospitals don't sleep and we know there will have been witnesses. It's vital people call us and let us know what they saw, so that we can build a timeline.

'We are asking anyone who was at the hospital that night to think back and think hard. Did you see the woman? She was wearing a blue tabard. We think she left the hospital carrying a brown leather holdall in which Sophie was hidden. She might have been behaving oddly, perhaps walking too fast, perhaps cradling the bag protectively instead of letting it swing at her side. We don't have a full physical description of her yet, but we know that she's white and has a young-sounding voice.

'If you think you saw someone who fits this description, what was your impression? How was she acting? Maybe you drove past the hospital. It was a stormy night – a woman out and about in those conditions would have drawn glances. Maybe you're a cab driver or bus driver. Did you pick her up?'

'There's a good chance she might have been at the hospital earlier, looking for an opportunity. She would have seemed anxious, even fearful. Our concern is that she's a recently bereaved mother herself, possibly suffering from temporary insanity at the loss of her own baby. If the person who abducted Sophie is watching this, please know that we are concerned for your welfare too.' She pauses. 'Think back to last night and earlier this morning, and search your memories for anything that seemed different or surprising. The main thing is we get Sophie back to her parents as soon as possible. If you have any information or think you know anything at all, this is the number to call. Thank you.'

'Do you think it was personal, Detective?' someone from the ranks of journalists asks. 'Does the perpetrator know the family?'

'We're not ruling anything out at this stage,' Parker replies. 'But it is conceivable this woman took the first baby she found and that the Creaseys were simply unlucky.'

'Do you think it was planned?'

'Again, we're not discounting any theory yet. But yes, I do think it was planned – to a degree, at least. We think the perpetrator left certain aspects to chance or didn't think them through. She was probably not in her right mind.'

A madwoman has Sophie. I break down, sobs racking my body. Leo takes me in his arms, drawing my head into the crook of his shoulder.

15

Leo

'LEO,' SOMEONE SHOUTED. 'WHERE WERE YOU WHEN your baby was kidnapped?'

There was a fine line between devastation and hysterical laughter, Leo realized. The whole shebang had a farcical quality, but black humour was his default as an author, so black and dry it could be misinterpreted. That was what this situation felt like. You couldn't get blacker than a stolen baby.

Being driven to the hospital in a squad car had given him time to gather his thoughts. He had been terrified of what he would find when he arrived – a broken wife, a police investigation, coming face to face with the direct and catastrophic result of his actions – but the journey at least gave him a chance to deal with each nightmare scenario in turn, to run through the worst that could happen and his own responses.

The reality had been as bad as he had expected. Jenny had been inconsolable and his in-laws were shocked and struggling to find a way to help their daughter. The

hospital was embarrassed and defensive about its inadequate security, its PR team fumbling in the dark, and the
police were reassuringly cack-handed. Leo didn't appear
to be in any immediate danger.

Everyone was looking at him. Before he could respond,
the detective raised the microphone.

'Mr and Mrs Creasey won't be answering questions
at this juncture. If you have any, please direct them to me.'

Leo could hear his own breathing, as though he were
underwater. He was trying so hard not to look shifty or
guilty that he was convinced it must be showing on his
face. He dreaded seeing himself on the television and in
the papers, and hoped to God the coverage would focus
on his wife, not on him. Jenny certainly looked the part.
Her hair was limp and she wore no make-up or jewel-
lery apart from her wedding ring. With her shadowed
eyes and jaundiced-looking skin, she came across as
exactly what she was: a woman to whom something
appalling had happened, who neither knew nor understood who she was now or how to exist in this grotesque
and unfamiliar world. Or was he projecting his own
feelings on to her? Perhaps.

She didn't deserve this. He remembered the woman
with whom he had fallen in love, the nerdy but pretty
twenty-two-year-old with hazel eyes and mousy hair
who'd had no idea how much more attractive she was
than her more knowing and flirtatious friends. He had
wanted to rescue her before they made her like them.

Leo trained his gaze above the heads of the journalists, trying not to wince at their increasingly intrusive
questions. Parker was doing a good job of batting them

away and sticking to her brief: persuading reluctant witnesses to come forward. Would the girl see this? He didn't remember there being a television set in her house, but he supposed there might have been one. At any rate, the story was growing so big, if she didn't see it now, she would soon. Some bastard from the *News of the World* had already slipped him a note, offering money for his story. More if Jenny would speak to them. He wouldn't be the last.

He wondered what his in-laws were thinking. Elaine had collapsed when he'd told her what had happened, and had to be supported to a chair. Charles had been Charles: staunch, rock-solid, ready to help. He felt terrible for the part he had played in Leo's absence from the hospital last night. *If only he knew.*

'I should never have interfered,' Charles had said. 'What does a fallen tree matter compared to this? If you'd been there—'

'Don't blame yourself. It was my choice to go. I'm so sorry, though. I did try to get back last night, but that damn flooding . . . Oh God. I can't believe this is happening.'

Jenny's hand was hot and damp in his, but he wouldn't let it go. Bafflingly, he found her alluring like this – frightened and almost blind in her confusion. Normally she was so together – her appearance, her actions, the way she made plans were all achieved without fuss. She created and maintained the framework of their lives. Now that framework had slipped, he appreciated what his throw of the dice was likely to have cost him. Because that was what it had been: chance had brought him to this pass.

They turned and walked back into the hospital, along the corridor to the room that had been set aside for the police inquiry. Elaine was sobbing quietly beside him and Jenny's tear-stained face was set like stone as she endeavoured to hold it together.

This was his life now, his new identity. Angry father, bitter husband. Liar, dissimulator. Criminal.

16

Jenny

I'M DISCHARGED THE FOLLOWING MORNING AND WE'RE driven home in two police cars: Leo, me and Tracy the family liaison officer in the first one; my parents and their suitcases in the second. Our drivers get out first and corral the journalists who have already gathered outside our house to greet us. They shout our names, but we ignore them. Mum, Dad and Tracy surround me while Leo runs up the steps and unlocks the door.

Tracy exudes compassion and a friendly efficiency that I find almost reassuring. She's wearing a black suit and her brown hair is pulled back in a ponytail. Gold-knot earrings decorate her ears and her open, pretty face is free of make-up. She is the epitome of approachable.

In the hall there are signs of our departure: my slippers kicked off at the bottom of the stairs; some old receipts that I pulled out of my handbag at the last minute, not wanting to take my clutter with me.

My father and Leo take the bags upstairs. Mum and Tracy steer me into the sitting room. It's cold. One of them wraps me in the throw that hangs over the arm of the sofa. Leo shouts that he's going to turn on the central heating and make everyone a cup of tea. Tracy goes downstairs to the kitchen to help him, leaving me alone with my parents.

Mum sits down beside me and Dad stands by the mantelpiece. Both of them have a grey pallor. Now that we're home, it's hard to know what to say to each other. Mum puts her arm around me and kisses the side of my head. Eventually, Dad picks up the newspaper from two days ago, flicks through to the games and folds it over on the crossword puzzle. He takes a pen out of the inside pocket of his jacket then sits down on the other sofa and reaches for a coffee-table book to press on.

Leo and Tracy come back upstairs bearing steaming mugs and a packet of chocolate digestives. After a while all I can hear is the crunch of biscuits and the quiet slurp of tea.

Tracy's radio crackles into life and she leaves the room, our heads turning to follow her as if we're tracking the ball at a tennis match. She returns with a quick shake of her head. No news. After a while, Dad breaks the silence.

'So what happens now?'

'I'm afraid all we can do is wait.'

I glance at the telephone on Leo's desk. It sits there silently.

'I can't just hang around,' Dad says. 'Give me a job.'

My father is a doer, a solution finder. When Kate and I were little, Dad was either at work or he was tinkering. While my mother was quite happy to put her feet up on the sofa and read a book, he would twitch if he didn't have a task. Our house was a shrine to his DIY efforts.

'Charles,' Leo says. 'Just settle down. We're all in the same boat.'

Dad frowns at Leo. He's never taken to him, probably because Leo, though respectful, considers himself leader of the pack.

'There's nothing you can do that our officers aren't doing already,' Tracy assures him. 'You're being a great help just by being here to support your daughter.'

Dad visibly bristles – he feels patronized – and Mum interrupts before he can retort.

'This area – it's quite rough, isn't it? I mean, the square is beautiful, but it's surrounded by those enormous council estates. They can see right into your back garden, can't they, Jenny? People can be jealous.'

'I don't think so, Mum,' I say tiredly.

'What about the lady who cleans for you?'

I shake my head.

'We've taken statements from her and her family,' Tracy says. 'They're not under suspicion.'

I make a move, releasing myself from Mum's embrace. She presses me down with a firm hand on my thigh.

'What do you need? Let me get it for you.'

'Nothing.'

Outside, a taxi draws up down the street, its engine ticks over and a front door thuds shut. The taxi drives away.

'Who lives next door?' Dad asks.

'I don't really know them,' I say.

'There are four sets of flats either side of this house,' Tracy tells him. 'All the occupants have been interviewed. Officers have gone door-to-door round the entire square. I can assure you, we haven't left a stone unturned.'

Where we are, in a slightly seedy but once grand Georgian square between Stockwell and Kennington, most of the houses were converted into flats sometime during the sixties and seventies. On our side of the square, only two remain entire houses, reconverted in the last couple of years. This is not the kind of area where people chat over their fences. The residents of the flats come and go. There's one community-spirited family who organized a street party in the gardens a couple of years ago, but they haven't repeated it. Their kids are teenagers and not interested. A few weeks ago, I bumped into their mother in the street and, with a laugh, she offered them up for babysitting duties. I wonder what she's thinking now. I expect she'll avoid me. It's easy to do that round here. We're anonymous. At least we were.

I get up, overwhelmed. Mum stands up too, as do Tracy and Leo. I walk to the door and they follow me. I stop at the bottom of the stairs and they stop. It's like that game we used to play at school, Grandmother's Footsteps.

'I'm going to run myself a bath,' I say.

'I'll do it,' Leo says. 'You just sit down.'

'No. I need to be by myself for a while.'

'Are you sure, darling?' Mum asks. 'I can sit in your bedroom, if you like. Then, if you need anything . . .'

'Stop it! I can't stand this.'

'Let her be,' Dad calls from the sitting room. He

appears, glasses slipping down his nose. 'Off you go,' he encourages. 'Get some peace.'

Tracy backs away discreetly, returning to her position near the window where she can keep an eye on the comings and goings, and make sure the reporters don't encroach too much on the house. Mum stands with her arms crossed, looking stricken. Leo regards me thoughtfully.

I trudge upstairs, hesitating outside our bedroom before carrying on to the top floor. The door to the room at the back is open and my parents' suitcases are on the bed. The room we chose for the nursery is at the front of the house, overlooking the garden square rather than the tower blocks behind us. I stand on the threshold. The room is flooded with light and the sun is out. The weather that would have greeted my baby when she came home is very different from the weather that greeted her birth. I resent its welcoming cheerfulness. It feels atrocious, insulting.

It still smells of paint and new carpet in here. The walls are pale yellow with stencils of farm animals running above the picture rail. A teddy-bear mobile hangs over the white cot. Next to the sash window there's a rocking chair with a folded cream cashmere blanket on the cushioned seat. I shake it out and drape it round my shoulders, then I sit down and rock. I imagine Sophie in the cot, lying on her stomach, her thumb in her mouth, her other hand curled round a rail and a teddy bear propped in the corner. A huge bubble of misery rises painfully through my chest and explodes out of my mouth in a cry of anguish.

Leo comes running upstairs. He drops to his knees beside me and I wrap my arms around his head, convulsing.

'Sorry, I'm so sorry,' he weeps.

It's the first time he's cried and I find myself praying that Mum and Dad don't follow him up here. But they have more tact. We hold one another for a long time, then he takes me down to our bedroom and I curl up on the bed, pulling the eiderdown over me while he runs me a bath.

'They will find her, won't they?' I say.

Leo strokes my hair. 'Of course they will. It's impossible to hide a baby.'

In the bath, milk leaks from my breasts and swirls into the hot water.

17

Leo

LEO'S SISTER-IN-LAW KATE CAME DOWN ON THE TRAIN
the following afternoon, leaving her husband to look
after the farm and their children. She burst into tears
the moment she walked into the house. It wasn't particularly helpful.

Tracy, the FLO, was in and out, dropping by even
when she had nothing to report. There had been little
progress – no useful witnesses and no suspects. The
ranks of journalists grew. They leaned against the rail-
ings on the other side of the road in a miasma of cigarette
smoke and frozen breath. Charles called them bottom-
feeders.

Every time a police car drew up, the members of the
press would go into a frenzy and Leo's brain would dull
with terror. He didn't know how he held it together, but
he would open the door, show in the officers, offer them
refreshments and wait, ears ringing, to be read his rights,
or at least be informed that a woman had been arrested
in Kent. But nothing like that happened. Instead, his

punishment was seeing his wife become someone else entirely as the hours and days went by.

The weight fell off him and he began to look gaunt. His skin was grey, his eyes yellow and unhealthy. He had four days' worth of beard. The worst times were when Jenny was sedated and asleep and he was left sitting at the kitchen table with his in-laws, knowing that he was responsible for destroying their precious daughter. He wished he could wind back the clock to before that phone call from Charles, to before he made the decision that changed all their lives. How could he have done this to his wife? And then he thought about that other baby and, in the small hours of the night when the scene of the accident spooled through his mind, he honestly believed he would not be able to bear the burden for the rest of his life.

'Leo?' Kate said.

He opened his eyes slowly and looked at her. In that moment, in the dim light, wearing one of Jenny's long cardigans, she resembled her sister so closely that he thought it was his wife, back to her normal self. Kate had come upstairs from the kitchen to find him sitting in the dark, his legs stretched out, hands clasped behind his head. He knew he looked like he was lost in thought, but his mind was empty, as if someone had wielded a leaf blower inside his skull.

'Sorry,' Kate apologized. 'I didn't realize you were asleep.'

'I wasn't. I was trying to . . .' His voice petered out. He had no idea what it was he was trying to do. Exist, he supposed.

Kate propped her bottom on the windowsill and peered out into darkness. Beyond the garden wall, the lights were on in a random selection of windows in the tower block, resembling an advent calendar. Leo straightened up and swivelled round. The chair had belonged to his father once upon a time. It was Victorian and mahogany with a back that curved into arms, a well-worn, green leather seat, legs that swept out, and feet on castors. His father had sat on it at this desk to write his book. Lola hadn't been interested in holding on to either item of furniture, so Leo had kept them as a reminder to himself of what could happen if you allowed your dreams to slip away.

'I probably should go tomorrow,' Kate said. 'Chris needs me. It's too much for him looking after the girls and the farm on his own, and his sister can only help out in the afternoons.'

Leo contemplated her through a haze of exhaustion.

'Can you stay one more day?' he asked. 'I need to go down to the cottage and talk to contractors about the roof.'

She stared at him. 'Can't that wait?'

He shrugged. 'James has contacted a couple of local roofers, but I need to meet them. He's been very kind, but I can't expect him to do any more than he has already.'

'For God's sake, Leo. Jenny is a mess, we've got journalists on the doorstep and the police in and out. How can you possibly think about leaving her?'

He might have known she would react like this. Kate had never liked him. She had always regarded him with a certain amount of scepticism, as if there were a selfish motive behind everything he did, every breath he took. He didn't really care what she thought. He knew what he had to do, and nothing she said would either deter or delay him.

'She'll be all right if she has her family round her,' he said shortly. 'But it's not just about the builders. I have a mother too, and she's distraught. I have to talk to her face to face or she'll come up here.'

'Well. OK, obviously you have to see your mum.'

The threat had hit its mark. Lola was renowned for sucking up the oxygen in any situation.

'I'll get a cab from the station, pick up my car from the cottage. It should have dried out by now. And thanks.' He made it sound as though he was grateful to have her blessing.

The house looked different in the light of day. Last time he'd been here, he had seen the dark shape of a house with a light glowing from the front door. In his memory it had taken on a menacing quality. Now, it was merely sad. There was an area of hardstanding, but he decided not to park there, even though it wasn't in use. Instead, he pulled in further along. He got out and stood still, listening to the birdsong, breathing in the fresh air. At his feet, primroses peeked through the long grass. On either side of the house, fields spread behind the hedgerow and rose in a gentle incline towards the horizon.

His tyres had left their mark, a black crescent of rubber tracks sweeping across the tarmac and on to a wedge of crushed and muddied verge. His stomach clenched.

He hadn't realized how close he had come to tipping into the ditch.

He swung round as the front door to the house opened.

Instead of the distraught girl he remembered, a young woman in a diagonally striped jumper and bleached jeans stood in front of him. He barely recognized her. She looked tired but pink-cheeked. The lank hair had gone, now washed and pinned back with tortoiseshell clips. She seemed transformed. The moment she realized who he was, she tried to shut the door. He slammed his hand against it and pushed his way into the house.

'Where is she?' he demanded. 'Where is my daughter?'

'She's not your daughter,' she hissed, pulling at his arm. 'What do you want? You shouldn't be here. What if someone saw you?'

He had driven with one eye on the rearview mirror, paranoid, but no one had followed him. He breathed out slowly. It was OK.

Sunlight flooded the house. It was bright and cheery, a parallel universe to the one into which he had been thrust only a few days ago. He heard a noise, like the mewl of a kitten, and followed it into the front room. The girl hurried after him, clucking and squawking. He didn't listen. The baby was in a carrycot on the sofa. As he looked at it, it opened its eyes and gazed at him. He reached out but the girl shoved him out of the way and scooped up the child. Immediately it began to root for her breast.

'Why are you here?'

'You have to give it back.' He felt breathless, his lungs constricted, his diaphragm rigid. 'This is not going to work. It's killing my wife. The plan was mad from the beginning. You're condemning yourself to a lifetime of lying, of looking over your shoulder. I'll help you. I'll come up with somewhere you can leave the baby where it'll be found quickly.'

'*She*,' the girl spat at him. 'Stop calling her "it". And she's not going back, not ever. She's my baby. You gave her to me.'

'Under duress!' He realized he was yelling, and pulled back. 'You didn't give me a chance to think.'

'You're a clever man. You're a lot older than me, you should have thought before you drove with a bottle of whisky in your hand.'

He saw the teenager again in the sly look she gave him, but for once in his life he had no words.

'I'll call the police,' she threatened. 'What you did was worse. I heard it on the radio. The policewoman said they think I might have gone insane because I lost a baby. She said "temporary insanity". You don't have any excuse for what you did.'

The baby began to whinge. Leo could feel the threat of its impending cries deep in his chest. The girl eased the knuckle of her little finger between its lips.

'I am begging you,' he said. 'I can give you money, a lot of money. Enough to get you out of this place and away from here.'

'I don't want your money and I don't want to leave. Go away.'

'Christ,' he exploded. 'You're young! You can have another baby. You can have a sodding houseful. You don't need this one. It doesn't belong to you.'

'She!' she screamed, and the baby gave an outraged cry.

The girl sat down on the sofa and lifted her top. She was trembling, but she still managed to put the baby to her breast with an efficiency that stunned Leo. She was so different from the girl he remembered. The panic-stricken, incoherent teenager had been replaced by a mother. He held his fists rigid at his side. After a moment, he realized he'd lost her attention.

He said quietly, 'What can I say to change your mind?'

She didn't so much as glance his way.

'Nothing,' she whispered, stroking the baby's head. 'Nothing.'

PART 2

Sixteen Years Later

2005

18

Jenny

I MOVE MY HAND TOWARDS LEO'S AND PRESS MY LITTLE finger against the side of his palm. He doesn't stir. He has always slept like a log. I slip quietly out of bed and put on my dressing gown. He can have a few more minutes, but I have to get on.

Downstairs, I close the kitchen door and sit down to answer emails from colleagues in Hong Kong. The only way to make bearable a life that has lost its meaning is to keep busy. I've stuffed mine with lists and tasks because if I have no time to think, I can't fall apart. In the sixteen years since Sophie was taken I've held down a job, I've set up a support group, which I run to this day, and I've gained a qualification in counselling.

A ping alerts me to a text. I get up and unplug my phone from the charger, smiling because I know who it will be; he always messages me on Sophie's birthday. I remember the first time he got in touch. It was about eighteen months after she'd been taken, and I was back at work. My line had rung and I'd picked it up, expecting an internal call. Around me, in the vast open-plan office, conversations clattered then melted away as I recognized his voice – that soft French lilt, like honey. I dropped into a vortex, where the people, machines and all sound and movement became a blur. I thought I was going to faint, or throw up, and gripped the desk with my free hand.

'Jenny?'

I couldn't say anything.

'Jenny. You remember me?'

I brought myself under control. 'Of course I remember.'

There was a long pause.

'I need to know. Is she mine?'

Someone popped their head round the door and I motioned for them to go away. I hoped they hadn't seen that my face was burning.

'I don't know. But I think so. I'm sorry. I should have got in touch.'

'I don't blame you, and you must not blame yourself.'

Silence again. I turned away from my screen and faced the window. A pigeon flew past.

'Have you told anyone?'

'No.'

'Are you going to?' He could get a lot of money for his story. My heart started to race again.

'No.'

I swallowed hard. 'Were you very angry when you realized?'

'Of course. It affected me deeply and I had to hide it

from my family. I'm not angry now. I don't want anything, Jenny. I just wanted to let you know that you are in my thoughts and I hope they find her.'

We haven't spoken since, but he's never forgotten her birthday.

I delete the message and answer one from my mum, fussing about arrangements for next week. I'm going to spend two weeks with her in Cascais. Kate and her daughters are coming out for the Easter weekend. We want to reassure ourselves that Mum's coping without our father, but for me the timing couldn't be better. I plan to escape the press attention that today's events are bound to unleash.

Upstairs, Leo is shaving in the en suite. I walk through the dressing room to join him, catching his eye in the mirror as I put down his mug of tea beside him. The blade rasps on his skin. My publicity-hungry husband is excited. The atmosphere crackles with it.

We are marking Sophie's sixteenth birthday with an appearance on ITV breakfast television and the six and ten o'clock news. The *Daily Mail* are featuring the case, along with an open letter to Sophie, which I wrote and Leo edited. The BBC interview was recorded last week.

Sophie's abduction was a huge story back in 1989, covered worldwide. As the years have gone by and there have been other child abductions and murders, less has been made of it, so Leo has felt justified in scheduling the publication of his three subsequent novels, *The Tea Party*, *Springfield Close* and *Threadbare*, within a week or two of 10 March as a way of keeping our daughter in the public consciousness. All these carnivals do is turn my baby into someone I don't know: the toddler, the child, the teenager.

It was Daisy, Leo's publicist, who suggested the big media push to mark Sophie's sixteenth. Yesterday, she came to the house to talk me through it; Leo didn't need instruction. She discussed the pros and cons of mentioning *In the Lake*. I wanted to say to her, 'It's not all about Leo, and it's definitely not about his new bloody book. I am dying inside, so stop wittering on and show some sensitivity.'

Of course, I didn't say anything.

Leo is keen. He is, in many ways, my surrogate child, absorbing my emotional energy: sometimes demanding attention, sometimes wanting to be left alone. But that's OK. I have a lot to make up for.

'What are you going to wear?' Leo asks as he saunters through from the bathroom with a towel wrapped round his waist, his skin shiny and pink.

He's still fit, and ageing well, his figure trim. His black hair is laced with grey and thinning at the temples. He replaced the round, wire-rimmed glasses for a trendier pair with tortoiseshell frames long ago. The gangly young man with a surfeit of self-confidence has grown into himself, and with success has come stature. He stands straighter, holds his head higher. He's doing better than me; I've put on a stone in the last couple of years. Sometimes I resent the contrasting effect the loss of Sophie has had on us.

I hold up a pale-green shirt. I've been reminded not to wear red because I'll disappear into the sofa, and equally not orange or bright pink because I'll clash with it. God forbid I clash.

'With my dark trousers and the lilac scarf.'

'Perfect,' Leo says.

Daisy warned me not to think my appearance doesn't matter, because it does. It's a 'big deal'. I wonder if she realizes I'm the main breadwinner in the Creasey household and don't need to be told to be careful about the impression I make. I know I'm going to be judged, more than Leo, as much by my choice of outfit as by the level of emotion I choose to show. I'm under no illusion – my appearance today will provoke a reaction. There will be pity and sympathy, but there will also be negativity, lurid speculation and righteous fury directed at me, the mother who slept while her baby was taken from her bedside.

There've been appeals before. In 1999, a computer whizz created a mock-up of what Sophie might have looked like at the age of ten, though how anyone can tell from a photograph of a newborn baby is a mystery to me. The artist studied both my and Leo's faces, as well as photographs of us as children, and made his calculations. He wasn't to know it was probably an exercise in futility because there's a strong chance my daughter's genetic make-up has nothing in common with Leo's. He produced a clumsy composite of a hazel-eyed, brown-haired child who could have belonged to anyone. I hate these circuses and question their usefulness. All they do is pick the scabs off old wounds.

With shaking fingers, I fit a pair of diamond-encrusted studs to my earlobes. A minute ago I was fine – as fine

103

as I could be, at least – but my pulse is racing now. Very soon, strangers will be opening their newspapers and finding the letter. Will their thoughts automatically go to girls they know who turn sixteen this week?

Sophie won't be one of those early-morning readers. There's no point dwelling on that outlandish possibility. How many sixteen-year-olds have time to read a newspaper over breakfast? Maybe, once they're home, they might idly turn the pages. The chances are one in a million that Sophie will be amongst their number. I understand probability.

In one of the few photographs we have of Sophie, her eyes are closed and she has a white cap pulled low over her forehead. We don't have any of her face without the cap. All you can see are her eyelids, pursed lips and tiny nose with its translucent nostrils. It sits on my dressing table. I pick it up and look at it, then glance at Leo. He's straightening the bed. That means he's uncomfortable.

'Why are we doing this?' I blurt out. 'What good will it do? It just encourages salacious interest. People don't want to help find Sophie, they want to imagine her in some pervert's dungeon. They love those kind of stories. I hate it.'

'We're doing it for Sophie. Never mind what other people say or think, we're reaching out to our daughter.'

'And you have a new novel to publicize.'

I sometimes suspect my husband of being entirely fulfilled, despite what happened. I, on the other hand, am incomplete, a money machine, a woman with no purpose but to wait for her missing daughter and to love and support her celebrity husband. Not that he needs my money in the way he used to. His royalties have softened in the last few years, with the advent of digital publishing, but he still makes enough to keep himself – if not in the lap of luxury, in comfort. And it isn't as if we've had a child to raise.

He drops his hands. 'You look ugly when you say things like that.'

'I'm not blaming you, Leo,' I say. 'I understand how these things work. But at least admit this suits you. Don't be a hypocrite.'

'What do you want me to say? That I'm glad our daughter was stolen because it means a bigger market for my books? You know that's not true. You can wallow in your misery, you can refuse to move on, but allow me at least to derive some pleasure from my life.'

'When have I ever stopped you doing that?'

He holds his hands up in surrender. 'You haven't. You're an angel.'

I scowl, refusing to be placated so easily.

'Come on,' Leo coaxes. 'Don't let's quarrel, today of all days. Let's celebrate our daughter on her sixteenth birthday.'

'You are such a bastard.'

But my anger has dissipated as quickly as it arrived. He's right – today is about Sophie, not us.

'It's been exactly sixteen years since one-day-old Sophie Creasey was abducted from St Thomas's Hospital while her mother slept only feet away. Her parents, Leo and Jennifer, have fought tirelessly to keep the story in the public eye, never giving up hope of finding their daughter. They join me now.'

The camera swings over to us, and I try not to look like a tailor's dummy. My hair has been brushed into a more flattering style and sprayed in place, my lipstick colour adjusted, my scarf draped becomingly round my neck. Beside me, I feel Leo bracing himself.

'Sixteen years,' the presenter, Camilla Richards, says. 'It feels like it happened only yesterday.'

Leo nods. 'Yes. Losing our daughter has done something odd with time.'

'I suppose it must be hard to have a normal life with that always in the back of your mind.'

'She isn't in the back of my mind.' I smile, so that Camilla doesn't think I'm offended. 'She's always in my thoughts. And our life is normal, it's just not the normal we expected.'

'You've both achieved so much over the years. Jenny, you're a partner at a prestigious accounting firm, and you've been a huge support to other bereaved families through the network you founded, Open Arms. You're an inspiration.'

'That's not the way we think about it,' Leo says. 'We just do what we have to do.'

'At the time,' Camilla says carefully, 'the case was huge. One of the biggest manhunts in history. The police had hundreds of leads. Interpol became involved. Do you blame the police for not finding her?'

I have a flash of Liane Parker's face, when she sat in our sitting room, a year after Sophie had gone, and told us that although the case wouldn't be closed, it was being wound down. I thought she was going to cry. Her eyes had reddened, and she had turned away from me. She took it personally.

'The only person I blame is myself,' I say to Camilla. 'The police did everything they could. I'm still in touch with the detective in charge of the investigation. We haven't given up on Sophie, and neither has she.'

'But no resources are being put into the case.'

'No,' Leo concedes. 'Of course we wish Sophie's abduction was still being fully investigated, but we're realists. Police have budgets to allocate.'

'Have you used a private investigator?'

Leo nodded. 'From time to time. Usually if someone gets in touch and we think there's a possibility a lead is real. But they've been false hopes, and that's so destructive.'

He takes my hand and gives it a quick squeeze. Camilla leaves a pause, her face full of sympathy.

'You've written an open letter to Sophie, haven't you, Jenny? Would you like to read it?'

I give her a quick, bright smile. 'Yes.'

'Go ahead,' Camilla prompts. 'Imagine Sophie is sitting at a kitchen table, eating her breakfast, and the television is on.'

I do a lot of presentations for work and I've talked to groups about Open Arms, but this is an audience I can't see and whose reactions I can't predict. It's unexpectedly terrifying. I look into the camera and pretend there's just one person looking back: Sophie. The letter is on the autocue. It starts to scroll as I begin to speak.

'My darling Sophie, today you are sixteen years old and

maybe you are reading this, watching us on the television or listening to the radio. You might not be celebrating your birthday today, but it may well fall this week, so happy birthday. We have never stopped loving you, and you are always in our minds and our hearts. Sophie, it's possible that you have been hidden in plain sight. You will be white, you may have brown hair and hazel eyes like me, or you might have your father's brown eyes and black hair. The woman you know as your mother might have a history of mental illness or postpartum depression. If you have any reason to think you might be our daughter, you can arrange to have your DNA tested in complete confidence. We will never stop looking for you and will never stop hoping that one day our family will be reunited.'

'That was beautiful, Jenny,' Camilla says. 'Is there anything you'd like to say to the woman who took Sophie?'

I look straight at the camera. 'If you have my child, I hope that you love her as much as we do. I hope that you've brought her up as we would have done.'

'For those sixteen-year-old girls out there,' Leo says, picking up when I fade out. 'If you were born between the fifth and tenth of March 1989, think about who you are and what you look like. Do you ever feel as though you don't belong? If you have the slightest doubt, get in touch.'

The camera switches back to Camilla.

'Thank you. Let's hope you get some calls.' She's leaning towards Leo, her face tipped to one side, her eyes wide. 'Your books have reached a huge audience in the years since the abduction, Leo. You've become a bestselling author – dare I say it, a household name. Would it be true to say that having your success tied up with the public's fascination with your personal tragedy in some sense creates a moral dilemma?'

Leo is curt. 'First, I would happily sacrifice any success if it meant getting Sophie back. But I suppose you have a point, in that before my daughter's abduction, people didn't know my name and after it they did, but frankly no amount of renown is going to help if the books are rubbish. That readers found their way to my work owes something to Sophie's disappearance, but the fact that they've stuck with me all these years owes more to my storytelling.'

Camilla's smile is stiff. Leo has made her look bad.

'Do you feel that the police gave up too soon?'

'They exhausted all lines of enquiry,' Leo says.

He's had enough, I think.

Camilla nods. 'And what about you two?'

'What about us? We're here, aren't we?' Leo snaps.

I put my hand on his forearm and exert gentle pressure. 'We've never given up and we never will. We know Sophie will find her way home.'

The interview is over. It lasted three minutes – a generous slot. When we were first interviewed on television, we were allotted ten minutes of airtime. On the first anniversary we were given eight, by the third five. On the fifth it was three. On the tenth we had just two minutes. Sixteen years is more interesting: a baby has become a teenager; a girl who can make decisions, question her life, turn it upside down. It earned us an extra minute.

109

19

Zoe

MUM HAS LEFT FOR WORK BY THE TIME I GET UP AND come downstairs. The kitchen is distinctly chilly, the outside world crisp and white with frost. The house is silent. I yawn and turn to the dresser to switch on the radio, but it's not there. She must have taken it with her, probably because she doesn't trust me to revise. God, it's bad enough living in a house without a television, but the radio is a lifeline. And it's not as if I don't study – there's nothing else to do around here.

I make porridge, scrape it into a bowl and swirl in some runny honey. On the table, I create a wall of canned tomatoes to lean my library book up against. I've almost finished reading *Carrie* by Stephen King. Mum doesn't know, and she wouldn't like it if she did – I should be reading stuff that improves my mind.

It's been hard for Mum. You need to know people to get anywhere these days, and she didn't have connections or qualifications, money or friends. Her education was half-hearted. No wonder she constantly lectures me about making the most of my opportunities and having a career. Fall in love and get married, but make sure you've got the wherewithal to look after yourself if it all goes wrong. Mum is a worst-case-scenario kind of person, but there's a fine line between preparing me for the ups and downs of life, and making me think it's not worth making the effort.

I pick at my food, reading and occasionally glancing out of the window. The sun is rising, the sky is blue. I'm not going to be like Carrie. I'm going to make a success of my life, even if it means gritting my teeth for another two and a half years of torture. And then I'll be off to university and the shiny new world that awaits. And I can help Mum if I get that high-flying job she keeps banging on about.

I finish my breakfast, make sure my guinea pig has enough food and water, then do the routine stuff: wash up my breakfast things, clean my teeth, pack my school rucksack and check I've got my keys. I put *Carrie* in my bag to finish at break and to change at the library in town later. I put on my coat, gloves, scarf and bicycle helmet, and leave the house. It's four miles to school and the journey takes half an hour – thirty-five minutes if the wind's against me. Most of it is country lanes, for the rest I use the pavement.

That half-hour on the road is precious. It's when I feel happiest and most alive, and when my brain switches on. I sort things out and make things up. I repeat my mantra: *I will not show weakness or shame.* That's the only way to survive school, in my particular situation.

By the time I jump off outside the gates, my body is

hot, but my face and fingers are frozen. I wheel my bike into the playground and lock it up. No one bothers me. Sometimes I get pushed, or flicked, or tripped. More often the attacks are verbal. I imagine the students in the playground as separate little darts of fire that I have to negotiate. Some are uninterested, others are aggressive and stupid with it. I avoid them. If they make themselves unavoidable, I keep moving, and if they surround me, I plaster a benign smile on my face and I don't react. Sticks and stones will break my bones, but words will never hurt me.

Sometime in the not too distant future, they're going to see me on television or in the papers or on a poster, and they won't be able to believe it, because I will be famous. They'll see how mediocre they really are. Mum says I shouldn't be arrogant, but being humble hasn't got her very far, has it? She doesn't talk about her upbringing much, but from what I can make out, it was very restricted, very patriarchal, and has left her struggling to cope with the real world. She was thrown out of the Jehovah's Witnesses and estranged from her family because of me, so even when I'm pissed off with her, I make allowances. It isn't her fault she's like she is, it isn't her fault she's wary of others when she was taught to consider outsiders as doomed sinners. She's rejected all that, but the indoctrination is so ingrained, so much a part of her, that it's bound to affect her. Poor Mum.

I always try to time my entrance into the classroom for three seconds before Miss Torrance arrives, so no one has a chance to pick on me. It means hovering outside until I see her coming round the corner. I like Miss Torrance. She has an acid tongue and a brilliant line in sarcastic put-downs.

My desk is four rows back, next to Jasmina's. Jasmina is OK because she doesn't actively bully me, but she doesn't engage with me either. I turn to smile at her, anticipating that she'll stare straight ahead at Jessie's ponytail. She doesn't want to be the butt of jokes either. Silly really, because she could do with a friend, but far be it from me to advise her on surviving this hellhole.

English Literature. We are studying Shakespeare's *Othello*. I know all about the green-eyed monster because he lurks inside me. Despite my efforts, I'm jealous of these girls with their happy families and intense friendships. I can get through this, no problem – Faulkner women are tough – but I would like a friend. I wouldn't care what she was like. She could be ugly, smelly, greasy-haired, even boring – although that would be hard to swallow. I just want someone who's pleased to see me.

Breaktime. I take *Carrie* into the cloakroom and finish the last chapter. Oh my God. I tuck the book into my waistband – it's very slim – and go outside. Four girls sashay over, swinging their glossy hair. I give them my neutral smile.

'Hey, Zoe.'

'Hey.'

'Do you watch breakfast telly?'

'Don't be an idiot, Jessie. She doesn't have a TV.'

'Oops, I forgot. Soz.'

I shrug and turn away. I can't comment on whatever it is they want to talk about. Becca sidles up beside me

113

and the others join her. I'm surrounded. One of those moments, then.

'It was your birthday on Tuesday, wasn't it?' she says. 'Sorry I didn't get you a card.'

I have no idea what to say to that.

'Did you get any nice presents?'

This is a trap. It doesn't matter what I tell them, they'll find something to sneer at, but if I remain mute, they'll only speculate, and that could get messy. I think about Carrie and the shower scene. That was horrific, but I can see how it could happen – a whiff of blood, a frenzy, and she's destroyed.

'I got tokens.'

That's a lie. I didn't get anything at all. Mum doesn't believe in celebrating birthdays. It's another unwanted remnant of her upbringing.

'I wish my mum would give me tokens,' Jessie says.

I'm taken by surprise by her friendly tone, but I know to tread carefully. Jessie's betrayed me in the past.

'Whatever.'

'Anyway,' Becca continues. 'We thought you'd like to know what they said on TV this morning.'

'Why?'

'Because your birthday was on Tuesday. It's like, there was this baby stolen from a hospital sixteen years ago today and the parents were on breakfast TV basically asking girls who were born the day before, or maybe the day before that, if there's any chance they could be her. It'll be in the papers too. The mum read out a letter to the baby.'

I frowned, not getting it.

'She's sixteen now, obviously,' Becca said, with a pained eye-roll.

'We thought of you.' Jessie giggled. 'Because your mum home-schooled you. Why would she do that if she didn't have something to hide?'

'She home-schooled me because she was home-schooled herself,' I say. *Do not show shame.* 'That was what she believed in. And anyway, if you're home-schooled, you're not on your own. The Department for Education keeps an eye on you.'

The trouble with being home-schooled until you're eleven is that you don't realize until too late that your house, your mother and you are different – and not in a good way. When you do realize, it's a humongous shock.

On the day I started school, Jessie asked who I liked best in Girls Aloud. I had no idea what she was talking about. That evening I persuaded my mother to buy a radio, arguing in the face of her obstinate refusal to engage with world issues that my life wouldn't be worth living if we didn't have one. I had seen the inside of Jessie's desk – the picture cut from a magazine and tacked to the underside of the lid. Five amazing-looking girls.

I don't blame Mum for the way she is, because she was conditioned. I only wish she hadn't accidentally transferred some of that conditioning on to me. I'm unravelling it though, stitch by stitch, ready to make a fresh version of myself once I get to university. Self-knowledge is painful, but an inevitable result of joining the real world late. I will be OK.

Mum and I don't look alike, but there are things we have in common. We're stronger than we look, we don't eat much and we don't feel the cold – a good thing, since we don't have central heating. We finish what we start. Come the apocalypse, I'll be more likely to survive than Jessie and Becca.

I am dying for my future.

'Ooh,' Jessie sneers. 'Wouldn't you want to belong to a normal family?'

I turn on her. 'What do you call normal?'

'Don't get your knickers in a twist,' she responds. 'I'd call it parents who wear reasonably fashionable clothes and make an effort to join in from time to time. We're only trying to help you. You can't deny your mum is weird. I saw her in town the other day. She was wearing this stupid hat pulled over her ears. She looked mental.'

She wrinkles her nose, like I'm a bad smell.

'She's hardly likely to be Leo Creasey's daughter,' Becca says. 'She's far too dull.'

'Who is he anyway?' another girl says. Sasha this time. 'I've never heard of him.'

'He's an author, you idiot. My dad says he's brilliant, but Mum thinks his books are dead boring.'

Becca sniggers. 'Maybe he is Zoe's dad, then.' She looks at me. 'Do you even know who your real father is?'

Mum always says, try not to judge other people too harshly, because you don't know what they're going through or what they've been through to make them the way they are. Most people are not born bad. I know nothing about Becca's home life and have never speculated about it in the way she appears to speculate about mine. For all I know, she's as much in need of a kind word as I am. She just has no idea how to ask.

116

'It's all right,' I say. 'Whatever it is that's hurting you, it's not for ever.'

Becca gapes, and so do the rest of them. There's a silence, and then someone splutters with laughter.

'What the fuck are you talking about, you freak?'

Becca turns on her heel, swings her hair and marches off, followed by her acolytes.

20

Jenny

OUTSIDE, A GROUP OF JOURNALISTS HURRIES TOWARDS us. There aren't many this time. We're still newsworthy, especially Leo, but there are other, fresher stories being told. I find it easy to smile, say a word or two and be gracious these days. It's become part of the job of being me.

'You were amazing in there, both of you,' Daisy chirps.

Amazing? What on earth does that mean in this context? We did loss well? We gave good grief?

'I'll deal with this,' Leo mutters into my ear.

He strides forward and greets a couple of them by name before launching into his prepared speech.

'Thank you all for your support over the years. Every anniversary brings back the horror and the sadness. It never goes away . . .'

I shouldn't assume I suffer more than Leo. There are things going on inside my husband's head to which I have no access. But he doesn't grieve in the same way. It's not that I don't have enough to do, I have plenty, but he has the ability to lose himself in his writing. He withdraws, and I can't do that. I don't resent him for it; he has to handle it in his own way. But I envy his ability to forget for chunks of time.

Daisy gives me a hug and I try to relax, but I catch myself wishing this warm body I'm holding is my daughter. Then she turns to Leo and he wraps an arm around her shoulders.

'That went well, don't you think?' she says, gazing adoringly up at him.

'Couldn't have gone better,' he agrees. 'Although I could have done without the insinuation that Sophie sells books.'

'You responded brilliantly. You could tell she realized she was out of order.'

'Leo, can we go?' I say. 'I need to get to work.'

It's early, but I'm keen to draw a line under the morning. Work is a good way of doing that.

'Oh, sorry, Jenny,' Daisy says, pulling her mouth down at the corners. 'Of course you want to escape.'

'I didn't say—'

'You must be feeling pretty grim. A couple of photos first, though. I'll get out of the way.'

'Thanks for coming with us,' Leo says.

'No problem. I'm always here for you. I'll call you tomorrow to go through the itinerary for the tour. I'm looking forward to it.'

I stare at Daisy, trying not to let my mouth drop open. We've just been pleading for news of our missing daughter and she's already moved on to the next subject: Leo traipsing round the home counties, giving talks to his legions of fawning fans. For God's sake.

I'm about to say goodbye when she holds up her hand. Her phone is ringing.

'Sorry, got to take this.'

'Fine by us,' Leo says.

We're promptly forgotten as she starts to dissect her latest argument with her boyfriend. 'And I was, like . . . And he was, like . . .'

Leo and I stare at one another and I feel a bubble of mirth. I stifle it as there are still journalists milling around and it wouldn't do to be caught wearing the wrong face. But sometimes I do laugh. Things are funny; life is funny. It's a spectrum of colours in many shades, not black and white. I force the muscles of my face to be still, and refuse to catch Leo's eye, because that would be a disaster.

Finally, Daisy signs off with a 'Thanks, babe. I'll see you in half an hour.'

Leo flags a taxi and we get in, shut the door and I collapse into giggles. Beside me, Leo's shoulders are shaking.

'I'm sorry,' I squeak. 'It's hysteria. I shouldn't be laughing.'

He takes off his glasses and rubs his face vigorously. I lean against his arm.

'I've got two weeks of that,' he says. 'The ups and downs of Daisy's relationship. You know she asks me for advice?'

I grin. 'What do you tell her?'

'Oh, I'm quite honest. I tell her she'd be better off without a boyfriend if he makes her that insecure.'

'Mr Compassionate. It should have been you training to be a counsellor, not me.'

'Well, if the next book flatlines . . .'

'Don't you dare.'

He looks silently out of the window as we cross Waterloo Bridge, then he turns to me. 'Jenny, you were amazing.'

'We both did well.'

'You were, like, and I was, like . . .'

I laugh and he grimaces.

'What Camilla said. She wasn't entirely wrong, was she? That's how it works. In this world, you're soon forgotten. I'm not saying Sophie is like one of my books, but if you apply the same rules, you get the same results. I want publicity for our daughter, I don't want her fading away. Whenever Sophie's story is told, I sell more books, but that's accident, not design. The point is people remember her name.'

'I know.'

I lean my head against his shoulder and he takes my hand. So often marriages break up under the strain of a tragedy, but not ours. Leo has never blamed me for what happened; he never even looks at me in a way that suggests he does. He's the only one. No one else understands why my mother's instinct didn't sense danger when I woke to find that woman leaning over the bassinet – my parents included. And me. I don't understand it, and I will never forgive myself for closing my eyes and drifting back to sleep.

The taxi drops Leo at Borough Market, where he's meeting his agent, then takes me to my office in the City. As I rise in the lift, I smooth down my clothes and snap open my compact mirror to check my mascara hasn't run. I'm wearing heavier make-up than usual and my clothes are colourful and studiedly casual, but I have a smart black jacket in my office that I can slip on.

I have a meeting followed by a client lunch and then more meetings to take me through to six o'clock. I watch the numbers on the lift display go up and tap my foot, impatient to be there, but when the doors open on the slick bright whiteness of the Joliffe, Langford & Morley offices, with the glass walls and brash gold lettering, I hesitate.

On the day when I should have been celebrating my daughter's sixteenth birthday, the thoughts that have been gathering in the corners of my mind for several months coalesce. I no longer want this. Everyone looks so busy, their glossy heads bent over keyboards, but I can imagine closing my eyes and opening them again to find the place empty. It's soulless.

As I step out of the lift and gaze around me, it feels as though I've disembarked from an aeroplane into a country I don't recognize.

I don't want these people, I don't want these values, I don't want what this whole shiny edifice represents. I wonder if I ever truly wanted any of it. Something has tipped my equilibrium and it's clear to me that I'm on my way out of here. I've changed; I'm no longer hungry for financial success. Money helps, but it doesn't keep the demons out.

My PA looks up as I pass her desk. 'How did it go?'

'It went all right,' I say, smiling at her. 'I could murder a coffee, if you've got time.'

I go into my office and close the door behind me, and I feel something I haven't felt in a long time. It's the first stirrings of excitement.

Later, as I make my way home and the more measured me has returned, I decide not to talk to Leo about my plans until I'm back from Portugal. It's a big decision and needs careful thought.

21

Zoe

WHEN THE BELL RINGS TO SIGNAL THE END OF THE school day, my rucksack is already packed. All I need to do is chuck in my pens, put my file in my desk and get out. I'm off like a shot. I burst through the doors seconds before the surge, and jog-walk to the bike lock-up, shoving my arms through my coat sleeves as I go. I fish my gloves out of my pocket, clip on my helmet and unlock my bike before anyone has a chance to accost me. It's silly, but I can't stop thinking about what Becca said.

I must be the only person in school not to have a computer at home. I could use the ICT Room to look up what I want, but the staff keep an eye on pupils' search histories, and I don't know how to hide mine. Also, Becca and Jessie have a weird interest in anything I do, and I can't trust them not to come sneaking up behind me.

Use of the computers at Maidstone Library is free. I've used them to find out more about Mum's background, to help me understand why she is the way she is. Becca wasn't wrong – she is a bit weird, but in a functioning unofficial way, like a lot of people. She holds down a job, and she's even a manager now. It's more than some of those girls' mothers have achieved.

What Becca and Jessie were talking about, despite it being impossible, has left me feeling jittery. I know Mum is my mum. There's no way she stole me. On the other hand, I've never felt I'm living the right life. When I was little I used to imagine there was another family out there, who had lost me in a forest one night. I didn't think they were kings and queens, or even dukes and duchesses, but I did think they were fun. I love Mum, but she isn't fun. She is suspicious, anxious and guarded. If we do things together, there's always an educational reason – we rarely do anything just for the hell of it. That's the other problem with home-schooling: school never closes.

The first thing I do after I've returned *Carrie* is pick up one of the well-thumbed newspapers and find myself a seat at a table. I turn the pages slowly, skimming the headlines, and find what I'm looking for on page 7.

Stolen Baby Sixteen Today

A baby, abducted in 1989, turns sixteen today. One-day-old Sophie Creasey was taken from her mother's bedside at St Thomas's Hospital, London on 10 March 1989. Her parents, Jennifer Creasey and acclaimed author Leo Creasey, are appealing for anyone who thinks they may know something to come forward. They are also asking sixteen-year-old girls, born in the week

preceding Sophie's abduction, to contact the police if
they have any doubt about their parentage.

    The Creaseys will appear on national TV today in
an attempt to jog the public's memory. 'She's out there
somewhere,' Jennifer Creasey told our reporter. 'And
we want her back. Not a single day goes by when I don't
think about her. No mother should have to go through
this.'

    Criminal psychiatrist Dr Jessica Robyn has described
Sophie's kidnapper as possibly isolated, nervous, a loner.
She may be prone to episodes of manic depression. She
is self-deluding, possibly dangerously so. If Sophie
Creasey is alive, she will have taken on some of her
abductor's personality traits. She may be secretive and
find it difficult to form relationships with her peers.
Her relationship with her false parent or parents will be
fraught with tension as she gets older.

I move on to the letter. I wish I'd seen her read it on the
television. It feels a little flat on the page, as if she's fiddled with it for ages, changing some words for better
ones and worrying about the punctuation.

I glance hopefully at the rank of computer monitors
but every one of them is in use. I should pick a new book
and go home. I leave the newspaper where I found it and
browse the shelves, running my fingers along the spines,
pulling books out and sliding them back in. I choose one
by Terry Pratchett.

The paper is still lying on the table. I walk over and
put my hand on it, then scoop it up with a quick glance
over my shoulder to check that no one is looking. I find

a space between the shelves where I can't be seen from the librarian's desk, surreptitiously rip out the article and tuck it between the pages of my new book.

I'm being ridiculous. There's no way I'm that missing girl. It's madness. My problem is I have no friends, no social life and I live with a virtual recluse. The idea of belonging to someone 'normal' – in Jessie-speak – is seductive. All I'm looking for is a chance to reinvent myself, but daydreaming about the Creaseys is akin to daydreaming about winning the lottery.

The only way to change your destiny is to do it yourself. University is the key, not some ridiculous pipe dream about being someone else's daughter. And yet.

As I'm about to leave, one of the computers becomes free and, after a moment's hesitation, I take off my coat again and settle myself in front of it, grimacing in revulsion as my bottom absorbs the warmth from the seat. Once I'm logged in, I go on the internet and type 'Sophie Creasey'. The picture that comes up of Leo and Jennifer is much better than the one in the newspaper, and I'm able to examine them properly. I'm disappointed by the husband. His face is properly sculpted whereas mine is round and soft. Jennifer Creasey, though. That's different. When I look into her eyes, I get a strong sense of déjà vu.

I discover that she's an accountant (which is not very exciting), was brought up in Kent, and married Leo in 1984. Since Sophie's disappearance she has supported many other families going through the trauma of losing a child and has never given up hope of finding her daughter alive.

I look at the picture again, but the feeling has gone – she's just a middle-aged woman with hazel eyes. She looks intelligent and kind, the sort of person who would never go around thinking they were better than everyone else, like Becca.

After that, I read the Wikipedia entry for Leo. He's a lot more interesting than Jenny.

Leo Creasey, born 12 November 1957, is an English writer.
He has published seven novels and two works of non-fiction.
Several of his novels have become international bestsellers. *Pig Lily* was shortlisted for the Booker Prize for Fiction in 1989.

Creasey was born in Brighton and wrote his first novel, *A Time for Bleeding*, in 1986, while working as a teacher. It sold approximately 10,000 copies in its first year. In 1989, Creasey's daughter by his wife Jennifer was abducted from St Thomas's Hospital in London. To date, she has not been recovered.

Before I leave, I go back to the shelves and browse the library's collection of Leo Creasey novels. I flick through them all and pick *Pig Lily* because it was published the year I was born and the year his daughter was stolen. I read the blurb. Apparently, it's about a man who has an existential crisis, brought on by having an affair with a wealthy ugly woman called Lily Kemp. There's a quote from the *Times Literary Supplement* that says it's 'a remarkable achievement'. It sounds dire but I'd like to read something of his, and this seems the obvious one.

I run my thumb over the cover's embossed lettering, then put it back on the shelf. On second thoughts, I'm not going to take it. If Mum were to find it, she'd want to know why I had it.

Mum isn't home when I get in. She isn't due back for another hour. I take the filched newspaper article from between the pages of the library book and unfold it on my desk, where a pine-framed mirror is propped up against the windowsill behind it. I hold up the photograph of the Creaseys and compare noses and eyes, lips and ear-lobes, shape of jaws, length of necks, but the only thing I can find that I have in common with Jennifer Creasey, apart from the colour of our eyes, is that the area between my nose and upper lip is a little short. Mum doesn't have that; hers is more bog-standard.

I reread the letter, this time imagining I actually am Sophie Creasey. Apart from my own desperation to get out of here, what would make me sit up and take notice? If, for instance, I lived in a reasonably normal house-hold, with a mother and father, several siblings and pets; if I was happy and well-adjusted, doing well at school and popular. My date of birth, but that's all.

I suppose if I was that girl, I might say something to my parents, jokingly, handing them the newspaper. Something like, 'I always thought there was something funny about you two.' They would snatch it out of my hand, read the article and the letter and laugh. Maybe they would make a sarcastic remark like, 'Well, you had to find out sometime.' Then my imaginary mum would say, 'Poor woman, how terrible. I don't think I would ever get over it.' And that girl would drop the newspaper into the recycling bin and think no more about it.

The only reason I ripped out the article and went online is discontent with my own life. The Creaseys are not going to save me. I am going to save myself.

22

Hannah

HANNAH LOCKED THE DOOR TO HER OFFICE AND strode along the corridor, stopping outside the TV room from where the familiar strains of the six o'clock news were clearly audible. She walked in. Ten residents were occupying the chairs arranged around the television. Some were asleep, their heads drooped; others were staring vacantly at the screen. A couple were more engaged. Anita, one of the longest-standing members of staff, smiled at her from her seat beside Prudence, a wheelchair-bound octogenarian with snowy-white hair so thin you could see her scalp.

'You off then, Mrs Faulkner?' Anita said. 'Have a nice evening.'

'In a few minutes.'

Hannah remained standing to catch the headlines and saw that the section on the Creaseys was way down the schedule. She rarely stayed later than six, and only then if there was something special going on, but she might not get another opportunity to see them.

'I think I'll just stop and watch the news,' she said, resting her hand on the back of a chair.

'I don't know why you don't get a telly. Then you could put your feet up of an evening and watch the soaps. It's how I wind down after a day in this place.'

Hannah smiled patiently. It wasn't the first time this had been said, and it wouldn't be the last.

'You may be right.'

'I bet your Zoe would like it.'

'I'm sure she would, but she'll have to wait until she's left home.'

'When she's gone, you'll be lonely,' Anita said. 'A telly is company.'

Ever since she'd taken Zoe, Hannah's life had been remarkably calm. There had been an anxious beginning, with Hannah expecting a policeman's knock at any moment, and the visit from Leo Creasey, which she had weathered remarkably well considering the mess she was in. She had anxiously anticipated the arrival of the community nurse, but the woman had seen nothing amiss; Zoe had been checked and weighed and given the all-clear. There had been friendly advice, cups of tea and cheap biscuits, a pointed interest in Hannah's circumstances that elicited nothing. After ten days, Hannah had been signed off, the nurse confident that she and Zoe were healthy, the house was clean and tidy, and there was food in the fridge. As far as the NHS was concerned, all was well.

Hannah was safe, and had been for years, but she had never felt secure.

The news item Hannah was waiting for wouldn't be

on for another fifteen minutes, and she was growing agitated. Zoe would be home and wondering where she had got to. But it couldn't be helped, she had to see this.

And then, there they were.

Hannah studied Leo's face with the urgency of a lover. That night, sixteen years ago, his hair had been wet, strands of fringe stuck to his forehead. He'd had dark circles around his eyes and wore a look of intense fury. This man was smoother, more urbane. The camera moved to his wife. Hannah had seen her sleeping face, but it'd been dark. It was the photograph that had been taken outside the hospital that had stayed with her; she had never forgotten the torment in Jennifer Creasey's eyes. That was still there, although it was less painful to see, smoothed away by the intervening years.

Jennifer was attractive in the way that girls who are unaware of their own beauty are, like the prettier women from the community in which Hannah had grown up. There was nothing showy about her. The first time Hannah had seen a photograph of Jennifer that wasn't taken in the aftermath, she had been surprised. She had expected Leo to have married someone with sharper edges.

The interview was pre-recorded and took place in the sort of room in which they always did these things, with a vase of flowers in the background. She wondered if it was the Creaseys' own house, but thought probably not. She listened as Jennifer Creasey described what her life had been like since that night.

In the early years, Hannah had avoided the Creaseys' annual appearances. It had been possible back then, but nowadays they could catch you off guard. Everyone sees everything whether they like it or not. She found it was better to get it over with. Watching Jenny stirred an inner turmoil, made her hate herself, caused a sleepless night or two, but then the media would mothball the story and move on, and Hannah's life would settle back into its reassuringly dull routine.

'Dreadful thing,' Prudence said. 'Imagine having your baby stolen from your arms. Poor girl. I hope they catch the bitch. She deserves hanging.'

'Now, Prudence, that's a bit harsh,' Anita said. 'Who-ever did it obviously has serious mental-health issues. If that child is found, then the lady will need help and compassion.'

Prudence cackled. 'Compassion. Ha. She wants locking up.'

'It was your Zoe's birthday yesterday, wasn't it, Mrs Faulkner?' Anita said. She raised her eyebrows. 'Any-thing you want to tell us?'

Hannah attempted to laugh it off. 'Sometimes I won-der. She's not like me at all. She's so much brighter. Zoe will go to university. She'll be the first woman in my family to do that.'

'You must be so proud of her,' Anita said, distracted, as Hannah had known she would be. 'I wish my Emily was that conscientious. Perhaps I should get rid of the telly.'

She chuckled to let Hannah know she wasn't serious, then started coughing.

Hannah stayed to watch the closing news item so that it didn't look as though she had only been there for the Creaseys' appeal, then she said goodbye and left the building.

'Zoe,' Hannah called as she let herself in. 'Sorry I'm late, love. Small crisis at work.'

Zoe came downstairs. 'What happened?'

'Storm in a teacup. Shall I get supper on? You must be starving.'

'I had some toast.'

Zoe took Hannah's coat and hung it on the hook in the hallway. She followed her mother into the kitchen and leaned against the wall.

'Why did you take the radio?'

'Oh Lord, I left it in the car.'

She rushed outside and came back with it, plugging it in beside the toaster. It was a stupid thing to have done, a spur-of-the-moment decision taken when the Creaseys' sixteenth-anniversary appeal was trailered. Zoe probably wouldn't even have noticed. She barely listened to what was being said, just liked it on in the background. And now Hannah had drawn attention to it.

'It's really annoying not having anything to listen to in the morning.'

'Sorry, love. The one in my office wasn't working and I didn't want to miss *The Archers*.'

Silence fell. Hannah moved from the fridge to the work surface. She took out a cutting board and chopped up an onion.

'Do you want me to do anything?' Zoe asked.

'No, it's all right. Were you revising?'

'Yes! What else would I have been doing?'

135

Hannah had been concentrating on not cutting her fingers, but she looked up. 'I don't know. Reading?'

It hadn't escaped her notice that Zoe's choice of reading matter had undergone a bit of a change lately, with trashy horror and romance novels taking precedence over the classics. She hadn't said anything because Zoe had so little freedom and it was nice for her to think she was rebelling in some small way. At her age, Hannah had done the same thing, sneaking into the library and hiding in a corner to read Barbara Cartland instead of her Bible.

It was the romances that had got her into trouble. Zoe had more sense. She wasn't going to fall under the spell of an unscrupulous man or get herself involved with one of the boys at school. Hannah found the idea of her daughter discovering sex terrifying. She hadn't had anything to do with that sort of thing since Michael Brady and had no intention of repeating the experience. Zoe had a good figure and a pleasant face; men would like her. Hannah had no choice but to trust her daughter. She prayed she would find her way in life without anything terrible happening to her.

'I've been doing a bit of both,' Zoe admitted.

She crossed the room and put her arms round Hannah's neck and Hannah reciprocated, smiling into Zoe's shoulder. Her daughter loved her. The fact that they had this beautiful relationship at all showed that it was meant to be. If not, it would never have worked. Zoe would have rejected her at some point, like oil repels water.

23

Leo

LEO COULD HEAR JENNY MOVING AROUND UPSTAIRS. The old floors creaked like something out of a horror film. They had lived in Albert Square Gardens for eighteen years now. He had been brought up in a 1930s semi, and then the executive home Lola had moved into with his stepfather, Alastair, and although he had nothing against those properties, this house was on a different plane altogether; more befitting to a writer.

Jenny had chosen it. Despite being clear-headed, number-crunching and practical, there was a streak of romance in her. The elegant sash windows still had their original shutters, intricate cornicing framed the high ceilings, and the wide floorboards – admittedly ineffi-cient when it came to keeping the place warm – had the patina of a hundred and sixty years of use trodden into them. There were two marble fireplaces in the sitting room, and from the back door a wrought-iron set of stairs spiralled down to a narrow garden, which was home to a huge cherry tree that billowed with white blossom in the spring, its petals falling like snow when the wind blew. It was in bud now.

It was a week since the appeal, and Jenny was about to leave for Portugal. Leo visited for a long weekend once a year and felt he did his duty. He disliked the society in Cascais, the coastal town to which Elaine and Charles had moved in 1987. Now that his father-in-law was dead, there seemed little point in Leo being there at all. He would only be in the way. He was glad Jenny was going, though; things had been intense these last few weeks, what with the anniversary of Sophie's abduction and the publicity campaign surrounding the hardback launch of *In the Lake*. Some breathing space would do both of them good.

There was a disconnect between him and Jenny that he had to work hard to hide. They'd both told lies, they both had secrets, but only he was privy to that fact. His lie was much worse than hers, of course, but what she had done to him still hurt.

Why had she done it? Was it simply the fact that she had gone away straight after that row?

It was the impetuousness of her action that astonished him. She had made a spur-of-the-moment decision. Sometimes the least likely people did that. It was like that old adage: it's the quiet ones you have to watch out for. They meander along, taking things in their stride, then out of the blue something happens and they explode from their normal, tranquil state and become accidental sinners.

Accidental sinners. He liked that. Perhaps he'd put it in the next book.

The sound of Jenny's feet thudding down the stairs

made him get up and dump the dregs of his coffee into the sink. This business of getting ready drove him crazy.

'Have you seen my reading glasses?' he asked. 'I had them at breakfast, but I can't find them anywhere.'

Jenny picked up the newspaper from the kitchen table, unfolded it and his glasses slid into her hand.

She passed them to Leo with a smile. 'What are you going to do without me?'

'I'll manage somehow.' He paused. 'Which reminds me.'

Jenny had moved away from him and was busy sifting through the contents of the capacious handbag she used for travelling. She threw some old tissues and receipts into the bin.

'Yeah?' she said without looking at him.

'Can you sign some cheques?' It galled him to ask.

'How much do you need?'

'I'm not sure. There'll be various costs, and I should allow for contingencies. I can bung them in the bank if and when. That's not a problem, is it?'

'Of course not. It's fine.' Jenny was always acutely attuned to his tone. 'I'll get the cheque book.'

'It's on the side.'

He listened to the scratch of pen on paper. Twice. Two cheques. One for each week; that was so like his wife. Everything neatly divisible.

She handed them to him and he folded them into his wallet. Her phone pinged.

'Taxi's here,' she said.

'Got everything? Passport? Keys?'

'I'm all set. If you hear anything . . .'

They'd had a call from Liane Parker that morning. The switchboard had received one hundred and thirty-eight calls following the appeal, the bulk of them on the day, but so far none of them had been helpful. A handful of the usual nutters, too.

'You mustn't get your hopes up,' Leo said.

'I'm not. I knew we'd attract attention-seekers, but there's always that tiny chance, isn't there?'

He rested his cheek on Jenny's head as he held her. Her hair was soft and clean and smelled of grapefruit shampoo. Even so many years later his guilt had the power to scorch him like a brand. He still couldn't believe it had happened. It was like the plot point that lost the reader by virtue of being too far-fetched.

Sometimes, when it was late and he couldn't sleep, he would invent scenarios in which the worst didn't happen. There was a storm, but he wasn't forced to take a detour, and he didn't find himself speeding down a country lane. Or he did, but he left the hospital a minute earlier and passed Hannah's house before she came running out. He drove on, reached Sparrow Cottage, dealt with the damage and returned home. The only thing these comforting versions of the story couldn't alter was Sophie not being his, because that was Jenny's mistake.

Maybe Jenny did the same, maybe she walked herself through that conference and saw herself saying no to the man's advances. Then there would have been no baby, no abduction, no life of self-flagellation.

'It's only been a week,' Jenny said as she broke off their embrace. 'Some things take a while to process. Maybe she's scared.'

'Jenny.' His voice was so sharp she jumped. 'Don't do this to yourself. We have to believe whoever took her wanted her and loves her, or we'll go mad. I think . . .' He paused, knowing what reaction he could expect, then choosing to say what he wanted to anyway because, for crying out loud, this had to end sometime. 'We need to draw a line and stop living our lives around her.'

Jenny stiffened instantly. 'I will never draw a line. You have your books to disappear into. I don't have that luxury.'

'You have Open Arms,' he pointed out. 'I've seen how much good it does you to help other people.'

'It's not the same.'

Of course she was right. Not only did he have his writing, but there were also the publicity events, the speaking engagements, appearances to be made at his rivals' book launches, and the spiritual balm of lunches with his admiring agent, Kirstie, and Reuben, his editor.

'If we'd had another baby—'

'Please, don't let's go there.'

'Can you not understand?' she said, 'a baby would have helped. But far be it for me to make you feel guilty or uncomfortable.'

He felt both those things. Guilt and discomfort were partly what drove him on year after year, and the memory of his father. Success was part of it too, but success, he had realized, wasn't a line drawn in the sky, it was fluid; something he would always chase, like a drug. He wished he could tell Jenny everything, but God Almighty, the fallout there would be. If she found out he knew Sophie wasn't his, it would be as though someone had withdrawn the fragile support that had been holding the whole stinking pile together. Jenny would put two and two together and they would come after him. He would go to prison and his fall from grace would be public and humiliating. Worst of all, she would hate him.

'That's not what this is about,' he said, knowing it was.

'Isn't it? I've got to go. I'll call you when I get there.'

She was doing up the buttons of her trench coat. He took hold of the belt and buckled it for her, and she let him. Old habits die hard. He walked her to the door and carried her case out to the waiting car, trying to mollify her, not wanting to part on a sour note. He relied on Jenny's devotion. He didn't like it when she went cold on him. It made him nervous. The driver got out and ran round to open the passenger door. Jenny folded herself in and Leo put his hand on the frame to stop her slamming it shut. He leaned towards her.

'Give my love to Elaine. And, Jenny?'

'Yes,' she said mutinously.

'I love you. You know that, don't you?'

'Yes.'

'Then kiss me properly.'

She kissed him on the lips. 'Look after yourself.'

With his arms folded and feeling mildly dissatisfied, Leo watched the taxi drive away, then turned on his heel and walked back inside. When he closed the door the house seemed to yawn. He didn't like being here on his own.

For something to do, he called Daisy to check arrangements for the tour. She told him the car would pick him up at seven o'clock the following morning and she would meet him at King's Cross with the train tickets.

'Everything's been organized. All you have to do is entertain the audiences and sell books.'

'I will certainly do my best.'

He wandered into the sitting room, feeling disconsolate, and picked up the framed photograph of his father that he kept on the little desk beside a formal portrait of himself. The one of his father had been taken when he was in his late thirties, the one of Leo about five years ago. The resemblance was striking. Two men with the same dreams who had taken different paths. What would have happened if his father had ignored the pressures of family life and carried on writing? He may or may not have found success; he may or may not have been happier. He might still be alive. Leo put the photo back and nudged it into position. One thing was indisputable, though: Lola would have left his father sooner.

24

Zoe

'WHY DON'T YOU COME TO WORK WITH ME TOMORROW?'
Mum asks.

It's just gone eight and we're washing up our supper
things. Nice though it is not to have to face the daily challenge of school, I am getting twitchy revising alone in the
house. I spent the best part of yesterday on my bed, going
back over my English Literature essays and skim-reading
Great Expectations.

'You're all right, Mum. I'm happier going into town.'

'But you can use the computer in my office. You'd
be much more comfortable there than in the library,
wouldn't you?'

'It's too distracting. They'll all want to talk to me.'

And I won't get any privacy.

Mum smiles. 'Would that be so bad?'

'No.' I nudge her with my shoulder. 'Honestly, it's fine.
I can have a wander round the shops when I need a break.'

Mum wrings out the dish cloth and wipes the surface,
which is old and stained. It has nicks in the veneer that

show the chipboard underneath, but there's no one except us to see it. I've convinced myself everyone at school has a showroom-quality kitchen, and the thought of anyone coming round here and seeing ours fills me with shame. I'm even ashamed of being ashamed. These things shouldn't matter.

To offer me the use of her computer is a huge step forward, but Mum has seen the writing on the wall. I'm going to be living in this century whether she likes it or not. If I revise at the Birches, she can keep an eye on me. I don't know what she thinks I'm going to get up to left to my own devices with the internet, but as far as she's concerned nothing but trouble can come of it. The devil apparently lurks in its inky depths.

At the beginning of the holidays I'm always so relieved to be away from Becca and her clique I barely notice I have nothing to do and no one to see. I usually start to get bored around now, four days in. This time, though, I have less time to brood or get angry. I have to revise properly because I'm determined to do well in my exams, and I'm on a mission to find out more about the Creaseys.

'Fair enough,' Mum says, taking a plate from me and drying it. 'But you are still working at the Birches this summer, aren't you? It's all been arranged.'

'I suppose so,' I say without enthusiasm.

'They love you there. And you're so good with the residents. Everyone's looking forward to you coming.'

I scrub the baking tray I grilled our sausages on, rinse off the suds and hand it to her.

'It's fine. I'm grateful for the job. But I can't think about anything except my exams at the moment.'

'I don't like leaving you on your own all holiday.'

'I'm a big girl. Don't worry about me. I can keep myself occupied.'

I chain up my bike outside Maidstone Library and walk up to the doors just as the librarian is unlocking them. I say good morning as I take off my helmet, and unzip my coat. I'm boiling underneath it. It's going to be an unseasonably hot day. I organize myself, taking my file out of my bag and placing it beside the keyboard. I have a list of things I need to research for History. I force myself to spend half an hour on Churchill before giving in.

It's the photographs of Jenny Creasey that obsess me, particularly the one taken right after her baby was stolen. She is so haunted, so broken. The more I study her, the more similarities I find between her face and mine, and the more I'm inclined to believe that, however unlikely, it isn't impossible that we're related. Then again, if I look hard enough, I can find similarities between myself and the Queen.

I open the public page for Open Arms, Jenny's support group, and read about its ethos and aims. Maybe I could request membership and get to know Jenny that way? But I'd have to come up with a good lie and I'd probably get found out. I close the web page reluctantly and google Leo. There's a lot more about him, and by him. He writes articles for newspapers and reviews other authors' books. I type in 'Leo Creasey events 2005' and find an announcement from Foyles bookshop on Charing Cross Road. He's going to be there this evening, on the final stop of a countrywide tour. Where else has he been?

I scroll back and find out that he was at Tunbridge Wells Library last night. Damn. I could have gone to that.

I tap my fingers on the desk, irritated at the missed opportunity, and earn a frown from the guy sitting at the next computer. I give him a swift smile, to which he doesn't respond. I log out, my face burning with shame, pack up my books and leave. I'm being ridiculous. I'm not lying to Mum and going to London to see this man. He's not my father.

Angry with myself, I cycle back home, pull my bike through the side gate and lean it against the wall. I feel sick from the waste of time, the two hours spent in front of a screen on a wild goose chase. Why can't I just accept who I am? Only three weeks ago I was focused – I knew what I wanted and how I was going to get it. Then Jessie and Becca dropped their bombshell, with their nasty insinuations.

Do you even know who your father is, Zoe?

Your mum home-schooled you. Why would she do that if she didn't have something to hide?

I search our house from top to bottom, which doesn't take long because it's small and the only places Mum would feasibly hide evidence are her bedroom or the tiny loft.

Mum's bedroom is plain, with cream walls, dun-brown carpet, and olive-green-and-mauve-striped curtains. It looks out on to the garden and the fields. The bed has an eiderdown over it, and there's a little table with a bedside light and a book; she likes memoirs. She has an old wooden wardrobe and matching chest of drawers.

I've never had much interest in this room or Mum's belongings – it's not as if she has anything I'd ever want to borrow, or old family snaps I can look at – but in the circumstances, being in here feels wrong. I feel distanced from her as I look round, as if she's a stranger, not the person I'm closest to, and I'm not the daughter she thinks she knows.

Mum doesn't have a dressing table – she uses the bathroom mirror if she needs to, which she doesn't because she never wears make-up. I search the chest of drawers first, then open the wardrobe. She has very few clothes, and they're all in shades of beige and brown. I move them aside, pat pockets, check the shelf above. I take out folded jumpers and, at the back, I find an envelope. There's nothing written on the front, so I open it and pull out a strip of rubbery plastic.

At first, my eyes and brain don't connect. There's another one in there. I take it out too and place them in my palm. One of them reads *Daughter of Hannah Faulkner 08.03.1989*. The other reads *Daughter of Jennifer Creasey 10.03.1989*.

Clutching the wristbands, I sit down on the bed. I feel as if my life has been ripped from me. Everything I've ever known has been a lie. The shock worms its way through my cells. How could Mum have stolen me? Should I call the number in the newspaper? And have Mum taken in for questioning? That kind of thing sticks, even when you're innocent. She'd definitely lose her job, and she would be hurt when she found out it was me who made the call. I'm not doing it, not until I've found out more.

It was only ever a silly fantasy. I never for one moment thought it was for real. Even when I was reading the articles, scanning their faces, looking for similarities, I didn't seriously believe it. It was a game I played because my life is so dull. Mum is my mother. It's just the two of us: Hannah and Zoe.

She stole me. I thought I knew everything there was to know about her, but that was childish arrogance and my perceptions are changing fast. She's never been overly emotional, but to have done this she must have felt such turmoil – far worse than anything I'm feeling now. I see her clearly for perhaps the first time in my life; not the mother with the job and the quiet, unassuming way of going about things, the often frustrating and sometimes embarrassing mother-person. I see her as a woman with agency, thoughts and deeds, and, above all, history. What did she do and why did she do it?

Downstairs, I wrap the wristbands in paper towel and put them in one of the zipped pockets of my rucksack. I have to see the Creaseys, even if I don't say anything, and I know where at least one of them is going to be tonight. I'll go back to the library for directions to Foyles from Victoria station, then catch a train to London. Leo's talk starts at six thirty and goes on till eight.

I won't hang around or force myself on him. I just need to see him in the flesh. And maybe Jenny will be there too, sitting in the audience, supporting her husband. My mother. My father.

I grimace, because I can't help thinking about how Mum will feel. She'll be waiting for me, growing anxious, not knowing what's happened. She is going to do

149

her nut. It's not as if I'm going away for ever; I'll be home by eleven. I could wait to hear her side of the story but the urge to get going, to see the Creaseys, is too strong; I'm popping with energy.

I can't even think what to put in a note to her. What can I say that wouldn't take me a month to write?

Gone to Jessie's to revise. Don't wait up for me.

25

Leo

LEO TOOK A LONG DRINK OF WATER AS HIS INTERVIEWER, Sam Portland, an up-and-coming literary journalist with a neatly shaped beard, opened the talk to questions from the audience.

At the beginning of each event, in each new town, the audience was told firmly that Leo would not be answering any questions of a personal nature. This was because on the first evening in Durham, it had quickly become clear that the only reason many members of the unusually large audience were there was because of Sophie and the recent appeal. The questions had been intrusive, and only the thought of the adverse publicity had stopped him either getting angry or just walking out. Hence the necessity to make things clear from the get-go. Since then, there had been the odd hiccup, but nothing his various hosts hadn't been able to handle.

He was pleased at the turnout. To his practised eye it looked as though the numbers were in the high forties. You never knew in London; sometimes there would be half a dozen, at other times up to fifty. He rubbed his chin and sat forward as hands shot up. At least Daisy wouldn't have to resort to asking a question to get the ball rolling. The first questioner was a woman in late middle-age. Typical of his audiences.

'Do you have first-hand experience of the issues in this book?'

Leo smiled as if he had never heard the question before.

'Not exactly, although my relationship with my father has certainly influenced my work and my career as a whole. My childhood was happy on the surface but underneath there were . . .' He paused. 'Shall we say, dark currents.'

He raised his eyebrows.

The audience chuckled, as he knew they would. Although to him it wasn't funny.

'Look, if a writer wants to be believed, if he strives for integrity and a book that resonates, he or she has to do their utmost to take a walk in their protagonist's shoes, be they good or bad. Not that I would do what Heath did.'

After that, the questions flowed. There was a good dynamic and he felt he was coming across well – impressive but not self-important. He preferred hearing from women, because he found that the men – particularly those of his generation and older – tried either to trip him up or to get one up on him. He had a competitive spirit himself and he could sense it in others.

'We've just got time for one last question,' Sam said. 'Yes, the young lady in the back row.'

A student? he wondered. They were the worst. If they were studying English Literature or Creative Writing and wanted to show off, they could be relied upon to come up with a question so convoluted that by the time they got to the end of it, he had often forgotten how it had begun. Leo craned his neck to get a better view of her, but could only see the top of her head. He didn't hear the question, and no one else did either, because she mumbled it.

'For those of you who didn't hear,' Sam said, 'the question is, how do you know when you've written something good?'

Leo's shoulders relaxed. The girl had been mercifully brief, and the question was an interesting one.

'I've never been asked that before. So thank you.'

He took off his glasses and polished them, smiling benignly at the sea of faces. Only one person had fallen asleep this evening. Pretty good going. Now, how to answer the girl?

'Everyone feels it sometime or other – that inner knowledge of a job well done. You get an instinct for it. Sometimes I reread the day's work and feel the energy drain out of me. If the chapter I've written doesn't have life, I delete it, because it's as difficult to resuscitate a dead scene as it is a dead body.' He paused for laughter. 'When I read it and it's good, I feel something physical going on inside me. I suppose it's that feeling . . .'

He lifted himself off his chair to better see the girl he was addressing. Nothing special. He sat down again.

'When you're a kid,' he continued, 'and you drive into town and you're looking out of the window and there's

nothing happening and you're bored stiff, but then someone appears wearing a chicken outfit and your whole
world brightens, that's kind of what I mean. Or when
you meet somebody at a party and you click. I don't
think it's an egotistical thing – I don't write stuff down
and think I'm bloody marvellous.'

He did sometimes, he conceded inwardly.

'I just get a feeling of a rush of air beneath it, of the
words taking flight.' He sat back. 'Hands up anyone in
the audience who's felt that way about something they've
done.'

Three-quarters of the audience raised their hand. The
girl didn't.

He glanced at Sam, who gave him an almost imperceptible nod. Their time was up, thank God. He was
longing to pour himself a whisky.

'Ladies and gentlemen,' Sam said. 'Let's give a big
round of applause to Leo Creasey. Thank you all so
much for coming tonight.'

Leo allowed himself a self-satisfied smirk.

The clapping died down to a trickle, the audience
stood, coats were lifted off the backs of seats and Sam
announced that Leo would be signing copies of *In the
Lake*. Some people – doubtless anxious to avoid the
embarrassment of walking past him without making a
purchase – dashed off, but others lingered. Amongst
them, the girl who had asked the final question.

Leo had sold a respectable number of books before she
reached the head of the queue. Now that he could assess
her properly, he could see she wasn't as plain as he had
thought initially, just one of those young women who

didn't make the best of themselves, either through lack of confidence or stubbornness. He knew the type. People didn't bother with them, so why should they bother with people? She was wearing jeans and a dark-blue jumper, and carried a quilted khaki coat over her arm.

Leo took a book from the top of the pile and opened it, glancing at her over his glasses, fountain pen poised. 'What shall I put?'

'I can't afford the book,' she said, then blushed. 'Sorry. I just wanted to say I enjoyed your talk and I'll get it out of the library and read it.'

Leo hesitated, then he saw that her hands were trembling and he realized she must have been building up to this. A genuine fan. 'What's your name?'

'Zoe.'

'Well, Zoe. Let this be my gift to you.'

He positioned his pen and wrote on the flyleaf *To Zoe, with best wishes*, and signed his name with a flourish.

'Thank you,' she said, surprised. 'Why did you do that?'

'Because it takes a certain amount of courage to do what you just did.' He held on to the book when she tried to take it, and forced her to meet his eyes. 'Thank you for coming.'

26

Zoe

I SHOULD LEAVE. I KNOW I SHOULD, BUT AFTER WHAT just happened I can't walk away, not yet. Leo was brilliant, really mesmerizing. The photographs don't show how mobile his face is, and his voice is great too – gravelly and deep.

I hang around, lurking beside the bookshelves on the floor below, my eyes glued to the staircase. Even though there's no way I could have done, I keep panicking that I've missed him. Perhaps he's taken the lift or there's a backstairs that the celebrity authors use to avoid persistent fans. Then, just as I'm about to give up, Leo comes running down the stairs, his coat slung over his arm. There's a slightly hectic look about his clothes, like he got dressed in a hurry or just doesn't care. One side of his shirt is coming untucked. It makes me like him even more.

At the door, Leo hesitates, then shrugs on the coat, does up the buttons, pulls up the collar. The guy who interviewed him appears, brandishing a pen. Leo pockets it and thanks him, shakes his hand and pats him on the upper arm, then strides into the evening crowd.

I go after him. After the peace of the after-hours bookshop, the bright, noisy mayhem of Central London at night is overwhelming. It's started to rain and the unfurling umbrellas add to the sense of being besieged. I feel a sudden yearning for the tranquillity of Tanyard Lane and the rolling fields that flank it.

Leo is easy to keep in my sights because he's walking with such purpose, cutting a path through ambling tourists. Outside the tube station he grabs a copy of the *Evening Standard* from the stack and pinions it under his arm. He doesn't turn round once, so doesn't see me pushing through the barriers or running down the escalator after him, my feet tapping against the metal treads. He heads through the tunnels to the southbound Northern Line. I'm not really following him, I tell myself; I'd be on this train anyway, changing at Embankment for Victoria. The train arrives and I get on and stand so that I can see him reflected in the darkened windows. He folds the paper to the front page article and holds on to the handrail, his body swaying with the movement of the carriage as he reads.

We're coming up to Embankment. I shift to face the doors. They slide open. Three people get out and two get in, but I don't move. My heart pounds. The doors close. Now I really am following him.

At Stockwell, Leo rolls the newspaper, stuffs it into his coat pocket and steps off the train, setting off at a brisk pace towards the exit. I follow him to a square with a railed garden in the middle. Sheltered from the drizzle under the covered entrance to a block of flats, I watch him let himself into the third house from the corner.

I ought to go. I've done what I set out to do, and seen one of the Creaseys face to face. I've even spoken to him. I should talk to Mum before I do anything else. I certainly shouldn't attempt to introduce myself.

I can still catch the ten o'clock train if I hurry.

My feet won't move, not in the direction they are supposed to go at least. It all feels a bit surreal, like an out-of-body experience. I'm crossing the road. I'm outside his front door. I'm lifting the heavy knocker and letting it drop. This was not the plan. What if he shuts the door in my face? Or calls the police?

I want to spin on my heel and run, but it's too late for that. Leo is standing before me, eyebrows raised, bemusement in his narrowed eyes, as if he can't believe someone has had the gall to interrupt his evening. He recognizes me and his brows snap together.

'What on earth are you doing here?'

I look past him, hoping that Jenny Creasey will appear. Stairs lead up into darkness behind him. The signed hardback weighs heavily in my rucksack. I make myself stand straighter. I'm not scared.

'I think you might be my father.'

27

Jenny

IT'S COOL OUTSIDE ON THE TERRACE, SO I'M WEARING
a jumper, a shawl around my shoulders, and my feet are
cosy in Mum's slippers. Kate sits beside me with her bare
feet up on the lounger, her arms wrapped comfortably
around her knees. She's only wearing a fine-knit sweater
and a pair of jeans. She doesn't feel the cold.

We watch the moonlight wobbling on the surface of
the sea while Mum cooks supper. Leo thinks it's all bridge
parties and golf here, but it isn't – it's peaceful. It's also
space in which to unwind after the press attention and
an opportunity to spend time with my sister. She's here
over Easter with Bella and Lara, leaving my brother-in-
law to run the farm.

The house is halfway up a hill and has a spectacular
view over the rooftops to the bay. I love the play of light
on the geometric shapes of the houses below and the
way the angles of the shadows they throw move, expanding and contracting as the hours go by. At night, the
white buildings become blue-tinged. The sun comes up

and the sun goes down and my life dissolves one day at a time. I dreamt about Sophie again last night, and the wispy memories of that dream still haunt me. Two weeks has felt too long on this trip. I'll be glad to get home tomorrow.

Below us, a neighbour's tortoiseshell cat slinks across the rooftops.

'What are you thinking about?' Kate asks.

'Hm?' I shrug. 'Nothing. I'm worried about Mum.'

'Me too.'

We talked to her yesterday, explaining that we didn't like her living here on her own so far away from family. Dad died suddenly two years ago; a massive heart attack while Mum was out shopping.

'What am I supposed to do in England?' Mum had responded, mildly indignant. 'You're at work all week, I'd be lonely.'

'That might change.'

Kate had darted me a look, her eyes raised in query. I'd shaken my head. *Not now.*

'All my friends are here,' Mum had said.

'You have us.'

She'd looked at us as though we were small children with limited understanding.

'That's very sweet, but I have a full social life, and we look out for each other. I don't want to disparage either of your living arrangements, but Jenny, I doubt anyone would notice if I dropped dead on the pavement in Stockwell.'

'Don't exaggerate, Mum. It's not like that at all.'

She'd widened her eyes slightly.

'And Kate, you and Chris never stop. I'm not going to live in the middle of a field. I like towns, and community, and people of my own age to chat to. I'm not keen on mud and rain. I play tennis three times a week. I swim every morning. I belong to several clubs. Of course I miss your father, but I don't dwell. I love this place, and I'm staying.'

Beside me, Kate stretches her arms above her head luxuriously and I'm reminded that, at home, she never has time to relax like this.

'Did you hear her last night?' she asks.

My skin prickles. 'Yup.'

Mum had called out to Dad in her sleep, an eerie wailing sound, drawing out his name. *Chaarlieee.*

'The girls heard it. They said it creeped them out.'

'It happened a couple of times before you got here. I think she's asleep. I don't think she's aware she's doing it.'

'Do you think we should mention it?'

'God, no! She'd be mortified.'

A door bangs. It's Kate's daughters, back from the shops with a large bag of crisps. Spending time with them is an exquisite form of torture, but I wouldn't avoid these annual get-togethers for the world. A dose of my nieces tops up my reserves of strength and insulates my nerves. Kate and I used to wait until they were asleep, then we'd sit up late, talking about marriage, life, Sophie. It's harder now that they're at an age when they go to bed later than us.

'What did you mean yesterday?' Kate asks. 'When we were talking to Mum.'

'About what?' I racked my brain. There had been a conversation, but I'd brushed over my plans, not wanting to worry my mother.

'You said something about change?'

'Oh, that.'

I feel myself blushing although there's no reason why I should. Only that I'm aware I can afford to throw away what – to Kate – is a staggering salary, to do something for me. At the heart of the tension between us is our grandmother's legacy. As the older sister, Kate was given first choice of Sparrow Cottage or its equivalent in cash. She chose cash, leaving me with what I thought, by 1988 when the housing market crashed, was the short straw. In the mid-nineties property values sky-rocketed, but Kate didn't benefit and her inheritance disappeared into the bottomless money pit of the farm she and Chris bought. I'm sure it rankled that Leo was the one who persuaded me to hang on to the cottage.

When I first brought Leo home to meet the family, Kate took an instant dislike to him. The cold front emanating from her was so obvious it was embarrassing. She and I had always been close, more like twins than older and younger sister. I had always looked up to her, but Leo coming into my life altered the balance, because I loved him and I wanted my entire family to love him, but Kate just wouldn't. She saw straight through him, and the faults that I brushed over – because I didn't care about them – she built into mountains.

You wouldn't know it, seeing where she's ended up, but as a young woman Kate was a lot more sophisticated than me. Before Chris came along she'd had a string of less than satisfactory relationships, whereas Leo was my first boyfriend, so she thought she knew all there was to know about men. She insisted she could tell he was the type who used people until they were of no use to him. She said I was being naive and that I'd get hurt, but she was the one who hurt me, not Leo. It took a while for us to get our relationship back on track, and even now it's not the same. I miss how we were as children, and I think she does too.

'I'm thinking of jacking in the job.'

'Wow. What's brought that on?'

I shrug. 'Life. I don't know, I want to do something different – help people.'

'I thought that was what you did. Help them maximize their filthy lucre.'

I laugh. 'I've had enough of all that. I don't like the politics. I don't care about the money. I hate fighting my way on to the tube and getting crushed and dealing with other people's stress. Everyone in the office seems to be younger than me, and they all want my job. They're welcome to it. I just want to get off.'

'That's quite a list you have there. Have you spoken to Leo?'

'Not yet, but I will.'

'He'll love that. No more fat-cat salary.'

I bristle. 'Leo is not all that concerned with money.'

'Only because he doesn't have to be.'

I study her profile. She's gazing into the distance. She turns her head and catches me looking at her.

'Sorry. I didn't mean it. I'm sure Leo will be very supportive of your decision.'

'No, you're not.' I shiver. 'Can we go inside?'

'Wuss,' Kate says.

'It's freezing.'

'Rubbish. You try milking at five in the morning.'

After the moonlit terrace, the kitchen, with its gleaming tiled floor and bright chandeliers, makes me blink. Bella is shaking the crisps into a bowl while Lara gets a tub of green-olive dip out of the fridge and decants it into a shallow pot. Athletically built and active, they are permanently hungry.

Kate dips her fingers into the crisp bowl and helps herself.

'Don't spoil your appetite,' Mum says.

Mum has her arm around Kate's waist and they're watching the girls fondly. Lara and Bella have requisitioned the big white leather sofa. They've changed into pyjamas and fluffy socks and have their feet up, facing one another as if on a boat, long hair flowing down their backs, while they languidly scoop up dip with their crisps. The picture makes me feel both unanchored and sad.

After Leo refused to consider trying for another baby, I played with the idea of having another 'accident', but, six months after Sophie was taken, before we started having sex again, Leo arrived home from what I had thought was a long lunch with his editor and announced he'd had a vasectomy. I very nearly left him then, and perhaps I should have done. The finality of it was shocking and hurtful. A savage cut.

I've never told my family. They think the decision not to have another child was mine and would never forgive

164

Leo if they knew the truth. It isn't as though my parents were denied the joy of being grandparents. Dad absolutely doted on Lara and Bella, and the girls lavish Mum with affection when they get to see her.

I forgave Leo eventually, but it took an effort of will, and only after he'd agreed to counselling. Predictably, that lasted all of three sessions. I was surprised he made it that far.

'How did your talk go?'

I climb on to the bed and push a pillow up behind my back, stretch my legs out and hook one ankle over the other. Facing the window, I can watch the aeroplanes crossing the night sky. Replete with dinner, a glass of wine inside me, I'm ready to hear about Leo's day.

'It went well. A decent audience.'

'How many books did you sell?'

'I don't know.' His voice is clipped. 'A couple of dozen? Something like that, anyway.'

'Have you had anything to eat?'

'No. I'll make myself a sandwich before I go to bed.' He sounds distant.

'How did you get home?'

'I took the tube.'

I picture Leo walking through a noisy, dirty Soho, jogging down into the tube station, the push of people, the bright lights, the smells and the dirt, and feel homesick for London.

'Is everything OK?' I ask.

'Everything's fine. Look . . . Sorry . . . I'll call you back. I'm just in the middle of something.'

Surprise makes me hesitate. 'I just wanted to chat.'

'Sure. Can't it wait? I'm starving, and I need a drink. It's been a long day.'

'I thought you said you were in the middle of something.'

'Yes. I'm writing.'

'OK,' I say sharply. 'I'll see you tomorrow.'

'What time's your plane arriving?'

'Six fifteen.'

I wait for him to offer to pick me up at Heathrow, but he doesn't. A taxi it is, then.

After I've hung up, I let my phone rest in my hands, irritated. Perhaps he was lying, perhaps no one turned up for his talk; it happens. Or someone's written something derogatory about *In the Lake*.

When a critic gave him a less than 100 per cent flattering review for *Pig Lily*, he sulked for days. But that was years ago. He's developed a thicker skin since, especially since the larger advances and royalties started rolling in. Success and validation are important to Leo. It's his ego. I'm glad I don't have one; it must make life exhausting. I check my watch. It's only nine thirty. I was going to go to bed, but I don't feel drowsy any more.

Downstairs, Kate is perched on the arm of the sofa, laughing at an episode of *Friends* and reaching across Lara's shoulder for the crisps. I open my laptop and check my notifications. Three for Open Arms. I read them. Someone has posted asking to join the group.

There are a list of questions, and I read the woman's answers, then press 'accept' and message her the letter I send to new members. Her seventeen-year-old son walked out of the family home eight years ago and hasn't been heard of since. She's wondering if that counts, if she can join. I reassure her that she has as much right to be in the group as anyone else. It's a slow process. Some join and you never hear from them again. Some are rarely off the site, some dip in when things get dark and ignore us when they're on an even keel. That's OK.

I explain to her how Open Arms works, that we offer support but we're not here to give advice, fix anyone's life or rescue anyone from a situation. We provide a shoulder to cry on and a listening ear and we don't judge. The words 'you should', 'you could' or 'you ought to' are banned. We listen to their stories when their friends don't want to be confronted with their pain any more. I find it immensely rewarding. I often find people just want to be heard.

'How's the great man?' Kate asks, her eyes glued to the TV screen.

I look up. 'He's fine.'

Mum turns to me with an impatient cluck.

'I don't know what's keeping your father. Could you call him on your mobile, darling? He'll just ignore mine if he's in the bar. It's getting late.'

Kate straightens up and comes over to the kitchen island.

'What did I say?' Mum glances from me to Kate.

'Mum . . .'

Kate gives me a warning look.

'Sorry,' Mum says, going pink. 'Sorry. I forgot.'

28

Leo

LEO REPLACED THE PHONE ON ITS CRADLE IN THE HALL. The girl was standing just inside the door on the door-mat, shivering in the draught, but he had no intention of inviting her any further into the house.

'My mother,' he said by way of explanation.

Some instinct of self-preservation had stopped him from saying Jenny's name, though it was hard to know why. Time to nip this in the bud.

'I don't understand why you thought you could just turn up here. Do you have any idea how many girls have called the hotline since that interview?'

She shook her head, her knuckles whitening as she gripped her hands tighter.

'One hundred and thirty-eight. But at least they had the decency to go through the proper channels. My wife is out this evening, but what if she had been here? She's fragile. She doesn't need to be doorstepped by every self-deluding, attention-seeking teenager who wants a shortcut to fame.'

The girl raised her eyes to his and he saw a spark of life.

'I don't want to be famous. I just wanted to see you.'

'Well, you've seen me now. You should go back to wherever you came from. It's been a long day and I haven't got time for this.'

'I didn't mean to cause problems.'

'I'm sure you didn't, but what the hell do you think gives you the right to follow me? I've had my fair share of nutters who think they know me or own me. None of them has had the temerity to knock at my door at nine thirty at night. I should call the police.'

'Sorry.' She hung her head.

She seemed vulnerable, but there was nothing he could do. Any hint of encouragement or sympathy from him and he'd never see the back of her.

'Good. I hope you realize how ridiculous you've been.'

He moved towards her, expecting her to take her cue and leave, but she stayed where she was, blocking his path to the door.

'I just thought . . . I wanted to talk to you first. I didn't want to speak to the police because . . .' She sniffed. 'If it's true, Mum will be in trouble. I didn't want to start anything unless I was absolutely sure.'

Leo narrowed his eyes. She didn't look much like Jenny. He felt strange, his mind crackling. It was part fear, part exhilaration. What if?

What if the past had come back to haunt him in the form of this unprepossessing girl?

'Your name's Zoe, isn't it?' He was amazed he could remember.

She nodded.

'Well, Zoe, I understand the power of the media,' he said, trying a different tack. Firm but reasonable. He was the grown-up, she was the child. 'It's manipulative. You're young and impressionable, and something or someone has planted the idea in your mind that you're special. But you're not my daughter. You should go home. Won't your mother be wondering where you are?'

Her jaw tightened in the way Jenny's did when she was determined to get her way. That was disconcerting.

'My mother's name is Hannah Faulkner.'

It meant nothing to him. But then he'd never known her name, had he? She hadn't told him and he hadn't asked.

'I've met several women called Hannah over the years,' he said carefully. 'I don't know anybody named Faulkner, though.'

'My birthday is the eighth of March nineteen eighty-nine. Two days before your daughter was born.'

He was unnerved. 'Did your mother live in London at the time?'

'No.'

'Well, then. Are you saying she travelled up to London to steal a baby? It seems a little far-fetched. Surely she could have got one from a hospital nearer to where she lived?'

'I don't know about any of that,' she answered. 'I just know it's true.'

Leo sighed. He was cold and irritated.

'So, you have a gut feeling about us. You can't go barging into people's lives because of your *feelings*.' He rubbed his temples with his thumb and middle finger. 'This is nuts. We're going round in circles.'

She met his eyes and he couldn't help scanning them. They were indeed Jenny's, or very much like them. This was ridiculous. So she had hazel eyes. So the dates matched. It didn't mean a thing.

The girl slipped her rucksack off her shoulder and unzipped one of its many pockets. She unwrapped the item she took out and concealed it in her fist. After a moment's hesitation, he offered his hand, palm up, and she dropped two small objects on to it. He ran his thumb over them. Baby identification wristbands. He turned away from her and held them under the hall light to read the labels. The whisky he'd drunk rose in his gullet and it was all he could do not to retch.

'Where did you get these?'

'From my mother's bedroom. You see? I'm not making it up. Will Jenny be home this evening?'

He thought rapidly, examining the implications. If this girl claimed she was his daughter, the authorities would demand DNA proof. They would discover she was related to Jenny but not to him. Her mother would tell some fabricated sob story that the media would believe because they love an underdog. They would stick it to him with the glee they always exhibited when bringing down a successful man. The act he had colluded in was unforgiveable, a brutal breach of trust and a heinous crime. His life would be over. He couldn't let that happen; he had to buy himself time.

'Come in, then. We'd better talk. Jenny's gone to see a friend but she won't be late.'

He reached behind her and closed the door. He felt her discomfort, a wrinkle of fear, and wondered if her mother had ever told her not to go into houses with strange men. He guided her into the sitting room, reasoning that leading her down to the basement kitchen might feel even more sinister.

'Where does your mother think you are?'

'I left a note. I said I was with a friend and would be home late. I told her not to wait up.'

'That was sensible,' Leo said, knowing there was scant chance of the girl's mother not waiting up anxiously for her daughter. He moved a pile of magazines and papers off the sofa on to the floor and indicated that she should take a seat while he perched on the arm.

'You know,' he said, 'now I look at you properly, you remind me of her.'

Her mouth stretched into a beam of pleasure that brought a sudden beauty to her features. He saw Jenny again, clearly and distinctly. He thought quickly. Whatever happened, if he pushed her away, even if he concocted a convincing excuse to keep her quiet, she wouldn't let it go; he could see she was stubborn. He felt his survival instinct kick in, and with it an animal cunning. He remembered his ruse with the car and Martin the farmer. He had thought his way out of a hole back then; he could do so again.

'I'm trying to work out what to do for the best. I think you should meet my wife before you tell your mother, because if it turns out to be true, which it appears to be, this is going to be a shock to everyone. Your mother might be arrested and go to prison, and you don't want that. If she did steal you, then I'm sure it was because she had some sort of mental breakdown. We need to have sorted all that out before the police get involved. We should protect her.'

Zoe nodded vigorously. 'Mum's not a bad person.'

He restrained his desire to roll his eyes. 'We're going to have to find a way of settling this, without doing harm. You can wait till Jenny comes home if you like. Did you tell anyone else what you were doing, because if so, perhaps you should call them?'

'I haven't told anyone.'

'No boyfriend, or best friend?'

'I don't have either of those.'

Thank God for small mercies.

'Right, well.' He looked at his watch. 'She'll only be an hour or so. You can read a book in the meantime. Or I'll put the television on, if you like.'

He felt rather pleased with the avuncular tone he had adopted.

'I'll read.' She delved into her rucksack for the signed copy of *In the Lake*.

Leo felt stymied. What was he planning on doing exactly? The truth was, as with his novels, he wasn't planning, merely going where the story led him. He felt imposed upon and angry. He didn't have time for this shit.

Zoe studied him, doubtless trying to find places where their DNA dovetailed. She'd have a job.

'What did you think of me when you saw me this evening?' she asked, resting the unopened novel on her knee.

173

'I meet hundreds of people every year at events like that. They all tend to merge into one.'

'But you said I had courage.'

'You've certainly got balls,' he agreed.

It was his own fault she had followed him home. If he hadn't paid her that compliment, if he hadn't made things personal, maybe she would have been on her way home by now. Even if the girl was right, he shouldn't have fed her fantasy. He was the worst kind of fool: a vain one.

'I'll be in the papers, won't I? People will know I belong to you and Jenny.'

Dear God, was she really that stupid?

'Let's take it one step at a time. We need to dot the i's and cross the t's.' Did he really say that? 'What I mean is, for legal reasons we'll have to confirm your DNA matches Sophie's before we go public with the good news.'

'I know, sorry. I'm just so excited. Do you think Jenny will like me? I hope I'm not a disappointment.'

Leo decided to humour her. He didn't want her to be upset, to turn this into something.

'If you are Sophie, she'll love you. We both will.'

She looked at him hopefully. 'But you're not particularly happy about it.'

He raked his fingers through his hair.

'You're very perceptive. If I seem cold, it's only because I'm protecting myself from disappointment. Jenny will be the same. You mustn't be hurt if she rejects you at first. We've had so many false starts. It'll be hard for her to take in, so you mustn't rush her or you'll overwhelm her. You must let me break it to her in my own way.'

'But the wristbands prove it.'

'I think they probably do. But Jenny and I, well, we only deal with hard facts. You do understand, don't you?'

He leaned forward and laid the wristbands on the arm of the sofa, smoothing them out. 'These things can be forged.'

Zoe frowned as she glanced at them. 'OK. Though I don't see—'

'Just bear with me.'

'Perhaps I've inherited your writing talent,' she said after a few seconds' silence. 'I read masses. Stephen King is my favourite at the moment. Do you like him?'

'I've never read his work.'

'You should. His books are brilliant. I've just read *Carrie*. I'd lend it to you, but I got it from the library.'

He fought the urge not to groan out loud.

'My wife is very good at maths. Maybe you've inherited that.'

'Yeah, maybe.'

That silenced her for a while. No romance in maths. Leo leaned back and closed his eyes but she didn't take the hint.

'It's just been me and my mum all along,' she said. 'Which is fine, you know, but it can make life a bit difficult, and—'

He was barely listening. He was thinking back to that dreadful night, to the rain and the moment he swerved and failed to avoid the young girl and her baby. Had he been sober, his reflexes would have kicked in faster. And now, sitting on his sofa, spinning ridiculous dreams, was a sixteen-year-old girl who could bring the whole house of cards crashing down. What the hell was he going to do?

She shivered and he asked if she was cold.

'No.' Zoe shook her head. 'We don't have central heating at home. I don't feel the cold.'

He raised his eyebrows. He remembered that house's damp chill. 'Well, I do. I'll make us both a hot chocolate.'

He ran up to his bedroom, opened the drawer beside the bed and fished out his sleeping pills. He flushed the loo so that she'd assume that was what he'd gone up for, and went downstairs. In the basement kitchen, he crumbled two pills into a mug with a spoonful of hot-chocolate powder, then added a generous splash of brandy and stirred it into a thick paste. The milk came to the boil and he poured it in, then tasted it. Bitter. He added another spoonful of chocolate and some sugar for good measure. He made a separate drink for himself, took the steaming mugs upstairs and watched while the girl blew on hers, holding his breath while she took a sip.

'It tastes funny,' she commented, wrinkling her nose.

'I put a little brandy in it. I thought we could both do with it.'

'Oh.' She smiled, looking as though she relished the experience. 'I've never had alcohol before.'

Leo remembered her mother saying she had never seen a film.

'I've texted Jenny. She's about to leave. She says she'll be home by half ten. Is that good?'

'Delicious.'

Seconds later, her eyes were closed, her head lolling.

'Zoe?' he whispered.

She didn't react, so he repeated her name, louder this time. She opened her eyes and tried to sit up.

'Wha . . . What?'

'Nothing. Go to sleep.'

He only ever took these pills when he was in the middle of one of his periods of insomnia. It often happened when he began a new book and all that pent-up excitement kept him awake. He normally took half a pill. The amount he'd given her would keep her out for hours.

She was stretched out now, one arm draped over the edge of the sofa, her breathing stertorous, like that of a drunk old man. Leo went outside, opened the rear door of his Range Rover, then stood for a while scanning the square. The house couldn't be seen from the main road, because there were trees and large shrubs directly in front of it in the communal garden. His upstairs windows would be visible, but he was confident no one across the square would be able to see what was going on in the street below. It was the houses on their side that he was worried about. It was late and quiet, but lights were still on. Reassuringly, where curtains and blinds were open he didn't detect any movement, just the blue flicker of television sets. That was the advantage of the anonymity of this place; for the most part, people minded their own business.

Whatever, he didn't really have a choice. He went back for her.

Taking a deep breath, Leo tucked his arms under Zoe's inert body and grunted as he picked her up. Unconscious, she was a dead weight, unwieldy and cumbersome, but he brought her outside and managed to get her on to the back seat without knocking her against the doorframe. He rubbed his back as he went back inside for his things.

Ninety minutes later he pulled up outside Sparrow Cottage.

Leo walked down the steps, opened the door and switched on the bare bulb, grimacing at the stale mildewy smell that flooded his nostrils. Under the soles of his shoes, the concrete floor felt unpleasantly gritty. A deep sigh escaped him. Was this really what he was contemplating doing? How did it fit with his view of himself as a reasonable man? He sighed again. One step at a time.

He had discovered the plans for this place when he was rooting around in the attic years ago. What had originally been a Second World War bomb shelter had been modified into a bunker by Jenny's grandfather at the end of the sixties. At the bottom of a set of wooden steps was a long narrow space, and behind a set of shelves cluttered with old paint pots and trays a door opened on to a room barely high enough to accommodate his frame. It was furnished with a bunk bed and a makeshift kitchen, and there was a ventilator system, which miraculously leaped into action when Leo flicked the switch, as well as a cramped cloakroom with a toilet and sink.

Leo knew very little about Edward Prest, only that he had gone to Canada to join a survivalist cult and never came back. He didn't think anyone knew about the bunker, least of all Jenny. Her grandmother had removed all trace of Edward from the house and never spoke of him, so perhaps its existence had been forgotten along with the man who built it.

The room was as cold as a fridge and a lot less

welcoming. He was glad now that he had never shared his discovery with Jenny, although the reason for that had been more to do with his antipathy towards his in-laws than any desire to keep it to himself. He hadn't wanted Charles getting overexcited and insisting on taking a look. But that had been before Sophie was born and Leo's life had taken a turn for the bizarre.

It was where he had hidden the baby's corpse after the police had left. He had brought it down here and put it under the bunk bed. Now he pulled it out, surprised at how light it felt, took it out of the room and tucked it under the steps in the darkest place.

He went back up for the girl, lifting her awkwardly from the car, staggering as he shifted her into a position where she wasn't going to slip. Her head was against his shoulder, his arms under her back and her knees. The last time he had carried her had been just before he handed her over to a stranger he met in a storm. He had breathed in her baby scent and been brought up short by it. Now he caught the smell of her hair and skin and again felt frightened at the enormity of what he was doing. Back then he'd had little choice. He didn't have any now either. It was a simple case of the girl or him. He had run out of options.

Getting her down the stairs without knocking her was impossible. Twice she blearily opened her eyes before slipping back into unconsciousness. The second time something lucid showed in their depths, a flicker of bewilderment turning to fear before he hushed her back to sleep.

He staggered down on to his knees and rolled her on

to the mattress, then rubbed his aching arms and back. He was too old for this. He fetched pillows and extra blankets, a bottle of water and a packet of biscuits. Then he covered her up and locked the door.

Later, unable to sleep, Leo found himself thinking about his father's unhappiness. It was a truth Leo hadn't been able to articulate as a child, even to himself, because it had seemed somehow shameful. He had endeavoured to hide it from his friends, often lying about what went on in their house. Hearing his father sob from behind the locked bathroom door had shocked him so much he hadn't been able to look him in the eye for days. It had shaped Leo's life, given him a determination to succeed and achieve what his father had missed out on.

What had happened today was not going to derail that. Not while it was in his power to do something about it.

29

Zoe

IT'S THE SMELL THAT WAKES ME: A PUNGENT ODOUR OF unwashed bedlinen and damp that I trace to the flattened pillow under my head. I'm thirsty and there's a bitter chemical taste in my mouth. I feel heavy, my body tugging me back into oblivion even while I try to make sense of my surroundings. Something is wrong. I almost don't want to open my eyes, but in the end I have to.

It's pitch dark and I have no way of telling what time of day or night it is. I only know I'm somewhere I'm not meant to be. I can feel thin metal ridges through the mattress, and when I stretch out my arm from under the blanket, I touch a wall. It's cold and softly blistered, reminding me of the damp spot just above the skirting on the wall of our kitchen, where the white paint bubbles and falls in dandruffy flakes to the floor.

As I roll over, a torch switches on, causing me to screw up my eyes. The yellow beam drops to the floor, allowing me to see the figure of the man seated on a wooden chair in the middle of the room. His hands and forearms rest on his knees. He slowly raises the torch again, this time not shining it straight in my face but against the wall close to my shoulder.

Through the fog in my head, I hear my own voice. 'Where am I?'

It sounds more like *whum-I*, as if there's fur on my tongue.

'You're safe,' he says.

I recognize his voice and even though his face is in darkness, I can see the gleam of his glasses. It's Leo Creasey. I wrap the blanket round my shoulders. It's freezing in here. Leo gets up and flicks a switch. Above us a bare bulb goes on. I squeeze my eyes shut again, then open them slowly and look around.

We are in a windowless room, about four metres by three. There are two closed doors. There's the wooden chair Leo is occupying and a small table with some crappy old kitchen cupboards above it. There's also a small, tired-looking armchair with stuffing bulging out from a tear in its side; the sort of furniture you'd find in a skip. Apart from the bed I'm sitting on, which appears to be a bunk, there's nothing else. Fear trickles down my spine.

'I don't understand.'

The last thing I remember is the taste of hot chocolate. Am I still in Leo's house? Maybe a bit they haven't got round to decorating yet? This place is dirty and cold, and the air is stale. My ears are blocked, like when you've got a really bad cold. I swallow to try to clear them, but it doesn't work.

Leo hands me a bottle of water. I'm about to unscrew

the lid when a reason for my lethargy suggests itself. Did he put something in my hot chocolate? Have I been drugged? What else has he done to me? My eyes widen and I thrust the bottle back, but he doesn't take it. He looks more amused than offended.

'You can see it hasn't been opened. It's perfectly safe to drink.'

I inspect the lid, satisfy myself he's telling the truth, then unscrew it and drink half the contents, glugging it back as if I've just crawled out of the desert.

'Are you hungry?'

He reaches behind him and produces a plate of toast, which I eye with suspicion. I shake my head.

He puts the plate back on the table with a shrug. 'I'm not going to hurt you.'

'I want to go home. Mum's going to be worried.'

'I'm sorry, but there's nothing I can do about that.'

'People will be looking for me.'

'I doubt that somehow.'

'What do you mean?'

Leo's face kind of folds. It's very expressive. Right now he looks sorry for me, and sort of haunted, which makes my stomach flip.

'Your mother won't report you missing.'

'Yes, she will.'

'Think about it.'

I swallow hard. Mum stole a baby. She'd have to confess.

'I'm not doing this because I want to,' Leo says. 'Please understand that. When you came to my house last night you gave me no choice.'

So it's the next day. I've been unconscious for hours.

'What have I ever done to you?'

'It's not what you've done, it's what you might do.' He sighs. 'You've stumbled into my private hell.'

'But you do have a choice. Please let me go. I won't say a word, I swear.'

'It's not that easy.'

'But you're my father.'

I say it with outrage. I've never had a father, but I know that if I had had one, he would have protected me from harm; he wouldn't have done this.

'I'm sorry to disappoint you, but I'm not. You're the result of a brief liaison my wife had with another man.'

My eyes are glued to his face as he tells me a story about a stormy night, a hysterical girl running out in front of his car and the accidental killing of a baby. He tells me how Mum blackmailed him into stealing his own newborn child and the nightmarish pact they made.

I shake my head, trying not to cry, my bottom lip trembling. 'Mum wouldn't do something like that. She wouldn't lie to me.'

He looks at me pityingly. 'It's all I have to tell you.'

Only a day ago, I'd dreamt about being the Creaseys' missing daughter. I'd thought it was a stupid fantasy, spun because I was unhappy and lonely, and because the girls at school thought I was nothing and I wanted to prove that I was something. A famous child, stolen from my mother's bedside. How could I have been so stupid? My entire life has been a lie.

'Why didn't you stop her?' I ask when I can speak without bursting into tears.

'Because it would have destroyed my career and ruined my life if it'd got out. I'd been drinking that night, and she knew it. I had no choice but to do what she wanted. I deeply regret it now.'

'If you regret it, then let me go. I won't even tell Mum I know and I won't go anywhere near your wife. I promise.'

I'm angry at myself for crying, but the tears keep coming. I wipe them away with the back of my hand. My head still feels muzzy.

'I'm sorry. I can't take the risk.'

He pushes up his glasses and pinches the bridge of his nose. He looks knackered. Perhaps he didn't sleep last night – that must mean he has a conscience. I wipe my nose with my sleeve.

'Please, let me go, Leo. I won't tell anyone. I'll just go back to school and forget it ever happened.'

He doesn't reply. He's getting ready to leave. I can feel it.

'Mum's going to be out of her mind when I don't come home.' I hesitate, then add, 'She loves me. She'll call the police.'

'You're being naive. She won't be able to prove she was mentally unwell when it happened, and I'm sure she's aware of what happens to other inmates who're inside for crimes against children. It's me or you, Zoe, and when it comes down to it, I'm more important than you. If you have to disappear in order for me to carry on doing what I do best, then so be it.'

'Are you going to kill me? Please don't kill me. I'll do whatever you say.'

He rubs at a crick in his neck and walks to the door. 'The last thing I want to do is hurt you, but it's up to you. You have to learn that what you do has consequences.'

'How long will I be here?'

My voice sounds small and scared.

Leo lifts his hand to the light switch. 'How long is a piece of string?'

I'm plunged into darkness. I hear the key turn in the lock. I hug my knees tight and listen to the hum of the pump, imagining my mother on that terrible day, and the decisions she made. She and Leo committed a terrible crime, but it's me who's being punished.

Why did I never sense something was wrong? She can't have held on to that secret without it affecting her. But of course it did. I just never knew, because I didn't know her before it happened.

30

Hannah

AT LUNCHTIME, HANNAH LEFT THE BIRCHES, CALLING
to Anita that she had to do a bit of shopping and would
be back by two. She jumped in her car and sped home,
her hands scrunched so tightly around the steering wheel
that her knuckles were white.

Please let her be back.

Hannah parked outside and sat for a while, not moving, just looking at the house. Zoe wasn't there. She knew
it even without going inside. She got out and trudged up
the front path.

Her instinct had been right. Today's post was still on
the mat; all junk. Hannah picked it up and went through
to the kitchen where everything was just as she had left
it. She ran upstairs to Zoe's bedroom in the slim hope
that she had come in and gone straight to sleep, but the
room was empty and the bed hadn't been slept in. She
moved into the bathroom they shared and ran the pad of
her thumb across Zoe's toothbrush. It was dry.

She sat down on the edge of the bath. What was going

on? Zoe had never done anything like this before. Could she still be at Jessie's? It seemed odd that she had been there at all; Zoe hated the girls in her class. If she'd stayed the night, she would have phoned. She would have known Hannah would be going crazy with worry.

Hannah wanted to call Jessie, find out what was going on, but she had no number for her; she didn't even know her surname. She'd have to talk to the school, persuade them to hand it over.

Their phone was one of those old-fashioned ones that had a coiled cord and a dial. Hannah had never seen the need to update it. Zoe, rather sneeringly, referred to it as 'vintage'. But if they had a cordless model, Zoe would be able to take calls in private, and Hannah couldn't have that. She hated secrecy, shut doors and whispered conversations. Her childhood had been spent with parents who never told her, or anyone, anything. In fact, they barely spoke at all.

She dialled the number for Maidstone Grammar, but after two rings she slammed the receiver back on its cradle. What was she thinking? If Zoe really was missing and Hannah involved the school and Jessie's family, she would be forced to go to the police and questions would be asked. What if they insisted on searching the house, on taking away Zoe's things for DNA testing? They would soon work out that Zoe Faulkner didn't exist, that she was Sophie Creasey. Hannah couldn't allow that to happen.

Why set a juggernaut in motion when Zoe might walk through the door any minute?

She took a long, steadying breath. This was an act of

rebellion. It was out of character, but when did teenagers ever do what their parents expected of them? Zoe was fine. She was still with Jessie.

Unless she had a friend Hannah didn't know about? A secret friend. A boy. Or a man. You heard such awful stories about things happening over the internet; about perverts. A cold piece of granite settled in the pit of Hannah's stomach. Zoe used the computer at the library. Maybe she'd been on one of those chatrooms. She fitted the profile of the type of teenager who might be tempted to do that kind of thing, because she didn't have friends.

Hannah searched Zoe's bedroom, rifling through her schoolwork, her drawers, and even taking books down from the shelves and flicking through them. She stood in the middle of the room and looked around. It was fairly spartan. Hannah couldn't afford to buy Zoe the latest fashions. Zoe didn't collect things either, unless you counted books.

Hannah's gaze rested on the bed. She pulled it away from the wall and ran her hand along the far side, reaching down to the floor. All she found was a stray sock. She checked under the pillow and raised the mattress and there it was: a torn-out piece of newspaper lying right in the middle. She picked it up.

Above a photograph of Jennifer and Leo Creasey, the headline read, *Stolen Baby Sixteen Today*. Was this her Armageddon? Panic immobilized her.

Maybe Zoe had found Leo Creasey. Maybe she was with him now. Maybe she had believed his version of what happened that night and couldn't forgive her. Hannah needed to speak to her, to explain, to make her understand that she'd had no choice.

Zoe wouldn't have gone looking for the Creaseys without talking to her first, would she? Had she failed as a mother? Anita's daughter, Emily, told her mother everything. She and Zoe weren't like that. Hannah had never tried to be her daughter's best friend. Maybe she should have, but it wasn't how she had been brought up. She had always rather despised women who behaved like that. It looked so needy.

How long should she wait? Maybe she should give her a few more hours. Zoe had probably already tried to call Hannah at work. She should go back and check if there were any messages.

There were indeed several messages waiting for her, but none from Zoe. How she got through the rest of the afternoon she couldn't remember. She barely recalled the conversations she had, and kept to her office when she'd normally spend time chatting to the residents.

She called home every fifteen minutes, but the phone rang out each time. Zoe had been out of touch for twenty-four hours now.

Hannah remembered the agonizing, bewildering pain she'd felt when she woke to find her baby dead beside her. Back then she had gone mad, she had run screaming out of the house. She had been young and frightened. The feeling that ran through her now was the same; it was just that age and experience meant that she didn't show it.

Zoe was a teenager, she reasoned. She was changing. Hannah had noticed the way she occasionally irritated her daughter, the pressures on Zoe that translated into demands her mother couldn't meet, the subtle and not-so-subtle signs that her daughter was humouring her. It was all natural. Zoe had found the article and gone off in a huff, but she would be back. All the same, it couldn't hurt to do a bit of research.

In the privacy of her office she used her computer to find out everything she could about the Creaseys, something she had never allowed herself to do in the past. She learned that they owned a house in Stockwell as well as a cottage somewhere in Kent. She called directory enquiries and asked for Leo Creasey in London but was told the number was ex-directory. In Kent there was no record.

She found another online article, this one an interview with a reviewer for a literary periodical. She skimmed the questions – mostly about Leo's writing motivation and style, and of no interest to her – then she read something that made her sit up.

NT: You talk about Chaffinch Cottage in your book. Was that house by any chance modelled on the house where you write?

LC: Loosely, yes. I do find houses are an inspiration. They are a window into characters, a way of adding a layer to the readers' knowledge of a protagonist without seeming to do so. I changed a few details, and the name, obviously, but otherwise it's a fair assessment.

NT: You like your birds, then?

* * *

Hannah found Prudence in the lounge doing *The Times* crossword puzzle. She closed the curtains against the gathering twilight, and drew up a chair.

'You're amazing, the way you whip through those,' she said. 'I never could learn. I don't have the general knowledge.'

Prudence patted the soft spring of her hair, looking pleased. 'It's like learning a language, dear. The more you use it, the better you get.'

'You need a good memory too, I expect.'

'Of course. It's a wonderful way of keeping it sharp.' She scrutinized Hannah. 'You look tired.'

'I didn't sleep well last night.'

'It's having a teenager in the house. Such a worry for you.'

Hannah stared at her, then realized she was generalizing. She coughed, then changed the subject.

'You've lived round here all your life, haven't you?'

'Apart from following my husband to various continents, yes. I was born not far away, and we retired here. My husband worked for Shell. My daughter-in-law is a consultant for them. She takes . . . Oh, she has . . .' She tutted, irritated at losing her train of thought.

'Do you know any houses with bird names?' Hannah asked.

'What an odd question. Do you mean in this area?'

'Yes.'

'Well, dear, I expect I do.' She picked up her pen and filled in a clue. 'Let me think.'

'Maybe a cottage?' Hannah said. 'Something like Chaffinch Cottage.'

Prudence sat up straight and clasped her hands together, resting them on her knees. She had the posture of a ballet dancer.

'There's Drake Farm, down near Nettlestead.'

'No, not there.' Hannah rubbed at the place on the back of her left hand where she had dug her thumbnail so hard it had left its imprint. 'More like one of those small garden birds.'

'Oh, well, there's the Prests' house.'

'The Prests' house?'

'Yes. What was its name? Sparrow Cottage! That was it. It's about three-quarters of a mile outside West Farleigh. Marjorie died a long time ago. He'd already buggered off. Canada, I think . . . I don't remember the details, but there was something wrong with him.' She tapped her head meaningfully. 'I seem to remember Marjorie left the house to one of the granddaughters. The younger girl – I can't remember her name. The one that married that author and had her baby stolen. I should have remembered that I knew her grandmother. Why do you ask?'

'Oh, no reason.' The back of Hannah's neck prickled. 'I thought I recognized the name, but I must have been mistaken.'

A black car sat parked on the gravel driveway. Hannah drove past the cottage and pulled up a little way down the lane. She walked back towards the property and rang the doorbell.

Standing there, waiting, she was reminded of the weekends of her childhood when she would follow her parents

193

from house to house. She and Deborah would wait in silence at their father's side, knowing they were likely to be met with indifference, and sometimes even hostility, but they would be ready with a smile and an offer of conversation – a friendly chat about the Bible. She could feel the flimsy copies of *The Watchtower* in her hands, the memory was so vivid.

The door opened and she looked into Leo Creasey's face. The shadows under his eyes were familiar, but his hair was sprinkled with grey and his face was craggier. In spite of the changes, he was very much the man she remembered. He still had that pulse of energy.

'Can I help you?'

'My name is Hannah Faulkner.'

'And?'

He waited, trying to pretend he didn't know who she was, but she knew he recognized her. She had seen it in his initial shock, the almost imperceptible widening of his eyes, the tension in his jaw.

'I want to know what you've done with my daughter.'

31

Leo

'I BEG YOUR PARDON?'

Leo stalled for time, even though it was hopeless. He'd guessed she would turn up at some point, but he didn't think she would find him so soon. The moment he opened the door he'd recognized her, with a sick jolt. Sixteen years is a long time, but she hadn't changed much. She was still relatively young but had an old look about her. It was the beige coat – a newer model but equally unenticing – her flat mousy hair and the deep lines etched between her brows. Sixteen years of worry about being exposed as a liar and a criminal would do that. He knew.

'Where is Zoe?'

'I'm sorry, but I'm on my way out and I don't know what you're talking about.'

Jenny's flight was coming in this evening and he needed her to believe he'd been at home all day, which would mean organizing supper on his return to Albert Square Gardens, and he had left it rather late. Because he wouldn't be coming back to the cottage before Tuesday, he'd had to ensure Zoe had plenty of food and water, warm blankets and something to read. He'd also needed to reinforce the internal door. It was either that or tie her up, and he couldn't in all conscience leave her unable to look after herself. Consequently, he didn't have time to spare for a row with Hannah.

'I don't believe you.'

'Well, I'm afraid that's your choice. I can't imagine why you think I would know anything about her. It's been sixteen years. I wouldn't know her if I saw her.'

He put on his coat then stepped outside, closing the door behind him. He did not want her inviting herself in. She had almost derailed his life once. She wasn't going to do it again.

He clicked his car's fob and strode towards the vehicle without giving her a second glance. In the quiet of the night, the crunch of gravel under his feet sounded overly loud.

'Don't lie to me.' She grabbed hold of his arm, her eyes glittering in the darkness. 'You know something.'

'I don't have time for this,' he snapped.

'I found a newspaper cutting in her room, about you and your wife. Zoe must have got it into her head somehow—'

He laughed. 'Really? Why on earth would she do that? Unless you've said something to her.'

'I haven't. But she's a dreamer. And why would she keep it if she didn't suspect something? You're lying. I know you are. Tell me where she is.'

Hannah's voice had risen to a pitch that made Leo's

head ache. Her hands were clenched into fists at her sides. He folded his arms and waited, reasoning that if he didn't add fuel to the flames she would calm down eventually. No one could sustain that level of hysteria without exhausting themselves.

He didn't have to wait long before being proven right. Hannah dissolved into tears, sobbing woefully, snot bubbling in her nostrils. He felt no urge to offer comfort, but she leaned against him anyway. He tentatively patted her back, then pushed her away. There was a damp patch on his coat. She made his skin crawl.

'I just want to find her.'

'I know you do,' he soothed, opening the car door and heaving himself up on to the driver's seat. 'Obviously you're worried, but you're not thinking straight. It's not as though my address is in the public domain.'

'I found you,' she said mutinously.

He hesitated. 'All I can tell you is she hasn't been in touch with me. I don't see how I can help.'

'She's very naive,' Hannah said, wiping her eyes with a crumpled tissue she had fished out of her sleeve. 'She doesn't know anything about the world. She's a young girl with no money, no phone, no way of getting herself out of difficulties. If she's gone to London, there's no one there to help her if things go wrong.' The words catch in her throat. 'What if someone's taken her?'

Leo resisted the urge to point out the irony. 'It's far more likely that she'll turn up.'

'If she's not home by the morning I'm going to the police. I don't care what happens to me.'

Leo leaped out of the car and grabbed her by the arm.

197

'Listen,' he hissed, bringing his face level with hers. 'You will not go to the police. If you do, it'll all come out. What you did, what you made me do. If this goes to trial, I might get sentenced as an accessory to a crime, but you'll go to prison for stealing another woman's baby after you killed your own.'

Hannah paled. 'I didn't kill her. You did.'

'Did I? I sometimes wonder about that, you know. Why were you outside with your baby in that weather? What had you done, Hannah?'

She shrank back.

'You know what they do to child-killers in prison? You'll be torn to pieces. I'm sure you've thought about that. Your name will be synonymous with evil.'

She yanked her arm out of his grasp and rubbed where he had gripped it.

'She was alive before you ran us down.'

'Maybe. Maybe not.'

He wasn't sure of his ground. He had touched the baby when they were outside, he remembered. He forced himself to recall the moment. She had felt cool, hadn't she? But then she'd been on the ground for a few seconds. In all honesty, he'd been too traumatized to assess the situation properly. He rarely thought about that day – he found it extremely hard to go back there – but in hindsight he was pretty sure she'd played him for a fool. She had deftly passed the blame for the death of her baby on to a stranger. And if he hadn't been drinking whisky, he might have realized it at the time. He was still being punished for that transgression; the gift that wouldn't stop giving.

'I'm sure forensics will be able to find out from an examination of the body.'

Hannah flinched and he paused.

'But I don't think either of us wants it to come to that. Go home and wait for her there. If she does get in touch with me I'll deal with it. I'll tell her that I'm not her father and that she needs to return home to you.'

Hannah's eyes were full of fear. 'And if she doesn't turn up?'

'Then there's nothing either of us can do for her. You'll have to tell her school some story, but for God's sake make it convincing. Send her off to cousins in Canada or something.'

She pulled in a sharp breath and he sighed. What did she want from him? Sensitivity? There wasn't time for that. A yellow glow in the distance told him a car was approaching.

'You'd better go,' he said.

'It would be convenient for you if I did, wouldn't it? If I just shut up and went away. You are a callous man, Leo Creasey. I saw that when we first met, and you haven't changed. You don't care about your daughter.'

'She never was my—'

'Oh, I know. You've denied her, washed your hands of her. Good for you. Well, you're involved whether you like it or not. You were there at her birth. You held her. If you weren't such a narcissist you'd see . . .' She started crying again. 'You would see that this matters far more than you, far more than your literary pretensions.'

'You're boring me now.'

'I'll talk to Jenny.'

Leo smiled contemptuously. 'If you ever go anywhere near my wife, I will kill you. I will eviscerate you, and I will enjoy it. Now, I have somewhere to be, so if you don't mind . . .'

Hannah cut a sad figure with her rounded shoulders and cheap lace-up shoes. He watched her get into her car and drive off, and only then did he allow himself to react, dragging in a long, painful breath.

That was the last time they were going to do a big media push on Sophie. He didn't care if it meant he sold fewer books, he could do without the aggro. Jenny hated it even more than he did, so she wouldn't argue. It was high time she gave up and got on with her life anyway. He was weary of the whole thing.

And now this. What the hell was he supposed to do with a sixteen-year-old girl?

32

Jenny

'THIS IS EXACTLY WHAT I NEED. THANK YOU.'

Leo has laid the table, lit a candle, warmed the plates and opened a bottle of crisp Fleurie. The curtains are closed in front of the French windows.

It's good to be home. The moment the cab turned on to the Clapham Road I felt a rush of happiness, despite the almost shocking contrast between the damp grey of South East London and the sun-drenched homes of Cascais.

'I should have cooked something,' Leo says, unwrapping my portion of fish and chips and carefully transferring it to my plate. 'This feels like cheating.'

I shake salt liberally over my chips. 'I don't care. I'm starving.'

I pop one in my mouth. Bliss.

Leo sits down. We tap glasses and smile at one another over the candle.

'You look well,' he says. 'You've got some colour in your cheeks.'

'I feel fat,' I groan. 'I've barely moved in the last two weeks. I needed it, though – I feel so much better.'

He nods. 'That was a tough few days, wasn't it? All that media intrusion. I'm not sure we should do it again.'

I don't say anything. He observes me over the top of his glasses.

'I've done a lot of thinking since you've been away,' he continues, 'and you were right, those public appeals do more harm than good. I saw what it did to you, Jenny. It drained the life out of you. Even I felt as if I'd been knocked for six. Frankly, the only people who gain from it are the press. It's voyeurism, it's repulsive and Sophie deserves better.'

'Well . . . I suppose so.'

'Jenny,' he adds, 'it seems to me the obvious thing to do would be to merge Open Arms with one of the larger missing-children's charities and take a back seat.'

'Why would I want to do that?'

'Because you're being pulled in too many directions and it means we can never progress beyond what happened.' He holds up his hand when I try to interrupt. 'Raking it over on an annual basis is a slow death. We'll always love Sophie, but it's time to focus on other things.'

I haven't told him what happened in Cascais yet, but even without the niggling suspicion that Mum might be developing dementia, her needs have become greater. So he does have a point.

'What with the job, the demands Open Arms makes on you, and your mum being on her own, you have no space for yourself these days. None for me either.'

Leo never thinks in those terms. Space and progress. I suspect he's been googling.

'I know that,' I say.

'So?'

'Did you get much of the book done?'

'Jenny.' He sighs at my attempt to change the subject. 'Not as much as I'd have liked, but the tour took so much mental energy. I thought I'd be able to write in the hotel rooms, but it was impossible.'

'Are the tours worth it?'

He shrugs. 'I don't know how well they translate into sales, but audiences seem to enjoy them, and I suppose they generate a bit of publicity.'

'It must be nice to get a little appreciation from time to time.'

'Can we go back to what we were talking about? I know that it's incredibly hard for you even to consider letting go of Open Arms, but you're exhausted.'

'You just said I was looking well.'

'You always look beautiful to me, but I can see what this is doing to you, and I'm worried. Something has to give.'

'But not Open Arms.'

'Why not? You have a close connection with missing-persons charities, it could be absorbed by one of them. There are overlaps all the time. And it's not as if it's particularly ambitious – it's just a Facebook page.'

My head snaps up. 'It is not just a Facebook page, Leo. It's about communication, trust and support. No one is on their own. If I let it get swallowed up by a big charity, there won't be that personal element.'

'No. Granted, there won't be Jenny Creasey sitting at

her kitchen table comforting anyone who feels like getting in touch at all hours of the day and night. But that's the point. You bear the brunt. Jenny . . .' He reaches for my hand. 'You can't be all things to all people. You have a high-powered job.'

'You're not the only one who's been doing some thinking.'

I pull my hand out of his and tuck my hair behind my ears. There's an imperceptible tightening around the muscles of his face.

'Oh, yes?'

'You're right. I have taken on too much. But it's not Open Arms I want to let go of.'

He narrows his eyes. 'What, then? Were you thinking of going part time? I'd support you if you wanted to go down to four days again.'

A while back I'd taken off one day a week to train as a counsellor at the local adult education college.

'I don't want to work part time. They're offering voluntary redundancy and I've decided to take them up on it. It's too good an opportunity to miss. I've come to the end of the line with the job. I've had enough.'

'I don't blame you. With your credentials you'll be snapped up. You're constantly being headhunted. I'm surprised you've stayed there so long.'

'I didn't mean that. I'm fed up with accountancy. I'm bored of the people I have to deal with and the obsession with money. I want to do something that makes a real difference.'

I lift my glass to my lips. My hands are trembling. Why is this such a big deal? He's my husband, not my boss.

'I'm a qualified therapist. I'm going to join a practice, maybe start my own in a couple of years.'

I examine Leo's face and see restrained dismay. He puts his elbows on the table, steeples his fingers and leans forward.

'I thought you were just doing the course as part of your therapy. I didn't think you would ever actually practise. You never said that.'

'It's a qualification, Leo. Not a hobby.'

Because I did the classes and the coursework on the days he was in Kent, I think he assumed it was part of my recovery. But surely it must have occurred to him that I might want to take it up as a career? I never actually came out and said that though, so I suppose I can't blame him for misconstruing things. The trouble with Leo is he sees everything through the prism of how it affects him.

He draws himself up and becomes Leo the man of letters, the authority on the world.

'I'm not convinced it would be the right thing for you to do. Don't you think it would make you dwell more?'

'I couldn't possibly dwell more,' I snap, jumping up.

'I'm sorry. I didn't mean that. Please, sit down.'

Mollified, I settle back into my chair. 'I believe I can help other people. I can empathize. I've learned ways of allowing myself to live when I'm in pain. I can share those skills and strategies. I want to.'

'Darling,' Leo says. 'I don't want to stop you doing anything you want to do, but I'm not sure this is for you. You're not strong enough. You need to stick to what you know. I don't want to have to pick up the pieces a couple of years down the line. You are brilliant at what you do. Look at what you've achieved. And . . .' He pauses, his gaze concerned. 'Think of the consequences if you fail. If something happened to one of your clients. How would you be able to bear it?'

I didn't expect Leo to greet my decision with huge enthusiasm, but nor did I expect him to cast me as a failure before I'd even started. I push my food around my plate.

'If you were scared to fail, Leo, you would never have written a book.'

'That's different. I don't have people's mental well-being in my hands. Psychology isn't an exact science, like maths.'

'I'm well aware of that,' I say, cross again. 'I think you should have more faith in me. I'm tired of there being only one correct answer. Human beings make a mess of things – that's what life is about. What I do now isn't real, it's all about formulae and spreadsheets and computers spewing numbers. It's sleight of hand. Even if there isn't a definitive answer to a problem, at least I'll have helped someone gather the tools they need to function.'

'That's all very well.'

'Leo. Listen to me, will you? Sometimes I think Sophie's absence is going to swallow me whole. Did you know that?' He opens his mouth to answer, but I rush on. 'But I'm still here and we're still together. Other couples in our situation might well have been driven apart by the strain. That's proof I'm capable of more, don't you think?'

I refuse to cry. I set my jaw and watch him. He tips the dregs of his wine into his mouth, then refills his glass and offers me the bottle. I wave it away.

'I didn't mean to imply you're weak,' he says. 'I happen to think we're getting along OK. We're comfortable. We have our pain but we both deal with it in our own way, we give each other strength. Why rock the boat?'

'I have no intention of rocking the boat. I just want to do something different. Something that helps people.'

He sighs. 'We're going round in circles. You help people through Open Arms.'

'Yes, and that's why I want to do this. I need to earn a living, but I want to do it in a way that I can square with my conscience. I'm just not that interested in numbers any more, I'm interested in people.'

He slumps back in his chair. 'I don't know.'

'If you're worried about the money, don't be. The redundancy package is generous, so we'll be cushioned while I build up my client list. And you make money.'

'We can't bank on my income, though. You know perfectly well what it's like – feast or famine. Financial security means I can write without worrying. If we'd had to rely on what I make over the years, we'd be in a pretty sorry place.'

'That's irrelevant. It's not as if I won't have an income. Just not as much. We live a simple life – we don't go on exotic holidays or spend money on expensive luxuries. I have savings. If I do this, we'll be able to spend more time together. I might even be able to come down to Sparrow Cottage from time to time.'

Leo places his knife and fork on his plate, slides them

together and picks up his glass again. He eyes me with hostility.

'No.'

He doesn't say it loudly, or sharply, he says it so coldly I shrink back in my chair. His eyes are like flint.

'I don't see why not,' I protest. 'That house is mine, after all. I don't need to come down on your working days. I only meant that instead of you coming back to London, I could join you for the occasional weekend. We could go for walks, do something with the garden. You said it needs a bit of TLC.'

'A little neglect doesn't hurt. In fact, it benefits the wildlife. I don't want manicured lawns or clipped hedges. Don't you understand, Jenny? The cottage is a scruffy, comfortable old friend. When I'm there I feel embraced. I don't want it to change. I've organized it the way I like it.'

'I would occasionally like to get out of London when I'm not working,' I say stiffly.

'Then we can do something else. We can hop on a train and go to Paris. We could go to Edinburgh. I promise I'll make more of an effort. Let's go somewhere next weekend. I'll book a hotel. What about the Cotswolds?'

I grow hot as tears pool in my eyes, and I drop my head so that he won't see. But Leo isn't blind or stupid. He jumps up and hunkers down beside me. He takes my hands and strokes them with his thumbs.

'I'm sorry, darling. I've been an idiot. I've neglected you when you've been nothing but generous, kind and forgiving. I'll be a better husband, I promise.'

He kisses me and I wind my arms around his neck.

He stands, drawing me up with him and we press the length of our bodies together. When I break the kiss, my tears are smudged on his cheeks.

'Let's go to bed,' he says, kissing me again.

As if all this can be sorted out with sex, I think, as I allow him to lead me upstairs. He unbuttons my shirt, flings off the eiderdown and we collapse on top of the snowy-white duvet. The sex feels different. Whereas before we flowed automatically into our groove, practised and familiar, this time I detect a sense of urgency in Leo; a quiet but powerful desperation that hasn't been there for a very long time, if ever. At one point I open my eyes and the expression of fierce concentration – of fury – on his face alarms me. It's as though I'm some other person, someone he hates and fears.

Afterwards, he lies beside me for an acceptable length of time, about one minute, stroking my hair and asking if I'm all right, then he gets up and disappears into the bathroom. I pretend to fall asleep. When he opens the door I sense the light through my eyelids. The light goes out. I wait for him to get into bed, but the bedroom door closes and he goes downstairs. I feel a mixture of relief and pique.

I won't let him down. We make mistakes, we do things we're not proud of. We make ourselves promises in order to salve our conscience. I allowed Leo to think he'd lost his own child, even though his pain would have been so much less if he knew the truth. There will always be enough money for Leo. Nothing has changed.

33

Zoe

I HAVE WATER AND A SMALL AMOUNT OF FOOD. THIS morning I ate the last of the digestives. What's left of the bread has gone mouldy, and I finished the fruit yesterday. Since he left, I've probably slept 70 per cent of the time. I'm getting used to the pungent smell down here, but I don't think it'll ever leave me. It's in my mouth, my nostrils and it's permeated my skin.

I've shouted and shouted until I've grown hoarse and my throat is sore, but no one has come, and I've stopped for now because it feels futile as well as painful. I was petrified when he first left. I banged on the door and screamed, then I was angry, but when nothing happens hour after hour, day after day, it's hard to keep it up. Maybe he knows and he's staying away on purpose to break me.

I don't think I'm in London. I remember now seeing a light on in the basement when I walked up to his front door, and he went down to the kitchen to make my hot chocolate. This is somewhere else. Somewhere his wife won't hear me shouting.

If he was going to kill me, I think he would have done so on the first evening, when I was drugged. He could have tipped me into a river or something. He could have made it look like suicide. He didn't. He's got me here because I surprised him, turning up like that. He didn't have time to think and now he's scared. If I can stop him being scared and make him trust me, maybe he'll let me go. I try to feel what he's feeling but that just makes it worse, because I wouldn't let me go if I were him.

I do another inspection of the room, but it's half-hearted because I've already searched thoroughly and nothing's changed. There are no weapons or tools. I slump on to the armchair and pick at the escaping fluff. What's Mum doing? What's he doing? Trying to come up with a plan? I imagine screwing up my own life that much and almost laugh.

Something occurs to me. I push myself up and open the cupboard on the wall. A mug. I take it and feel its weight. It's one of those thin porcelain ones; pretty and old-fashioned, with garden birds and sprigs of wild flowers on it. I like it, and feel a moment's regret as I slam it on to the floor. It shatters into three big pieces and lots of smaller ones, tiny shards and white dust. I hide the two larger sections between the wall and the mattress of the top bunk, and keep hold of the third piece. It's shaped like a curved triangle and fits snugly in my back pocket. I carefully scoop up the rest and drop it behind the toilet. The dust I blow away.

Hours go by. When I move again, my limbs feel stiff.

If that's happened in the space of a few days, what am I going to be like in a week? A month? I'm not particularly keen on exercise. I'm useless at netball, and I hate going to the gym because people are always watching you as they wait for their turn on the equipment. I should do something, though. It's better than counting the marks on the wall.

I start by pacing the room. It takes eleven of my steps, so I do fifty lengths. Then I do stretches and star jumps, but they make me feel clumsy and self-conscious, even though no one's here to witness me making a prat of myself. I run on the spot until I'm out of breath, which doesn't take long; it's much harder work than cycling. I have a break on the bunk, then start again. I went to yoga club after school for a term last year, so I do some of that. I attempt the warrior pose, but my legs ache and tremble. I stick at it because if I have to run, I'll need strong thighs. I count to twenty, then collapse on to the floor.

There's a sound, a scraping. I count the number of times his shoes tap the stairs. One, two, three, four, five, six, seven. Details are important.

'Zoe.'

I don't answer because fear seems to have taken my voice away.

'Zoe,' he says, louder this time. 'OK. Suit yourself.'

The moment I hear his footsteps on the stairs again, I fling myself against the door, pounding it, my voice coming back. I scream his name.

'Move away from the door and I'll open it.'

I back up against the bunk bed. He comes in.

'Turn around and put your hands behind your back.'

I do as I'm told, but before I turn I take the piece of porcelain out of my pocket and conceal it in my palm, the sharp edge poking between my fingers. As soon as Leo touches me I spin on my heel. I go for his face, knocking his glasses askew.

He catches my wrist, holding it so tightly I cry out. He bangs it back against the metal edge of the upper bunk and my hand opens, the pain sending a hot arrow through my entire body. My improvised weapon falls to the floor at his feet and he kicks it far under the bed. He flings me down, kneeling on my back while I kick and scream.

Once my wrists are bound Leo rolls me over, wraps his hands around my neck and squeezes. His glasses have slipped down his nose, his eyes bulge, his mouth widens into a maniacal grimace. Through my blurred vision he looks like a mad professor. Tears pour down my cheeks, wetting my ears. He squeezes harder and I begin to go slack. My hands press into the small of my back. My feet thud against the floor. I'm going to die.

I fix my eyes to his. At first, he seems to have gone somewhere else in his mind, somewhere disconnected from me, but then something odd happens. It's as though he suddenly realizes what he's doing. He rises without warning and rushes into the toilet to throw up. I lie flat on my back, my chest heaving, my choking sobs almost as noisy as his retching.

Leo blunders out of the room, slamming and locking the door behind him. I hear him stumble and swear on

213

his way up the steps. I roll from one side to the other until I've worked up enough momentum to flip on to my stomach, then I drag my knees under me and start the difficult job of standing up. When I'm there I go to the door and check it's locked. It is. I sit down on the chair, stunned. Leo just tried to kill me, but he couldn't do it.

So what now?

He's gone a long time. Two hours, maybe three. I can't see my watch. I get into bed because I might not be able to get up quickly enough when he comes back, so I remain seated, waiting. My head droops between my shoulders, but each time I fall asleep I dream I'm tumbling, and jerk awake.

Leo stands framed in the doorway, a carrier bag in each hand. He looks sorry. I expect I have bright-red marks around my neck. My throat hurts more than ever and my head aches.

He locks the door behind him and starts emptying the bags. He's bought more biscuits, cereal, packets of dried French toast, three apples, three bananas and a bag of tangerines. A bag of carrots too. There's nothing I can't eat without a knife. From the other bag he pulls three ready-made sandwiches from Marks & Spencer. There's a choice of chocolate too – three bars – and a box of Easter-themed mini cupcakes.

'I didn't know what you'd like,' he says. 'You're not a vegetarian, are you?'

I shake my head. He tears the wrapper off a pack of

loo rolls, pulls off a strip of tissue and uses it to wipe my face.

'That's better,' he says.

He gets down on his hands and knees, and reaches all the way under the bunk bed to retrieve the broken shard of mug.

'Where's the rest of it?' he asks, holding out his hand.

When I don't reply, he pulls my blanket and pillow off the bed, then the mattress, and does the same on the top bunk until he finds what he's looking for. He rattles the pieces in his hand, then puts them in his pocket.

I sit stiffly, watching him, saying nothing.

'I'm not angry with you, Zoe,' he says. 'You only did what anyone would do in the circumstances.'

'Are you going to kill me?'

It hurts to speak.

Leo rakes his fingers through his hair, then drops his hand as if he's embarrassed to be caught using such clear body language. He's wearing a loose, rather scruffy jacket, frayed at the collar. He reaches into his pocket and takes out a penknife, which he opens. He grasps my shoulder and pulls me towards him roughly. I scream, but he doesn't slice it through my neck; instead, he eases it between my wrists and cuts the cable tie binding my hands. I rub at the red marks left on my skin, then take the sandwich he proffers and rip open the packet.

Leo's voice becomes business-like. 'I'm here every week from Tuesday morning until Thursday afternoon. Friday through to Monday I'm in London with my wife. While I'm here, I write every day from six until three, then I either go for a walk or do some maintenance on the property. I'll bring you food three times a day while I'm here and leave you with enough provisions to last when I'm not. Is there anything else you need?'

He hasn't answered my original question. I reach for the bottle of water and take a long swig, swallowing painfully.

'Books.' I sound like I did when I had tonsillitis last year.

'Good idea, I'll bring a selection. Do you prefer the classics, or something contemporary?'

It's as if he's an English Literature teacher doing me a special favour. He tried to kill me and now that he's not going to, he's being nice, like this is reasonable, like he's not telling a sixteen-year-old girl she's not going to get out of here. Ever. Does he think I should be happy and grateful if he shows a bit of thoughtfulness?

'Some classics, but I like horror and science fiction too.' I put my hand to my throat and swallow. 'What if I need . . . something else?'

'Like what?'

I just look at him. Then I say, 'I'm sixteen.'

I can't bring myself to spell it out. I'm not used to talking about things like that.

'Oh,' he says, the penny dropping. 'OK. I'll see what I can do. Right,' he adds, as if he's dismissing a class. 'I need to get back to work.' He takes a pencil and a folded sheet of typing paper out of his pocket and hands them to me. 'If there's anything else you need, write it down on this. Within reason, of course. I want you to be comfortable, Zoe. It might be hard to believe, but I'm not a monster.'

'Can you bring me a book now?' The thought of the hours stretching ahead, with nothing to do, scares me more than the future does.

Ten minutes later, he's back with a selection: well-thumbed copies of Charles Dickens's *Little Dorrit*, Thackeray's *Vanity Fair* and Wilkie Collins's *The Woman in White*.

'These should keep you going. I don't have anything lighter, I'm afraid, but I'll get you something next time I'm in town.'

'I've read them already.' I see the look on his face and add hurriedly, 'But I can read them again. Please don't take them away.'

When he leaves I sit for a long time, staring at the door. Then I unwrap a Mars bar and eat it. I wonder what Mum's doing. She'll be desperately worried. She must have gone to the police by now. She'll tell them what's happened. I imagine them treating her with disbelief, sneering maybe, making jokes behind her back, then she'll hand them some kind of proof, something with my DNA on it. They'll swing into action.

Will I hear the sirens from down here? I hope so. Scotland Yard will probably be involved. They'll break the door down and find me cowering on the bed, dirty and bedraggled, quivering with fear. One of them will put their arm around me and tell me, with a catch in their throat, that I'm safe now.

Jessie and Becca will be doing their homework when their parents call out, 'Hey, isn't that the girl who's missing?' They'll rush to the TV and watch open-mouthed as I'm hurried through a barrage of press, lights flashing

217

like a strobe as they try to get a picture. 'Zoe!' the journalists will shout. 'How did it feel being held prisoner?'

The image disappears abruptly from my mind. My stomach begins to feel tight. She can't go to the police, can she? She stole me. The moment she involves them, they'll figure it out. A light will flash up on a central database somewhere, and the connection will be made. She won't be able to bear the shame.

And if it's true she replaced her dead baby, then what would she do for her pretend daughter? Would she sacrifice herself to save me? She must. She will. She loves me. Maybe a jury would be sympathetic towards her. She can say she wasn't of sound mind. How long does it take to get the results of a DNA test? I have no idea whether it's two days, two weeks or two months. But what if she's too frightened to come forward? Where does that leave me?

34

Leo

LEO LEANED OVER THE BUTLER SINK, HIS HANDS ON the counter, staring out of the window into the sinister gloom of the garden. He blinked away the image of Zoe's distorted face. He had been overcome by rage and the sheer stress of his situation; anyone would have reacted the same way. He was proud of himself for pulling back from the brink – not many men would have been capable of that. It had been Zoe's eyes that had knocked some sense back into him, locking with his, causing a physical reaction in him. They were Jenny's eyes. He didn't know whether to be grateful or to despair.

He felt alive, that was the extraordinary thing. His brain was literally buzzing, his pulse jumping. He was so full of adrenalin he felt he would burst if he didn't find an outlet.

He took his mug of black coffee into the study, put on Tchaikovsky's 'Violin Concerto in D Major', then sat down at his desk and pressed 'enter' on his keyboard. The screen lit up, he opened the latest draft of *Still*

Lives, spread his fingers over the keys and focused his thoughts.

Nothing. He adjusted his posture. Where had that feeling of flying gone? He grimaced, scrolled back a few pages and read what he'd written last. It was pretty good. More than good. So what was the problem? He tipped his head back and stared at the ancient beam above him. He stuck out his jaw and ruminated. He tried again. Some words came: a sentence, two paragraphs, but there was no hit. That indefinable thing, the sudden stirring of his mental juices that had sent him rushing to his desk, had dissipated. Damn it.

Leo huffed and rolled back his chair, spun round and stared at the bookcase on the opposite wall, scratching his jaw. Irritated, he sprang up, put on his caped oilskin coat, shoved an old baseball cap on to his head, and stomped outside.

There had been something there, he thought as he strode along the lane. An imperative. That slippery muse who sometimes gave freely, sometimes held back, had been with him. He should have listened.

He stopped walking and dug his hands deep into his pockets. The rain pattered on the hedgerow. He breathed in the heady odours of wet tarmac and grass. A car approached, and he stood to one side. James Turner, the neighbour whose phone call sixteen years ago had started all this, lifted a hand in greeting as he slowed to avoid splashing him. James's dog gazed at Leo with her big brown eyes. She looked, to his heated imagination, as though she saw right through him. Did she know? Had she detected the scent of Zoe on her walks?

Watching Turner's brake lights fade into the dark, Leo's brain stuttered like a strip light. It was there. He knew exactly what it was that he needed to do. *Still Lives* could wait. He turned on his heel and set off back to the cottage, almost at a run he was so scared of losing his train of thought.

Back at his desk, Leo closed *Still Lives*, opened a blank document and began to type. Nothing felt beyond him. He had sold his soul and the knowledge had injected a blazing energy into his mind and body. The idea that he could keep a girl prisoner was astounding. Her presence, like a butterfly in a jar, galvanized him, made him feel potent and alive.

Words leaped from the page, phrases danced, the dialogue sang with integrity and truth. He felt breathless with excitement. His emotions were intensified, his thoughts sharpened. He would complete *Still Lives* because he had signed a contract, and it would be brilliant, but this story had taken control of his voice. It wouldn't release him until it had been told. The pity of it was that no one would ever read it.

35

Hannah

ON SATURDAY, WHEN HANNAH DROVE BACK FROM work along the dark and winding lane, she had little hope of doing anything other than watching Sparrow Cottage, but there were no lights on and the driveway was empty. She experienced a little thrill. Leo Creasey wasn't there.

To be safe, she drove on, looking for a place where she could leave the car unseen. After about two hundred metres she spotted a mud track leading along the edge of the field towards some woodland. She drove up it and parked.

The last week had been hell beyond anything she could have imagined, worse even than when she lost the baby. Zoe was part of her and, to Hannah, her absence was like losing half of her beating heart, half of her soul.

Leo was somehow responsible. Zoe would never have behaved like this of her own accord. She was stubborn but she wasn't cruel. If, as Hannah firmly believed, Zoe had approached Leo, claiming to be his daughter, he would have been as terrified of being exposed as Hannah was. She couldn't go to the police, but if her daughter was here, Hannah was going to find her and get her out.

At the cottage, her flat shoes shifted the gravel, and the noise of stone grating against stone seemed to carry across the surrounding fields. The air was crisp and fresh. She bent to look through the letterbox, but it was too dark to see anything. She walked round the side, cupping her hands around her eyes and pressing them against the windows. All she could see were shapes and shadows. In the kitchen, the oven clock bathed the room in a greenish glow. She tried the back door, rattling the handle, but it didn't give.

She could remember her father drumming into her that she must not make important decisions on her own. She mustn't be ruled by her heart, but by the guidance of those more experienced than her. The men. She had proved them wrong; she had been making important decisions on her own for a long time now. But still, it was there at the back of her mind, that nagging voice. *You aren't equipped to deal with this, Hannah.* Well, that might be the case, but for want of anyone else, she would do what had to be done.

Hannah took her bank card out of her purse and tried sliding it into the lock, between the door and its frame. It didn't work. She turned to face the garden. The place reeked of neglect – the roses were straggly and needed cutting back hard, and leaves had been left to curl and brown where they fell. Weeds grew in the flowerbeds and rotting apples lay at the foot of gnarled trees. The place smelled of damp earth and decomposing organic matter. She wasn't surprised. She knew Leo Creasey well enough to understand his mind was set on one track. He came here to write.

She walked across the patio, tripped on a step and landed on her hands and knees. She absorbed the shock then picked herself up, brushing the dirt from her gloves and trousers. Something rustled close by, and she started with fright, but it was only a bird of some kind, displacing the fallen leaves beneath the hedge in its search for insects.

Below the low-hanging roof, the windows of the cottage resembled troubled eyes. They seemed to pity her. What had those rooms witnessed? She stamped her feet. She wasn't wearing the right shoes for traipsing through damp grass and her feet were getting cold.

A large, solidly built shed stood in the garden. It was locked but the key was in the door. She was surprised Leo was so careless. Inside were garden tools and a toolbox. From the box's contents Hannah selected a hammer. A car drove by and she froze, waiting until its headlights vanished before returning to the house.

Glass panels sat in the top half of the cottage's back door. Hannah tapped a pane experimentally. Something small scuttled across the paving – a mouse running for cover. The next time she hit the glass she did it with conviction and it shattered, breaking the stillness. Somewhere close by, a bird burst out of the hedge. She reached through, careful not to catch her wrist on the jagged edges, and turned the latch.

'Zoe?' she whispered.

When there was no response she shouted her daughter's name.

Nothing.

Leo's house smelled of old wood fires and unwashed mustiness. She wandered around like a thief, poking her head into rooms, opening cupboards, nervous but exhilarated. Upstairs, she wrinkled her nose at the state of his bedroom. He hadn't made the bed, there were discarded clothes on the floor, and God knows when he'd last cleaned his bathroom. It was disgusting. The spare bedrooms looked as if they hadn't seen guests for a very long time – the beds were used as extra surfaces and were cluttered with papers. His manuscripts, she guessed. She picked up a sheet, cast her eye over it and put it down.

Opening a door and finding a set of narrow stairs leading to a loft space got her excited for all of two minutes, but it was clear Zoe wasn't up there – just boxes and carrier bags full of paperwork. She hoped Leo didn't smoke. The place was a fire hazard.

Back in the kitchen she saw how he'd left mugs and plates unwashed in the sink. A pair of slippers had been kicked off under the table, the floor felt sticky underfoot and the surfaces needed a wipe. How could he live like this? She picked up a pad he'd left lying on the table and flicked through it. Illegible scrawls, partly shorthand. She pictured him sitting here, drinking his coffee, putting down his thoughts. She itched to tidy things away, hoover up the cobwebs, clean the windows and beat the dust out of the cushions.

As a child she'd been the tidy one. Deborah had been messy – a reluctant little housewife – though when she married, all that changed. Hannah remembered her shock at the shiny spotlessness of her sister's marital home. The odd thing was that if Deborah did tidy anything, she was always praised for it. Hannah, who was always on hand to help her mother, was rarely commended, and if she let things slide, she was punished.

She was beginning to lose hope when she spotted the narrow tongue-and-groove door. Various aprons and a raincoat hung from hooks on the front of it, so she hadn't noticed it at first. She could see, from where it was placed, that it would lead under the stairs. The hairs on the back of her neck stood up. She wiped her damp hands on her coat and tried the handle. It turned easily.

Hannah took a deep breath and pulled open the door. A broom fell against her shoulder. She pushed it back. Beside it sat a vacuum cleaner and a mop and bucket. An ironing board leaned against the wall. She put her hand over her mouth to stifle a sob. Zoe wasn't here and the disappointment was devastating.

She left through the back door, picked up the hammer and took it back to the shed, and then scanned the garden. No other outbuildings. A scuffle somewhere close by startled her, and she shrank into the space between a wheelbarrow leaning on its front brace against the shed and the hedge.

'Maggie! Here, girl! Out of there.'

The dog raced up to her, panting and wagging its tail. She pushed at its nose, but it wouldn't leave her alone, sniffing around her feet before giving a sharp bark. She almost collapsed in terror.

'Maggie! Come on, girl. You know you're not supposed to be in here.'

Footsteps sounded on the gravel, then the patio. Whoever it was was coming towards her. She gave the dog a shove. Maggie looked at her with her big eyes, then ran off.

'Did you smell a fox?' the man asked. 'Good girl. Good dog.'

The sound of the dog being given a congratulatory slap on the flank made Hannah jump. The man strode back across the lawn and she allowed herself to breathe. Then his footsteps stopped.

'What's that you've found, Maggie?'

A scraping noise. She guessed he had seen the broken window and picked up a piece of glass. He expelled a long whistling breath. Her eyes wide, Hannah stared into the blackness, trying to find an escape route, but the hedge stretched on, dense and unbroken. The dog came racing back to her.

An authoritative voice filled the night. 'I know you're there. I'm calling the police.'

Hannah cringed against the hedge, trying to disappear into it. The dog was snuffling around her again and the man's heavy footsteps sounded across the patio once more.

A crack rang out, followed by a shout of annoyance.

Realizing the man must have tripped over the same step, Hannah pulled the hood of her coat over her head, ran out from behind the shed and charged towards the gate. She skirted him as he picked himself up off the ground and cut through the soft earth of the flowerbed.

He lunged for her, but she evaded him and, chased by the dog who obviously thought the whole thing was a game, she ran up the lane.

Hannah hadn't moved faster than a brisk walk for a very long time and within seconds she was crippled by a stitch, the sharp ache stabbing into the tender space between her hip and her ribcage. She gripped her side and struggled on for the final few metres, losing her shoe in the muddy track behind her car. She turned back and whipped it up before Maggie got there.

The man was running towards them – although it could hardly be called running, more an awkward power walk – his hand outstretched as if to grab her, too out of breath to yell. A bulky man, she doubted he was any fitter than she was. He needed to be careful or he'd have a stroke.

Hannah scratched the car door as she fumbled for the lock. She jumped in, cranked the car into reverse and, swerving horrifically, accelerated backwards into the lane. She braked, her body jerking. A hand slapped the car and she shot forward, speeding off with a sob of relief.

'Please tell Zoe that we wish all the best for her,' Miss Colville said.

It had long been obvious to teachers, parents and pupils at Maidstone Grammar that her daughter didn't fit in there. So when, two weeks after Zoe's disappearance, Hannah informed the head that she and Zoe had come to the decision to remove her and send her to live with family in Canada, Miss Colville hadn't been surprised. Insultingly, she was barely able to contain her pleasure and didn't ask the questions any reasonable person in her position might be expected to. All that had mattered was that she would no longer have Zoe in the school as a constant reminder of her inadequacies.

Hannah was unable to let that smug dismissal pass.

'You allowed this to happen. I hold you to blame for the fact that I don't have my daughter at home with me.'

'Ms Faulkner, it's hardly my fault that you didn't give Zoe the necessary skills to negotiate school life. If you hadn't insisted on isolating her as a young child, she might have found it easier to make friends. I sincerely hope a new country and a new family will go some way to undoing the damage you did.'

'She was bullied and ostracized while you were in charge. You were negligent.'

Miss Colville drew herself up to her full height. 'If you wish, you can take your complaint to the board of governors.'

'I hope it won't come to that, but only because neither Zoe nor I want anything more to do with this place. If you don't harass me, I won't take it any further.'

Hannah stalked out of the office, slamming the door behind her just as the bell went and the classrooms released their laughing and catcalling charges. Pushing through the chaotic rush of boys and girls, she held her breath until she was outside, before turning to look back at the ugly concrete-and-glass building.

You didn't give your daughter the necessary skills.

She had failed as a mother. It was her fault. Everything was her fault. Even Michael Brady.

* * *

The weekends were the worst. The house was empty and the worry gnawed at her as she tried not to imagine Zoe dead somewhere, her body dumped in a shallow grave. Or the image of her alive but cold and scared and in darkness. The loneliness of her life without Zoe in it – the grey monotony of her days – was equally unbearable. As was the crippling anxiety, waiting for a visit from the police, flinching at shadows. But the days turned into weeks and the weeks into months, and her sense of loss was only equalled by her fear of being found out. When the police didn't come in the first days, she at least knew her secret was safe. But at what cost?

At work, Anita was the trickiest to handle. Hannah didn't get close to people, but if anyone could profess to knowing her, Anita could. They had swapped stories of their daughters for years, and Anita was voraciously curious, always wanting to know if Hannah had heard from Zoe, how she was doing, whether she'd made some friends, met a nice boy. It meant a constant watchfulness on Hannah's part. As for the residents, they would forget what she told them from one day to the next. It eventually sank in, with the help of Zoe's 'letters from Vancouver', but it didn't diminish the agony of missing her daughter, the fear for her safety, or her conviction that Leo knew something.

He too thought he was safe, but she was watching him.

36

Leo

LEO TUGGED SHARDS OF BROKEN GLASS OUT OF THE doorframe and dropped them into the dustpan. Outside, the overgrown lawn was wet with dew. The flowerbeds were dominated by uncontrolled shrubs, several of which were deciduous and looked woody and unkempt in the winter months. He should do something about them.

Towards the back of the garden, in what had once been an orchard, budding fruit trees threw out their gnarled fingers. Close by, a thick mat of ivy covered the entrance to the bunker. That's what he needed to think about.

What if Hannah came back? That phone call from James telling him about the break-in had been a wake-up call. Leo almost had a heart attack when James announced that he'd already called the police. Thank God Jenny hadn't been home, because by the time James called him again later, he was a nervous wreck. The police had had a cursory look round, told James that country house break-ins were on the rise and left a leaflet about security on the kitchen table, leaving James to make the back door safe with a piece of plywood nailed over the broken pane. There was unlikely to be a follow-up, unless Leo made a fuss. He wasn't going to do that.

The ivy was an inadequate cover. Leo knew Maggie often trespassed during her walks, chasing the scent of foxes. What if she picked up Zoe's scent and started sniffing round the hatch? It would only take a little curiosity on James's part to discover it.

He would have to design and build a permanent camouflage that could be moved easily if you knew the trick – like a secret door in a stately home – and he'd have to do it sooner rather than later. He had some ideas. The locals were used to him doing the odd bit of DIY, so the work wouldn't raise any eyebrows.

It was frustrating because he was itching to get back to his new story, but he had no choice. He folded the broken glass into a newspaper and shoved it into the kitchen bin, then pulled on an old fleece and went outside. No time like the present.

There was one advantage to the intrusion. Hannah must now be convinced that Zoe wasn't in the house. She had gone to ground, but he was under no illusion. She was like a terrier. He hadn't heard the last of her.

PART 3

Two Years Later

2007

37

Jenny

THE WOMAN SITTING OPPOSITE ME HAS HER HANDS folded in her lap. She's silent. She'll speak in her own time. Her name is Tessa Dudley and this is her first appointment.

This morning began with a call from Mum. She was confused. She thought Kate was supposed to be there. That segued into something about Kate's last school report and her neighbour's middle-aged son stealing food from her freezer. My heart was thumping painfully when I got off the phone. I hate her being so far away. I called the neighbour and asked her to pop round, but the situation is unsustainable. Mum can no longer look after herself, and the house in Portugal has to go. I've been over four times in the last nine months, but each time, Mum accuses me of never coming to see her.

Leo complains that I'm being pulled in too many directions, and he's right, I'm almost at breaking point. I've decided to do something about it.

Mum needs to be in a home, close to at least one of

her daughters, and since Kate lives in the middle of nowhere and is tied up with the farm, that responsibility has fallen on me. Things are going to have to change radically. Of course, I've already mentioned this to Leo, but I don't think it's registered, at least not the financial implications and how that might impact on him personally. It's going to be tricky.

Tessa still hasn't spoken. I nod and sit up straighter. I can see she's the quiet type, the type for whom articulating problems is like climbing a mountain. Self-sufficient, lonely. I have other clients who barely pause for breath, filling silences with words so that the bad stuff can't get in.

I have no regrets about changing careers. It's been hard for me to believe that my life is worth anything since Sophie was taken, but counselling has helped me find a sense of purpose again. To people not in my peculiar world, eighteen years must seem an adequate time to stop grieving and get on with life, especially since I never had a chance to get to know my child. At the beginning of 1989, before this nightmare began, I might have thought the same, but it doesn't work like that.

Tessa speaks. 'My daughter died sixteen years ago. She only lived for a few hours.'

I wait for her to go on, ignoring the hot flare of desperation inside me. I've had to learn to cope with these triggers, to put my own feelings to one side and focus on the client. It's the biggest challenge of the job.

'I feel so stupid,' Tessa says. 'I'm still finding it difficult, even though it was such a long time ago. She would have been an adult now and I've done nothing worthwhile with my life. I can't seem to allow myself to recover.'

'It's natural. There's no right or wrong way to grieve and no prescribed time to stop grieving. You've taken a positive step towards recovery today. You should try to think of this as a brand-new journey, not an extension of an old one. What was your baby's name?'

'Abigail.' She closes her eyes. 'She was born on the third of February nineteen ninety-one at two fifty-five in the morning. She died at eleven thirty-five.'

'At the time she died, did you have anyone with you?'

Tessa shakes her head. 'Her father wasn't around and my parents . . . Well, they didn't approve of my choices, so they kept their distance.'

'Would you like to talk about that?'

Her face hardens. 'No.'

'What about Abigail? You can tell me anything you like.'

Tessa looks down at her hands. I remember that empty feeling. I'd only had Sophie for a few hours too, but I missed holding her more than I could possibly express. That unspeakable, pressing void never goes away. You have to learn to carve a path round it.

'She was perfect. She was my baby and I let her down. I should have been awake.'

She takes a tissue from the box at her side, blows her nose and smiles wanly.

'I'm so sorry,' she says.

'Don't be. I'm glad you came to see me. I think I can help you.'

* * *

237

'Tell me,' I say, as I wind up the session, 'why did you pick my practice? I saw from your notes that you don't live in London.'

I had questioned Carys, our administrator, about it, but she hadn't been able to shed any light. It's unusual, but Tessa isn't my only client who comes from further afield, because of Open Arms. In the end, it's up to them how far they travel.

There's a small hesitation before she replies, as I expect her to.

'Because I knew about Open Arms, and obviously I'd heard your story. Everyone has. I wanted to talk to someone who would understand that it makes no difference how long you knew your child for. Was it wrong of me? If you'd rather I went elsewhere, I'll understand.'

'Of course not. As long as you're comfortable, we can carry on.'

The truth is, I feel exposed. But that's what the years of training were for, I remind myself. To cope with situations like this.

I find myself thinking about Tessa later. Clients don't usually get to me. I'm well-trained, I listen, ask questions and explore the answers I'm given, but I don't allow their unhappiness to touch me. Of course, it does from time to time – I'm only human – but I've learned to accept it, then put it to one side and talk it over with my supervisor later. With Tessa, though, her story resonates. I probably should have agreed with her when she offered to find another therapist. Have I made a mistake? If I have, it isn't too late. I can explain that, on reflection, it would be better if she found a different counsellor, someone closer to home.

I set that aside as my mind moves to the next big hurdle. Telling Leo I have to sell Sparrow Cottage.

38

Hannah

PEOPLE WALKED PURPOSEFULLY ALONG ST GEORGE'S
Road, their faces braced against the chill. Jenny was
taller than Hannah and had changed into trainers, so
Hannah had to increase her speed to keep up.

She couldn't quite believe Jenny hadn't seen through
her. When she thought about the hell she had put that
woman through, she felt almost drunk with horror, but
it was done and couldn't be undone. Her feelings of guilt
had to be kept under control.

She had been watching Leo for almost two years,
although she drove down the lane less often these days
than she had done in that first terrible year, when the
loss of Zoe was a yawning chasm in her life and she still
reeled with disbelief. That had settled into a hard core of
determination. As far as stalking Leo was concerned, it
was glaringly obvious that she was causing herself more
inconvenience than she was causing him. She also suspected he obtained a malicious pleasure from it, as if it
were a game to him.

Some months ago she had been a member of an audience gathered to hear him talk, and he'd spotted her as they filed out of the venue. He had held her gaze for a few seconds before turning his attention to an elderly couple, unfazed, even bored by her presence. Familiarity breeds contempt.

At any rate, he hadn't put a foot wrong. As far as she could ascertain – by turning up at random times, nipping out from work on fictional errands whenever she had the chance – when Leo was at the cottage, he was at his desk. He occasionally went for walks or to the supermarket, but he had never done anything to bring her any closer to finding out what had happened to her daughter. Which was why Hannah had turned her attention to his wife.

She followed Jenny along Kennington Road, keeping about twenty paces behind her. Jenny's hair bounced as she walked. Even as she weaved her way through the commuters entering Kennington tube station, she wasn't hard to spot.

The false name came from a game Hannah and Zoe used to play when Zoe was little. It was a combination of the name of the dog that Hannah and Deborah had as children and their childhood home on Dudley Street. Tessa Dudley. Zoe's alter ego had been Dottie Tanyard, named after her first guinea pig and the lane they lived on.

After her session with Jenny, Hannah had spent the afternoon in the Natural History Museum. Entry was free, there was a nice café, it was warm, and nobody cared how long she stayed. At half past four, she had made her way back to St George's Road, where she waited in the gardens of the Imperial War Museum for Jenny to leave work. She'd hoped it would be five o'clock, but her quarry didn't leave the building until six, by which time Hannah was frozen.

They passed Oval station and continued along the Clapham Road. What Hannah was doing wasn't brave, it was necessary. Either she proved one way or another that Zoe had found Leo and that he had acted to stop her from destroying his reputation, career and marriage, or she moved on. Moving on was not an option – she owed it to her child to find out the truth. She needed to study the other facets of Leo's life. Getting close to Jenny felt like a natural progression.

Tracking down Jenny's place of work hadn't been difficult – it was listed on the public page for the support group she ran – and booking that first appointment had given Hannah a sense of purpose. For the first time in ages she didn't feel flat. The expense was crippling, but she reasoned that she would have to pay a private detective more.

When Jenny turned right a couple of minutes later, Hannah broke into a run. She turned the corner and found herself on a wide, tree-lined road, pitted with potholes and dominated by a council block. The street led to a square of grand semi-detached Georgian houses.

Hannah melted into the shadows and watched Jenny let herself into the house. She gave it a couple of minutes, then crossed the road and peered down into the basement area. A light was on. Leo was sitting at the kitchen table.

Hannah scuttled back to the safety of the other side of the road. She was satisfied. There were bars on the basement and ground floor windows, but no burglar alarm shield on the wall.

The key to Zoe's whereabouts must be in that house. It was just a matter of working out how to get in.

39

Leo

'HOW WAS LUNCH?' JENNY ASKED, BENDING TO UNTIE the laces of her trainers.

Leo looked up from the email he was composing, pulling together the thoughts he'd had on his walk back from Covent Garden. He and his agent had had lunch at The Ivy with a film producer who was interested in making one of his earlier novels into a movie. A couple of Leo's books had come close to being optioned before, but negotiations had always come to nothing. He couldn't put his finger on the reason, but this meeting had felt different.

He smiled at his wife. Best to be circumspect and curb his excitement. Marriage these days seemed to be a case of being one step ahead. He loved her, but their relationship had changed after he confessed to his vasectomy. He had tarnished himself in her eyes, become less deserving of her respect. He had done his best to make up for it, but even now, so many years later, he wasn't sure that he had been forgiven.

His mistake had been to announce it as a fait accompli,

but he had been scared that if she'd been persuaded to come round to the idea, he would have had to have gone through the rigmarole of pretending he had an appointment and coming home looking shaken. As it was, he'd had to lie about being in pain and had taken to sleeping in the spare room so that she wouldn't discover that all was well down there. Sometimes he felt Jenny totted up his shortcomings in a ledger, and that made him wary. Something was making him wary now.

But Jenny's eyebrows were raised, her head tipped to one side, and in the end he couldn't resist.

'Actually, it went rather well. Obviously, he didn't give much away, but I wouldn't be surprised if he came up with an offer.'

He took off his glasses and wiped them vigorously.

'Oh, goodness! That's fantastic. How much money's involved?'

He laughed. 'That's not very romantic of you.'

She flushed. 'No. Sorry. Forget I said it.'

He put his glasses back on.

'Don't get carried away. It might never happen, and even if it does, it won't be life-changing.' He saw her face fall and added quickly, 'But a film will boost sales of the book, so there's that. Kirstie says to expect a figure between sixty and eighty thousand pounds.'

Was she disappointed? It was hard to tell, but he thought so. Since walking away from the City, her more-than-generous six-figure salary had dipped into five figures. Simultaneously, the whole ebook thing had exploded and his royalties had shrunk. Money was a niggle these days, but he was surprised it mattered that much to her. Maybe she was concerned about his pride. That was sweet.

He stood and put his arms around her, breathing in the sweet, herby smell of her hair. Jenny didn't wear perfume but she liked expensive shampoo. However difficult things had been over the years – and at times they had been sheer hell – he was still tied to her, and not just because he was honour-bound to make up for the wrong he'd done. It was because of something deeper, more primal, that had to do with her scent, her being. And to be honest, the slight detachment he had noticed in her lately was quite attractive. He let her go and poured her a glass of wine.

'Congratulations on getting this far,' she said, and kissed his cheek. 'You're brilliant.'

'Do you want to go out for supper?'

'You've just been out for lunch.'

'There's not much in the fridge.'

He was annoyed. Still buoyed by the massive ego boost today had given him, he didn't want it to end here, in the basement of their house.

'You could have picked something up on your way home,' Jenny pointed out.

She moved to the table and pulled out a chair.

'I was going to, but what with all the excitement, it went out of my head.'

She smiled. 'OK. That's understandable.' She scrolled through her messages with her thumb. 'Leo, there's something we need to talk about.'

'That sounds ominous.'

'It is. You'd better sit down.' She shoved her phone to

one side and turned the stem of her glass with her fingers. The shifting light on the surface of the wine, with its slick of colour, was mesmerizing.

'You won't like it, I'm afraid,' Jenny said. Something odd played over her face – part fear, part challenge. 'I have to sell Sparrow Cottage to pay for Mum's care.'

A long silence followed. It was a silence of held breath, of yellow-tinged clouds foreshadowing a storm.

'No, you don't,' Leo said. 'You are not selling Sparrow Cottage. I won't let you.'

Jenny stared him down. He noticed that the lines between her brows had deepened.

'You know what the situation is,' she said. 'I can't go on like this, having to fly off to Cascais at a moment's notice. The only thing to do is to bring Mum back to the UK and sort out long-term care here. Selling the cottage is the only way we can afford to do that. Her pension won't cover anything like what we need. You do see, don't you? I have a responsibility.'

'Can't the sale of her house pay for it?'

'Unfortunately not. Mum and Dad funded their retirement through equity release. What's left will barely cover two years of care-home fees.'

Leo grimaced. Elaine might be losing her marbles, but otherwise she was fit and healthy. She could easily live for another decade.

'Why can't Kate pay her fair share?'

'Kate will pay what she can, but she and Chris don't have much money. There's no way they can contribute as much as we can. We are ...' She hesitated. 'Less encumbered.'

He didn't take the bait. 'You know how much the place means to me, how many books I've written there. It's not just a house, it's a friend and a sanctuary.'

He closed his laptop, pushed it aside and stretched across the table to take her hand. 'There has to be another way. We could have her here.'

Jenny's eyebrows flew up. 'The house is totally unsuitable, but even if it were perfect, you wouldn't last five minutes. I have a job and you're not here half the week. It would mean getting home help. How much do you think that would cost?'

'I don't know,' Leo said. He had never been concerned with money, as long as he could do what he wanted. He was happy with the simple things in life. Despite coming of age in Thatcher's Britain, he considered himself remarkably lacking in material values. 'But I'm sure you do.'

'It's way more than we can afford.'

He was indignant. She had thought all this through, but expected him to take it in immediately. 'Perhaps if we'd had this conversation earlier, it wouldn't have got to this point.'

'Leo.' She sounded exasperated. 'We have. Or at least I have. You don't listen to anything I say. I know how wrapped up you get in your writing, but real life goes on, and from time to time you have to engage with it. You can't blame me if you miss something. Be reasonable. Having my mother here is a ridiculous idea. Do you want to help her go to the lavatory? Clean up after her? Do you want to watch television with her, spoon-feed her when she can't do it for herself?'

He scowled. 'Lecture over?'

'I'm not lecturing you. I'm telling you what you need to know. I've found a lovely care home in Clapham. I'll be able to see her every day. And Leo, this house is big enough for you to work in without being disturbed. We can clear out one of the spare bedrooms. You can make it your own.'

'They both get used.'

For a moment he thought there was no way she could challenge him. Since Kate's girls had started university, they'd been treating the house as free lodging whenever they wanted to meet friends in London, go to interviews or take up work experience placements. Leo was perfectly relaxed about having them, although if Kate had known at what time and in what state they came in some nights she might have thought twice about allowing it.

'We can put both single beds in the larger room,' Jenny was saying. 'They can share. They won't mind. It's not that often the girls are both here at the same time anyway.'

'It's not a question of physical space, it's a question of mental space. I cannot write in this house. I need Sparrow Cottage. I won't allow you to sell it, and that's that.'

'It's not your choice. I do understand how much the place means to you, but it's time to let go.'

'What about if we downsize in London? We're rattling around in here by ourselves.'

In the silence that followed he saw the end: the policemen at the door, the courtroom, the bars of a prison window.

Jenny pushed back her chair, went to the fridge and topped up her glass.

'Why should I be the one to suffer?' Leo demanded. 'She's your mother.'

Jenny turned on him, slopping her wine. 'For once in your life can you think about somebody else? It's like everything we do is for your convenience. I worked my socks off for years to fund you when you weren't making any money. I gave over the house my grandmother left me because it made you happy. I accepted it when you told me I couldn't go there, because I was in awe of your talent. I still am, but it's always been about you: your books, your needs. Kirstie needs to do better for you. You need to make a lot of money from optioning the rights to that book or frankly we're sunk. It's your turn to make the sacrifice. Heaven knows I've made enough of them.'

'Don't throw that in my face.'

This is what it was all about. The baby he wouldn't give her. Did she never think about what she had deprived him of when she passed Sophie off as his? She owed him Sparrow Cottage.

'Yes, I know. I can't mention the fact that you wouldn't let me have another child. I can't tell you how it feels to see my friends' and my sister's children grow up and become adults. I can't look into the future and picture myself in Mum's situation, my husband dead, my mind falling apart, for fear of upsetting you. I won't have the luxury of children to take care of me, Leo, and nor will you. Have you ever thought about that?'

'Stop it, Jenny. This isn't achieving anything.'

He was beginning to feel weary. He shouldn't have had that third glass of wine with his lunch.

'Listen to me. Either you make enough money to make up the shortfall in Mum's care, or Sparrow Cottage goes on the market. I'll give you six months.'

Leo jumped up and left the room, pounding upstairs. He grabbed his coat and slammed out of the house. Bloody woman. She was being unreasonable. She knew he couldn't risk everything on a film deal that might never happen. Without the producer and his lavish compliments, the confidence he had felt earlier was beginning to fade.

He needed something else. He needed alchemy. And, he realized with a jolt, he had it, hidden in a password-protected file on his computer at Sparrow Cottage. A tale born of a moment of heightened awareness and inspiration two years ago. It had practically written itself, a force propelling him to commit to paper the extraordinary story of the abduction of a baby. It was unedited, a first draft, and nobody, not even Kirstie, knew about it. It was something he had done for himself, never intending that anyone would read it. But no writer genuinely writes with that thought in mind.

Could he use it? He picked up his pace, his stride lengthening, his fists rammed into his jacket pockets. Possibly. It was a bloody good story. It was like he had told the audience at Foyles, in answer to Zoe's question – how do you know when you've written something good? He could feel it physically – a repressed euphoria, an ache that started deep in his solar plexus.

There were always ways round problems if you had

the stomach for lies. He felt a scratchiness at the back of his throat and coughed. He supposed he could tell people that he had long felt the desire to give his baby daughter a history that made some kind of sense, to exorcize his own demons and help other people going through a similar trauma. It was a risk, but it made sense. It would get him out of a potentially catastrophic situation.

40

Jenny

I ROLL OVER AND OPEN MY EYES SLEEPILY. LEO IS sitting up in bed, his shoulders hunched. It's very early.

'What's wrong?' I mumble.

'I feel like shit.' His voice is barely audible. 'I feel like I'm swallowing razor blades.'

I shuffle up and he takes my hand and places it on his forehead. It's hot and clammy.

'You're running a temperature. I'll see if we've got any painkillers.'

He must have sweated buckets, because when I try to straighten out his pillow, it's cold and wet. I tip it on to the floor and give him mine, then climb out of bed reluctantly and root around the bathroom cupboard until I find some paracetamol. Leo winces as he swallows two of them.

'Christ,' he croaks. 'This is all I need.'

'How's your head?'

'Feels like a truck ran over it.'

* * *

253

I transfer Leo to one of the spare rooms, strip our bed and go about my day. On Tuesday mornings I don't have clients, but I set aside two solid hours for replying to messages from people who've got in touch with Open Arms. At eleven, I close my laptop, put the kettle on and make Leo a mug of honey and lemon. It's frustrating. I don't feel as though we finished that conversation last night. I'd been hoping he would sleep on it and wake up in a more reasonable frame of mind.

Upstairs, I put the drink down beside him and tiptoe to the door. He murmurs something and I turn to see what he wants. He says something else, but I don't understand a word. Then I realize he's still asleep.

Intrigued, I move closer. He's quiet for a second or two, then he starts again, spouting dreamlike non-sense with the occasional almost-coherent sentence. I stroke his head and he goes quiet. I back away from the bed.

'Zoe.'

Zoe?

I wait for him to say something else. When he doesn't, I whisper, 'Who is Zoe, Leo?'

His breathing deepens. I sigh and step out of the room.

By twelve, Leo is awake and claiming he's feeling bet-ter. In the meantime, I've been out to the supermarket and bought soup, Ribena and soluble aspirin – all the things Mum used to give me and Kate when we were ill. I bring him up a mug of the soup but he barely manages two mouthfuls.

I want to tell him he's been talking in his sleep, and

ask him about Zoe, but I don't. I'll wait until he's better. I have an early lunch and go to work.

That evening, I find Leo sitting on the bathroom floor, leaning against the bath, his face sweaty, his eyes bloodshot and his neck swollen. I dissolve a couple of aspirin and help him drink up, holding the glass to his lips and waiting patiently between each agonizing swallow. I rinse a flannel in cold water, wring it out and hold it to his forehead. He takes it from me and presses it against his neck. I chivvy him back into bed and watch over him until he falls asleep.

Even after he drifts off I stay, wondering whether he'll say that name again. He doesn't. It's chased all thoughts of my mother's plight out of my mind. My imagination is working overtime. I even check his contacts on his phone. No Zoe.

By the following morning, Leo has lost his voice completely. He demands I accompany him to our GP to make sure the doctor understands the importance of his plight, and gives him drugs. As I don't have a client until eleven, I comply. The doctor diagnoses a particularly virulent case of flu and prescribes bed rest, decongestants and plenty of fluids. This is not what my husband wants to hear.

'How long will it last?' I ask.

'Five to seven days.'

Leo grunts.

'You should be on the mend by the weekend,' the doctor tells him. 'Although you may find yourself drained of energy for a good few days afterwards. Don't overdo it.'

Leo forces out a couple of words. The doctor turns to me, eyebrows raised in query.

'He says he has to work,' I translate. 'He normally goes down to Kent three days a week. It's part of his routine. It's very important to him.'

'Oh, I don't think so, Mr Creasey. Surely your publisher isn't cracking the whip that hard?' He chuckles at his joke.

Leo isn't remotely amused. He scowls and tries to speak, then snatches a piece of paper and a pen off the desk and scribbles in angry caps: ANTIBIOTICS???

'Antibiotics work for illnesses caused by bacteria, not viruses, and influenza is a virus. There would be no point prescribing them in your case. You'll have to tough it out, I'm afraid.'

The doctor brings his hands down on to his thighs with a slap, indicating the appointment is over.

'But you have your lovely wife to take care of you. I can give you a prescription for codeine. That should help with the pain.'

Leo looks as though he's about to argue, then the fight goes out of him. We leave and he shivers beside me in the car. He doesn't even attempt to speak. When we get home, after stopping off at the chemist, he tries to make himself comfortable at the kitchen table, but soon gives up and crawls back up to the spare bedroom. Leo has never been an easy patient, and this time is no exception. He keeps insisting he's going down to Kent tomorrow, and I keep repeating, 'No, you're not.'

* * *

That night I give him two codeine tablets. When I check on him in the morning, he's sitting on the edge of the bed in his underpants, pulling on a pair of blue-and-grey-striped socks. His face is still clammy and his glands are still swollen. He waves, a flick of the wrist, as though he wants me to go away, but I stand my ground.

'What're you doing?' I ask, then realize the answer is obvious. 'Leo, you can't possibly go to the cottage.'

'I can,' he grates, wincing. He puts on his glasses.

'You look terrible. How's your head?'

'Better.'

He's lying. He has pain written all over his face. His eyes are half closed, there are pink spots on his cheekbones and his skin has a waxy tinge. His hair is crying out for a wash, and two days' worth of stubble shadows his chin and jaw.

'This is insane. You're not going anywhere.'

He lifts his head with difficulty and glowers. 'I need to write.'

'Can't you just type up a few notes?'

'No.' He swallows, his body tensing. I wince in sympathy. 'I need to be there.'

'It's the last thing you need.' I'm thinking of the cottage and its draughty rooms. 'But if you insist on going when you're in no condition to drive, I'll take the rest of the week off and come with you. So you won't get anything done anyway. Don't be childish. I'll get you a pad and paper. If it's that important, you'll write it down.'

He scowls, but I can tell he's almost grateful. I kiss the top of his head, and when I bring him a glass of warm Ribena before I set off for work, he's asleep. I'm not used to having Leo under my authority. It feels good to have won a small battle.

I see one of my more long-standing clients first, a City trader with work-related anxiety bordering on paranoia. She accepts her thoughts are extreme, but cannot rid herself of the idea that younger employees are actively plotting to oust her, and is particularly fixated on the women. She has other anxieties too that sprout from that same branch.

Being a therapist isn't so very different from being an accountant, at least the kind I was. I used to look after private clients with varied portfolios of assets. Now I look after clients with varied portfolios of problems. In both situations, you have to understand them. An identical financial transaction for different clients can have very different outcomes because of who they are as people. The same goes for therapy.

After we've finished up, I see her out, then scoot back into my consulting room and close the door. With ten minutes' thinking space before my next appointment, my mind goes blank. I tap my desk, tune out the white noise and my thoughts consolidate. I have two major problems: Sparrow Cottage and Mum. There is no question that the sale of the cottage will rock my marriage, but if I don't sell it, Mum will suffer.

I understand how Leo feels. I've seen it happen with clients back in my City days – certain assets have more emotional resonance than others, and more often than not they're of the bricks-and-mortar variety.

Leo is ridiculously dependent on that house. Ten years

ago, when he was turning forty, I contemplated gifting it to him. I even went as far as getting contracts drawn up, considering it fair recompense for the lie I had told him. But I'm not a complete sap. I changed my mind because what if that place is all he wants from me? Why would he stay with me once he had it? When Dad was alive, he never missed an opportunity to point out that it might prove legally problematic if ever Leo and I split up.

The fact that I'm forbidden to cross the threshold rankles, but I'd only want to change things; update, tweak, renew, renovate. It would be as irresistible a project as Albert Square Gardens was, and I wouldn't be allowed to touch it. That would frustrate me.

Losing it will affect me almost as much as Leo. I've grown used to having our house to myself on Tuesday and Wednesday evenings. I can watch what I want on TV, eat baked beans if that's what I fancy, and go to bed early without feeling I'm neglecting him. But things happen, lives get shaken up, and if we're inflexible, we risk being broken.

To be safe, when I left the house, I took his car keys with me, but I needn't have worried. When I get home, he's barely moved.

I'm sitting at the kitchen table, making notes for the quarterly Open Arms newsletter, when I start thinking about Zoe again. It isn't very nice when your husband mutters the name of another woman in his delirium. I don't know any Zoes and as far as I know he doesn't either, but the publishing world is full of attractive young women and it may well be that she's one of them. I don't believe she's an author. He wouldn't like the competition.

I lean back in my chair and massage the tension out of my right shoulder. Leo has never given me reason to suspect him of infidelity. Flirtation with fans, maybe – women fawn over him at signings. But this is different, this is a name.

By Friday, Leo is on the mend and this time, when I try to persuade him out of going to Kent, he refuses to listen.

'I'll get a couple of days' work done and come home. I won't overdo it, I promise.'

'Are you sure you're all right to drive?'

'For God's sake, stop fussing. I'll go mad if I don't get out of the house. I'll take it slowly. You've been a brilliant nurse. You need some time off as well. I'll get out of your hair.'

'You aren't in my hair. You're my husband.'

I give up. I should get off to work, and he's a grown man. If he's determined to go, I can't stop him. But when he gets into his car, I panic and run outside. He lowers the window.

'What have I forgotten?'

'Who is Zoe?'

'What?'

'You were talking in your sleep. You said "Zoe". Who is she?'

I detect a slight narrowing of his eyes, a nanosecond of concealed shock, before he laughs.

'I've been talking in my sleep?'

I nod.

'Wow. Well, Zoe is a character in my novel, of course.'

Of course. I drop my hands from the window frame, he waves and pulls off. I suppose it makes sense. At any rate, I'll find out sooner or later. I shouldn't be so insecure; I'm too old for that. The trouble is, I'm not. I'm not sure anyone ever is. I don't want to lose him.

41

Zoe

SOMETHING TERRIBLE MUST HAVE HAPPENED. THAT'S the only explanation. No one's going to find me, the food will run out and I'll slowly starve to death.

Huddled under my duvet I list everything in my bedroom in Tanyard Lane, the names of the girls in my class at school, the flowers and vegetables we grew in the garden, the names of the guinea pigs I've had over the years. I hope Mum has been taking care of Smartie. I keep forgetting things and have to start again. I have days when my mind never quite switches on. This is one of them, and it's his fault.

In the two years I've been here, Leo has never not told me his plans. If his routine changes he explains why and makes sure there's enough food, books and videos to last me. He brought a television down here a couple of weeks after he kidnapped me. There's no reception, so I can't watch TV programmes, but it has a built-in video player. It's ancient, but it works fine. The videos belonged to Jenny's grandmother, so they're mostly costume dramas and old movies. From time to time he buys me more recent films from charity shops.

On Tuesday, when he didn't turn up, I got so frightened. I waited and waited, thinking he was just delayed, that maybe his car had broken down or there had been some difficulty at home. I reassured myself he would come, because he would never leave me for this long without a good reason. By the afternoon I was pacing the room, banging on the door and screaming, maddened with fear and claustrophobia. It felt like those first weeks all over again.

My digital clock, another gift from Leo, says it's nine fifteen in the morning. I have been on my own for a week. I've finished the fresh food and I'm living off biscuits and crisps. I lurch between periods of acute terror and moments of hope when I hear, or imagine I hear, something move up above.

He's not coming back. Why has he done this? Is he dead? Maybe he's had a heart attack. My own heart starts to race at the thought. Nobody knows I'm here.

Don't think that.

What will happen to me if he doesn't come back? Which part of me will shut down first?

I eat one of the remaining biscuits, take a vitamin D pill, then clean my teeth. I spit in the basin and, as usual, my saliva is rippled with blood. The vitamin D supplement is supposed to make up for the lack of sunlight, but I doubt it works. Mum always said vitamin pills were a waste of money but Leo likes me to take them. It makes him feel as if he's being caring and responsible.

I take off my socks and jumper and start my exercise routine, which includes stretches, some yoga poses from a video Leo bought me and then some cardio stuff – running on the spot. I watch the clock until I've completed twenty minutes. It's boring but necessary.

Mostly I enjoy it, motivated by imagining the day I finally escape. I'll be able to run for a mile at least. Wherever I am, that should be enough surely to find a house and throw myself on some kind person's mercy. I sometimes allow myself to picture their surprise when I say I'm Zoe Faulkner. Today it hardly feels worth it.

I attempt twenty stomach crunches, but only manage seven before I throw myself back into bed. I roll on to my side and hook my arms over my face. My body is warm but if he doesn't come back, it'll go cold. Before long it'll decompose into the mattress, leaving my skeleton lying under the covers, my skull on the pillow.

I don't want to die. The panic comes rushing back. I curl up into a ball and try to block it out, pumping my feet and balling my hands into fists. My breath is shallow and fast.

I go to the air vent and yell, then slump over to the armchair and pick up the spiralbound notebook I've been using as a diary. It's for Jenny. One day she might want to know about my life and I don't want to forget the little details. When I flick back, I find times when Leo was kind, when I even liked him. She needs to know both sides of my story. It's not all fear and hate. There have been highs as well – like in anyone's life, I suppose. When I write, I try to convey what I'm feeling, but even that creates difficulties. Do I admit to looking forward to seeing him when he's been away? Do I admit to listening for the sounds of his arrival, or to enjoying our conversations, even our rows?

After a while I put down my pen, sit with my hands in my lap and lapse into gloom again. There is no beautiful way to be found dead here. It's so squalid. I'll look like a homeless person, not a young girl. I try to remain optimistic but the overriding voice in my head says Leo is taking the coward's way out. He's hoping I'll die. Maybe he and Jenny have gone on holiday. I hate him. I hate her and I hate my mum. None of them cares about me. I'm a lost child, dead already. They are moving on.

He's back. At the first tap of his foot on the step, I leap up. He shoots the bolts and fits the key into the lock, and when he opens the door I charge at him. He grabs my wrists and kicks the door shut. I fight him until he wraps his arms around me and pinions me against his body.

'I'm sorry, I'm sorry,' he repeats. 'I was ill. I'm so sorry, Zoe.'

'You left me,' I shout. 'You left me all by myself. I didn't know what was going on. I thought you'd died.'

He soothes me, apologizing over and over again. In all the time I've been here he's never held me like this, for comfort; only to restrain me. Being hugged is like getting hooked on a drug. I can't get enough of it. I can feel his ribcage under his shirt and smell the soap he uses. His hands are splayed on my back, our thighs are pressed together. My chest rises and falls against his. My deadened senses come alive.

Too soon he detaches from me with an awkward cough. He leads me to the armchair and sits me down, holding me firmly by the shoulders until I relax. Then he backs away, feeling for the door. He locks it and drops the key into his jacket pocket.

He pulls out the kitchen chair, swivels it round on one leg and straddles it, his arms crossed over the back. He watches me. After a while my tears dry up. He has dark shadows under his eyes and his cheeks are sunken. He does look as though he's been ill.

'What if you had died?' I say fiercely. 'I would've starved to death all by myself.'

He rubs the space between his eyebrows.

'You must have been very scared. I apologize.'

I raise my chin. 'You have to do something. You have to write it in your will. You have to tell people I'm here.'

He thinks about it, then shakes his head. 'It's too dangerous. And quite apart from that, it would affect my legacy.'

'What's that supposed to mean?'

'I wouldn't be remembered as an author. I'd be remembered as the man who kept a young woman prisoner in a bunker.'

'You'd be dead, so you wouldn't care.'

'It matters to me now.'

'So it's perfectly fine if I die in here, so long as your reputation isn't damaged? Even though you won't know anything about it, you would prefer I suffer a slow, painful and lonely death? I'll probably go mad before I die. Have you ever been so lonely it eats your flesh?'

Leo laughs, but his laughter is uneasy.

266

'You've been reading too much Stephen King.'

'I'm just telling you what it feels like. I want you to understand what it is you're refusing me. You're old. You could die at any time of a heart attack or cancer. There's loads of diseases people get when they get older. You could end up in a wheelchair.'

'You don't have to be quite so pessimistic,' Leo says, disconcerted. 'I lead a healthy life. I gave up smoking years ago. There's no reason why I shouldn't live to a grand old age.'

'Is your father still alive?'

'No,' he says curtly.

'Then maybe you'll get whatever he had.'

'My father killed himself.'

I sit forward and hiss at him, 'Well, maybe you'll do that too. Out of guilt. But if you do, please make sure you unlock the door first.'

He gives me an exasperated look and gets up to leave.

'For what it's worth, I really was worried about you, and if I could have driven down earlier, I would have done.'

I ignore him, but when the door closes I clamp my hand over my mouth to stifle a sob.

42

Leo

YOU'RE OLD.

Leo sat in front of his computer, working his jaw. On the CD player, Maria Callas sang a lament. He was impatient to get to work, but what had happened with Zoe had stymied him. What had he wanted to say? He pushed the keyboard under the screen, set his elbows on the desk and pressed his forehead into the soft pads of flesh at the base of his thumbs, rocking his head to massage it. He still felt like shit.

Sugar. That was what he needed. He headed to the kitchen and took a can of Coke out of the fridge, popped the tab and poured it into a glass. It fizzed up over the rim. He felt a growing sense of unease. Something had changed. There had been a small but nonetheless significant shift in their relationship, and he didn't like it. He didn't trust it.

He was not old. He was in the prime of his life.

When she'd flung herself at him like a wildcat, he had been moved. He couldn't deny that. Zoe had always been human to him, but he had never been tempted to make himself vulnerable to her. He obviously wasn't completely well yet, and she had taken him by surprise. When he had held her and splayed his hands against the small of her back, he had felt an emotional response, and that was not good.

He knew how destructive ignoring boundaries could be to a perfectly workable relationship. Six years ago he had lost an extremely good publicist because she had become fixated on him. Not that anything like that would happen with Zoe Faulkner. She was more than thirty years younger than him, for Christ's sake. Ironically, he was more of a father figure to her.

Which brought him back to those two little words: 'You're old.' He would be fifty in November. Jenny thought he should throw a party, but he wasn't sure he wanted to broadcast his half-century. He couldn't believe it had been two years since he had abducted Zoe. Two years, and he'd got away with it. It amazed him.

He finished the Coke and felt better for it, returning to his desk with renewed vigour. He had dealt with the climax of the novel already. This final section would be where he tied up the loose ends. He would give his readers some clue as to the future life trajectories of the characters to whom they were saying goodbye so that they could, if they so wished, imagine them progressing through life, like friends who had moved to another country.

The story was exciting and pacy, and he was pleased with how he had portrayed the main characters. He'd worked hard to make the parents as far removed from him and Jenny as possible in personality and life experience. His alter ego was a surgeon, Jenny's was a booker at a modelling agency.

Zoe's character had been called Clare originally – obviously he couldn't call her Sophie – but thanks to his fever-induced mumblings, he'd have to change that. He could always swap it back in the final draft, if he felt strongly. Whatever it ended up being, Jenny wouldn't question it, since he often altered names over the course of a rewrite. But that had been a near miss.

He had finished by three. He needed someone to read it now. A fresh pair of eyes. He usually asked his agent, and he knew Kirstie would be only too happy.

He poured himself a generous measure of whisky, lit a fire, flopped down on the scruffy old sofa and put his feet up on the footstool. On second thoughts, Kirstie would get overexcited and there would be endless conversations. Maybe he should sit on it for a while.

This novel had to work, and he was confident that it would. It was brilliant. He just wished the stakes weren't so high. His eyes felt heavy and he decided to let go, just for a few minutes.

Three hours later, Leo woke up on the sofa, hungry and groggy. He hated sleeping in the daytime, despised naps. He put a frozen lasagne in the oven and set the timer for forty-five minutes then sat down at his computer, started a fresh document and typed 'To be opened in the event of my death . . .'

He paused. If he didn't do it, he would be a monster. If he did, he would be a monster. Either way, his secret would be out once his time was up. He had held Zoe in his arms while she sobbed. He had seen the desperation on her face when she threw herself at him. She was not an idea, she was a living, breathing woman. His wife's child. He began to type.

My darling Jenny, in the event of my death you will find a padlock key in the drawer in the kitchen. At the back of the garden there's a raised bed built from scaffold planks. It's on castors and can be moved easily. You'll find a metal hatch underneath it. Open it. The girl you will find is Sophie. I stole her twice and this is our story . . .

Leo stretched his arms behind his head and uncricked his neck. Then he ran his hands through his hair, shoved back his chair and jumped up. Of course. Zoe was the answer.

'What do you mean?'

By the sound of it, Zoe was still in a strop. He scratched at a small scab on the back of his hand.

'There's something I've been working on – a thriller. I need to make some serious money. Jenny has threatened to sell this house.'

'She can do that?'

'It belongs to her.'

'Oh.'

He could almost see the cogs working.

'What will happen to me?'

He didn't say anything, just looked at her. He saw

himself scooping her into his arms, then felt so unsettled his face became hot. He turned away from her abruptly and pretended to inspect a crack beside the doorframe.

'Leo,' she repeated, her voice a higher pitch. 'What will happen to me?'

He turned to face her. 'I should have killed you right at the beginning. I should never have allowed things to get this far.'

Zoe moved and Leo grabbed her wrist. In the silence, they stared at one another. He knew she understood. If the house had to go, then she would too.

Her voice trembled when she spoke. 'Tell me about the other book. Why do you think it will make more money than *Still Lives*?'

He still held her gaze. 'Because it's based on you.'

'On me?'

'It's about the abduction of a baby.'

'Won't you be taking a bit of a risk?'

He relaxed his shoulders. 'No. Because I'll be upfront about it. I'll admit it was inspired by the abduction of my child. It'll get a lot of publicity.'

'But that's so cynical. People won't like it. They'll accuse you of using Sophie to sell books.'

'They'll buy it, though. I can guarantee you that. Prurient interest is an effective marketing tool.'

'Right,' Zoe said, wrinkling her nose in distaste. 'What about Jenny? Does she know?'

'I haven't said anything to her yet,' Leo admitted.

'How far have you got?'

'The first draft is finished.'

'Quick work. Well, in that case, it's bound to be brilliant.'

He shot her a penetrating look. 'It has integrity. That's why it works. I can't afford to be high-minded. I need a surefire bestseller or things are going to get bad.'

'You just want to get rid of me.'

'No, I don't. You must trust me.'

She glared at him. 'Why should I?'

'Because I have your best interests at heart. This is life or death for both of us, because my life will be over if this place is sold. The novel needs work, but if we're going to do this, it has to be done quickly and you're going to have to play your part. I want you to read the whole thing through. I want to know what you think.'

'As if you even care.'

'Funnily enough, I do.'

She waited a good few seconds before giving him her answer, but he knew it was going to be a yes. She was malleable. That knowledge gave him a sense of power, of infinite possibilities.

'All right. I'll do it.'

'Good.'

He handed her a pencil. 'I want you to write down your thoughts as they occur to you. You don't have to spare my feelings.'

She cocked her head, disbelieving.

'I'm serious, Zoe. I need you to be honest.'

43

Jenny

TESSA DUDLEY SITS STRAIGHT-BACKED, HER HANDS clasped on her lap. We've been talking about her parents, about their beliefs and the way love was used as a bargaining tool when she was growing up. And of living in fear of Jehovah. She had to please him at all costs, and that meant pleasing her parents and any figures of authority, however undeserving they were.

'Including Michael Brady,' Tessa says.

'Who is Michael Brady?'

'My best friend's father and the father of my baby.'

'Ah. How do you feel about what happened between you?'

Tessa shakes her head. A tear drops on to her hand. She plucks a tissue from the box beside her and blows her nose.

'Stupid, ashamed, bad.'

'And?'

There's a question in Tessa's eyes when she looks at me. 'What do you mean?'

'Are all your negative feelings directed at yourself?'

'I don't know.'

'Yes, you do. There were people who ought to have protected you from predatory men, Tessa: your community, your family and your school. Think about how it made you feel when they failed you.'

She's torn the tissue into tiny shreds. 'It hurt. I felt robbed and humiliated.'

'Why robbed?'

Tessa pauses.

'Robbed of my future. I expected to get married and have a family and a position in the community. I didn't think I'd have to look after myself.' She raises her eyes to my face. 'I expect you think that's pathetic.'

'I don't judge you. You know that.'

She takes a sip from the mug of tea she's ignored up till now.

'When I woke up and found Abigail dead in her crib, that was the end of everything for me. I'd fallen into hell. I'm still there. I don't know how to get out. I live my life one day at a time and I pretend I'm all right. I do my job well and then I come home and I wander around the house where I lost her and I can't . . . I can't always snap out of it. It's like it has a hold on my mind, like there are tentacles there, clinging on.' She presses her fingers to the sides of her head as if to demonstrate. 'I wanted to love her, to prove to her that she deserved love.'

'Like you did?'

'Yes.' She looks pleased to have been understood. 'I didn't understand when I was a child, but I did by the time I had her. Love doesn't demand good behaviour,

275

love just exists. They taught us love had to be merited. They wanted us to feel insecure around each other, especially children with their parents. If we were loved unconditionally, they wouldn't have had the same power over us.'

This feels like a breakthrough.

'Perhaps by learning to love yourself, without putting conditions on that love or worrying about falling short of your own expectations, you'll find some peace and a way to move forward.'

'How have you been able to do that?'

'We're not talking about me, Tessa,' I remind her. 'These sessions are about you.'

'But you do understand what I'm talking about, don't you? You live with this too. I'm sorry,' she adds when my lips compress. 'I've crossed a line.'

Then she reaches for another tissue and knocks over her tea, sending it spilling over the tabletop.

'Oh!'

She dabs ineffectually at the puddle with a soggy tissue, but it drips on to the cream carpet. She gets down on her hands and knees.

'Leave it.' I jump up and go to the door. 'I'll get a cloth.'

I hurry across the reception to the little galley kitchen and squeeze out a cloth under the hot tap. Carys raises her eyebrows as I dash past her.

'Spilt tea,' I say. 'Not a sea of tears.'

'I can't believe I was so clumsy,' Tessa says, moving her feet out of the way to allow me to work on the stain.

The session ends with Tessa still apologizing as she closes the door behind her.

I breathe a sigh of relief. I'm going to talk to my supervisor later, but I know what she's going to say. Stop seeing this client. It's the right thing to do. Tessa is overinterested in me and my tragedy. It's as though she wants to turn the tables and have me unburden myself to her. Perhaps she just wants a friend. Poor thing.

There's always a risk that patients will get too attached or become curious about their therapist's personal life. I am sympathetic and I can see where all this is coming from with Tessa. She clearly had unconventional – even warped – relationships with those around her as a child and, as an adult, she still doesn't understand the unwritten rules. I don't want to crush her already fragile self-esteem but I need to be absolutely clear. I'll speak to her. It's for her own good. I'm sure she'll understand.

44

Hannah

AFTER SHE LEFT JENNY CREASEY, HANNAH CAUGHT the 155 bus from Elephant and Castle, having memorized the route, got off just before the turning to Albert Square Gardens and crossed the road. She walked past the Creaseys' house and completed a nervous circuit of the square, feeling sick and agitated, a familiar band of dull pain tightening round her head. Her heart sank. She did not need a migraine now. Getting hold of Jenny's keys had been unbelievably stressful – that's what must have brought it on. That and lying awake in the small hours, worrying about what she was going to do.

When Jenny had come back in with the damp cloth, Hannah thought she must have sensed her anxiety and excitement, but amazingly she hadn't. Or if she had, she put it down to what they'd been talking about. Jenny was so hard to faze it had been difficult to find a chink. But her enquiries about Jenny's own situation had done the trick, and had given Hannah a reason for her own clumsiness. At any rate, it had worked and she was here now. Ready for the next part of the plan.

An old man came out of one of the houses with his dog. He nodded at her, then let himself into the garden square. Hannah darted up the steps to the Creaseys', her hands shaking as she fumbled in her pocket for the set of keys she'd stolen from Jenny's bag. She unlocked the front door. It opened to silence.

She walked into a double-length sitting room where the milky daylight threw the suggestion of a shadow from the barred windows. Two large, comfortable-looking sofas upholstered in a soft, silvery-grey fabric and two stone fireplaces dominated the room. Broad floorboards that looked ancient were partly covered by a thick pile rug. At the far end of the room, tucked into an alcove, was an old-fashioned rolltop desk. Hannah opened it. She knew she was alone – over the last two years she had worked out Leo was always in Kent on a Tuesday – but the instinct to be silent was powerful. The desk was empty except for a few pens and a drawer containing miscellaneous bits and pieces. The drawers beneath it contained salvaged giftwrap and Sellotape.

Hannah closed them, disappointed. On another wall, bookshelves housed a collection of Leo's novels in their various editions and languages. She ran her fingers over the spines and pulled out the hardback edition of *The Emerald Cuckoo*, the book she had seen in a shop window shortly before all this started. The dedication read, 'To Jenny, without whom I could not have done any of this.' She replaced it and spun on her heel. This house was a lot fresher and cleaner than Sparrow Cottage, though she doubted Leo lifted a finger here either.

She climbed the stairs and glanced through an open door into a bedroom. It was lovely – like something out of the interiors magazines she flicked through while she waited for her appointments. The bed was covered by a sumptuous quilted eiderdown made from shimmering grey velvet, and above it hung a French chandelier constructed from prisms of pale-purple glass. She wandered in and ran her hand across the eiderdown, imagining a sleeping Jenny and Leo spooned together under the cover. He had everything he wanted. He hadn't suffered for what he'd done.

She could tell which side of the bed was Jenny's because of the Penny Vincenzi novel on the bedside table. She pulled open the drawer and found a spare pair of glasses, a packet of antihistamines, some eyedrops and a magnifying glass. She found nothing unexpected in Leo's cabinet either – just a torch, notebook, a collection of pens and pencils, and a half-empty blister-pack of sleeping pills. What was keeping him awake? As if she didn't know.

Between the bedroom, which overlooked the square, and bathroom, which looked out on to the back garden, was a dressing room with Jenny's clothes hanging on the right and Leo's on the left. The shelves below were lined with shoeboxes. Hannah opened them one by one. Finally, just as she was about to give up, she removed a lid and, instead of finding a pair of shoes, came across a book hidden under tissue paper. She took it out, opened it and read the inscription on the flyleaf twice before she could believe her eyes.

To Zoe, with best wishes, Leo Creasey

Hannah sat back on her heels. She had been right all along: Leo was lying. Two years he'd had her. What had he done to her in that time? If she wasn't at Sparrow Cottage, then where was he keeping her?

She clung to the book. Perhaps Zoe was dead, after all. No one could keep a grown woman prisoner all this time without someone getting suspicious.

A knock came from the floor above her and she froze. Wasn't she alone after all? The floorboards creaked. Hannah got up slowly. She tried to remember if the bedroom door had been closed. It hadn't – she was almost sure. She stood behind it and pushed it so that it was only a few inches ajar.

'Don't, you idiot!' a girl squealed.

'I'm not doing it on purpose,' a male voice responded.

'Have you seen my phone?'

'You're sitting on it.'

A peal of giggles followed. Hannah pressed herself back against the wall, her heart beating wildly. Who were these people? Did the Creaseys have lodgers?

Someone thudded downstairs, and she caught a flash of a teenage boy in jeans and a dark jacket, followed by a girl with long blonde hair. She shrank back into her corner.

'Can I look in here?'

'No, you can't. That's my aunt and uncle's bedroom.'

'They won't care.'

The boy pushed at the door and Hannah closed her eyes and prayed.

'No, you don't. It's private. Come on, I need coffee.'

The door stopped moving.

'Is there food? I'm bloody starving.'

'When aren't you? There's a loaf of bread with your name on it.'

'Wicked.'

The pair charged down the stairs. From the smack of bare feet on the wood floor, it sounded as if they jumped the last few. After a couple of seconds, Hannah stepped out on to the landing and peered over the banister. A light was coming from the basement.

She realized she still had the book in her hand and turned it over thoughtfully. If it was going to be used as evidence one day, it was important that it should be found here. She replaced it in the shoebox in the dressing room.

Hannah crept down to the hall, barely daring to breathe, grimacing as she tugged the security lock on the front door. It clicked noisily. She held her breath, but they hadn't heard. If they had, she would have had to run and hope for the best. Music blasted up from the basement – something modern and harsh to the ear. It stopped abruptly then started again – a different track but equally grating. Hannah left the house, closing the door as quietly as she could, then forced herself to walk to the bus stop at a normal pace.

Fifteen minutes later Hannah was back on St George's Road. The receptionist looked up in surprise when she came through the practice's doors.

'I think I may have lost one of my earrings here earlier.'

She hoped she didn't sound too flustered. She was a bag of nerves.

'I don't suppose you could pop your head round Jenny's door and check it's not in there. It might have come off when I was trying to mop up the tea.'

'I don't like to disturb her,' the receptionist said. 'She's with a client.'

'I'm just worried it might be vacuumed up by your cleaner. I wouldn't ask, only I've got a train to catch.'

The receptionist hesitated, then smiled. She came round the desk and knocked on Jenny's door, then went in. Hannah snatched Jenny's keys out of her bag and placed them on the floor beside the umbrella stand, out of the receptionist's line of vision. Jenny would panic later. They would search the place and find them.

'Can't find it, I'm afraid,' the receptionist said, returning to her desk.

'Oh dear.' Hannah frowned as if she was recalling something. 'Wait, I used the loo. I'll check in there.'

She went in and came out brandishing the earring.

'Thank goodness for that. They belonged to my mother. See you next week.'

45

Zoe

I HAVE THIS NICE FANTASY. I'M WORKING IN A PUBLISH-
ing house. It's old-fashioned with panelled walls and
shelves bowing under the weight of hundreds of books.
I'm the quiet and unassuming intern who's stepped in to
edit an important author's new novel after his regular
editor became ill and everybody else was too busy. The
boss, an elegant woman in a short black dress, comes
and stands beside me, reading over my shoulder. She's
making me nervous, and I jump when she puts her finger
on a note I've made in the margin. I'm sure she's going to
tell me off, but she merely comments, 'Very perceptive,
Zoe.'

I feel a brief sense of achievement before my bubble
bursts. I'm never going to be a real editor and have colleagues and friends. I'm going to grow old down here
and probably die.

Thoughts of Leo dying crowd their way in. I drop my
head between my knees and take deep breaths. Slowly
the panic recedes and its physical manifestations – the

aching limbs, racing heart and tense diaphragm – vanish. This is what my life is like: a lot of bumps and the odd moment when something Leo says makes me smile. Days of calm punctuated by massive downers.

When I hear Leo's footsteps I position myself beside the table, with my fingertips resting lightly on his manuscript. My palms are damp and I wipe them on my sweatpants. I'm nervous. I tell myself it's only because I'm excited about his book, but I know it's more than that. It's because on some subconscious level the hate I feel for him has fused with something else, something more complicated.

I do hate him, but when he's near me I change – I feel more alive, I move differently, I even speak and stand differently. I despise myself for it.

His eyes slide towards the pile of pages. 'What did you think?'

'I thought we could talk about it. I've made some notes.'

'How was my punctuation?'

He sounds as though he's humouring me. I frown, annoyed.

'It was fine, but I was more interested in the story and the language. I made a note of words you repeat.' That'll pop his self-satisfied bubble.

He shrugs. 'Verbal tics. That's great, Zoe. It's always useful to have those pointed out.'

I drag the armchair over to the table, sit on the arm and shove the kitchen chair towards him with my foot. Leo rolls his eyes, but he takes a seat.

'Why did you call her Zoe?'

'Hm?' He looks at me quizzically. 'Do you have a problem with that?'

'No.'

I turn each page. At first Leo is dismissive of my scrawls and underlinings.

'Yes, I know about that . . . My copy editor will spot that kind of thing . . . Fine.'

I go faster, embarrassed, beginning to lose confidence and worry that what I've done is trivial and irritating. It's only when we get about eighty pages in and I begin to point out issues that aren't cosmetic, that Leo becomes prickly.

'This bit doesn't really work,' I say.

'Why not?'

'It's up to you, obviously. But it feels like you haven't put yourself inside Zoe's head properly. She's angry and determined to show her mother she's an independent person, but she's not confused. Anyway . . .'

'OK,' Leo says impatiently. 'I've got the point. I'll think about it. What else?'

'Well, it's all small stuff. There's really only one major problem with the book that I can see.'

He folds his arms. 'Major?'

I flick through, looking for the right page.

'This section could be more powerful if you held back on the information, don't you think? You've told the reader more than they need to know. It would mean rethinking parts of it, but it might be worth doing. If there's time, I mean.'

The end of that speech sounded weak. It's not how I

meant it to come out. It was only because I sensed him bristling. I shift my gaze to my feet and when I look up again his face is hard. I can feel myself reddening.

'I only mean,' I say, fidgeting with my hair, 'that if you hold off on that bit, there'll be more of a chance to build up suspense.'

I wait, and when he doesn't respond I rush into the void. 'Apart from that it's brilliant.'

'I don't need to be told my work is "brilliant" by you, thanks all the same.'

His voice is an ugly sneer. He reaches for the manuscript and stands up.

'I might as well dump the entire thing and start again.'

'But that's stupid. All I meant was that when I read it I felt it lost tension. I was just looking for a way to fix that.'

'Well, you obviously know better than me.'

'I don't.' The disappointment and frustration make me want to stamp my foot. 'I thought you needed my help.'

'I did,' he says, struggling to unlock the door with his free hand. 'I foolishly believed you might appreciate good writing.'

'Fine,' I snap. 'Just ignore everything I've said. I've obviously got it completely wrong.'

'Don't be petulant, Zoe.'

'I'm not the petulant one.'

I rip the pages from my notebook and drop them into the bin.

Leo leaves the room without a word. As soon as the hatch closes my mind goes dark, as if his departure has switched off the light. Why do I need his approval so badly? Why does he haunt me when he's not here?

I wrap my arms around myself and squeeze my eyes shut. I just want to be held. It's been days since he hugged me, but I can still smell him, still feel his heartbeat against my cheek, still feel his muscular hands on my back and his chin on my skull. I want to be held and held and held. Sometimes I want that even more than I want to be free.

46

Leo

DRIVING BACK FROM THE SHOPS, HAVING HAD A chance to cool down, Leo found it strange that he'd been so defensive and so arrogant. He was fine with Reuben's critiques, but then Reuben was an experienced editor, not a schoolgirl. Still, he shouldn't have behaved like an over-indulged child, and when he came to think about it she was absolutely right. He could leave it as it was, but he wouldn't be satisfied. He'd know it was wrong, not good enough. If you're going to do something, his father had always told him, do it properly and finish the job.

He pulled into the driveway and sat in the warmth of the car for a moment, thinking about it. It was these little incidences, these moments of conflict and tension, that were creating a worrying dynamic between him and Zoe. He didn't want to be her friend, and yet he felt drawn in. He was beginning to understand her a little. He knew her moods. He could tell just from her demeanour if her period was due – her lack of energy and snappishness. She rarely smiled, so rarely in fact, that when she did it honestly was like the sun coming out.

Once again, he regretted the hug he had given her. How amazing that something so natural and simple could so thoroughly undermine the status quo.

Well, time to face the music. He took the keys out of the ignition and opened the door.

'I apologize.' Leo handed Zoe the bag containing her groceries. 'You were right. It's a pain in the arse, but I'm going to do what you suggest.'

He reached under the table for the bin, rescued her notes and shuffled them together neatly.

'Really?'

'And all the little bits and pieces you picked up on are really helpful. There's stuff I don't agree with—'

'I was probably wrong about lots of it,' she interrupted. 'I probably got a bit anal. But I think it's going to be brilliant. And I liked doing it.'

There it was, that word again. Brilliant. He let it go. 'We're both happy, then.'

He started helping her put away the things he'd bought, then stopped. This was what he did when Jenny came home with the shopping. It was too cosy, too couply. Zoe was his prisoner not his wife. He closed the cupboard door. Zoe was watching him. She had that look on her face, the one where she was feeling a little confident, a little cocky. Women often fall into the trap of believing they can manipulate a man.

He felt they were circling each other, and that wasn't good. He needed to get things back on track. He had no intention of using his position to his advantage. That wasn't what this was about. This was a case of needs must. He was a famous author. She was somebody no one missed, here because of a quirk of fate, not because she had crossed paths with a psycho. He would care for her and keep her safe. He had written the letter she wanted, so that was off his conscience.

He wondered what Jenny would make of it, if and when she discovered it. It pained him to think of her love for him turning to ashes.

Zoe had finished emptying the bag. She stripped the wrapper off a Mars bar and took a bite. She held it out.

'Want some?'

'No, thanks.'

He flicked through the manuscript, then put it on the table, picked up her pencil and made a note.

'Leo?'

He glanced at her. 'Yup?'

'Can I be in the acknowledgements?'

'Nice try.'

'I don't mean my real name. I can make one up.'

'Jenny reads them. If there's a name she doesn't recognize, she'll ask about it.'

'You could say it's someone who helped with your research.'

He grunted.

'Don't you think I deserve it?'

'Let me think about it.'

'I'll put something in, shall I?'

She smiled and, despite himself, he felt a comfortable warmth suffuse him. He handed her the page with the acknowledgements. She sat down and laid it on the table in front of her, her head resting on one hand while the other slowly spun her pencil. He'd already written what he wanted, thanking his agent and editor, and Jenny of course, but also emphasizing that this was a work of fiction, that nothing else should be read into it. He had written a life for his daughter and ultimately given her a happy ending. He would sell it as the work of a grieving father trying to find closure.

While she read, he leaned his hip against the table and flicked through her notes. Zoe wrote something in the margin, then turned the sheet of paper face-down and stood up. She was far too close to him, so close that if he'd moved his hand an inch he would have touched hers. He went still, alert to the charged atmosphere.

When she slid her hand round his upper arm and clung to him, raising herself up and pressing her lips against his, just for one moment, he was liquid. Then he came to his senses.

'Shit. For God's sake, Zoe. Get off me.'

He pushed her away, none too gently.

Heat flared in her cheeks. 'Sorry. Sorry. I don't know why I did that.'

'I've got to go.'

'Please don't leave yet. I don't want to be on my own.'

'I've got work to do.'

He rammed the key into the lock, desperate to get away, not just from temptation but from the morbid horror of being confined with her, with her warm, pulsing body, her scent and the unpleasantly competing odours of food, stale air and damp.

He could feel her stricken gaze, with all its neediness and anger, on his profile. He turned once to look at her, then shot out of the room, slammed the door and locked it.

'Fuck.'

This would not do.

Leo threw himself on to the sagging leather sofa and put his feet up. They were so close to finishing, why had he allowed her to muddy the waters? He tried to focus his mind, but he kept reliving that moment. He could feel her hand on his arm, the pressure of her breasts.

He flicked through the manuscript to the end and lifted the corners of his mouth in grudging admiration. He had to hand it to her, she had initiative.

I owe eternal thanks to Tessa Dudley, for her invaluable input.

Did she think he was born yesterday? He had no doubt it was a coded message of some kind. He screwed up the sheet of paper and aimed it at the bin, then got up with a grunt. At his computer, he scrolled to the acknowledgements page, positioned the cursor and typed, 'I am indebted to . . .' He scratched his head. What name would placate and flatter Zoe but mean nothing to Jenny, or Hannah Faulkner for that matter? Maisie, he decided. After Maisie Gallagher, the heroine of *In the Lake*, the book Zoe had left behind in Albert Square Gardens. Maisie what, though? Something clever. Faulkner, he thought. Falconer. Hunter.

I am indebted to Maisie Hunter, for her wisdom.

Zoe would appreciate that.

On the other hand, would it provoke questions from Jenny? He deleted it and started again.

... to Maisie Hunter, for her generous help in researching this novel.

If Jenny asked, he would explain that Maisie was an American lawyer, specializing in family law. But she wouldn't ask because she never did. At any rate, he might think of something better down the line. There was no hurry.

He rocked back and laced his fingers behind his neck. For a moment, he allowed himself to reimagine that kiss, to wonder what it would have been like to take it further. Then he shut down the thought with a shout of annoyance and reached for the whisky bottle.

47

Hannah

HANNAH HAD CONSIDERED TRAVELLING STRAIGHT TO
Sparrow Cottage from London, but by the time she
reached Maidstone station her headache had developed
into such a bad migraine that it was all she could do to
drive home and crawl into bed. Any movement induced
an agony so crippling she almost threw up.

She took an over-the-counter sleeping pill and slept,
waking in the morning with the right side of her head
feeling as though it had been sliced through. She rang
Anita and told her she wouldn't be coming in. By late
afternoon the pain had begun to abate and she found
she could think again. Zoe had seen the article and it
had made her question her life. What else had she seen?
With shaking hands, she opened her wardrobe door and
felt around for the envelope. It was still there, but it was
empty. She burst into tears.

Why couldn't Zoe have confronted her with the
wristbands? Why did she have to go after the Creaseys?
She knew her daughter. She would have been profoundly

shocked, but she would also have been lost in the romance of it all. Zoe was a daydreamer – had been since childhood – only this time the daydream had turned out to be real.

Oh, Zoe.

Instead of demanding the truth from Hannah, she had gone for the dramatic reunion and found herself alone with Leo. She had no way of knowing that she held his reputation in her hands, that she could bring his life tumbling down. In her naivety she would have expected him to be happy to see her, but Leo would have been horrified and afraid.

Zoe would be eighteen tomorrow, and she would spend her birthday a prisoner of her own father. Hannah put her head in her hands. She could blame other people; Michael Brady, her parents, but really it was her fault her daughter was suffering; it was all the bad decisions she had made, the weakness she had shown. Zoe was stronger than her. She had long known that. She prayed for her and for the strength to outwit Leo.

What did Leo do with her? He must have brought her into the house. Would he have drugged her? But she couldn't think like that. Zoe wasn't stupid – she would have realized what was happening and tried to escape.

Her mind wouldn't stop. Had he persuaded Zoe she could never go home? What if he'd told her Hannah had killed her baby, had shaken it? Hannah's stomach churned. She had done just that, hadn't she? She would go to prison and be an object of hatred. If Leo had poisoned Zoe with his lies, she would never want to see Hannah again. That was reason enough for her to disappear. She might have changed her identity and found a new life in London. Hannah shuddered. She knew what could happen to innocent and friendless young girls who arrived in the city in search of work.

She left the house and drove to Sparrow Cottage, turning on to the track that led up towards the woods. Just above the trees, the clouds drifted over a sliver of moon. She lingered until she felt ready to confront Leo, thinking back to that night. She didn't often take herself there. Despite the passage of time, it was still raw. She still occasionally gasped when a memory came back unbidden.

Who was she back then? How had she had the gall to lie to Leo Creasey and steal a baby? At seventeen, a little younger than Zoe was now, she'd been so certain that there was no other way that she hadn't questioned the choice she made. Leo would still have had alcohol in his bloodstream when he drove them to London and he'd been in shock, yet she hadn't given it a second thought. There was no way she would do anything like that now. She was a very different person these days. She drew a sigh and opened the door. Her feet sank into the ridges left by a tractor.

There were lights on in the cottage and his car was parked on the driveway. She could hear classical music playing; a dramatic, sweeping melody. She rang the doorbell hard. The music went off. Leo opened the door in his socked feet, a big brown cable-knit cardigan that looked like it belonged to someone else draped over his black shirt. When he saw her he scowled.

'What do you want?'

'I want to know where my daughter is.'

'This is getting boring. Go away, Hannah.'

'I know that she came looking for you. I have proof.'

He folded his arms and cocked his head to one side, considering her. 'What proof?'

She had intended to throw the discovery of the book in his face, but that would mean he would know she had been in his house and he would find out about Tessa Dudley. She remembered when she had confronted him outside Sparrow Cottage. He had smiled at her unpleasantly, and told her that if she ever went near his wife he would kill her. He had used the word 'eviscerate'. And here they were again, only this time it was just the two of them. If he had killed Zoe, he would have no qualms about killing her.

'Enough for the police to be interested in you.'

'So, what's changed?' he drawled. 'I take it you no longer care if the world finds out what you did.'

She would not be bullied. 'Why should they believe you over me? You killed my baby, you suggested I take Sophie because you knew she wasn't yours. You wanted to get back at your wife, to hurt her like she'd hurt you. You were drunk and angry, and you made me do it. I was seventeen years old and I didn't know anything about anything. You were in your thirties. I had no one to turn to – you had your wife and your mother. You took advantage of my distress. I'd given birth and lost my baby in the space of two days. I wasn't in my right mind.

'The thing is, Leo,' she added. 'People just love seeing the mighty fall. I'm the underdog. You're arrogant and smug. Think about it.'

She surprised herself. She had never made such a long speech before.

'No, I will not "think about it". Why the hell should I? I don't know where your daughter is, or anything about her.'

She raised her eyebrows.

'You're delusional. Feeding off your own fantasies. You need help.'

He didn't sound 100 per cent confident.

'Why don't you just tell me where she is? You don't want trouble any more than I do. Give her back to me. I've told everyone she's living in Canada. I'll say she's coming back to go to university here. No one's going to question it.'

'Give me credit for having some intelligence.' He sighed. 'Can't you see that you're fixated on me for the wrong reasons? You've spent your entire adult life looking for someone to blame and I'm the obvious target. I helped you eighteen years ago and, in doing so, ruined any hope my wife had of happiness. I pay my dues every minute of every day, knowing it's my fault she's in torment. I could blame you, I could stalk you like you do me, but frankly I'd rather get on with what life I have left. At least I've made something good out of the horror. What have you done? Nothing, except whine and blame others for your misfortunes. I've run out of sympathy. Now go on, get lost.'

'I'm not going anywhere.'

'Then you leave me no alternative.'

He grabbed her by the arm, frog-marched her back to the lane, and shoved her so hard she fell to her knees.

She scrambled up and turned on him, but he was quicker. He held her wrists and pulled her to him, whispering into her ear.

'What is it you really want, you stupid bitch?'

He pushed his hand under her coat and clasped her breast hard. Hannah whimpered with pain. He let her go and laughed as she scuttled away. She could feel him watching her as she stumbled up the lane, her arms crossed.

Leo had no conscience. How did you get through to a man like that? He was no better than Michael Brady.

Hearing a car approaching, Hannah panicked, thinking Leo was coming after her. She set off at a run. Was he planning to get rid of her once and for all? The headlights caught her as she staggered off the lane and on to the track. The vehicle pulled in beside her.

'Jenny?' came a voice.

She turned to find an elderly man eyeing her through the lowered window of a Land Rover.

'Sorry,' he said gruffly. 'I thought you were someone I knew.' His eyes narrowed. 'Friend of Leo's, are you?'

'It's none of your business who I am,' she said, walking away. She remembered him from the last time she had been here. He didn't seem to recognize her, though.

'Actually,' he called after her, his voice plump with self-importance, 'as a local magistrate, it is my business to interfere if I see any suspicious activity.'

She ignored him, getting in her own car and turning on the engine.

He waited, blocking her path, his engine running. Hannah gripped the steering wheel and stared at him in the rearview mirror. After a moment, he drove on. She followed him, drawing a sigh of relief when he turned in through his gate.

This wasn't over. For all Leo's bravado, she had rattled him.

48

Leo

'I THOUGHT OF A GREAT NAME FOR THE BOOK,' ZOE SAID.

Leo looked up. He was slouched on the armchair, reading through Zoe's comments while she fed him pages from a steadily diminishing stack. They had been working flat out. His back and shoulders were aching, and the vague warning of trouble in his wrists and hands had become a loud alarm. He opened and closed his fists and flexed his fingers. These days he ached in unexpected places. Once this damn thing was finished, he would have a rest. He would wait three months before he even thought about completing *Still Lives*.

'Oh yes?' he said.

He already had a title in mind: *The Nowhere Girl*. He liked the way it sounded, the rhythm of it. It had a literary resonance he felt it deserved.

'Go on.'

'*The Girl Who Never Was*.'

He rested the pages on his knees and raised his eyebrows. 'Really?'

'It suits the book.' She paused. 'It's what she was, right? Mum's baby, I mean.'

'It's not bad. Let me think about it.'

Leo pushed his glasses up. This had been a sprint; he had never worked so intensely. Zoe pored over every phrase and called him up on things he hadn't had a chance to think through properly. He was used to bringing out a book every three to four years, and having time to allow each draft to percolate. This was how other authors worked; normal authors who reliably provided their publisher with a three-hundred-page novel each year. And made more money than him, damn them. But that was the point, wasn't it? It was about saving Sparrow Cottage, not his ego or his reputation as a literary genius.

Zoe rubbed the small of her back then stood up, raised her arms above her head and stretched. Her breasts lifted under her jumper. Leo looked away.

The Girl Who Never Was. She was right, the title was good. He could see it in gold letters, embossed, his name huge above them. Please God, it would be enough. If Jenny stuck to her threat, he didn't know what he would do.

'Just one more hour,' he said.

He was feeling distinctly twitchy. He'd go for a walk along the Downs to get some perspective. He might even drop in at the Tickled Trout.

'I can do more if you like,' she said, handing him another page.

Leo ran his eye over her notes. One of the advantages of having someone so young annotate the manuscript was that her handwriting was still bordering on school-girlish, as though she was anxious to win a gold star for it. Rounded, regular letters, nothing scrawled or slipshod like Reuben's could be on occasion – or his own, for that matter.

' "Pace drops off here"?' He raised his eyebrows.

'It does, Leo. You need to cut the whole scene. It's irrelevant. I drifted off a bit.'

'Ah.'

It was a scene to which he was particularly attached, where the heroine harks back to her youth. He picked up his pen and ran a diagonal line through it. Sometimes you had to make a decision about who to trust, and he had decided to trust Zoe – in this, at least.

He liked being with her. He didn't love her, he assured himself. He loved Jenny. But Zoe gave him the kind of attention Jenny never had. Jenny supported him and saw to his physical and material needs, but deep down she didn't care about his writing. She respected what he did, in an abstract sense, but the idea of her sitting for hours, reading and critiquing his work like Zoe had been doing, was unimaginable. He had never suggested it and neither had she. She read his novels once they were physical books, but even then he wasn't sure she read them properly. They weren't her thing – she preferred romances. He didn't resent it, just felt mildly dissatisfied. He had always felt mildly dissatisfied.

Zoe filled that vacuum. When she loved something he had written it made him euphoric. If she accused him of being boring, like she had just now, it could throw him off-kilter for hours. He had grown to live for her approbation, he realized, as ridiculous as that sounded. He cast her a wary glance. Was she drawing him in? Lulling him? Last night he'd had a fraught sexual dream about her and had woken feeling pleasantly shocked at himself.

How had it come to this? Never mind this novel, his life had turned into something out of a Hitchcock movie. He groaned inwardly. He was lonely, that was all. Jenny was so wrapped up in her new career, far more interested in her clients than she was in him. It couldn't last, and it would be cruel of him to allow Zoe to think it could. But for the time being, he was enjoying himself, and that was allowable, wasn't it? So much of his life was hard work, painful and filled with guilt. He deserved the respite these hours gave him.

She'd said something. He had been so lost in his thoughts that he hadn't heard her.

'Sorry. What?'

'Take me upstairs, Leo.' Her voice was soft. 'Please.'

'Zoe, I . . .'

His stomach muscles clenched. Had she read his mind?

'I just want to get out into the fresh air.'

No, he realized, embarrassed at his mistake. That's not what she meant.

49

Zoe

HE LOOKS AT ME LIKE I'M MAD.

'You are joking, aren't you?'

'I don't mean let me go, I just mean take me up there and give me a few minutes outside. You can tie my hands behind my back. Please, Leo. Nothing's going to happen.'

I watch his face. I'm sure he's thinking that if he does it once, I'll expect it again. And what if my demands grow greater? What if one thing leads to another? I hold his gaze and feel a change going on in my body; a warming, a softening. Does he feel it too?

'I won't ask for anything else, I promise,' I said. 'I've worked so hard. You're going to make money out of this book. I deserve a reward, don't I?'

I hold my wrists together behind my back. Leo secures them with a black cable tie. He goes ahead of me and I follow him up the wooden staircase. When I step out of the hatch, he takes my arm to stop me falling over. The night air on my face is a shock. I expected a room of some sort, but instead I see the shadowy outline of shrubs, some bare-branched trees and, in the sky, the bright disc of a full moon. There is no house upstairs after all. I feel a bit of a fool for thinking there was.

My senses are invaded. I can hear strains of opera – it's almost surreal. I can taste the air, I can smell green things. Leo draws me away from the opening on to a path and I lean back and look up at the stars.

'Are you cold?' he asks.

'No.'

I lie because I don't want to go back inside, not yet, but the truth is I'm freezing.

'You're shivering,' he says matter-of-factly.

Leo takes off his jacket and arranges it over my shoulders. I turn three hundred and sixty degrees, slowly taking everything in. I breathe 'oh' into the air.

He holds my arm and we walk around the garden, like lovers taking a stroll. I have my trainers on but I wish I didn't. I want to feel the dewy grass between my toes, I want the gravel to dig into the soles of my feet.

The cottage is old and brick-built, with a bowed roof like a horse's back. It looks like the kind of house you'd find in a fairy tale – the woodcutter's cottage. There's even a pile of logs stacked neatly to the side. The lights are on downstairs. Through the window I see a brass tap, a bottle of washing-up liquid and beyond that, a table with a glass, a plate and a newspaper on it. I want to stay longer, but Leo moves me on.

The garden is disproportionately large and neglected, but romantic for it, especially in the pale moonlight.

Rose stems sprouting new growth clamber over walls and trees. Curled brown leaves that must have fallen in autumn still litter the ground.

Leo leads me across grass and along paths. The ground at the foot of a large camellia is scattered with its blooms. We have one in our garden at home. When we pass the far corner, a powerful smell of fox hits my nostrils.

My time is up all too soon. I don't make a fuss because I want him to allow it again, but this has changed me. I've sniffed the air, I've felt it on my cheeks, I've breathed in the outside.

The jacket is still round my shoulders when he locks us back in the room. He unbuttons it slowly, our heads close together. We are silent. I shift a little so that his hair brushes my lips. It's coarse, and smells nice and clean. He raises his head and holds my gaze for a second, then peels the jacket off me and hangs it over the back of the chair. When he frees my wrists, I wrap my arms around him, pressing my face into the muscular dip beneath his shoulder. I don't move and he doesn't push me away. Slowly his arms come round me. He rests his chin on my head.

'Zoe.'

He pulls away slightly and I raise my face to his. Our mouths hesitate, a hair's breadth between them, and then they touch and it's as though I've been electrocuted. I bunch the fabric of his shirt into my fists and hold on tight. He cups the back of my head and we stand pressed together so hard I can feel his heart beating through our clothes. I don't fight him off.

I lose everything in him. I lose my mind, my worries

and my control. I feel frantic and I feel ready. I feel him and only him. I am no longer me alone. When he takes me, I can't contain myself, I feel as though someone has opened the door to my cage and I've flown out.

Leo has arranged the two bunk bed mattresses on the floor, where they take up all the available space. We lie side by side, facing each other, our eyes locked. He strokes my cheek and trails his fingers along my arm, over the curve of my hip and down my thigh.

Above me, on the table, the figures on the digital clock creep towards seven. Time is my only reality. This dirty little room, with the smells that I no longer notice – it's not real. There is time and there is Leo. My cage hasn't gone, it's just different. He spoons his body around mine, and I allow my breathing to slow.

Minutes go by, half an hour. He doesn't move. His arm has grown heavier. The fridge has been humming but it stops abruptly, leaving only his breathing to alleviate the deathly silence. It's the breathing of a sleeping man.

I edge myself out from beneath his arm. He doesn't move when I replace my body with my pillow. Asleep he is vulnerable and I feel regret. I wanted what happened between us; I still want it. I understand Leo. He's my guard but he's also a man. I think he's lonely, despite Jenny and all the people he meets in his work. I'm lonely too.

None of this changes the fact that I have an opportunity to get out of here, and I have to take it. I look round for something to knock him unconscious. The television, perhaps? I dismiss the idea. It'll make too much noise.

Also, being cracked over the skull by a television set might result in his death, even if I only mean to knock him out. I don't want to kill him. When I get out, I'm going to visit him in prison, perhaps hold his hand across the table. Do they let you do that? Do they let you kiss?

I feel something by my foot. His glasses. I tread on them. That should slow him down.

I slip the key out of his jacket pocket, find my sweat-pants and top, and pull them on. I wait for a moment, holding my breath. Leo sleeps on. Emboldened, I ease the key into the lock. It makes a scraping sound. He doesn't stir. It won't move. I try again, pulling it out a fraction, but it still sticks. There must be a knack to it.

On the third go it gives and I depress the handle. The fridge noise starts up with a juddering vibration and startles me, its hum seeming even louder than usual to my hypersensitized ears. I glance at Leo just as his eyes open, confusion sharpening quickly into comprehension. My time has run out. I open the door and charge up the stairs, but he's up and after me.

Seven steps. I'm younger and faster than him and I've kept myself fit. The hatch is open and I'm through, my hands scrabbling in the dirt as I lift my knee on to the edge. Leo grabs the waistband of my sweatpants and I swing at him. He lets go and grasps my ankle, yanking me down. My chin hits the lip of a step, causing me to bite my tongue. I cry out in pain and kick blindly. The heel of my foot connects with his face.

He pounces on me, pinning me at the bottom of the stairs. I'm crushed under the weight of his body and his hot breath is in my ear. He's naked and it's almost as though we're making love again, but in anger this time. He takes hold of my wrist, twists my arm into a half nelson, pulls me up and propels me back into the room and on to the mattresses.

'Now, that was stupid,' he says, panting.

He switches on the light. He has a bright-red graze on his face and without his glasses or his clothes he looks a bit ridiculous. But he isn't. I know that now.

He frowns as he picks up the glasses, and dangles them in front of me.

'Did you do this?'

I don't answer. I can taste metal. My mouth is full of blood, my tongue swollen and sore. I wipe the blood away with the back of my hand. He bends the glasses back into shape and puts them on. They sit on the bridge of his nose at an angle. He gets dressed, pulling on his jeans with jerky, angry movements.

'I'll see you before I go tomorrow morning. I'm being lenient, but if you try anything like that again, I'll be forced to remove some of your privileges.'

I cry when he leaves the room, thinking about what I've done, about the futility of it all. He knows he has me now. I had a chance and I blew it. He'll never take me above ground again. I wonder if Jenny will smell me on him.

And then I start imagining what I'll feel if I ever do meet her. I hope that we will recognize that we are blood, and the fact that we don't know each other won't matter. But I'm scared that it will, that she'll feel nothing. I refuse to entertain the possibility that it won't happen. I am not going to die down here.

311

50

Jenny

MY PHONE STARTS RINGING AS I'M CROSSING KENNING-ton Road on my way home on Wednesday evening. I don't recognize the number.

'It's Kirstie,' Leo's agent says as I answer. 'Sorry to bother you, Jenny, but he's not answering his phone. I was wondering whether he was with you.'

'No, he's in Kent. He's a bit useless when he's down there. Is there a problem?'

It's very unusual for her to call me. In fact, I don't remember it ever happening.

'Absolutely not. I've got some news. Big news. Could you ask him to get in touch as soon as you hear from him?'

'I'm intrigued,' I say. 'What's happened?'

'My lips are sealed. Sorry, but it wouldn't be right to tell you before I've spoken to Leo. This is so annoying, I'm literally twitching with excitement.'

Leo isn't due to call me for a couple of hours. I try his number, but he's switched off his mobile. Typical. I'm willing to bet Kirstie's call was about the film deal. I wonder how much money it means and whether, in spite of what Leo said, it's enough to save Sparrow Cottage. That would be fantastic.

James Turner, I think. He might be able to get hold of him. I move under a street lamp and scroll through my contacts until I find his number. He picks up after the third ring.

'Hello, Jenny.' His voice is raised, as if he's standing on a mountain somewhere.

It's been a long time since I last spoke to James. He's probably a little deaf. I speak clearly.

'I'm so sorry to disturb you, James, but something urgent has come up and I can't seem to get hold of Leo. I don't suppose there's any chance you could nip down to the cottage and ask him to call home. Don't worry if it's a bother.'

'Not at all. I'll walk the dog there now. Funny thing, Jenny. I must be going mad in my old age, because I thought I saw you in the lane the other day.'

My brow creases. 'You thought you saw me? I haven't been there.'

'No, I realized straight away it wasn't you, of course, so I felt a bit of a fool. It was dark and she was running. Mind you, I haven't seen you in years.' It sounds like a reproach. If it is, I deserve it. 'She was rather fierce when I challenged her. Thing is, I did recognize her. I think she might have been the woman I caught trying to break in a couple of years ago.'

This is news to me. Why has Leo never mentioned an

attempted break-in? It's very unlike him not to have persuaded me to deal with the insurance. I make a mental note to ask for an explanation.

'Are you sure it wasn't Lola Creasey, Leo's mother?'

Lola sometimes turns up unannounced and it drives Leo crazy.

'No, I know her. This one was younger. In her late thirties, I'd say. She looked upset. She told me to mind my own business when I asked her what she was doing there. She was most uncivil.'

'I'll ask Leo if he knows anything about her,' I say, quelling any further discussion. 'And thank you for offering to knock on the door.'

'I'm sorry we don't see you down here any more, Jenny. It all looks a little dilapidated these days. I remember, when I was a lad, your grandfather used to pay me a few pounds to help—'

'James, I have to go. I'll talk to Leo about getting someone in to do repairs. He doesn't always see when things need doing.'

'Too busy creating his marvellous books, I expect,' James says with a throaty laugh. 'Not concerned with the mundanities of life like us lesser mortals, eh?'

'No.' That's certainly true. 'Oh, and, James?'

'Yes.'

'Please don't mention the woman to Leo. I wouldn't like him to think he's under scrutiny. You know what I mean. He values his privacy.'

I walk the rest of the way home in a daze. A woman seen leaving Sparrow Cottage in a state? Who was she? Could it possibly have been *the* Zoe, or is that too big a leap? I did think his excuse about her being a character in his novel was rather thin, especially in view of the expression on his face when I asked him. If he's having an affair, how long has it been going on? Months? Years? And why was she running? A lovers' tiff, then? My gorge rises. Is that what the fuss over Sparrow Cottage has been about? Not a place to work, but love nest? No wonder I'm not allowed anywhere near it. That makes me angry. That house is rightfully mine. I didn't mind when I thought he was writing his books, but if there's a woman involved, that's another matter altogether. It explains a lot. I've been stupidly trusting.

Kate's youngest, Bella, who's staying with me for a few days – a typically last-minute arrangement – appears as I'm letting myself in, her phone in her hand. As she comes into the light, I think that it should be Sophie. It should be my daughter pounding down the stairs and throwing herself at me.

'Hi, Auntie Jenny,' she says, giving me a hug as she pulls on the green parka with faux-fur-trimmed hood that I bought her for Christmas. 'I'm off out. I finished the cheese. Sorry! Have a nice evening.'

Then she's gone, taking with her the scent of strawberry lip gloss and youth.

Sometime this evening, possibly quite soon, Leo will ring to find out what the emergency was. I have time to pour myself a glass of wine and change out of my work clothes into sweatpants and a slouchy pullover. I sit, cradling my glass, with the telephone on the table beside me. I've been ignoring the obvious for too long. Leo and I live almost separate lives.

In the old days, every time he returned home was like a reunion. I justified the way we lived to our friends by explaining that the unusual arrangement kept our marriage fresh, that there was excitement, that we missed each other, that Leo needed isolation or he wasn't able to write.

Nowadays, even though my hours are more civilized, we still seem to miss one another. Leo has so many functions to attend and sometimes I wonder if he even sees me these days, or if I've blended into the furniture as far as he's concerned. I kid myself that his head is in his latest novel, but maybe the truth is that his head is with her.

I glance at the wedding photograph in the silver frame on the mantlepiece and scowl. I remember something Tessa Dudley said to me at our last session. *Love doesn't demand good behaviour, love just exists.* Can I feel that way about my husband? I'm not sure I even want to try at the moment. There is love, but I'm not sure I want the compromises that come with it any more, since they all seem to be made on my part. I have to think about this.

I jump up and turn the frame round so I can't see us looking young and in love and full of optimism. He's been using me. I'm a means to an end, the woman who pays the bills, a facilitator. I angrily brush away a tear. He might think I'm a pushover, but I'm not. He needs me more than I need him.

The phone rings and my heart misses a beat.

I won't say anything. It would be stupid to knee-jerk. I need to think this through, tackle it as I would any other problem – by not acting in haste. There will be one difference. This time I'll work out not what's best for Leo, but what's best for me.

I pick up. 'Hello, darling.'

51

Zoe

A WALL CALENDAR HANGS ON THE BACK OF THE TOILET door. It features spectacular images of beautiful land-scapes from across the globe. March is the Khlong Lan waterfall in Thailand. It's a magical place where silver sheets of misted water spring from lush greenery to pummel the rocks. I often sit here for longer than I need to, making up stories. This one has fairies in it. They dart from fern to branch, slip in and out of the water-fall, spin ever-increasing circles on the surface of the lake.

It's my birthday today – my Zoe Faulkner birthday, not the Sophie Creasey one. It occurs to me that keeping up the Jehovah's Witness tradition of not celebrating birthdays must have been very convenient for Mum, because it saved confusion over the dates.

I'd like to spend the day beside the waterfall with a picnic and a rug and a friend, or at the very least a dog. Maybe I will. I only have to shut my eyes and imagine myself there to catch a sense of the thick heat of the day and the cool of the mist rising from the river. I clamber behind the waterfall to the hidden overhang where the rocks are wet and shaded. I hold my hand out and feel the water pounding it, splitting between my fingers and meeting again beneath them, like threads on a loom. I dive from the rocks and roll on to my back in the water, laughing as my friend dive-bombs in after me.

I had a chance and I blew it. I shouldn't have worried about putting on clothes, I should have just run. If I hadn't been wearing clothes, it would have been harder for him to hold on to me. I would have kicked him hard enough to drive him back, then slammed down the hatch and locked it. I would have got some clothes from the cottage and walked to the nearest house. It's my fault I'm still here.

I write down what happened. At least it's something exciting. I find it extremely hard to write about the sex, but I make myself do it. One word after another. Details are important. Things I remember. That I started it. That Leo wanted me. That it was passionate, but weird because I was scared. Losing your virginity is a big enough deal in the best of circumstances. When I get to the bit where I attempt to escape, it's a lot easier to describe.

I hear the hatch lift and his feet on the steps. The key turns. He sets down two large carrier bags on the floor. He's wearing a different pair of glasses and his face sports a nasty bruise but I feel all loose inside at the sight of him. Does he feel it too, or does he just feel awkward? We've seen one another naked and kissed each other's bodies, but I've also kicked him in the face,

319

scratched him and tried to escape. The chances of a relationship are going to be low.

The bags are stuffed with groceries. He doesn't usually buy this much. Maybe there are some extra treats in there, to show I mean something to him. He keeps a safe distance. He's hard to read but there is something going on. He's very tense. Is it because he loves me more than he's angry with me? Will we make love again? I wish he'd talk to me.

'What's going on?' I ask, trying to sound casual.

'What makes you think anything's going on?'

'You're different.'

He doesn't touch me, even though I'm close enough for him to. I'm surprised at how disappointed I feel.

'I had some good news last night. *In the Lake* has been optioned for two hundred thousand pounds. It's a lot more than I expected.'

My jaw drops. That is an unimaginable amount of money.

'And that's not all. They're flying me to LA tomorrow to meet the director and screenwriter. This time it's going to happen, Zoe. They want to start casting straight away. Big names. It means the house will be safe.'

He means I will be safe. I don't know whether to laugh or cry so I don't smile, I just wait to see what he says.

'Aren't you pleased?' he says.

'Why should I be? It doesn't change anything for me. I'm still trapped down here. I'm still your prisoner.'

'I'm going to look after you. There'll be more money. I can make improvements. Give you more space. Maybe even a shower. You can work with me. You have a real talent for editing.'

His eyes are glowing. He honestly believes his own crap.

'How long will you be away for?'

He runs his fingers through his hair, so I know it's bad news.

'That's what I need to talk to you about. I'll be back in London on Tuesday, but I have a meeting on Wednesday and . . . Well, I'm out on Wednesday evening and I have commitments on Thursday, so I won't be with you until Friday.' He indicates the bags. 'There's more than enough to last you in there.'

I'll be alone for a week. Again. Just the thought makes my chest go tight. I suppose at least this time I've had some warning, not like when he was ill. Loneliness snakes around me, shadowy figures trailing their gossamer fingers over my flesh. Leo comes to sit beside me on the arm of the chair. He absently strokes my hair away from my face. No kiss.

'What happened between us,' he says. 'It was a mistake.'

I push his hand away. 'I don't care about that.'

His face softens. 'Yes, you do. And so do I. I should have controlled myself, and I'm sorry. It was unforgivable.'

'As unforgivable as keeping me here?'

He grimaces. 'Well, perhaps not.'

'Then don't make it worse by leaving me for so long. It's not fair.'

'You'll survive.'

I give him a hard shove. 'Survive? What the hell do

you think I've been doing all this time? You think giving me food is enough? What about my sanity? I need you. I can't be isolated; it makes my head do strange things.'

'Zoe, Zoe,' he soothes. 'Don't you understand? This is in your interest. Without Sparrow Cottage there is no you.'

'Don't talk about that.' I cover my ears but he just raises his voice.

'I don't want to hurt you, you know I don't. I've tried my best to make life bearable for you. I've involved you in this book, and you've been incredible. I owe you so much for that, but you have to allow me some flexibility. You can't expect to control me.'

'So this is how it's going to be?' I say. 'You are all I have, and now you're going to meet all these famous people, and you'll spend longer and longer away from me, and I won't be able to cope. You're just going to discard me.'

He frowns. 'Don't be childish. That won't happen.'

The 'childish' stings. 'It will. You'll probably end up discarding Jenny too, once you don't need her money.'

'Stop it.'

'No, I won't. Admit it, Leo. This is a big change for you. I'll be a nuisance, holding you back.'

I don't know why I said that. I don't want to believe it. All I'm doing is making things easier for him. I don't mean for him to forget me, ever. His conscience might torment him, but he still feels entitled to take what he wants. It's how he's always lived his life, I think. From what he's told me, his mother is to blame. Greedy, flaky, parasitic Lola. But then nothing is ever Leo's fault, is it?

322

He takes off his glasses and pinches his fingers into his eye sockets. 'I wish none of this had ever happened. I honestly don't know how to go on.'

'Oh, poor Leo,' I sneer. 'I don't know how you go on either.'

'You have the right to despise me,' he says. 'I've hurt you. I wish it could be different.'

He looks tired and despondent when he gets up and moves towards the door. I've got under his skin, but I'm not stupid. When he drives away from here this evening, that feeling will dissipate. The lure of his Hollywood dream will be more attractive than the guilt I provoke, and the cord between us will break – until the next time he's here.

I stand up and walk towards him slowly. He has his hand in his pocket, feeling for the keys. His eyes glitter; he thinks I'm coming for sex. Maybe deep down that is what I want.

'If you open the door, I will fight you,' I say.

'I don't doubt it.'

I take hold of his lapels with as much aggression as I can muster and wind my leg round his. He loses his balance and rams his hand against the door to steady himself.

'Get off me, Zoe. Don't play stupid games.'

'This isn't a game. This is my life.'

I hang on so tightly that my body responds. Leo moves forward, half carrying me, until I hit the metal frame of the bunk. I cry out and clutch the back of my head.

He's panting. 'I have this much patience, Zoe.' He raises his hand, his forefinger about a centimetre away from his thumb. 'If you don't behave, I will be forced to restrain you.'

'Restrain me more than you already do?'

'Yes,' he says coldly. 'I don't like being manipulated. I can get a chain, if that's what you want, and treat you like a dog.'

He has the key out and I stare at him, ready to rush him again, but he shakes his head slowly.

'Is it worth the risk?' he asks. 'I will hurt you.'

I scream and run at him anyway, my teeth bared, but this time he's ready for me. He punches me in the face so that I ricochet against the wall and slump to my knees, my mouth bleeding. He unlocks the door, exits swiftly and locks it behind him.

'Happy birthday to you too!' I scream. 'Bastard,' I add morosely.

I wet some kitchen towel and clean the blood off my face. The inside of my mouth is cut. A drop of blood lands on the back of my hand and I smear it away with my finger.

I hate him. I wish I had dropped the television on his head.

Seven days. One hundred and sixty-eight hours. I'll sleep for sixty of them at the most, leaving me with one hundred and eight hours to fill. Six thousand, four hundred and eighty minutes. I'll have to create a world for myself that will keep the darkness at bay. I can't think about the walls or the ceiling because if I think too much I'll drive myself mad.

52

Jenny

'ARE YOU SURE YOU'VE GOT EVERYTHING?' I ASK. 'PASS-port, phone, keys, sunglasses?'

I study Leo's face while he pats his pockets and checks the contents of his black leather bag. Could he be having an affair? I need concrete evidence before I demand answers. All I have is an elderly man's description of a distressed woman running away from Sparrow Cottage. It's suspicious, but she could be a fantasist; a bitter, lonely, middle-aged woman, sustaining herself with an imagined relationship with her favourite author. Perhaps Leo was kind to her and she chose to interpret that as reciproca-tion. He could have put her straight and told her to get lost. Leo can also be cruel. The scene James described might have been the aftermath of that conversation.

Leo hugs me. I breathe in his scent and return the embrace. I feel angry and betrayed. I don't care about the money, I'm still selling Sparrow Cottage if it turns out he's been entertaining his mistress there.

'I wish you were coming with me,' he says.

I keep my answer light and playful. 'No, you don't.'

I needn't have worried that he would suspect anything is wrong. He's so excited to be going to LA, so caught up in the drama and the possibilities. He's already putting London and me behind him, thinking ahead to a long lunch with Hollywood royalty. I'm glad, not because it stops him noticing that I'm not myself, but because I want this for him as much as he does.

His worry lines deepen when he sees my expression. 'I'm only going to be gone four days. You look like the sky's about to fall on your head.'

I glance at myself in the hallway mirror. I do look a bit miserable. I'm not as good an actress as I thought.

'I'm fine.'

'No, you're not. It's Sophie's birthday tomorrow. We always spend it together, and I'm letting you down.'

'It's OK. I'm meeting a friend for lunch.' It's Sophie's eighteenth – another important milestone in our daughter's life – but he doesn't mention that. 'I don't want you to feel bad. This is your time, Leo.'

'I'm not as important as Sophie. I won't go if you don't want me to.' He takes his phone out of his pocket. 'I can text and cancel right now.'

I smile. 'Don't be silly. We can speak on the phone.'

He lets me go, picks up his case and moves to the door. My heart aches. He turns as he opens it and I'm not quick enough to hide my expression.

He frowns, scrutinizing my face. 'What is it? There's something else, isn't there?'

I can't tell him my fears. I'll just irritate him. Proof first.

I need to say something, though.

'I just feel like you're leaving me behind.'

It feels true.

'You had your chance,' he says, not unreasonably.

'You know that's not what I mean. You're going to meet famous and glamorous people, and I'll seem very dull by comparison.'

His face clouds and I'm not sure, because it was fleeting, but he looked hunted. What did I say?

'Don't be silly, Jenny. I'm too old to be impressed by that sort of thing.'

I smile and think, *Rubbish*.

The Addison Lee driver takes his suitcase and swings it into the boot. Leo sinks into the back seat.

'I'll call you as soon as I touch down,' he says.

I find what I'm looking for at the back of the drawer in my dressing table. I remember being given the keys to Sparrow Cottage by my grandmother's solicitor. There were two sets, and while I gave Leo one, I retained the other.

After her funeral I considered moving in, caught up in a pleasant fantasy about the rural idyll, but came to my senses after two weeks. My parents and Kate had stayed for the first week while we sorted through Granny's possessions, then they left me to it. I remember the hollow feeling in my chest as Dad's car disappeared around the bend in the lane, and how reluctant I had been to go back inside and face the empty rooms. I was young and embarking on a career, and knew no one in the area under the age of fifty. Fresh out of university, I was used to having friends on tap. The romance waned with the first rainy day on my own and had vanished altogether by the third. I wanted to be in London.

The Turners, Granny's closest neighbours, had been welcoming and keen to help me settle in, but they were a different generation to me and so woven into country life that they didn't understand where I was coming from. Their sons were still at school at the time, so whenever I went for supper at their house I was treated like an extra teen, not an adult.

Patricia Turner is dead now, the boys have long since flown the nest and James is on his own. Kind, pompous James. I feel guilty for neglecting him. I could have said life got in the way, but it didn't. Leo got in the way.

I would have sold Sparrow Cottage if I hadn't fallen in love with Leo. I'd arranged to meet the estate agent and, at the last minute, Leo had insisted on coming with me and making a day of it with lunch in a country pub and a stroll along the Medway towpath. At that point, early on in our relationship, we couldn't bear to be parted from one another.

He had walked into the cottage and started to explore while I picked up the post and opened the windows to air the rooms. When the estate agent arrived, Leo hovered close by, his hands in his pockets, glowering. The agent gave me an estimate then and there, for thirty thousand pounds, but when he left Leo grabbed me and whirled me round until I was giddy and fell against him.

'Don't sell this place, Jenny.'

I'd argued, but Leo was the man with the words. He persuaded me to hang on to it and in return I lived in his grotty flat in Streatham rent-free until my earnings outstripped his. Our life fell into a pattern that has worked, despite the dire predictions of friends and the disapproval of my family, for twenty-five years.

I hold the key in the palm of my hand. It's been a long time since I last used it.

I reach the cottage sometime after two. James wasn't exaggerating. The property has been neglected. I'm more exasperated than angry as I survey the overgrown garden. Why can't Leo employ a gardener? It wouldn't cost much.

It isn't about the money with Leo, though. I've spoiled him by dealing with everything to do with Albert Square Gardens: all the boring bits of admin, all the renovations and ongoing maintenance. He hasn't been obliged to exert himself or worry about anything except his writing. In London, as far as he's concerned, things happen as if by magic: workmen turn up, elderly washing machines and fridges get replaced, fresh bedlinen appears on the bed, and his shirts reappear on their hangers perfectly ironed.

The paintwork is flaking on the cottage's front door, a used and grubby cable tie has found a home in a corner of the unswept porch, and spiders have spun webs around the carriage light. Great. My house-proud grandmother would turn in her grave. If I do decide to sell, it'll need an overhaul before I allow an estate agent anywhere near it.

I sigh and let myself in. As I cross the threshold, a wave of nostalgia throws me straight back to my childhood. I see myself running in from the rain with Kate, eating teacakes toasted over the fire and spread with melting butter and syrupy plum jam, Dad outside chopping firewood, Mum and Granny gossiping in the kitchen. Only the smell is different: Leo's coffee rather than tea and toast. I switch on the kettle and drop a teabag into a stained mug. Beneath the coffee aroma is a faint smell of burnt plastic. I'm actually quite shocked at the state of the place. I had no idea Leo was still capable of living like a student, but evidently he is.

While I'm waiting for the kettle to boil I wander into the sitting room. It's smaller than I remember and the ceiling, with its blackened and split beams, is lower. Leo has altered little beyond moving the position of the sofa. Perhaps it would have been easier if he had changed everything, because I feel a cool stream of envy flowing through my veins. I could have used this place as a country retreat. Instead, I bowed to pressure and put his needs before mine. And for what? So that he can bring his women here?

But perhaps I've misjudged him. So far I've seen no evidence of a woman's touch. Quite the opposite, in fact.

Only one of the sofa cushions is indented. That's interesting, but not proof of his innocence. I climb the creaky stairs with their threadbare bottle-green carpet and enter the master bedroom, where I'm pleasantly surprised to see Leo has made the bed, although from the slightly musky odour, I deduce he hasn't changed the sheets recently.

I scoop up one of the pillows and press it to my nose. Definitely Leo. The other doesn't smell of anything in particular, never mind a woman's perfume, and there's no incriminating smudge of foundation on the white cotton. I pinch the corner of the duvet and throw it back to inspect the sheet for any evidence of love-making. It's rumpled but there's nothing to indicate anything has gone on.

In fact, there're no obvious signs of a woman's presence; no hairbrush or discarded clothes. Either Leo is paranoid about detection, which I doubt, or he hasn't had a woman in here. My examination of the bathroom proves equally fruitless: no feminine products, no make-up, no women's underwear amongst his boxers in the washing basket. I'm surprised to find I'm more disappointed than relieved. Am I looking for an excuse to air my grievances? Do I want the simmering volcano to erupt? I'm not sure. Perhaps I merely want something to change.

I return to the kitchen, finish making my tea and take it into Leo's study. Amazingly, this room is immaculate, or as immaculate as a room filled with ageing furniture can be. He's even dusted. The small leather sofa is well-used, its sagging upholstery telling of evenings spent ensconced there, reading through his work.

I plant myself at his desk. Aside from the computer, keyboard and mouse mat, there are few distractions; just a notepad covered with barely legible scrawls, a block of Post-it notes and an old jam jar filled with the rollerball pens Leo favours for marking up.

The top drawer contains an unopened pack of pens, a hole punch and stapler, and various items of correspondence. Curious, I shuffle through it. At the bottom of the sheaf is an envelope. It makes the hairs on my neck stand up. On the front, in Leo's masculine handwriting, it reads, *To be opened in the event of my death.* I flip it over to inspect the seal. It's been firmly glued down. From its weight and thickness, I can tell it contains more than one folded sheet of paper.

Strange. Leo and I have written wills and deposited them with our solicitor. Why would he need this separate document? And it's such a melodramatic thing to do, as if he has some deathbed confession to make. I'm tempted to steam it open. If I replace it exactly where I found it, Leo won't notice it's been tampered with. I might live to regret it – eavesdroppers rarely hear anything good about themselves, after all – but I can't resist. Having found nothing else of interest, I'm loath to go home empty-handed.

Something else catches my eye. The wastepaper bin is empty except for a balled-up sheet of paper. I'm not sure what prompts me to retrieve it and smooth it out, but I have a strong sense of foreboding, almost as though this is what I've come here for. It's Leo's acknowledgements – for *Still Lives*, presumably.

I read, expecting to see my name. Leo always adds me – he likes me to know that he appreciates the support I give him. And there it is: *my beloved and endlessly patient wife.* He thanks Kirstie and her assistant, then Reuben and the rest of the team at his publisher, and the various people he's interviewed for research purposes. He's added something in pen, between the lines. I blink to clear my blurring vision and read it again, in case I'm mistaken. I am not.

I owe eternal thanks to Tessa Dudley, for her invaluable input.

It's there in black and white. It can't be a coincidence. Tessa Dudley, my client, the woman who insists on coming all the way from Kent to see me when there are bound to be several excellent psychotherapists within a five-mile radius of where she lives, has been thanked by Leo for her help on his novel.

It takes a moment to process this, then the implications hit me. This woman has been stalking me. She's sat in my consulting room and lied about losing her baby in order to manufacture an emotional connection. I feel exposed, stripped of my dignity. What a vile thing to do. How dare she? And why? The only reason that suggests itself is that she's obsessed with him and jealous of me.

Is this why they rowed? Because he discovered what she was up to? Was he in love with her until that moment? He must have been. Either that or he was using her. Why else thank her in his acknowledgements?

Something else occurs to me, and I scrutinize the piece of paper again. How did I miss this? This isn't his handwriting, not even close. Tessa must have written it. My hands feel big and clumsy. What happened? One of them must have discarded it. Leo, I would imagine. No doubt since he ended the relationship, he didn't want her name in the book. Leo, you stupid idiot.

I phone the practice and ask Carys to look up Tessa Dudley's contact details on the database. She hesitates, probably wondering why I might want a client's address, and I kick myself for not having an excuse ready.

'I have a leaflet I meant to give her,' I improvise. 'I thought I'd drop it in the post so she can look at it before our next session.'

333

'Oh.' Another pregnant pause. But Carys is employed to assist me and the other practitioners, so she does her job. 'OK. Here we go. Got a pen?'

'Yup.'

'Tanyard Cottage, Tanyard Lane, ME18 3QL.'

I replace the unopened envelope in the drawer and carefully arrange the other papers, the hole punch and stapler on top of it. The urge to snoop has left me.

In the car, I type Tessa's postcode into the satnav. Sixteen minutes to my destination. What has Leo got himself into? No doubt he slept with her before he realized she had mental-health issues. I'm the idiot. I believed her when she told me she had come to see me to work through her grief. I've been manipulated as cleverly as my husband.

I arrive outside a modest redbrick house and walk up the quarry-tiled path. No one answers my knock. Through the letterbox it's possible to see a narrow hallway leading to a dated kitchen. There's no clue as to the woman who lives here, no familiar belted coat hanging from a hook. I step back and look up at the darkened windows. This is a waste of time. Tessa isn't here.

She's due to have her fourth session with me on Wednesday. I can wait till then – it'll give me time to work out what to do. Right now, I feel destructive. I want to go home, stuff Leo's clothes into black plastic sacks and chuck them out into the street.

Leo is the first man I slept with, and would have been the only man if it hadn't been for my one-night stand. Apart from that aberration, I've never needed or desired anyone else but Leo. It hurts to think I'm not enough for him. I don't know what to do, how to react. I could follow my instinct, get angry and risk the destruction of my marriage; I could say nothing and fume silently; or I could have a reasonable discussion with him.

I just want to be content, that's all. I don't need the ups and downs of a volatile relationship; I need to feel safe and loved. This throws all my assumptions about Leo in the air and I don't know what to think. Maybe he craves drama in his life. It certainly looks as if he's found some.

One thing I do know, though: I'll fight for him. No one is walking off into the sunset with my husband.

I pull up at a set of traffic lights. I can't make up my mind. I still suspect he is or has been sleeping with Tessa, but if so, he must be unaware of the malignant side to her character. And, if I'm logical about it, there are other possible scenarios. What James saw could be interpreted differently: Tessa might have been running from the house because she had ended the relationship. Leo wouldn't have liked that. He might have lost his temper.

I picture him touching her and grimace with distaste. It doesn't feel right. Leo likes to be with people who make him look good. So if they aren't lovers, why has she been at the cottage? And how has she helped my husband with his book?

A car toots impatiently. The lights have switched to green without me noticing. I raise my hand in apology and accelerate away.

By the time I reach home I've calmed down and my head is clear. I'll keep my thoughts to myself until I've tested my theories. There's a chance I've misread the situation, isn't there? What if there never was an affair? What if Leo is being stalked by Tessa? What if he's done his best to reason with her, even to help her, and she's become worse, spiralling out of control? Thank God I never discuss my clients with him.

53

Leo

DOWNSTAIRS, THE FRONT DOOR SLAMMED SHUT, WAKing Leo. He turned his head then lifted himself up on his elbow so that he could see the face of the digital clock hidden behind the doorstop of a book Jenny was reading. Nine fifteen. It must have been Bella. Jenny would have left by now, and anyway, she would have shut the door quietly. It would never occur to his niece to keep the noise down. He had heard her come in at about midnight.

He liked coming home – the smell of his bed, Jenny's toiletries in the bathroom – but yesterday had felt different. Jenny's greeting hadn't been quite warm enough. And they hadn't had sex. Jenny had said, 'You must be exhausted, why don't you get an early night?' She had wanted to catch up on some work. He hadn't argued, but had gone to bed feeling uneasy. And now she had gone off to work without even bringing him a cup of tea. He flopped back down and sighed.

The thought of sex reminded him unpleasantly of

what he had done. What had he been thinking? He felt a frisson as he recalled the clumsy, almost painful wrangling between him and Zoe. He hadn't realized it at the time, or if he had, he'd either ignored or stifled the voice, but the tension between them had been there almost from the beginning. She was like a young Jenny: coltish, unaware of her allure, sweet. It was that hug that had changed everything.

He had a mental picture of her hair strewn out across the dirty mattress, tangled in his fingers, the 'oh' of her mouth as she moaned; the sense-stirring scent of her skin mingling with the damp mustiness of the room; a reminder that she was in his power. Her fingers, little claws digging into his back. He felt himself grow hard. Shit, he was a mess.

It had been a mistake and it wouldn't happen again. Having sex with her had nullified the promise he had made to keep her safe. If she had been a one-night stand they both could have walked away, but she was there, a constant reminder, a ticking time bomb.

Men made mistakes when they became sexually obsessed with women, something that had been a strong theme running through at least two of his books. Sleeping with her had created yet another winding, screwed-up path down which his mind didn't want to travel.

Christ, what if she had got away? It didn't bear thinking about.

Did Zoe think things were going to be different? That he would become her lover and she would be able to wind him round her little finger? He thought not. He had extinguished that small flame of hope the last time he saw her.

338

His time spent away from both women had been liberating, as though a huge weight had been lifted simply by being on a different continent with different people. With sunshine, blue skies and good food. Perhaps he would move there alone, become a screenwriter. Throw his troubles to the winds. He could forget his past mistakes and start afresh. He grimaced. He could forget what he did just before he left the cottage on Friday morning.

He felt bad about missing Sophie's eighteenth, but if he'd been here, Jenny would have wanted to talk, and he didn't want to talk any more. From that point of view as well, the trip had been a godsend, forcing them out of that annual rut, into doing something different.

Unfortunately, Jenny would always be stuck in March 1989, at five in the morning, waking up in a hospital bed seconds before realizing her baby was gone. Those last precious moments when life was still normal. He had done this to her, and, of course, he would always regret it, but he also felt there should be a statute of limitations on regret and guilt. This film would give him a reason to move on. Jenny even seemed to expect him to. A new life in America? Yes, he could see that.

He rubbed his eyes. Bloody pipe dreams taunting him. It was all impossible while he had the millstone of Zoe around his neck. One second later or earlier – that's all it would have taken – and he wouldn't have hit that girl in the road. One fucking second. Why him? He should have driven Hannah straight to the hospital. He should have allowed due process to take its course. It would have been over and done with then. He would have been punished and it would have been over and done with. Perhaps he would have written a novel in prison.

He groaned. He should get his act together. He was meeting Kirstie today and she would be expecting him to be his usual urbane and amusing self. She would want to hear about the meetings in LA, eager for every morsel, when he felt as if he'd just crawled out of a sleeping bag in a field on a camping trip with his father.

He tore himself away from the bed and went into the bathroom. He turned on the shower and stood under the jet for a long time, thinking. He loved his wife. He squirted shampoo into the palm of his hand and rubbed it into his hair, squeezing his eyes shut as he rinsed it. He did love Jenny.

It was hard to fathom how he felt about Zoe. Since those early, difficult weeks, they'd settled into a routine. He came and went, and after a while he had stopped thinking about her when he was in London. She was part of what happened when he was down at Sparrow Cottage.

He turned off the shower and towelled himself dry. When the mist cleared from the mirror, he saw a middle-aged man with salt-and-pepper hair, strong-featured, striking. 'Old', Zoe had called him. He pasted shaving cream over his jaw and picked up his razor.

He never should have allowed her to become emotionally reliant on him. But what could he do? He wasn't a monster. He was as aware as the next man that food and water weren't enough. She needed human interaction.

He'd had time to think while he was away, and the

conclusion he kept reaching was that this situation had to end. Various solutions had presented themselves, none of them satisfactory. He could persuade Jenny to join him on a three-month research trip to some far-flung country during which time Zoe would quietly fade away. The sadness this engendered in him surprised him in its intensity.

The other possibility was to spirit Zoe out of the country with enough money to start a new life. But even if he could manage that, which was debatable, could he trust her? She would swear that he could, but deep down he was convinced she would sell him out to the highest bidder.

So he was going to have to kill her. He looked at his hands and shuddered. It would have to be a long-distance death, one where he could pretend it wasn't happening. He could dispose of the body before Jenny put the cottage on the market. He'd have to. Those surveyors stuck their noses everywhere.

The important thing was to make sure nothing linked him to Zoe or Hannah. He crouched down and pulled out the shoebox, took off the lid and sighed with relief. He hadn't realized until his heart rate slowed, but he'd had a pinprick of anxiety that the book wouldn't be there, that Jenny had found it and was biding her time. He opened it, tore out the flyleaf and moved through to the bathroom. There, he ripped the page into little pieces and flushed them down the loo. He'd get rid of the book too, but that wasn't so urgent. Maybe he'd just leave it somewhere. On a park bench, perhaps.

* * *

Leo pocketed his wallet and reading glasses and scooped up the change from the sideboard. He went to the bowl where he and Jenny kept their keys but his weren't there. He could have sworn that was where he'd put them when he came in last night.

What the hell had he done with them? He glanced at his watch; he was going to be late if he didn't get a move on. He knew from old that there was nothing more guaranteed to piss off his agent than unpunctuality. Mind you, he was about to make her a lot of money, so she would have to forgive him. He had left them in the bowl, he knew he had. Jenny must have used them and failed to put them back.

Downstairs, after another scout around, Leo called Jenny at work. The receptionist told her she was with a client, so he explained what had happened.

After a few seconds, she came back on the line. 'She says she's really sorry, Leo. She put them in her bag by mistake. What do you want to do? Shall I send a courier?'

'No, I need to get going. I'll come and pick them up.'

He glanced at his watch. He would take a taxi to the practice, then get the tube the rest of the way.

54

Jenny

I CLOSE THE DOOR AND SIT BACK DOWN, FOLDING MY hands on my lap. Leo is on his way. There is no going back.

'Sorry about that. My husband had an emergency.'

'Don't worry.'

Tessa waits for me to settle myself. She has an unusual quality; a face that can light up momentarily and transform, but is otherwise a blank canvas. I ask myself what might have attracted my charismatic husband to her. There's nothing about this plain woman, with her flat shoes and old-fashioned shirt and skirt, that could make me feel threatened. I don't understand how James Turner could have mistaken her for me.

'You were telling me about your sister?' I say. 'You told me she gave you her old baby things. Did you try to get in touch with her after that?'

'No. I didn't want to push her. I thought she would come and see me when the time was right. And I was ashamed.'

'About your baby dying?'

'Yes.'

She goes silent, and I wait. Outside, the sun is shining. A bus goes by.

'I know this is a difficult time of year for you,' she says at last.

'Tessa . . .'

'Are you OK?'

If everything she's told me so far has been a lie, and she's used the kidnapping of my baby to forge a relationship between us, then the question is outrageous. Anger congeals inside me. It's the concerned voice, the emphasis on the *you*, the deliberate attempt to switch roles.

I mirror her body language, wrapping my arms across my chest. She thinks I'm going to talk about my own child, but I decide to make the most of the opportunity to catch her off-guard.

'Not good,' I say.

'I understand,' Tessa responds.

'No . . . No, you don't. I've found out my husband is having an affair.'

Her mouth drops open. 'I'm so sorry.'

I shrug off her commiserations. 'I'm the one who should apologize. I shouldn't have said that. Tell me about Deborah. How close were you when you were younger?'

She hesitates. I imagine she's trying to read between the lines. Does she think she has a rival, or that I'm on to her?

She speaks so quietly I don't hear what she says and have to lean in.

'I'm sorry, Tessa, could you repeat that?'

344

'I don't want to talk about Deborah.'

'We can talk about whatever you like. This is your space.'

'I've been thinking that maybe it was a good thing Abigail died, because I might have treated her in the same way my parents treated me. I mightn't have been able to help it.'

It's all lies, but I play along.

'You don't know that. We've talked about letting go of your anger, and I know you've tried to forgive your family—'

'I have forgiven them.'

'I'm not sure that's true. There's still anger there, only you've deflected it towards yourself instead. Try to describe how you feel, deep down inside you. Think about unlocking those last doors. There's no hurry – you can take as long as you like – but don't lie to me, Tessa, because I'll know.'

I couldn't resist. Her eyes flicker, and I sit back to give her the impression I have all the time in the world.

The session is almost at an end. If Leo doesn't appear soon, all this planning and angst will have been for nothing. Frankly, it would be a relief. I'm already regretting it.

'I haven't asked this before, and you haven't talked about it, but has there been anyone else in your life since the man who fathered your baby?'

Am I imagining it or does her expression close?

'No,' she says. 'I haven't met anyone.'

'And why do you think that might be?'

345

She looks surprised by the question. 'I'm not interested in a relationship.'

'Tell me why you feel that way.'

I flick my gaze up to the clock. Six minutes to the end of the session, and then Tessa will be gone. I feel able to breathe. He isn't coming, or if he is, it seems likely he'll miss her.

Tessa presses her thumbnail into the soft space between the thumb and forefinger of her other hand. It's something she does frequently. I don't think she's aware of it. I wait, imagining the second hand revolving slowly, counting down. Tick tock.

'I suppose I think they'll see through me,' she says at last.

'And what will they see?'

'I'm not sure.'

'I think you do know. I promise you, if you talk about it, it won't feel so awful.'

'I've done bad things,' she says, gazing straight at me.

There's a glow in her eyes and it's painful to look at her. Her voice is full of conviction.

'I've stolen and I have hurt people. I can't love another person when I feel so unlovable myself. I don't deserve it.'

Now that's a surprise. I adjust my reading of her. Is she about to own up to sleeping with Leo? Feeling a little shaken, I make my voice soft.

'Whatever you've done, it's in the past.'

Did you try to steal my husband? Did you lie to me and stalk me?

'You're allowed a second chance,' I continue.

346

Two minutes until eleven fifty. I'm alert to every sound, my body primed. There's a click and bump. The outside door opening and closing.

My stomach flips. What have I done? It's like poking a tiger with a stick.

I could stop this. I could take his keys out of my bag and pass them through the door. He need never know Tessa was here. One minute to go. Tessa is still speaking. My hands are on my lap, one covering the other. Anyone watching me would be forgiven for thinking I'm engrossed in what she's saying, when the truth is I don't take in a word.

'Jenny.' Tessa says my name sharply.

'Sorry.'

'Why do you think your husband has been unfaithful?'

I put on my stern face.

'I'm very sorry, Tessa. I shouldn't have said that. It slipped out because I had a tough few days. Now,' I say, sitting forward, as if I'm about to stand, so that she understands our session is at an end. 'Can I leave you with one thought?'

She nods. I search her eyes for the truth. I want to say, 'Did you really lose your baby?' If she didn't, then how much must she hate me to come here every week. I can't help her with that.

'I want you to try to see your grief as a dear friend. That friend has accepted a job abroad and is going to move her life there. She will keep in touch with an email from time to time, maybe even visit once in a blue moon. But you'll learn to live without her.'

I see it then, the raw grief, and instantly regret the

trite metaphor. Whatever she's doing, and for whatever reason she's here, she isn't faking it.

'Tessa.' I'm so terrified of what I've put in motion that I try to delay the moment of truth. 'Of course you can book more sessions if you want, but I think it might be time to find someone closer to home.'

'Yes.' She appears to be thinking. 'You're probably right. I wish you well. And I'm sorry.'

'For what?'

But she's already moved towards the door.

Leo's keys are in my bag where I dropped them this morning. There was no guarantee that it would work, but it has, and now I wish I hadn't interfered. I stand to one side and she walks out ahead of me. What have I started?

55

Leo

'OH, HERE SHE IS,' THE RECEPTIONIST SAID, GLANCING over his shoulder.

Leo had been trying to remember her name. Carrie? Something like that. He turned and saw Jenny walk out of the room behind her client. At first his brain didn't make the connection, then he felt like someone had punched him in the gut. He almost swore.

'Goodbye, Tessa,' Jenny said. 'Safe journey home.'

Jenny didn't acknowledge Leo immediately, but Leo wouldn't have noticed if she had. His gaze was fixed on Hannah, who was staring at him, her face grey with shock. If he had been taken by surprise, then so had she.

Why had Jenny called her Tessa? A wisp of memory fluttered in the back of his mind but he couldn't pin it down. And now Hannah had left, rushing out of the building so abruptly that Jenny stared after her, her eyebrows raised.

Jenny held out her hand, dangling his keys from her

fingers. Her eyes were bright, but it was the brightness of a sharpened knife.

'I'm so sorry, darling,' she said. 'I was in such a rush this morning I grabbed both sets by mistake.'

Did she? he wondered. Or was this a trap? Of course it was. Somewhere along the line he must have slipped up, but there was no time to go into that now. He took the keys out of her hand, threw them into the air and caught them with a nonchalance he was far from feeling.

'Don't worry about it. Listen, I've got to go or I'll be late for Kirstie. Nice talking to you, Carrie.'

'Carys,' Carys corrected, oblivious to the highly charged atmosphere. 'But everyone gets it wrong.'

He had to get out of there. He thought he was going to have a heart attack.

Jenny was talking to him, but he could barely make out what she was saying above the sound of blood rushing in his ears. He tried to analyse her expression, but she was giving nothing away. He wanted to demand answers, but he couldn't, not in front of the receptionist and the waiting client, and not until he had spoken to Hannah and found out what the hell this meant.

He ran down the steps into the street and looked up and down St George's Road, spotting her heading in the direction of Elephant and Castle, her open coat flapping, the unbuckled belt fluttering at her sides like kite ribbons. She was already halfway to the end of the road.

He set off after her, his long strides eating up the gap between them. She barely looked as she crossed the side streets. From the way her shoulders were twitching and her hands were moving, he suspected she might be talking to herself.

How long had Hannah been seeing Jenny? What had she told her? Jenny must have guessed something, or she wouldn't have contrived the meeting. He hadn't imagined the challenge in her eyes as she handed him the keys. She knew something. But what exactly? And how had she found out? He could understand Hannah stalking Jenny to get at him in some oblique way, but she'd been as shocked to see him standing there as he had her, so he didn't think she had told Jenny anything.

So Jenny had found out some other way. Was it something he had done?

The book. He hadn't hidden it very well, but Jenny had never been the curious type. She must have come across it and decided to trick him into an admission rather than just asking him. He had called out Zoe's name in his sleep, and Jenny must have sensed that he was lying when he'd passed it off as a character's name in his novel. He had underestimated her.

Tessa. Now he remembered. Tessa had been the name Zoe had used when she had thanked herself in the acknowledgements. Tessa something. But even that made no sense because how could Jenny have connected him or Zoe with Tessa Dudley? Hannah must have dropped hints in her sessions; maybe even mentioned Zoe. Yes, that must be it. Jenny would have picked up on that. His wife had been busy.

If he wasn't careful this was going to turn into a shitstorm, with him at the centre.

He sped along the pavement, galvanized by dread. He was not looking forward to the conversation he and Jenny would be having later. He would have to bluff and tell her that Hannah was a deluded nymphomaniac who'd been stalking him for weeks. He'd say that he hadn't wanted to worry her. He was confident Hannah hadn't mentioned the babies, because if that had been the case, Jenny wouldn't have played games like she had this morning.

Dudley; that was it. He was going out of his mind. He needed to get to Hannah, to defuse whatever it was she had started, before Jenny worked things out.

At Elephant and Castle his view was blocked by a double-decker, and when it had passed he could no longer see her. He guessed she had gone into the tube station, making it safely into the lift as the doors closed, the back of her head visible through the window panel. He slapped his Oyster card on the reader and clattered down the spiral stairs, his heel slipping on one of the treads. He grabbed the handrail and only just prevented himself from falling on his arse. At the bottom he followed the signs for the Bakerloo Line platform, weaving impatiently through the slower walkers.

It wasn't particularly busy and he easily followed Hannah's progress towards the end, where the crowd thinned out. He passed two elderly women sitting on one of the benches, their hands resting on their knees, and a young man leaning against the wall beside them. A group of tourists was studying a tube map.

Hannah had stopped close to the edge of the platform, her bag held tightly under her right arm, her left hand gripping the strap. Leo glanced up at the display board as he approached her. The next train was due in two minutes. He would get on it if she did.

Reaching Hannah's side, he could feel the tension pulse from her.

56

Hannah

HANNAH STUDIED THE ADVERT ON THE OTHER SIDE OF the tracks. It was for Cunard cruises and featured an enormous cruise liner against a backdrop of the Norwegian fjords. In one of the corners, a young couple drank champagne under an improbably starry night sky.

'I found the book in your house,' she said.

'What book?'

Leo removed his glasses and wiped them with a cloth he took from his pocket. From that little tell, she inferred that he knew exactly what she was talking about.

'The one you signed for my daughter.'

'Even if that's true, it doesn't make you any less guilty.'

She gazed at him steadily. 'I don't care what happens to me.'

He laughed. 'Of course you do.'

She was so scared and high on adrenalin that she was trembling. She wondered if he could tell; if he could smell her fear. But it was too late now. She had made her decision.

'I will be going to the police and I'll be making a statement. Once I've told my story, they'll arrest you. The only way you can make this any better for yourself is to tell me where Zoe is. They might not come down so hard on you.'

'You don't get to threaten me,' he snarled. 'You mealy-mouthed little nobody.'

'It's your choice what happens next,' she said, lifting her chin. 'But I'm not leaving you alone until I know where my daughter is.'

Leo seemed to grow taller, his shoulders expanding as he brought his face close to hers.

'For fuck's sake, you stupid cow. Why couldn't you leave me alone? Your daughter is dead, she's been dead for two years. I killed her when she came to my house in two thousand and five.'

Hannah recoiled and Leo turned on his heel, striding off down the platform. Dazed, she watched him go before running after him in a burst of fury. Before she could question what she was doing, she shoved him so hard that he was flung off the platform and on to the tracks.

Time slowed down. His body was suddenly and terribly illuminated by the lights of the approaching train, her own screams drowned out by the high-pitched shriek of its brakes. She braced to throw herself in front of it, but someone roared, 'Don't!' and she hesitated.

It was enough. She was grabbed by the arms and

thrown back. She landed on the cold concrete floor, bruising her shoulder and hip. Strangers pulled her up, dragged her along the platform and pushed her down on to a bench. People were screaming, chaos erupted and somewhere an alarm rang. A crowd gathered. This was the end. It was too late for her. All too late.

Too late for Zoe. Too late for Leo.

PART 4

57

Jenny

I CAN BARELY REMEMBER THE LAST FEW HOURS, JUST that moment when Carys interrupted my session to tell me the police were here. After that, the images are blurred. I hear the words 'I'm afraid your husband is dead, Mrs Creasey' over and over again, and feel that terrible sinking sensation.

I suppose I answered their questions. I can't remember what they asked, or even when they left. I remember Carys bringing in a cup of sweet tea, which I didn't drink. I don't remember the taxi journey to Albert Square Gardens, but I do remember the jarring unfamiliarity of the house when I walked through the front door. It was as though I'd stepped into a universe where everything was the same, and yet it wasn't.

I touched my belongings to try to find that sense of being home, but nothing spoke to me. I should have taken Carys up on her offer to come back with me, but I instinctively said, 'No. You get off. I'll be fine.' She has a long commute and a family waiting for her. It wouldn't have been fair. To the police I said, 'I'll be all right.' Of course I did.

I phone Kate from the kitchen. Chris answers. She's gone to pick up Bella from the station. I'd forgotten my niece had been leaving today. So much has happened.

'I'll get her to call you,' he says. 'You sound odd. Is there something wrong?'

'No. I'm fine.'

What a strange thing to say, I think as I set the phone down on the table beside me and put my head in my hands.

How can Leo be dead? It's all my fault. If I hadn't meddled, if I'd considered things more carefully before I tricked him and Tessa into meeting, he would still be alive. I could simply have asked him to tell me the truth. Why did I feel the need to play games?

It transpires Tessa Dudley isn't her real name. Her name is Hannah Faulkner and she's a care-home manager from Maidstone. It makes no sense. The police haven't found any obvious connection between her and my husband, but they're confident it's only a matter of time before something emerges. She hasn't spoken yet, they told me. She's in shock. She isn't the only one.

I thought she and Leo might have been having an affair. I thought if I brought them together, they would be unable to hide the truth. It never occurred to me she could be violent. What have I done, allowing her into my life? I'm her therapist. If anyone knew about her state of mind, I did. How could I have been so blind?

I assumed her fragility was an act, that she had set up the appointments to get close to me because she was jealous. I thought it was some warped plot to drive a wedge between us. The police can't accuse me of anything criminal, can they? Just unprofessional behaviour.

I don't care what happens to me at this stage, though. It's Leo I care about. He was so happy, happier than I've seen him in ages; excited about the film deal and enjoying life. Now, because of me, he'll never get to see *In the Lake* on the big screen. It would have been the crowning moment of an illustrious career. Whatever he's done, I find it unbearable that he'll miss that. I wonder if it'll even get made now. Poor Leo.

The phone rings, and it's a relief to have my thoughts interrupted. It'll be Kate.

But it isn't. The voice belongs to a man.

'Mrs Creasey, my name is Detective Inspector Braithwaite. I'm in charge of your husband's case. I'm very sorry for your loss.'

'Thank you.'

'Do you have a moment?'

I quickly dry my tears. 'Um . . . yes. What do you need? I gave a statement earlier.'

'I know, and I'm sorry to disturb you again. You're aware that we have a woman by the name of Hannah Faulkner in custody?'

'Yes.'

'The thing is, Mrs Creasey, Ms Faulkner has asked for you. She's refusing to talk to anyone else, but she's said that if you'll come, she'll tell you what happened. I know it might seem odd, but we need to hear her side of the story while it's still fresh in her mind. May I send a car for you?'

I doubt I have a choice. 'Yes. That would be fine.' There's that word again. The most inappropriate word in my vocabulary.

He tells me someone will be outside my door in ten minutes and hangs up.

I badly want to phone Mum and tell her everything. I want to have her comfort me and offer practical suggestions, but those days are gone. Even if she happens to be lucid today, she wouldn't understand.

DI Braithwaite possesses an air of gruff competence. He's tall, broad-shouldered and square-jawed, with jet-black hair and blue eyes. He doesn't waste time in collecting me from reception and showing me straight into the interview room where Tessa is already sitting. But I should try to remember: her name is Hannah.

She looks lonely and frightened as I take my place opposite her, her eyes meeting mine for an instant before sliding away. This is the woman who inveigled her way into my life, who stalked me and murdered my husband in a seemingly unprovoked attack. She's a plain creature, but you don't have to stand out in a crowd to be dangerous.

Is it that conflict that attracted Leo to her? Is that why our lives collided?

The detective switches on the tape recorder and shunts his chair back a few inches to make it clear he isn't part of the conversation. I wait in silence for Hannah to start. I don't feel the need to be polite.

'I'm sorry,' she says. 'I didn't mean to kill him, but he went too far.'

The expression on her face expects a response from

362

me, but I pick up my plastic cup of water and take a sip, my eyes trained on hers.

'This is about Zoe,' she says after a false start.

I frown. 'Who?'

'Zoe is . . . was my daughter.'

'You told me your daughter was called Abigail.'

'That wasn't her real name.'

'You said she died a cot death. Was that a lie too?'

Hannah brings her hands on to the table, placing them flat, palms down, as though she's bracing herself.

'Yes. Zoe was sixteen when she died and it was your husband who killed her.'

I choke on my water and wipe my mouth with the tissue Braithwaite passes me. 'That's a lie. Leo has never killed anyone. He couldn't.'

'Mrs Creasey, perhaps you could let Ms Faulkner explain,' Braithwaite says.

Hannah hesitates. I have a feeling that whatever she says now will shatter everything I thought I knew about my life with Leo.

'This morning, after I left you,' Hannah begins, 'Leo followed me down to the platform at Elephant and Castle station. I told him I had evidence to prove he had abducted Zoe.'

This is not real. I've stepped into a nightmare. 'What evidence?'

Hannah's eyes dare me to lose my cool. 'I found a book with a handwritten dedication to Zoe in a box in your house.'

'Sparrow Cottage?' I say. That makes some kind of sense at least.

'No. The London house. I stole your keys from your bag and broke in.'

'I don't believe you.'

She shrugs. 'Remember when I spilled the tea?'

'Can we back up a bit?' Braithwaite says, looking confused. 'You're accusing Leo Creasey of the abduction of your teenage daughter?'

'Yes.' She takes a long, deep breath. 'Zoe has been missing for two years.'

I frown. 'You must have the wrong man.'

'When did you report this?' Braithwaite asks.

'I didn't,' Hannah says. 'If I'd reported it, the police would have wanted her DNA.'

I lean on the table and put my head in my hands. 'I don't understand.'

But as soon as the words leave my mouth, I remember Leo saying the name Zoe in his sleep when he was ill. I haven't eaten anything apart from a biscuit since breakfast and I feel queasy.

'I don't think you knew your husband very well,' Hannah says. 'He had a lot to hide.'

'But why did you kill him? Did he know things about you? You lied to me about who you were. What other lies have you told?'

She gives me a pitying look. It's as if she's already made the journey and is waiting for me to catch up.

'Leo and I were in the same boat,' she continues. 'I threatened to go to the police. I said I didn't care what happened to me. I was ready to take my share of the blame.'

'The blame for what?'

She gives me an appraising look. 'For a different crime.'

Braithwaite shifts in his chair.

'I tried one more time to persuade him to tell me where Zoe was. He lost his temper and told me that he had killed her in two thousand and five. She's been dead all along. I didn't know what I was doing, I just reacted.'

This has something to do with Sophie. I can feel it in every screaming molecule of my being. I forget all about not putting pressure on her and the questions spill from my mouth.

'Why should I believe you when you've been lying to me for weeks? Why would Leo have killed your daughter? It doesn't make any sense. How did you meet him?'

Tessa stiffens. *Hannah*, I remind myself. Hannah.

Braithwaite mutters a quiet warning. 'Calm down, Mrs Creasey, or I'll have to end the interview.'

I can't calm down.

Hannah's lashes glitter with tears. She glances at the detective but, getting nothing from him, locks her eyes with mine. Her gaze is fierce.

'My baby was born on the eighth of March nineteen eighty-nine.'

As she struggles with herself a shrill, scared voice hisses in my ear. *Here it comes.*

'She died two days later on the tenth of March.'

My stomach churns. 'Did you steal my baby?'

She looks petrified.

I jump up and lean over the table, shouting at her. 'Did you steal my baby?'

'Mrs Creasey!' Braithwaite booms, leaping to his feet.

He grabs me by the shoulders and pushes me down. 'I'm going to pause the interview here. We can pick it up again later.'

'No,' I say. 'I want to know everything now.'

'Mrs Creasey . . .'

'It's all right,' Hannah says. 'I'm OK to carry on.'

'Ms Faulkner, are you sure you wouldn't prefer to wait until there's a lawyer present?'

I bristle with anger. Why should this woman be treated like she's a fragile flower when the detective has just yelled at me?

'Tell me the truth,' I say. 'You owe me that.'

Hannah holds my gaze then turns to Braithwaite. 'I don't need a lawyer.' She takes a long breath. 'I stole Sophie and I was helped by your husband. I called her Zoe and brought her up as mine.'

The truth takes a moment to sink in, but when it does I slide off the chair and sink to my knees. If Zoe Faulkner is dead, then Sophie is too, and Leo murdered them . . . murdered her.

58

Hannah

HANNAH WATCHED AS HER WORDS SANK IN. SHE FELT cold and numb. She'd had nightmares about this moment for years. It hadn't been like lancing a boil; it had been much worse. She had destroyed an innocent woman, killed her hope and stolen her reason for living. She would go to prison for a long time. Leo had had a lucky escape, in her view. She had done him a favour. At some point she supposed she would feel remorse, but for the moment there was nothing, not even relief.

Leo and Zoe were dead. Without the hope of seeing her daughter again or the idea of punishing Leo to sustain her, there was nothing much in her life, just a job and a roof over her head. Looking at it that way, prison didn't seem such a bad option.

It surprised her that she could kill, that she had felt enough passion to lash out like that. It had been the final flash of light and colour before she faded away. Because she would fade. No one would remember her.

'Do you need a doctor?' Braithwaite asked Jenny as he helped her back on to the chair.

Jenny shook her head. She directed her gaze at Hannah. 'How could you?'

'I don't know. I was desperate.' She explained about the crash. 'Leo came out of nowhere. He'd been drinking and I was out of my mind. It just happened. I convinced him that he'd killed my child when he hit us. He said you'd had a baby but he didn't want it.'

Hannah saw the flash of hurt in Jenny's eyes. She wished Braithwaite would take her away and lock her up so that she didn't have to look at her any more.

'You took my baby,' Jenny hissed. 'That kind of thing doesn't "just happen". You weren't Leo's passive victim, you went ahead and did it because I had something you wanted and you put yourself first.'

Hannah fiddled with the cuff of her sleeve. 'Leo was too stricken with shock to realize that my baby was already dead. But he took Zoe from me when she came looking for him, and he didn't give her back to you because he was too much of a coward. I lost everything.'

'Don't pretend that you lost more than me when you had my daughter for sixteen years. You saw her grow up. You took that from me.'

Hannah held Jenny's gaze. She made herself do it; partly as punishment, partly to prove to herself that she was capable of honesty. The silence in the room stretched, until Braithwaite coughed. Hannah took a sip of water.

'How did you find out I knew Leo?' she asked.

The look Jenny gave her was one of utter contempt. 'What does that matter now?'

'Please. I need to know.'

Jenny sighed. 'I found a piece of writing in the cottage with the name Tessa Dudley on it.'

'But that's . . .' Hannah felt a flicker of hope. 'What piece of writing?'

'The draft acknowledgements for Leo's new book. He thanked you. I mean, he thanked Tessa Dudley. And since you're the same person . . .' Jenny turned to Braithwaite. 'Please can I go now?'

'You were at the cottage?' Braithwaite asks. 'When was this?'

'Last Friday.'

'Wait,' Hannah said, leaning forward eagerly. 'Tessa Dudley was part of a game we used to play when Zoe was little. It's a message from her. Leo lied.' Her voice rose. 'She can't have died two years ago if she wrote that. There's a chance he's been hiding her all this time.'

Jenny's hands flew to her mouth. 'The cottage. She must be there.'

She turned frantically to Braithwaite, but the detective had already opened the door and was calling for a colleague.

'Take me too,' Hannah pleaded, scraping back her chair. 'Please. I'm her mother.'

Jenny turned to regard her. 'No, you're not.'

'But I'm the only mother she knows. You have to take me. She's going to be confused, she'll want me. I know I've done a terrible thing and I know I have to pay for it, but at least let me be there when you find her. Please, I can't stay here.' Her voice became a wail. 'Zoe will need me. She doesn't know you.'

'She has a point, Mrs Creasey,' Braithwaite said. 'We don't know what kind of state we'll find Sophie in, if we find her. It might be just as well to have Ms Faulkner with us.'

Hannah sat in the back of the car with a constable who looked all of seventeen, while Jenny rode in the front. She felt curiously calm. Leo had paid the ultimate price for his crime, and Hannah would be judged and made to pay for hers. In her mind, she already had – many times over – and prison couldn't really be worse than what she'd been through. If she pleaded guilty, then presumably there would be no need for a trial. She almost looked forward to her cell, the monotonous regularity of her days with no decisions to make and, most of all, nothing to hide.

'Why would Leo tell you Sophie was dead?' Jenny asked after they had been driving for about half an hour.

Braithwaite briefly caught her eyes in the rear-view mirror. He was probably hoping that in the intimacy of the car she would talk. He didn't know how badly she wanted it all to be out in the open.

'Because I wouldn't let up. I kept pushing him. He knew I'd been watching him since she went missing, but finding out that I'd tricked my way into seeing you was the final straw. I went too far. He just wanted to say the thing that would hurt me most and he wanted to get me off his back.'

'You should have gone to the police. Why didn't you?'

'I was scared. I would have had to explain that I stole her from you. Leo said I'd be accused of killing my own baby. There had been so much media attention. I knew what would happen to me if the truth got out.'

Jenny twisted round. 'You sacrificed her to save yourself? What kind of mother does that?'

'I was only seventeen.' Hannah's voice cracked. 'I'd grown up in a very sheltered community. I was naive and terrified.'

'Excuses.'

They lapsed into silence. Hannah watched the suburbs glide by. Ordinary people with ordinary lives. How she envied them.

'Leo left a letter,' Jenny said abruptly. 'Oh my God, how could I have forgotten?'

Hannah leaned forward. 'What letter?'

Braithwaite shot Jenny a glance. 'Go on.'

'He'd written "To be opened in the event of my death" on an envelope. It's in his desk drawer. It must be about Sophie.' Jenny strained forward. 'Can't you drive any faster?'

Braithwaite accelerated, switched on the blue lights and gave a quick blast of his siren. The cars ahead pulled over to let them pass. Within minutes they'd hit the motorway and were breaking the speed limit.

No one spoke. Hannah gripped her seatbelt. What would they find? She didn't want to think about that, she just wanted Zoe to be safe and well. Everything else could wait.

'He won't have hurt her.' Jenny's voice cut through the silence. 'Leo wouldn't have hurt her.'

No one responded. Braithwaite's attention on the road

was fierce, and Hannah was too tense to speak. Forty minutes later they turned in to the lane leading to Sparrow Cottage. Hannah craned her neck. She had been here countless times over the last two years, but she'd never seen a fog like the one rising from behind the trees now.

'What's going on up there?' Braithwaite asked, leaning over the steering wheel to peer through the windscreen.

He slowed to a halt and lowered his window. Hannah could smell burning. This was no fog. It was fire. Up ahead, the sky was bathed in orange, and blue lights throbbed through the gaps in the trees and hedgerows.

Braithwaite swore and drove on, and Hannah started to pray, but the cottage was the only house down the lane, apart from the one belonging to the old man, and they'd already passed his. In fact, he was the first person Hannah saw as they sped round the bend. He was watching the firefighters douse the cottage with water while flames belched from the windows. From inside the car, Hannah could feel the heat. The sky was lit with a million sparks, and the sound of crackling was audible even from that distance. Jenny was screaming.

59

Zoe

THIS HAS BEEN A LONG WEEK. I HAVEN'T HAD THE energy or will to do anything except watch films and eat. My life has become so narrow and uneventful that I still daydream like a child. I have no sense of reality, my emotions veer between extremes. I'm up or down, or utterly, catatonically, dangerously bored.

I've thought about killing myself because if this is to be my life, then I'd rather let it go. Leo could live for another thirty years.

I carry on with my diary for Jenny, but the words, which were all there in my head when I woke up this morning, sparkling with precision, kind of seep away. What I write is dull, to me at least. I try to describe what it's like being here, and realize most of what happens is boring. But perhaps it won't be boring to her. I write bits about my childhood, although that's quite boring too. There's the bullying at school, but I don't want this to be one big whinge. I don't want to talk about Leo today either; I'm too confused about him. I tell her a bit about my life with Mum instead.

We didn't have the perfect relationship. Jenny will want to know that. Before school it was one thing; after I started at Maidstone Grammar it was another. School made me look at her with fresh eyes, eyes that were mean and judgemental. Jessie and Becca's eyes. My mum was different, she wore the wrong clothes, thought the wrong things, feared life, feared fun and, most of all, feared her own demons. Just because you leave a religion does not mean you stop believing everything you've been taught from the day you were born. She rejected a lot of it, but, of course, there were aspects she agreed with. She couldn't help it, and those things had a bearing on the way I behaved and the way I was treated.

But she was loving, kind, patient and intelligent. And vulnerable. I want Jenny to know that, because one day she's going to sit in judgement over my mother. It's important that she understands that she wasn't bad. She was just screwed up.

My nose twitches. I smell smoke. A bonfire? Leo lit one once and practically choked me. By the time he came down I could barely breathe. If he'd waited much longer, he would have been greeted by the sight of my dead body. I can still smell it, especially when I'm doing yoga and my face is close to the floor.

I doubt it's Leo, so maybe it's a local farmer burning his fields. I don't think that happens in March, though. Don't they do it at the end of the summer when the crops have been harvested? I think I'd remember if it had happened last year. And also, surely it's a bit late in the day?

Smoke begins to drift through the air vent, grey wisps of it curling upwards, floating on the current of air towards the exhaust flue at the far end of the room. I tear out the sheet of paper I've been writing on and slide it into its hiding place with the others under the rug before looking up at the miasma of smoke swirling around the ceiling. Then the lights go off and I'm plunged into darkness. The fridge and ventilation unit go silent. I wait for my eyes to adjust, forgetting that there's nothing for them to adjust to. The light switch doesn't work when I try it. I reach blindly for the chair, pull it towards me and sit down. It must be a power cut. The electricity will come back on eventually. There's no need to worry.

There's something . . . I don't know what it is, but the silence has been rudely broken. I barely hear a thing down here, just Leo opening the hatch, the occasional rumble of a tractor in the lane. I've become used to the deathly quiet, but now it sounds like there's a battle going on above me. There are a lot of heavy footsteps, thudding and banging, shouting.

Of course. I'm so stupid! The smoke. Leo's house must be on fire. Those are firefighters I can hear. Surely someone will have told him what's going on? He'll come. He wouldn't just leave me, would he?

I pull the chair over to the wall, climb up and yell into the air vent. Even though it isn't working, the smoke is still getting through. I cough as it hits my throat and lungs. When I can't take any more, I get down, crawl over to the bed and curl up underneath the duvet, away from the smoke-filled air. My eyes sting.

They'll put the fire out, then they'll go away. If the cottage has burnt to the ground, what will Leo do? Without it, this might be the thing that makes the difference. I'll be more trouble than I'm worth.

60

Jenny

BRAITHWAITE SWERVES INTO THE VERGE, GETS OUT OF the car and runs towards the cottage. Behind me, on the back seat, the young constable fidgets, itching to be where the action is instead of babysitting a couple of hysterical women. A fire officer approaches Braithwaite. The DI shows him his badge and points towards us. I wonder how he's describing the situation.

Owner's dead. I've got the wife in the car and . . . well . . . a baby-stealing murderess.

I cannot sit here doing nothing. I slide my hand to the clasp of my seatbelt and release it while opening the door at the same time.

'Hey!' the constable shouts as I shoot out and run.

I know he'll hesitate, torn between coming after me and staying to guard Hannah, but Hannah is the criminal. I keep as close to the hedge as the ditch will allow, squeezing between the gate and the fire engine. The noise of the fire and the hoses drowns out the sound of my feet on the gravel, but no one is looking my way. At the front of the house, plumes of water arc above me.

I hurry round the side, through the area where Leo keeps the bins, and into the garden. The back door is ajar, the fire already having been brought under control in the blackened ruins of the kitchen. I step in, sloshing through filthy water, and open the internal door.

The fire is still burning this side of the cottage and smoke billows through the warren of low-ceilinged rooms and up the stairs. 'Sophie!' I scream my daughter's name. Then I scream 'Zoe!', and cough convulsively. Barely able to see three metres in front of me, I scoop up the hem of my coat to create a makeshift mask. My eyes sting so badly I can't keep them open, the muscles surrounding them going into spasm. Eventually I manage to squint through slits.

In Leo's study, flames climb the curtains and feed off the spines of his books. The sofa smoulders, releasing toxic fumes. I try not to breathe but my lungs are bursting. The desk. I make my way through acrid smoke with my coat still over my mouth. A coughing fit consumes me and I grab hold of the back of the chair to steady myself. I pull open the drawer and rummage amongst its contents. There it is.

'Jenny.'

I turn, narrowing my eyes. Through the smoke I can see a figure standing in the doorway. Hannah. I hold up the envelope.

'I've got it.'

'That's good,' she says. 'We've got to get out of here now.'

'You go. I won't be long.'

She takes a step forward. 'What're you doing?'

I follow a wire with my fingers. 'Unplugging his computer. I'm not leaving it.'

'Don't be stupid,' she shouts. 'There's no time for that.'

'No, I have to, or it'll be destroyed. There's his work and evidence . . .'

An explosion of noise makes me look up in horror. Fire pours over the ceiling like liquid, flames dripping to the floor.

'He's dead,' Hannah yells, running forward, her cuffed wrists held up to her chin. 'What does evidence matter now? Come on.'

There's a loud crack, like a gunshot, and I duck as a beam comes down, bringing with it a gust of embers and plaster dust. We're trapped behind it and Hannah's clothes have caught fire. I pull my sleeves down over my hands and throw my arms around her. I can't see a thing. Sparks burn my exposed skin, sharp darts pricking my neck and cheeks. There's a stench of singed hair in my nostrils, but I keep hold of Hannah, clinging to her as if everything in my life depends on saving her. As if she's my last link to Sophie.

We are pulled apart. Two burly arms scoop me up and another firefighter lifts Hannah.

Everything goes black.

The next thing I know, I'm in an ambulance and someone is fitting an oxygen mask over my face. Braithwaite is there, his mouth drawn in a thin line of fury. The constable stands at his side, looking petrified.

'What the hell did you think you were doing?'

I can't answer.

'Do you have it?' Hannah is sitting next to me, a silver blanket around her shoulders.

I look down at my empty hands. I must have dropped it when I blacked out. No one's going to go back in and risk their life for a piece of paper. It's probably ashes by now, anyway.

I shake my head. I failed. She stares at me then looks away.

Is this the end? It can't be. Sophie is alive somewhere. Not here, maybe, but close by. There'll be barns and cellars to search. There'll be sniffer dogs and heat-seeking drones. How much time do we have?

I gaze out at the smoke and the lights, the firefighters and their hoses. The old house was a tinderbox. I should have been firmer, I should have insisted that Leo had the wiring overhauled.

Braithwaite leans into the ambulance. 'Are you badly hurt?'

Hannah doesn't react. I shake my head. I can't feel pain now, but it'll come soon enough.

'Why on earth did you let them get out of the car?' the paramedic demands. 'They could have been killed.'

Braithwaite's forehead creases. He doesn't take kindly to being reprimanded.

The paramedic sighs and turns to Hannah, teasing up her sleeve to reveal angry red welts.

Hannah winces.

'Could you at least unlock this woman's handcuffs so I can make her comfortable?'

'She's in my custody.'

'Not when she's in my ambulance, she isn't. Unlock them now.'

Braithwaite scowls, but he pulls the keys out of his pocket. Hannah holds out her wrists and the cuffs are removed.

'On your head be it if anything happens,' Braithwaite says. 'Mrs Creasey, where do you think you're going?'

I'm half in, half out of the ambulance. 'To look for Sophie.'

'You're staying right here.' He beckons to the constable. 'Don't let them out of your sight this time.'

Braithwaite marches off, his phone pressed to his ear. I glance at Hannah, silently pleading with her to do something. She holds my gaze, then gives me an almost imperceptible nod. Now all I need is to distract the constable.

'I need to pee,' I say. 'Could you take me somewhere, please?'

61

Zoe

I'M COUGHING LIKE CRAZY. IT'S SO VIOLENT I RETCH and a bit of sick scalds my throat. Leo must know what's happening by now, I tell myself. He'll be on his way.

What will he do when he gets here? Perhaps, with everyone's attention on the fire, he'll take a risk and get me out. But I can't see the fire brigade and police not noticing him vanishing into a hole in the garden and reappearing with an eighteen-year-old girl in tow. Of course he won't come for me straight away. Maybe tomorrow, once the fire engines have gone.

Perhaps he's out there, watching his precious cottage burn. I bet he's saved his computer. Perhaps he's thinking this is the answer to his prayers, that the question of what to do about me has been taken out of his hands, the decision made for him. He'll have no reason to come here, so he'll stay away and block any thoughts of me. Out of sight, out of mind. Maybe he'll go abroad and only come back after I'm well and truly dead. It's not much of a stretch to imagine Leo crossing his fingers and hoping the problem will solve itself. I start coughing again, hacking like an old man. Even my saliva tastes of smoke.

Even though the smoke is at its densest just beneath the ceiling, I get back up on the chair and shout into the air vent until I can't breathe and have to go back to bed and pull the duvet over me. The darkness is disorientating; I feel safer lying down.

When I was younger and life was relatively normal, I had dreams. I used to go to the careers office at breaktime and pore over university prospectuses. I'd picture myself in the landscaped grounds of prestigious institutions with a group of attractive, intelligent-looking friends, or in a lecture theatre, my notebook open in front of me, my pen poised. I would have found my tribe there. One of those places would have been my world if I'd never heard of Leo and Jenny Creasey.

One of two things will happen to me: I'll die or someone will find me. But how will they do that if the cottage has burnt down and Leo's letter has gone with it? Someone might chance upon the hatch eventually, but it's unlikely that will happen before the bulldozers move in and demolish the house. Maybe they'll dump a diggerload of rubble on top of the hatch. The new owners will get a shock once they start on the garden. Then again, Leo might be too scared to sell.

My biggest regret about dying is not being able to say the things I want to say to him.

If the smoke doesn't kill me, I have two weeks' worth of food. If I ration it, I can make it last three. Then I remember I don't have a working fridge any more.

If I get out, I promise myself, I will have a brilliant career. If I get out I will try to forgive my mother. If Mum has taught me anything, it's that life isn't worth living if you can't forgive those who've done you harm. I will forgive Jessie and Becca, and all the other girls who treated me like vermin, and I'll forgive my teachers for turning a blind eye. If I get out, I will do my best to forgive Leo. These are promises I make to myself, not to any God. I owe it to myself to fulfil my potential and not let these people, and what they did to me, drag me down. I am worth more.

I'm struck with a horrible thought. The destruction of the house may mean the water pipes no longer work. I fling aside the duvet, make my way to the toilet and turn on the taps. The stream of water dwindles to a trickle, then stops.

'Shit.'

I lean back against the wall and slide down it. This is the end, then. It's not fair. On second thoughts, I'm not even going to try to forgive Leo. He doesn't deserve the enormous mental effort it would take. He can go to hell.

62

Hannah

HANNAH THOUGHT THAT THE CONSTABLE WAS GOING to say no, that he wasn't an idiot and wouldn't make the same mistake twice, getting stuck with one woman while the other made a run for it.

The paramedic gave him an impatient glance.

'Take her behind a tree, for God's sake, man. I'll keep an eye on this lady.'

Hannah waited until the pair were out of sight, then climbed out of the ambulance, ignoring the medic's exasperated shout, and ran into the lane. She wasn't sure what she was going to do, but she spotted Leo's officious neighbour. He was the type that would know if Leo owned any land around here.

His brow knitted when he saw her hurrying towards him. She must have been a frightening sight, her face blackened with soot, her hair and eyebrows singed.

'What're you doing back here?' he demanded.

She swiped her wet hair away from her face. Her throat was seared, but she managed to speak.

'How well did you know Leo?'

'Extremely well. He's a good friend.'

'Well, then, you might be able to help me. He kidnapped my daughter.'

'I beg your pardon?'

'Please, just listen to me. It's going to be public knowledge soon. He took my daughter two years ago, and he's hidden her somewhere. Do you have any idea where that might be? Does he own any other buildings in the area?'

'Are you mad, woman?' he blustered. 'Leo wouldn't do a thing like that.'

'What do you think Jenny and I are doing here? Why do you think the police brought us?'

'The fire—'

'We knew nothing about the fire until we got here. We came to find my daughter.'

The old man looked torn. Hannah waited, shaking, while he mulled over what she'd said. He glanced over her shoulder and, turning, Hannah saw Braithwaite steaming towards them.

'What do you know?' she urged. 'You must have seen something.'

The dog growled a warning, a low rumble at the back of its throat, then barked once.

Braithwaite grabbed Hannah from behind and dragged her back to the car. The pain from her burns was excruciating, and she whimpered in agony. He pushed her inside unceremoniously, and leaned over her to fasten her seatbelt. Then he threw himself into the driver's seat and ground the car into gear.

'I think you've done enough damage,' he said, looking

over his shoulder as he reversed into a three-point turn. 'I should never have brought you.'

A figure emerged from the shadows and slapped the car's bonnet. Braithwaite slammed on the brakes and squinted into the darkness. Leo's neighbour signalled the detective to wind down his window.

'I told him he should get the place rewired,' Turner said, bending to Braithwaite's level. 'Accident waiting to happen.'

'Sir?' Braithwaite said. 'Is that all?'

'Not quite,' he said, leaving a dramatic pause. 'I've thought of something.'

He was breathless, unused to so much excitement.

'Name's James Turner. I knew the family. It's about what she said.' He indicated Hannah. 'About Leo kidnapping a girl.'

'Go on.'

'In the summer of nineteen sixty-nine,' Turner began, 'I was at home before I went to university. I earned money doing odd jobs for Mr and Mrs Prest – the previous owners. To cut a long story short, Edward Prest paid me to dig. It was bloody hard work, but I was a strong lad.'

'What did you dig?'

'A bunker. There was already a bomb shelter there, so it was just a matter of extending it. Prest was convinced we were in imminent danger of a nuclear attack. I thought he was mad, but I wasn't complaining – I needed the money. I helped him and then I went off to university. By the time I got back at Christmas, he'd gone. I was just thinking—'

387

'Where is it?' Braithwaite interrupted.

'It was a very long time ago, but I can show you, if you'll follow me.'

'Wait here. Don't move.'

Braithwaite jumped out of the car and ran back towards the house. Hannah twisted round to see where he was going. The ambulance was leaving but the detective stepped in its path and waved it down. A few words were exchanged with the paramedic, then Turner joined them and together they walked back through the gates.

Braithwaite appeared to have forgotten about her, so Hannah climbed through the gap between the front seats and opened the driver's door. There were now three of them following the old man and his dog: DI Braithwaite, the medic, and a fire officer brandishing a battering ram and a pair of bolt cutters.

She kept to the back of the flowerbeds, crouching low behind the shrubs and roses, ignoring the thorns that tore at her clothes and caught in her hair, the soil that spilled over into her shoes. Turner stopped about four metres from the end of the garden and looked around, stooping to pat his dog.

'It's somewhere here,' he was saying. 'The entrance should be via a hole in the ground. I didn't see it finished, but I remember him saying there would be a hatch of some sort.'

Braithwaite shone his torch across the garden, then rubbed at his neck. He seemed exasperated.

Turner scanned the area. To Hannah, watching, he seemed anxious not to appear a fool in front of the younger professionals.

'I imagine Marjorie wanted to cover it up and forget all about it after Edward left. So maybe . . .'

He crouched with difficulty and pressed his hands against the wooden frame of a raised bed while the dog sniffed at the ground beside him.

'Oof,' he grunted, rocking back as the frame slid smoothly on to the path, revealing a metal cover. 'There you go. Thought I wasn't mistaken.'

Hannah ran from her hiding place. Braithwaite swore and grabbed her, shoving her into the arms of the paramedic.

'Just get her out of the way,' he ordered, infuriated. 'Take her to the ambulance.'

'Please let me stay,' Hannah begged.

Braithwaite turned his back on her.

'She's my daughter!'

Braithwaite went still, his shoulders tensing, before he nodded at the medic.

'OK,' he conceded. 'She can stay, but keep her under control.'

The fire officer cut the padlock on the hatch, then together, Braithwaite and Turner lifted the lid. In the light from the torch, Hannah caught sight of a set of open wooden steps. Braithwaite shone the beam at them, then descended.

'There's another locked door down here,' he shouted. 'I'll need some help.'

63

Zoe

THERE'S A THUD DIRECTLY ABOVE ME, AND VOICES. I get up and stand in front of the door.

'Please, please,' I murmur, touching it with my fingers.

I hear the low rumble of the cover rolling off the hatch.

'Hey!' I bang on the door with my fists. 'I'm here, I'm in here!'

I start coughing again, bent double, my eyes stinging.

'Zoe?' a man shouts. 'Zoe, it's all right, we're going to get you out of there. Stand back.'

I move to the bunk and cling to its frame, my knees like jelly. Something crashes against the door. It shudders but doesn't give. Another crash, and this time the lock splinters. On the third attempt, the door bursts open. I'm blinded by a torch, then the beam dips. It's a fireman. He's handsome, dirty-faced and big. I grin stupidly.

'My name's John,' he says. 'Now let's get you out of here.'

Behind him, another man holds out his hand tentatively,

like you would do with a dog, as if he's worried he's going to scare me.

I walk forward and the two of them stand to one side. At the bottom of the stairs I look up through the hatch to the faces peering in, and I see my mother.

I don't care what she's done, her face is beautiful, haloed by a hazy, smoke-fogged light. I hold on to the banister and walk up the stairs. I start to laugh, then keel forward in another paroxysm of coughing as hands stretch out to take hold of me.

I bury my face in Mum's neck and wrap my arms around her. I must have grown, because we're the same height now. She reeks of smoke.

Around us, everyone is moving and shouting, torch beams bobbing. It's a lovely, joyful chaos. The fire is out and Leo's cottage smoulders. It wouldn't have surprised me if Wagner had been belting from the ruins. I look for Leo's face amongst the figures milling around, but he's not there. He could still be on his way, or maybe he's already been arrested. I actually feel sorry for him, for the waste of his career, for the book we've spent so many hours on and that probably will never be published. I feel a weird sadness at the thought that the next time I'll see him will be in court.

A woman is silhouetted in the lights of the emergency vehicles, and the sight of her makes me feel a sudden fear for the future. This is good now, but bad things are going to happen.

I know who she is. It's something about her stillness that tells me she's my real mother. I can't look away. It feels to me as though she's extraordinary, bigger and more powerful than us. Then someone raises their torch and Jenny Creasey's face crumples as she staggers forward.

Mum senses a shift in me. She loosens her grip and turns round. I watch her face as she stares at Jenny. It's full of fear and regret. I suddenly feel much older than her. I want to tell her it's going to be all right, but I can't because it isn't.

'I'm sorry,' she says. 'I'm so sorry.'

Jenny walks towards us. She's a mess. Her face is smeared with black, her clothes burnt and her hands bandaged. A blood-stained pad is stuck to her forehead, and blood and dirt cake her hair. Her eyes meet mine and she smiles, but her smile isn't easy to see. It's asking for something so huge that I have to look away. I don't know her and I can't give her what she wants.

I hold Mum, pressing her against me, trying to stop the involuntary trembling. I don't know whether it's her or me, or both of us. She's going to be hurt by what happens next and I won't be able to protect her. So, just for now, I want to reassure her that it's still the two of us together. I'm still her child.

It's bizarre. My mother is driven away in one car and I'm put in another with Jenny Creasey. She's stunned. I stare out of my window, rigid with tension, and she stares at the back of the driver's head. Why won't anyone talk to me about Leo? I can feel Jenny's anxiety; it's filling the car. Without looking at her, I know she's trying desperately not to cry. I do understand that this isn't the big reunion she dreamt of. I thought I'd throw myself into her arms, but I couldn't do it. I had the same dreams as she must have had, but the reality is that we are strangers, and I can't behave in a way I don't feel.

I pick at the skin at the edge of my thumbnail. 'Where's Leo?'

She misunderstands. 'It's OK, he can't hurt you now.'

The driver glances into the mirror and I see him catch her eye.

'I know he can't hurt me. I'm not scared of him. I just want to know where he is. Why won't anyone tell me?'

There's a pause, and I feel a trickle of dread.

'Leo is dead, Sophie,' Jenny says. 'I'm afraid your mother killed him. She pushed him in front of a train.'

I'm so shocked that I respond to the one thing that doesn't matter. 'Please don't call me that. My name is Zoe.'

'I'm sorry.'

She sounds so unhappy.

'It's not your fault.'

I don't say another word, not for the entire journey. It would be futile to try to make Jenny understand how I feel or describe the fissure that has cracked open inside me. It's as if my life force has been sucked away; as if I've been slammed against a wall and winded. I was going to forgive him. I was going to sit across a table from him in a prison visiting room and talk about what he did. I was going to get inside his head like he got inside mine. And now I can't. And none of them will ever get that.

64

Jenny

'READY?' I ASK.

Zoe nods. She's pale and shell-shocked. I'm not exactly relaxed myself.

Cameras flash as the protection officer takes our bags out of the boot of the car and uses my keys to let himself into the house. Two more officers shield us as we cross the pavement, walk up the steps and make our way through the front door. We ignore the shouts, the pleas for a statement.

I switch on the light and turn to Zoe. There's a fierce gleam in her eyes.

When the police leave, silence descends.

Zoe is wearing clothes that I nipped into Marks & Spencer to buy: a long-sleeved white T-shirt, a russet-coloured pullover and jeans. The trainers are her own. I had to buy clothes for myself as well because there's been no opportunity to come home until now.

She glances through the door into the sitting room and frowns.

'Let's go down to the kitchen, shall we?' I say, knowing that the sitting room is where my husband drugged her.

I have barely touched her since the night of the fire. Even then, our contact was embarrassed, almost brusque; like when two people meeting for the first time realize they already have a history that's too big and emotional to mention. I've been careful not to push too hard. I keep reminding myself that we have plenty of time, but sometimes it doesn't feel like that and I get overwhelmed with sadness and a sense of futility and failure, thinking that it's too late, that I've lost her already. That I lost her eighteen years ago.

Down in the kitchen I bustle around making tea and toast while Zoe sits quietly at the table, watching me. After the last few days, I've realized that silence is better than gabbling inanely to fill it. I speak when I need to speak and she does the same. She isn't being stubborn or even unfriendly, she's feeling her way. Two years is a long time in the life of a teenager.

When Zoe yawns, I'm relieved. It's not even eight o'clock, but the strain of the last few days has been extreme and I'm exhausted. I show her up to her room, the one that faces the square and which would have been her nursery, although I don't tell her that. I would have liked to have freshened it up with brand-new linen and filled a vase with fragrant daffodils from the garden, but there hasn't been time.

It's been a mad week. From my temporary accommodation near the hospital, I've spoken to lawyers and detectives, coroners and undertakers. I've had Lola screaming at me one moment, crying all over me the next, and Leo's brothers offering unwanted advice from a safe distance.

Only Kate has kept me sane. She'll be here in a few days. I smile, buoyed by the thought. Her common-sense approach will relax the tension between me and my daughter, ease the oddness, and make it easier for us to be together.

I peek through the closed curtains and wonder idly if any of the assembled journalists were here eighteen years ago. Parked up are three broadcast vans with antennae, and numerous motorbikes and cars. The neighbours are going to get fed up, if they aren't already, with their precious parking spaces being commandeered. I let the curtain drop and turn slowly to find Zoe perched on the edge of the bed, gripping the mattress. Déjà vu, I think, as my heart skips a beat. How extraordinary, after almost nineteen years, that I should get a glimpse of the man I slept with in my daughter's face.

I've spoken to him. I called him before the news hit the airwaves. He wants to meet Zoe at a time when she's ready. I want to see him again too.

'Is there anything you need?' I ask Zoe.

'No.'

'Then I'll say goodnight, shall I?'

I move towards the door and her eyes follow me. I hesitate. Does she want me to stay? I wish I could see inside her mind.

'G'night,' she says, reaching for the carrier bag.

I go down to the sitting room, to the desk in the

corner that belonged to Leo's father, and sit on his chair, swivelling it slowly to and fro. In the gloom I seem to see Leo standing over by the fireplace in his black trousers and fashionably scruffy jacket. He smiles slowly. I blink and the image has gone. How am I going to survive this on my own?

There's a noise. Do I go back up? Does she want me? She's crying audibly, so perhaps she does. I follow the sound upstairs, and find her where I left her. I sit down and, to my delight, she leans into me.

'I miss him,' she says. 'Do you think that's weird?'

I press my cheek to her head. She's warm and smells of the hospital and the lemon-scented soap I brought in.

'Not really. I miss him too,' I admit. 'We can be weird together.'

'He wrote the letter. He wasn't going to let me die in there.'

I'm surprised that she could even think he was. 'Yes, he did.'

She wipes her eyes. 'I had to persuade him. He wasn't going to, you know? He was worried about what people would think about him after he was gone.'

That shocks me. 'What he did was unforgivable, but he wasn't a killer.'

'He killed my mother's baby.'

'No, he didn't.' I look at her, surprised. 'I'm sorry, I thought you knew. Hannah's admitted that her child was already dead. She'd smothered her in her sleep by accident. She tricked Leo into thinking it was his fault.'

397

She looks unconvinced.

'You can ask her to tell you about it tomorrow. Zoe, it's important. Everything Leo did, he did because he was scared. He was a coward, but he wasn't a killer. Your mother as well. They both acted through fear.'

65

John

JOHN FINDS THE ENVELOPE WHEN HE CHECKS THE pockets of his uniform before taking it to be cleaned. He puts it into a plastic bag and takes it home.

The envelope reads, *To be opened in the event of my death.* He tries to remember the circumstances – that night was so chaotic, what with those lunatic women running into the house and putting their lives, not to mention his and his colleagues', at risk. Then it comes back to him. Carl had one screaming woman in his arms, and he had hold of the other one. He saw her drop the envelope, so he whipped it up and stuffed it in his pocket, meaning to hand it over later. He carried the lady out of the house to the waiting ambulance and forgot all about it. There was so much going on, what with the fire and finding the girl in the bunker.

Lisa is at work. John cracks open a beer and takes it into the lounge with a cold sausage left over from last night's supper.

The letter doesn't state who should open it, and the

other criteria have been met. The guy died under a train.

John sets down his can on the coffee table and teases open the envelope at the burnt edge. He pulls out a single folded sheet of paper and smooths it open on his broad thigh. Parts of it are burnt, but most of it is there, and the rest he can fill in himself.

My darling Jenny,

If you are the first person to read this letter then I'm glad, because it's how I would have wanted it.

I've debated long and hard whether to write this, but in the end I didn't want to leave this life not having said anything. I have always known Sophie is not my daughter, and I forgive you wholeheartedly. There are two reasons for my decision to overlook your infidelity, one less generous than the other. I did it because I didn't want to break your heart, but also because I enjoyed the life we had together and I was too comfortable and too much of a coward to abandon it. I've been able to write my books because of you. I've had the success I've had because of you. Your generosity and love has sustained and inspired me ever since we met. I am grateful, and only sorry I couldn't give you what you so evidently needed. I underestimated that need and I've been punished for it. We both have, I think.

Please don't feel guilty about your mistake. These things happen, and I'm big enough to acknowledge it was my fault. I put work before family. This was not something I could help. Writing is who I am, and my books are proof of that. They will continue to have a life

*in libraries and homes throughout the world, long after
we both are dead. Fatherhood was never part of the
deal. I wish it could have been, but such is my nature. I
was always honest about that at least. I weigh that
decision against my body of work. I have to believe it
was worth it and that you believe it too, in your heart.*

*My darling, I hope that I reached a grand old age
before I died, that I've lived a good life and have made
you happy, despite everything.*

Leo

John frowns. In the days since the fire there have been
loads of articles in the papers and he's looked at online
coverage as well, because he's felt invested. Someone on
the telly said the guy had left a letter to tell his wife
where the girl was, in case something happened to him.
He must have changed his mind and written a new one
somewhere down the line.

Bastard, he thinks. *You selfish fucking bastard.*
There's a postscript.

*If Jenny dies before me and someone else is reading
this, there is nothing more to say, only that human lives
are complicated and we should be judged by our deeds
and not by the things that we neglected to do. I have
not always acted with consideration towards others,
but I have done my best with the hand I've been dealt.
I don't believe in God, but I hope to be forgiven my sins.*

Yours,
Leo Creasey

John knows he should have handed it into the police immediately. In his defence, he's been sorting out a family drama of his own. Lisa's sister has moved in with them because her partner kicked her out. He forgot, simple as that. It's hardly surprising he hasn't been focused. The pair of them are doing his head in.

The girl is going to be devastated when she finds out her father didn't give a rat's arse about her and the only person he cared about was himself. What a wanker.

John has two choices, as he sees it. Make sure everyone knows what an arsehole the guy was, or let sleeping dogs lie. He'll never forget the young lady's face when he smashed open the door to her prison. She looked him straight in the eye and broke into a smile that gave him a head rush. As a firefighter, you don't always get outcomes as good as that.

John reads the letter again, working his jaw. This is evidence of the man's character, but he's dead anyway, so who would John be helping by revealing that he was a nastier piece of work than people already thought he was? He can't work out what to do for the best. He could wait until Lisa gets home and ask her advice, but he already knows what she would say.

Give it to the police, babes. It's got nothing to do with you.

John folds the letter and puts it back into its envelope, props it against his empty can and contemplates it gravely. This kind of thing changes lives. He has a duty to give it some serious thought.

Of course, the woman who kidnapped Zoe as a baby was as much to blame. How could a mother put her own interests before those of her family? In his book, the pair of them were as bad as each other. He scratches his head. The writer is dead and the woman is going to prison. Do the girl and her real mother need more crap in their lives?

He heaves his large frame off the settee and takes the letter into the kitchen. He opens a drawer under the counter and finds an old plastic cigarette lighter. He flicks it on and brings the flame to the corner of the envelope.

66

Jenny

MORE PEOPLE THAN I EXPECTED HAVE TOLD ME they're coming to Leo's funeral, but since I only expected to count them on one hand, that doesn't mean many. Lola phoned to say she and Alastair would be there. Kirstie and Reuben are coming, but not Daisy. She's too busy. James Turner. Kate and her daughters. My brother-in-law has stayed on the farm, but I don't think he would have come, even without the cows to milk. Maybe he would have. Maybe I'm being unjust.

Jake, Leo's youngest brother, is borrowing a mate's van to make the journey from the depths of rural Wales. I have my doubts as to whether he'll make it on time, or at all, but at least he's showing solidarity. Marcus sent me a kind message but didn't want to schlep all the way from Australia for his criminal brother. I don't blame him.

God knows how many journalists will be hanging around. The service hasn't been advertised, but I wouldn't be surprised if they got wind of it. If they come, they will see that Zoe is there and draw their own conclusions. I haven't tried to talk her out of it. His death is one of the hardest things she has to deal with. She can't tell him how she feels about what he did, and he will never have to face her in court. Apart from that, I didn't feel she was ready to be left alone in the house.

Kate's girls are lively and funny, and it's lovely to see Zoe dissolving into childish giggles with them. For an hour or so, they seem to forget the reason we're in the car and the grimness of our task. Kate glances at me from time to time, her eyebrows lifted, wanting to reassure herself I'm OK. I am, for the time being at least. It's a relief to have somewhere to go and something to do that has a clearly defined beginning and end.

There is a small police presence at the entrance to the cemetery, preventing the press from coming further than the gates. It doesn't stop them poking their cameras against the car windows. Zoe shrinks back.

Kirstie and Reuben are already there, standing near the entrance to the crematorium. Kirstie waves and they hurry over to greet me. I endure their hugs and murmured sympathies.

'I don't know what to say.' Kirstie looks at me glumly.

'You don't have to say anything. It's very kind of you both to come.'

Reuben gives my arm a friendly squeeze. 'This is all so strange. I've known Leo for a long time. I'd never have thought him capable—'

'He was a complex character,' Kirstie says, interrupting his flow.

I give her a grateful smile. It's kind of them, but I wish

they hadn't come. I should have said family only. James Turner is on his own, so I go over to him. It's all a bit surreal.

Finally, they are ready for us, and we file into the chapel. I sit next to the aisle so that I can get up to speak. Zoe sits next to me, then Kate, then my nieces.

Jake arrives, running in just as the service begins. He takes a seat behind me and puts his hand on my shoulder. I twist round.

'You made it,' I whisper. 'Thank you.'

That's when I see the man sitting across the aisle. He has big, broad shoulders, cropped hair, and a face so freshly shaved it looks squeaky. He nods when I catch his eye. I have no idea who he is. Leo rarely socialized in Kent, unless coerced into it by James.

I've chosen a humanist service because Leo wasn't interested in religion. There isn't going to be a eulogy – why eulogize someone like Leo? – but I walk up to the lectern when the celebrant asks if anyone would like to speak.

'Thank you all for being here. It means such a lot to me to have your support. We all know Leo did some terrible things, but today I would like to remember the good times as well. He was a loving husband.'

I notice a couple of sceptical faces, namely Kate's and Alastair's. It makes me angry.

'He was a loving husband,' I repeat. 'He was a fantastic writer.'

I look at Zoe, but she's staring at the coffin. Laid on it are the white roses I brought and a bunch of lilies from Lola. Their cloying scent fills the chapel.

'Whatever you may think about Leo, I loved him and we had a happy life together for many years. I will never forgive him for giving my baby to another woman or for what he did to Zoe, but he was tortured by it and he lost his life because of it. I hope he rests in peace.'

I stumble away from the lectern in tears. It's all been too much. My emotions are ragged from being torn apart so many times. Kate jumps up and supports me back to the pew. To my surprise, Zoe gets up. The shuffling stops. The chapel is absolutely quiet.

Her voice is measured and clear. Almost unemotional.

'Leo Creasey kidnapped me. He kept me prisoner for two years, but I forgive him, because he has changed my life. When he took me I didn't know who I was. I was miserable. I feel so much stronger now than I did before.'

She focuses on me.

'I think I probably knew him better than anyone, because I knew what he was – and what he wasn't – capable of. He couldn't kill me. He tried once, but he couldn't.'

I gasp, and Kate puts her hand on mine, gripping it.

'He taught me that I could survive. He taught me that human beings are rarely who they want you to think they are. We all wear masks and disguises. Leo was a weak man who wanted to be great, so that was the mask he wore. He was hiding so much that it made him mad.'

She looks at me again, and I brace myself.

'Leo had always known that he wasn't my father.'

My ears ring. I can feel everyone's eyes on me.

'What's she talking about?' Kate whispers.

I shake my head and she swears softly under her breath.

'I don't hate him,' Zoe goes on. 'I don't want to hate anyone, even my mother . . . I mean, the mother I grew up with. My true life starts now. So no more lies, no more secrets. Thank you.'

She nods, almost to herself, then walks towards me. Kate and I shuffle down for her. She sits, her back straight, her hands trembling, as the celebrant concludes the service.

Barely two minutes later, the strains of 'Ave Maria' fill the chapel as the curtains close around Leo's coffin. I'm desperate to get out, to get Zoe on her own. Leo knew? How? Why didn't he tell me?

Outside, in the crisp April sunlight, the air smells of cut grass. We mill around politely, but no one wants to extend the misery. There isn't going to be a wake. Lola, Alastair and Jake say they're going for lunch at a local pub and try to persuade us to come too, but I can't bear the thought of it. I want to go home.

I turn to look for Zoe. She's standing by a little paper card attached to a stake planted in the gravel. It says 'Leo Creasey'. The only flowers laid beside it are mine and Lola's.

'Zoe.'

She doesn't hear me, or if she does, she's ignoring me. She's right if she is; this isn't the place. The bombshell she's just dropped needs to be digested, not discussed in the presence of other people. I have a feeling that's why she said it when she did, so that I couldn't react immediately. But now everyone knows.

I realize I don't mind all that much. Zoe's right – it's time to stop the lies and bring the secrets out into the light of day. No one here will go to the press with this, but all the same, things have a habit of getting out. I can imagine Kirstie saying to a friend, 'You must swear not to tell a soul, but . . .'

I feel someone at my side, wanting my attention.

'Mrs Creasey.'

It's the stranger from the chapel. He's taller than I expected, and attractive in an earnest way.

'Thank you for coming,' I say. 'I don't think we've met.'

Closer up, his ease with himself vanishes and he scratches his ear.

'I just wanted to pay my respects.'

'Thank you.' I watch my daughter out of the corner of my eye. Jake's talking to her now. I call my attention back to the man. 'Were you a friend of my husband's?'

'No. I didn't know him.'

Something odd flickers behind his eyes. Hostility. He glances around as though he's worried about being overheard. That turns out to be an accurate assessment, because he asks if we can have a private chat.

Mystified, I signal to Kate that I'll be a couple of minutes, then I follow the man back inside. He stands awkwardly, his hands tucked into his trouser pockets.

'My name's John Crouch and I'm a fire officer,' he begins. 'I was attending that night.'

'I'm so grateful,' I gush. 'You lot did a fantastic job.'

'Yeah, well. Didn't save the house, did we?'

'No, but you saved us.'

'That's what I want to talk about. It was me and my colleague who pulled you and the other lady out. You shouldn't have gone in. You could have been killed, and so could we. If you don't mind me saying so, it was a stupid thing to do.'

I feel crushed. 'I wanted to find my daughter.'

'It's all right. I just wanted to make sure you never do anything like that again. Part of the job.'

I smile uncertainly. 'Well, thank you for not telling me off in front of my family.'

I move towards the door.

'Wait. That isn't what I came for.'

He pulls an envelope out of the inside pocket of his jacket and holds it out. I take it and turn it over. *To be opened in the event of my death.*

'Where did you find this?'

'I picked it up when you dropped it. There was so much happening it immediately went out of my head. I only found it when I was turning out the pockets of my uniform.'

The edges have been teased apart. I search his face. 'Have you read it?'

He hesitates, then nods.

'But it wasn't yours to read.'

John flushes. 'I'm sorry—'

'Thank you.' I cut him short. I have more important things to think about. 'For everything.'

Fragile scraps of charred paper float to the ground but most of the letter is legible. As I take it closer to the light and read it, the thinly veneered walls that I've erected to shield myself fall away.

Outside, in the courtyard, Zoe comes into sharp focus. So sharp that my eyes prick. She's standing beside

Kate, who's chatting away to James Turner. She's trying to look comfortable, but she obviously isn't. Her eyes flicker round, as though she's looking for somewhere she can go – like searching your partner out at a party when you lose confidence – and I realize, all at once, that she's looking for me. I'm her safe place. I glance at the letter, then back at my daughter.

Over the years, I have made so many excuses for Leo, to myself as well as to other people, but it turns out he was utterly selfish. Zoe wants no more secrets, but no way am I showing her Leo's letter. I tear it up and drop the pieces into the paper towel bin in the cloakroom and walk out into the sunshine. I can at least protect her from this. I'm protecting myself as well, from the shame of people knowing how little my husband cared.

'Let's go,' I say firmly as I walk towards my family.

I put my arm around Zoe's waist and, for a few moments at least, she allows me to hold her. As Kate scoots past, she taps me on the shoulder and grins when I turn to her. I know what she's trying to say in that clumsy way of hers; what she said to me yesterday evening when I expressed my frustration at not being able to connect with Zoe. *Baby steps*. The pain of missing my child growing up dissolves into little more than a mist. I try not to cry, but it's hard. The ache in my throat is a happy one. The tears I want to shed are tears of joy.

The sun is shining. The cemetery looks almost cheerful. We pile into the car and I drive away.

67

Jenny

A WEEK LATER, I'M AWAKE EARLY DEALING WITH THE mountain of red tape occasioned by Leo's death. I glance up from my laptop screen to find Zoe standing in the doorway in her pyjamas. Her hair is unbrushed and she looks younger, more like the teenager I imagine she was when Leo met her in Foyles that evening.

'Coffee?' I ask. 'I've just made a pot.'

'Yes, please.'

Her manners are impeccable. I get up and pour her a mug and she takes it from me, then leans against the counter.

'What would you like to do today?' I ask.

'I'm going to see Mum.' She adds in a rush, 'I can get the train.'

'I can drive you.'

'No, that's OK. I've worked out the route. It's easy. I get off at Ashford and walk.'

She doesn't even need me as a chauffeur. Maybe she will never need me.

'When Leo died, we were working on a book,' she says, before blowing the surface of her coffee.

'What do you mean?' She's never said anything about working with Leo. My idea of her circumstances shifts a little as I recalibrate.

'I was editing it for him.'

'Oh? When did that start?'

'When you told him you were going to sell Sparrow Cottage.'

'*Still Lives*?' I frown when she shakes her head. 'A different one?'

'It's about stealing me.' She sets down her mug. 'He thought it could make a lot of money and then you wouldn't have to sell, and I would be safe.'

Christ, I think. Had I signed her death warrant when I made that decision? I feel dizzy and have to sit down. She gazes at me steadily.

'Do you mean it's a confession?'

'No. It's a thriller based on what happened.'

The look on her face when she talks about Leo scares me. What else went on between them? I can't ask her that.

Zoe flushes. 'I liked doing it. I was so bored.'

'Yes. Yes. I can see that.'

'It's really good.'

I'll bet it is. 'Well, his computer was destroyed in the fire, so I suppose I'll never know.'

Zoe chews at her bottom lip then pushes herself away from the counter. She picks up the newspaper and reads the headlines. I get up and wash up the coffee pot for something to do, chasing the grounds down the sink with the tap's extendable nozzle.

'There's a hard copy in my room,' she says.

'Really? I didn't see . . .'

'Not here.'

'Oh, you mean . . . ?'

I can't cancel my appointments, so I drive down to Kent the next morning. Zoe stays in London. She doesn't want to go back there. When I open my car door I'm assaulted by birdsong. I breathe in the cold, damp air; it still smells strongly of the fire.

Sparrow Cottage is a ruin of blackened beams and scorched walls, but the chimney is still standing. There's a squirrel perched on what's left of the kitchen wall. The garden is wet with dew, the lawn ruined from the emergency services tramping all over it, but the flowerbeds are untouched and the apple trees are in blossom. Black-and-yellow crime-scene tape loops around the ruins of the house, the garden and the hatch.

I check my watch. I'm a little early. I get back into my warm car to wait.

'Beautiful morning,' the constable says cheerfully as I follow him to the far end of the garden.

He deals with the padlock, pulls up the hatch and switches on his torch. Stupidly, I didn't think to bring one, and there's no electricity down there now. The door to the room is open. We go inside and he swings the beam around.

'There it is,' I say, spying a pile of paper on the table.

I look around the room, at the dirty walls and grotty

bunk bed. This is where my daughter spent two precious years of her life. A flying visit seems wrong.

'Would you give me a minute alone?' I ask. 'With the torch.'

The constable hesitates, then hands it to me and leaves. I close the door; not completely, because I can already feel the quiet menace of isolation, but enough to experience something of what Zoe must have felt every time Leo locked the door and walked away. As I arc the beam, a spider freezes in its path, like an actor with stage fright. Forensics have left a trail of dusted fingerprints.

I get on to the bunk and lie down, gingerly resting my head on the pillow. It has an unwashed, pungent odour that catches in the back of my throat. I can't stand it for longer than a few seconds. If I wanted to feel a connection with my daughter, I'm not going to get it by sniffing her pillow.

The manuscript is fanned out on the table, so I put down the torch while I attempt to shuffle it into a neat stack. The torch starts to roll and I make a grab for it, but I'm holding the manuscript, so it clatters to the floor and goes off, plunging me into darkness. I get down on my hands and knees and feel around, and my fingers touch the edge of the rug. There's something poking out. I locate the torch and switch it back on. Zoe has hidden some sheets of lined paper, torn from a spiralbound pad, underneath it. It begins, *Dear Jenny* . . .

I take them to the armchair and sit how I imagine Zoe sitting, with my feet against the arm, the pages propped against my thighs. She's written pages and pages describing her childhood, her upbringing, her troubles at school. When she talks about Leo, which she inevitably does, it reads like a young girl's crush; sometimes angry and hating, sometimes lost in daydreams, missing him when he isn't there, argumentative when he is.

She doesn't say one bad word about Hannah. Not one. Not many people would be so loyal. Every so often she reiterates, *I am going to survive this*. Then I turn a page and the words blur into a grey mass, like insects in a cloud of dust.

When I hear the constable's footsteps on the stairs, I fold the pages and tuck them inside my coat.

I return the sheets of paper to Zoe that afternoon. She hands them back to me without looking at them.

'It was for you,' she says.

'Thank you.'

I wait. We both wait. There's a long silence – the kind where you can hear your heartbeat.

'Did you read it all?' she asks.

Her gaze is unwavering and I feel a surge of pride. I made this incredible girl.

'Most of it, yes.'

'It wasn't rape. But it wasn't love either.'

'I know.'

I would like to hug her, but I feel clumsy and awkward and unsure of myself, so the moment passes. There is a chink of light in the knowledge that by writing it down she reached out to me. I can settle for that.

Epilogue

Jenny

KIRSTIE THINKS THE NEW BOOK IS AMAZING, BUT suggested publishing it under a pseudonym, and possibly even offering it to a different publishing house because Leo's name has become toxic. Reuben nipped that idea in the bud by making his substantial offer conditional on keeping it. So I've signed a contract, with a headline-grabbing advance, all of which, including eventual royalties, will go to Zoe. It's bound to do well, and I'm glad, because it means Zoe will have financial security.

The story staggers me. Not that it's so good, but because it reads like true crime. Leo was so scared of losing Sparrow Cottage that he wrote a potboiler about the two nights, sixteen years apart, on which Zoe was taken. What was he intending to do when it was published? His gall and arrogance are beyond belief.

I've had to explain over and over again that I knew nothing and I suspected nothing, but I know there will always be people out there who don't believe me, who think that in the same situation they would have put two and two together.

How did I not know that something was wrong? Was I so wrapped up in my grief that I didn't notice that the Leo after our baby's abduction was not the Leo I married? His grief was different to mine; he talked about moving on, about having a life to live. It was as if for him Sophie went only skin deep. In hindsight, I did sense something was off, but I made allowances because I loved him so much.

As well as Zoe's request to be called by the name Hannah gave her, there have been other setbacks for which I wasn't prepared. There's been hostility, confusion, denial and a resolute defence of Hannah. Zoe's a mess – we both are – but she has more to deal with than I do. If one more person asks me if I'm counselling her, I'll scream. She's seeing a therapist, but it isn't me. Of course it isn't me.

I've learned not to allow my anger to spill out round Zoe. I only ever speak ill of Hannah to my sister, otherwise I hold my peace. But this dispensation for the woman who stole her, who didn't tell a soul when she disappeared at the age of sixteen, who was too much of a coward to sacrifice her freedom for her daughter's, is particularly galling. I would have done anything, but that's the difference between us. The important thing is not to tear Zoe apart.

I had no conception of how this would be. It's my fault for being focused on my own feelings and not properly considering hers. In my heart, Zoe has only ever been an infant, but she's an adult with a mind of her own. It's been hard to accept that these things aren't maths formulae that either work or don't. Emotions are messy. You wouldn't think I was a therapist, seeing what a dog's dinner I made of those early days.

Zoe has already found a school where she can take her GCSEs in the summer, and she's applied to a sixth-form college for September. She does nothing but revise. She is, I've realized, possessed of a steely determination.

My husband was a highly manipulative liar and I have been a gullible fool. He was also a vain man, so vain that he would have let Zoe die rather than make sure she was found if he went first. He was a monster.

And yet, I miss him. When he was alive, he absorbed so much of my energy that there's now a huge Leo-shaped hole inside me, and I don't know what to fill it with. In an ideal world it would be Zoe, but this isn't an ideal world. She has her life to lead. I have work and Open Arms, but I need more. Kate assures me that there are all sorts of things I can do – teaching, for instance. Ironically, the career that Leo had worked so hard to escape. I like the idea and will think about it once the dust settles.

I worry that Zoe is going to leave. Every morning I wake up, certain in the knowledge that she'll pack up her meagre belongings and tell me it isn't working; she can't be my daughter. It's too late, we have nothing but our DNA in common. Sometimes, when we're in the same room, I'm aware of her eyes on me. I imagine she's trying to work out who it is she's got herself involved with. I am a stranger.

They found the baby; the original Zoe. Leo had left her in the leather bag I took to the hospital all those years ago. I have a memory of it on our bed while I carefully packed it with all the things I'd need immediately after her birth. The lies my husband has told . . .

Hannah is being held in a women's remand centre in Middlesex, pending her bail hearing. Ordinarily, she would have been let go until that time, but the media has whipped up such a frenzy of speculation, ill-informed judgement and righteous anger that it's been deemed too dangerous. Her house has already been vandalized: a brick through the window, graffiti on the walls. *Bitch*.

Even I'm uncomfortable with it.

Zoe refuses to be part of that story. She spent the first sixteen years of her life as Hannah Faulkner's daughter, being loved by her and loving her. I can't expect her to switch off those emotions. There's anger and resentment, even hatred at times, but underneath it all she cares deeply.

Zoe's visited her, but I get to see her for the first time since all this happened when we attend the inquest into the death of baby Zoe Faulkner. Hannah looks thin and drawn. Her sister, Deborah, draws a picture of an introverted and naive teenager, young for her years, preyed on by an unscrupulous man. She explains how her family and the wider community believed him and rejected Hannah. Hannah covered up the death of her baby because she no longer trusted those in authority.

At the end of the proceedings the coroner sums up the evidence and concludes that the first Zoe Faulkner died by asphyxiation while sleeping in her mother's bed. He records a verdict of death by misadventure. Zoe had braced herself for involuntary manslaughter. This is marginally better. When Hannah leaves the courtroom, Zoe runs out after her. The date still hasn't been set for Hannah to be tried for the theft of Sophie, but we're expecting it to happen before the end of the year. After that, I'm hoping life will settle down.

Try as I might, I cannot hate Hannah. She is too sad a character to merit such a visceral emotion.

Sometimes, when little things remind me that Zoe saw a side of my husband that was hidden from me, I feel a profound jealousy. Then I remind myself that she was only trying to survive. I will not let Leo ruin our fledgling relationship from the grave. I'm glad he's dead. I've wasted enough time on him. I have my own life to get on with.

My problem is people. Namely Lola Creasey, who picks up the phone on a daily basis to tell me how dreadful she's feeling. And Hannah. Poor, lonely Hannah, who has no one to fight her corner apart from the daughter she let down. Her sister visits her once every couple of months, but Deborah has no intention of getting involved beyond that, so Hannah has become my responsibility. I find I mind less about that than about Lola's encroachment into my headspace. I think it might be because by showing Hannah compassion I'm earning Zoe's love, and I do want my daughter to love me. I want that so much.

I've accepted that I've lost Sophie for ever. I've accepted that I can't expect Zoe to spend her life trying to make up for that. I've accepted my happiness is not her responsibility, it's my own. And funnily enough, this acceptance has made me more relaxed around her. And today, when I took her up to Leeds University to look round, she gave me a hug just before we got back in the car.

Acknowledgements

Keep Her Quiet is my fourth novel with Transworld, and I love being part of this book-mad family. I am so happy to have worked with Tash Barsby on three novels now. I couldn't wish for a better, more perceptive and more patient editor. Thank you to the designers and marketing team, my publicist Isabella Ghaffari, and my copy-editor Rebecca Wright and the proofreaders for saving my blushes.

Thank you to Becky Ritchie, my agent at A.M. Heath, for patiently brainstorming story ideas, for reading and critiquing early drafts and for the supportive chats. Like all Becky's authors, I'm also hugely grateful to her for tweeting like mad when our books are published.

The writing community in the UK is fantastic. While writing these acknowledgements during Coronavirus lockdown, it's become even more apparent to me how incredibly lucky I am to have writing and writers in my life. Thank you to the Prime Writers, the Psychological Suspense Authors' Association, the Petersham Writers' Group and to all the good friends I've made along the way.

Thank you to the book blogging community, to the readers, reviewers and tweeters. We authors rely on you more and more these days, and your support is highly valued.

Thank you, Steve, for being my first reader once again, and for coming up with the title. One day I hope to be able to keep you in the manner to which I've become accustomed.

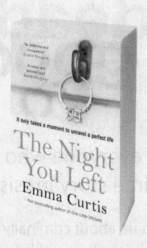

It only takes a moment to unravel a perfect life

The Night You Left
Emma Curtis
the bestselling author of One Little Mistake

When Grace's fiancé vanishes without a trace the night after proposing, her life is turned upside down. But has Nick walked out on her, or is he in danger?

As Grace desperately searches for answers, it soon becomes clear that Nick wasn't the uncomplicated man she thought she knew. And when she uncovers a hidden tragedy from his childhood, she realizes an awful truth: that you can run from your past – but your secrets will always catch up with you . . .

'So addictive and compulsive'
Claire Douglas

'A tense and twisted read'
Sarah Vaughan

AVAILABLE NOW IN PAPERBACK AND EBOOK

dead good

For everyone who finds a
crime story irresistible.

Find out more about criminally good reads at
Dead Good – the home of killer crime books,
drama and film.

We'll introduce you to our favourite authors and
the brightest new talent. Discover exclusive extracts,
features by bestselling writers, discounted books,
reviews of top crime dramas and exciting film news
– and don't forget to enter our competitions for the
chance to win some cracking prizes too.

Sign up:
www.deadgoodbooks.co.uk/signup

Join the conversation on: